THE CELTIC RING

First published in Sweden as:

Den keltishka ringen

THE CELTIC RING

Björn Larsson

Translated by George Simpson

SEAFARER BOOKS

SHERIDAN HOUSE

First published in 1992 by
Albert Bonniers Fõrlag AB, Stockholm

First published in 1997
in the UK
by Seafarer Books
2 Rendlesham Mews, Rendlesham, Woodbridge
Suffolk IP12 2SZ

and in the USA by Sheridan House
145 Palisade Street, Dobbs Ferry, N.Y. 10522

UK   ISBN 0 85036 437 X
USA   ISBN 1 57409 024 0

Printed in Finland by WSOY

Sea of the Hebrides

EILEAN MOR

FORT AUGUSTUS

INVERGARRY

CORPACH

FORT WILLIAM

ARDMORE POINT

TOBERMORY

STAFFA   ULVA   KERRARA

OBAN

SHUNA SOUND

GULF OF CORRYVRECKAN

IRELAND

MULL OF KINTYRE

WEST COAST OF SCOTLAND

Chapter 1

IT was the eighteenth of January, 1990. A stiff breeze, rising at times to a moderate gale, swept in from the south and brought gusts of heavy rain.

In Limhamn, a port town on the Swedish side of the Sound, Station Street was deserted except for an occasional car of which the headlights flashed on shop-windows or were reflected by the wet asphalt.

The wind at my back made walking easy. The strongest blasts lifted me forward on my way to the ferry terminal. Not that I had any reason to hurry. There would be no crowd to worry about on a Thursday evening in the first month of the year, when the ferries sailed off half empty. And in any case the waiting room was far from inviting.

Otherwise, I didn't mind waiting. I had gradually learned how to wait, to forget that my time was merely slipping by without bringing anything of value to me or to anyone else. But although constantly on the move, I had not been able to repress the feeling that time was slipping by. There was always something that had to be finished, always something that could not be put off and it was always somebody else who set the deadline.

When I had left Sweden to live in Denmark it had been a first attempt to escape from the treadmill. But my work remained in Sweden, and the punch-clock continued to measure my time, exactly as before. So I never arrived anywhere, only went back and forth.

Year in and year out, three times a week, I had commuted across the water. The only variation was offered by the different ferry-lines I took. These changed in accordance with where my 'home' happened to be at the moment. Although always the same, my home moved about. As a matter of fact, I lived on a sailing-boat, and she could be moored anywhere along the coast from Elsinore in the north to Dragør in the south.

At present, she was laid up for the winter at Dragør, that being one of the few ports on the Sound which remained astir whatever the season. The pilots, the fishing-boats and the ferries kept sailing in and out as usual, and that relieved the worst feelings of desolation. But in the summer, me and my boat were constantly on the move. *Rustica*, as she was called, did not have a fixed home port.

In the eyes of the authorities my transient way of life made me a 'border-crosser': a person who lives in one country and works in another. But I saw myself rather more as a bird of passage that has paused and fed too long. Viewed either way, I overstepped no bounds. In spite of this, there was a certain charm in my daily travelling and in the knowledge that I had emigrated from Sweden. Sometimes I indulged in the delusive belief that all would not be quite the same when I left the ferry on the other side. Of course this usually proved to be nothing else but wishful thinking.

As for the crossing this evening, something a bit special could at least be expected. For the ferry *Ofelia,* which plied between Limhamn and Dragør, had undergone a complete renovation and was now - presented as *Queen of the Sound* -

back in service. I would be taking her for the first time since her elevation, and I was curious to know how she would suit me. Being in winter harbour at Dragør and with four dark months ahead when I would probably have to use the same ferry-line, it was a matter of genuine interest to me. If ice should suddenly form, *Rustica* and I couldn't move to a port with another ferry-line to Sweden.

So far, there hadn't been any trace of ice. We were certainly having a mild winter. Snow had fallen for some days in December, but it didn't remain long on the ground. One night the temperature crept down to under -10°C.; but for the most part it was close to zero. The weather had been grey, with much rain and wind. Twice, the wind had reached hurricane force, and 11 Beaufort was registered at Kastrup Airport. The following day, water rose over the quay, and I couldn't get ashore. The Baltic being a non-tidal water, extreme changes in the water-level caught everybody unawares, including the fixed quays. That night even the pilots were rowed out to their boat, moored as it were in the middle of the Sound. We were, in short, having a typical Danish and South Swedish winter: wet, raw, overcast and dreary.

But there might be an abrupt change. According to the fishermen, you could never be sure of an ice-free winter until after the middle of February, which was still a month away. Moreover, the weather had been unstable during recent days. After a grudging northerly wind yesterday, we now had a wet one from the south; and an entire day of rain indicated that the front had passed over and that the wind would shift to north or northwest. There was a restlessness in the air which affected my state of mind and I was not inclined to take anything for granted.

That is probably the reason why I felt no surprise when, on reaching the ferry-terminal, I found the waiting-room entirely empty. I had never previously been alone on a crossing, but it had sometimes occurred to me that sooner or later I would be, considering the hours at which I travelled.

I inquired at the ticket-office if the ferry putting out was the new queenly *Ofelia.*

'Why shouldn't it be?' came the answer.

'I only wondered. Where are all the others?'

'What others? There are no other passengers', the ticket-seller replied in an indifferent tone, as if the ferries could sail empty for all he cared.

But he was mistaken. As the Second Mate punched my ticket, we heard rapid footsteps. We turned at the same time to look at the late-coming passenger: a large, red-haired man of middle age, who wore a sailor's jacket, a thick woollen sweater and rubber boots.

'Are you waiting for me?' he asked in English, with an accent which I placed as Scottish or, possibly, Irish.

I looked at the Second Mate who didn't react at all.

'I thought I was going to have the whole ferry to myself', I answered.

'Are we alone?' asked the man.

He scratched his head, running his fingers through his tangled hair.

'The weather is so bad,' the Second Mate explained. 'Those who come for the restaurant have stayed at home. There will only be the two of you and a couple of lorry-drivers.'

The stranger included me in a smile.

'Then we will have the boat to ourselves.'

He presented his ticket, which I happened to note was a single one. And the door slammed behind us.

'Perhaps we could keep each other company?' he suggested, and his voice resounded between the walls of corrugated plate. 'If you don't mind?'

'Not at all,' I answered immediately.

But at the next instant I regretted not having been a bit restrictive. After all, I had wanted to make an inspection of the 'Queen', as she had already been named by the elderly who crossed the Sound regularly with the ferry and who had been my only fellow-passengers on the early morning ferry from Dragør to Limhamn at half past four.

Every morning the usual retired people would be sitting faithfully in the waiting-room when I arrived. They never went ashore on the other side, but always returned with the same ferry. They bought the same cigarettes, sat at the same tables, played the same card-games, drank coffee from the same plastic mugs which they brought with them. Their outing probably gave them something to do and talk about. For them, that was enough. But I realised how much they must have needed it when I learned that they lived in Copenhagen and had to get up before four in the morning to catch the bus to Dragør. If it hadn't been for them, I would have had the ferry to myself many times already. Now, when I finally had the chance, I would have preferred to look around on my own.

The red-haired man seemed to guess my reluctance.

'Nothing compulsory about your joining me, you know.'

'It doesn't matter.'

I regarded him very closely. He looked like a fisherman or a seaman. But his self-assurance and something in his bearing made me believe that his place was on the bridge rather than on deck or in the engine-room.

'MacDuff', the stranger said as we got over the gangway and he extended his hand.

'Ulf', I mumbled, reluctantly.

I had always disliked giving away my name, and this time I should have kept it to myself, if I had known better.

'Good to meet you, Ulf,' he said. 'How about a beer?'

I was struck by his immediate use of my name which I so easily and carelessly had revealed. Scandinavians can spend hours together without exchanging names; and if names are given, they are by no means certainly remembered.

Later I have come to understand that names are of consequence in Scotland and Ireland, maybe the result of a thousand-year-old Celtic tradition. For the Celts, to be anonymous was the same as being dead, and to forget a name was the same as to kill the person who bore the name.

I proposed to MacDuff that we go to the 'Tavern' on the upper deck. According to the papers, the old reddish-brown and brass fittings had been preserved as they always had been and this part of the boat looked as it had always done. A single, silent waiter was in attendance. He served a Sort Guld to each of us, accepted payment and was seen no more.

MacDuff and I faced each other.

'Where do you come from?' I asked tentatively. 'Scotland perhaps?'

'Why d'ye ask?' came the answer.

He didn't seem to take this as an entirely innocent question.

My first impression was that he was a man on his guard. But this could just as well have been a fruit of my imagination. One of my weaknesses was that I sometimes thought I knew better far too readily.

'Aren't all 'Macs' from Scotland?' I said as an explanation.

'Not nowadays,' he answered and made it sound like a reproach.

'In any case,' I said, 'your accent is neither American nor English.'

'Heaven deliver me from either one! I'm as Scottish and Celtic as it's possible to be - born and bred on the Isle of Lewis. If you know where that is.'

I nodded. Actually, I knew it quite well. I told him that for years I had dreamed of sailing to Scotland and that I had spent a great many hours studying charts and pilot books of both Scotland and Ireland. But especially the Hebrides.

With enthusiasm and genuine pride, MacDuff began at once to portray the Hebrides as a paradise on earth. It was obvious that he knew where he belonged and why. The more he talked about the place, the more I envied him; for I have never had any roots myself, neither of a geographical nor any other kind. My country, Sweden, and my people, if the Swedes could be called that, was only a distant background in my life. As an adult, I had not spent more than a few years in Sweden. Sentimentally, homesickness was unknown to me, but perhaps not a nostalgic sense of lacking it. And this may have been why I was captivated by MacDuff. It wasn't the only reason, however. He also possessed an intensity, a fervour, that stimulated and even dazzled. When I asked him about the waters of the Hebrides, he became an inexhaustible spring of knowledge that obviously arose from experience. He was spontaneous and frank about everything, except about what pertained to himself and what he might be doing on the Sound in the middle of winter.

This became very clear when I guilelessly asked him if perhaps he was a seaman. As he seemed to know so much about sailing, he must surely have something to do with the sea and ships.

'In fact,' I added, 'you look as if you've just gone ashore.'

MacDuff did not answer. I again felt that he suspected me of trying to find out something he did not wish to divulge.

I explained that I didn't mean to be curious, but that I lived in a sailing-boat, and consequently that I was a sailor of sorts myself. When I then told him that I had already sailed to Brittany and that my next destination would be Ireland or Scotland, it was as if my first question had never been asked. Half humorously and half in earnest, I went so far as to say that Celtic blood flowed in my veins. I made an allusion to my own lack of roots and remarked that the only place where I had felt at home was Brittany. It had something to do with the light and the atmosphere, the blend of French pleasantness and Breton bareness. It was the cliffs and the sea and a sense that people had a history. MacDuff didn't smile. He took what I said more seriously than I did myself.

Afterwards, our conversation remained open and agreeable, even at periods confidential. But all the time there was around MacDuff a sphere which it seemed forbidden to try to enter. A balance had to be maintained between this and the confidentiality that had sprung from our being alone together in the ferry. But I did ask what brought a Scot to Sweden in mid-winter.

'Looking for support,' he answered, and asked if I had heard about the nuclear power-station being planned in the north of Scotland.

The English, he told me, were about to destroy one of the country's most beautiful natural landscapes and many historical relics. Not that this was anything new.

'But what has that got to do with Sweden and nuclear power?' I wondered.

'Nuclear power's only a symbol,' said MacDuff. 'The important question is how to put up resistance. You obviously know how to do that in Sweden. They haven't decided to give up nuclear energy anywhere else. We must be able to learn from your example.'

As I had in some small way been involved in the movement myself, I was curious to know whom he had talked to in Sweden. He did mention some people, but I had never heard of them before. When I asked what he thought of the 'The People's Campaign Against Nuclear Energy', he seemed not to know about it. If I understood him correctly, he had visited only a few places and for some reason it struck me that they were all ports. Of course his story might quite well be true, but it wasn't credible.

Very soon, he gave me to understand that we had talked enough about him and his affairs. He wanted to hear more about my life aboard *Rustica*. In what harbours had I moored of late? Were there other people who lived as I did? Or who went out sailing in the middle of winter? I couldn't tell him very much. Only that I'd lived at Dragør for the last three months. That the only winter sailors I'd met were some friends of mine who had a ship chandler's in Limhamn. Earlier on, I had to be sure sailed about among the ports of the Sound and had met lots of yachtsmen. But MacDuff's interest seemed to be centred on people who sailed in the winter.

At the same instant as the ferry heeled over in the turn towards the harbour of Dragør, he disclosed that he was really only interested in one single person.

'You haven't by any chance met a Finn called Pekka?' he asked casually, or in a feigned casual tone.

'It's not impossible,' I answered, mostly to see how MacDuff would react.

I didn't care in the least who Pekka was or what MacDuff wanted of him. But MacDuff's deviousness on the subject took away something of our mutual confidence. As I had guessed, my reply was taken up with more interest than his indifferent tone had seemed to show.

MacDuff hastened to explain that he had met Pekka about a month earlier, when Pekka was sailing around in the Hebrides in a catamaran.

'In November,' MacDuff remarked in a manner that showed what he thought of such showing-off. They had last met in Oban, on the west coast of the Scottish mainland. Pekka had then declared that he was on his way home to Finland, through the Caledonian Canal, across the North Sea and down through the Sound. MacDuff said that he had done everything to make Pekka wait until spring - hadn't been far from stopping him physically if he tried to sail. The more so since Pekka had a woman on board, a Scotswoman he'd picked up on one of the islands. There was now an undertone of anger in MacDuff's voice. If Pekka had been risking merely his own life, it would have been a private matter. But to imperil the woman's life for nothing. That was unforgivable.

Pekka had promised to wait for a few days before making up his mind. But the next morning the catamaran was gone. MacDuff had telephoned to the lock-keeper at Corpach, whom he knew well. But no Finnish catamaran had passed into the canal. But some days later MacDuff had met a fisherman from Kirkwall, on the Orkneys, who told him that Pekka and the woman had sailed round the north of Scotland. They had gone through the notoriously dangerous Pentland Firth south of the Orkneys, and survived.

'Not that they deserved to,' said MacDuff disparagingly. After that, in spite of the warnings from the fishermen, they had steered for Skagen on the northern tip of Jutland, at the entrance to the Kattegat. And God alone knew where the pair now found themselves. At the bottom of the North Sea, presumably. In the best of cases, blown up on a sandbank along the coast of northern Jutland.

'You haven't seen him?' MacDuff asked with unconcealed urgency.

'No, I haven't. But I'm sure I would have remembered him. Somebody like him must have a lot to tell.'

'Yes,' MacDuff answered sharply, 'stories that must not be told. Others might be tempted to follow his example and risk their lives. For no good purpose at all.'

He was interrupted by the captain's voice coming over the loudspeakers:

'A message to our two passengers. Please leave the ferry by the car-deck. The electricity is cut off in Dragør. If you look out at the town you will see that it is in complete darkness. Without electricity the gangway cannot be lowered. We hope that you have enjoyed the crossing and will be with us again.'

I translated for MacDuff, but he started to smile before I had finished, as if he had already guessed what the captain had said.

'That's what I call service,' he said. 'I'm going to remember this!'

We left by the car-deck, where a gang-plank had been laid out for us. The Second Mate was there to make sure we would reach firm ground. Without hesitation, MacDuff crossed first; he was obviously used to planks that were narrower and less steady. And from my experience on *Rustica*'s narrow stem, I too had no need to worry about where I was setting my feet.

When we had got ashore, the second Mate warned us: 'Careful the rest of the way! The place is pitch dark.'

It was.

You had to know that there was a harbour before us in order to make out the outlines of quays and boats and houses. I was not used to moving around in darkness. MacDuff, however, seemed quite untroubled.

I asked him where he was heading. He seemed uncertain for an instant, then said that he was only going to Copenhagen.

'Why don't you come down to *Rustica* and have a drink,' I said, and meant it.

Much is said about falling in love at first sight, much less about becoming friends at first sight, the immediate feeling that some people could become your friends if time and circumstance permitted the friendship to flourish. Something of that kind of was what I felt when standing with MacDuff on the quay of Dragør's harbour, in spite of his exaggerated suspiciousness. Not for a second did I guess how misdirected, and at the same time well-founded, this feeling was.

MacDuff accepted my invitation.

'But first,' he said, 'you must show me the harbour. If I haven't told you before, I'm a pilot by profession. So I have a special interest in harbours.'

'We can't see a thing now,' I objected.

'Just wait a minute or two. Darkness is never quite impenetrable, you know. There is always some light.'

Of course this was true. Before long I thought that I saw quite clearly boats, fishing-tackle, quay-sides and water. But I continued to move warily. The quay was slippery and the temperature of the water at close to freezing-point.

I pointed out the few sailing-boats still in the water, expressed my sincere admiration for the pilots and told him what I knew about the port in general. MacDuff seemed moderately interested, in spite of what he had said, but he looked everywhere. Nothing escaped him.

'Is this the only harbour?' he asked when we had looked at everything and stood before *Rustica*. 'I had the idea there was another one.'

'There is a small marina.'

'Where is it?'

'Wouldn't it be better to have a whisky here in *Rustica*?'

'First the marina, then the whisky,' said MacDuff peremptorily.

MacDuff was already on his way.

I showed him the way to the marina, although I knew that there wasn't much to see in the new harbour: only a few unoccupied boats. But when we stood at the end of the northern-most pier-head and looked out over the harbour basin, MacDuff pointed at the outline of a boat, a catamaran, moored to a buoy.

'What's the boat there?'

I realised why MacDuff had been so anxious to see the

harbour. It came to my mind that Pekka had perhaps sailed away with MacDuff's woman and that I was witnessing nothing but a drama of jealousy.

I explained that the catamaran was used only in sailing races, and that it had been for three years at Dragør. In the darkness, I couldn't tell if MacDuff was disappointed. In any case, he came back with me to *Rustica* and drank some whisky, a fifteen year-old Old Fettercairn, which surprised him. Evidently, he hadn't expected to be served a whisky of that quality in a Swedish boat in Dragør.

I soon forgot about his secrets, even more quickly as, speaking as a pilot, he had many good things to say about *Rustica*. It's to be hoped that there is a way to everyone's heart. The one to mine led through *Rustica*, but I don't believe MacDuff was aware of it. He meant what he said. And consequently his words bore weight. Among other remarks of his, I clearly remember him calling her 'a boat that breathes security'. But when I think about that now, after all that has happened since, and perhaps goes on happening, it seems inconceivable to me that *Rustica* once breathed security.

MacDuff left at about eleven. I accompanied him to the bus-stop. But when we had got there, he decided that he would walk in the direction of Copenhagen. I advised against this. After all, it was nearly ten miles to the centre of the town. Before we parted, he gave me his address and telephone-number and made me promise to get in touch with him if I came to Scotland. But when I watched him disappear into the night, I was convinced that we would not see each other again.

Chapter 2

THE town was still plunged in darkness when I walked back down through Dragør towards the harbour. My footsteps resounded desolately from the cobblestones. The narrow streets, with their low yellow houses under thatched roofs, usually possessed a genuinely idyllic charm. But tonight the ground-floor windows didn't allow passers-by to see directly into cosy interiors, and this gave me a ghostly and alien feeling. The light of candles flickering here and there within fought an uneven battle with the impenetrable darkness.

On reaching the harbour, I walked past *Rustica* and on out to the end of the pier. The wind still blew hard enough to tear the crests off waves and turn them into tattered silver strips. But its gusts seemed to be losing force. Out in the Sound you could see the flashing lights from the buoys and the lighthouses: Drogden, Nordre Röse, Flinten and Oskarsgrundet. An aeroplane with searchlights on was coming in to land at Kastrup airport. The rays touched the pier where I was standing, then caught a freighter on its way northward. A passing ship, a descending plane ... One reason why I had chosen Dragør as winter harbour was my being so often reminded here of the world beyond the horizon.

When I came back to *Rustica*, I was still wondering why MacDuff should be so anxious to get hold of this Pekka. I was unwilling to believe that he had travelled so far merely because Pekka was supposed to have a certain Scotswoman on board his boat. Not that I could find a better explanation. But I was quite certain of one thing, and that was that MacDuff had concealed his true reason for being in Denmark.

It was warm and pleasant in *Rustica*'s cabin. I paused in the dark and watched reflections play on the ceiling; they came from a flame just visible through the little inspection-hole in the cooking-plate of the heater. The hole was there simply to show if the heater was burning, but nowadays I never peeped through it. To know if the heater needed cleaning, I only had to watch the reflections from the flames on the ceiling.

The heater never gave trouble. It was an old, traditional type of drip-fed diesel heater used by fishermen for half a century. No electricity was required, and not so much as a wick needed to be changed. Heat came from two metal flame-rings at the bottom; fueling was controlled by a simple regulator. The sound construction of the heater made it infallible, and it had heated *Rustica* during four long winters without my doing more than remove the soot every second month.

The heater had become so much a part of the boat that it might easily have been taken for granted. I often looked at it with a kind of gratitude. It was, after all, the heater that made my way of life possible. Not only could I depend on it in all winds and weather, but with its polished stainless-steel and curved lines, it was also an adornment to *Rustica*'s saloon.

I had much the same feelings for my paraffin-lamp, a Danish Stelton design, which hung from the ceiling over the table. Like the heater, it was solidly made, handsome and functional. Although modern in design, it possessed a type of

15

burner renowned for many years. With the wick turned up all the way, the lamp gave as much light as a forty-watt electric-bulb. And I got seven hundred watts of heating into the bargain.

To port hung my paraffin cooker, also an elderly model, now difficult to get hold of. The newer models, I'd found, being pre-heated with paraffin instead of methylated spirits, were difficult to light and had to be tended like babies.

All in all, I had chosen the right equipment, simple, functional and beautiful. I had also been lucky with the boat itself: a Rustler 31, bought second-hand. She was thirty-one feet long, nine-foot beam, long-keeled and strongly-made by Anstey Yachts in England. She had all the good qualities common to well-built, long-keeled boats, that is, all of them except speed and manoeuverability in tight quarters. She was traditionally planned, with pantry to port, navigation and working table to starboard, then a berth to either side, after that an oilskin locker and the toilet opposite each other, and the forepeak, my sleeping quarters. *Rustica* wasn't fitted out in the usual dark teak but in light ashwood. In the summer, teak is doubtless a cosy and inviting wood, but on rainy and gloomy November afternoons and evenings you realise what it means to have a white-painted bulkhead and light-hued wood elsewhere.

Throughout the years, I had acquired routines. Coming on board, I took a look at the heater and filled it up with diesel if required. Then I took off the glass of the paraffin-lamp and trimmed the wick with my fingers as I had learned from an old woman keeping a shop with nothing but paraffin-lamps in Copenhagen. I then waited for the first bluish flame to steady, begin casting a mild glow over the saloon and giving the pale wood a golden lustre. That done, I put water for coffee on the heater and took out a thermos flask. I hid my briefcase as far away as possible. Finally, I got myself something to eat.

When the coffee was ready, I lay down in the bunk, propped up by a pillow, and began reading. During the week, coming home from work, I seldom devoted an evening to the boat, except possibly in the summer when the evenings were light and warm. Although there was no-one about in the winter, or because of that, I never had a social problem. That came only in the summer. A lot of sailors livened up during their vacation and tried to compensate for a dearth of human contact at other seasons. People who would never so much as greet their neighbours at home, all of a sudden seemed to have an irresistible urge to get in touch and make new acquaintances. When more and more pleasure-boats were cropping up around *Rustica*, I often missed the solitariness and the empty horizons of winter. The fact was that nothing brought me such peace as a winter evening alone on board, with only wind, waves and seagulls for company.

That night, however, the expected tranquillity refused to descend on me. I became restless, and restlessness in a boat is a troublesome malady. There would have been a simple cure in summer: to cast off and sail away. But in the middle of the winter, with the risk of ice locking you in any day? And I couldn't wander about my home otherwise than like an animal in a cage, which is no cure for restlessness; that is walking three yards or so back and forth, with lowered head if you don't have enough headroom. To be restless in a boat is a severe ailment. No wonder that nearly all sailors detest being becalmed, often more than being in a storm. If restlessness creeps up on you when you are becalmed at sea, there is no known remedy.

This particular evening, I tried to find some relief by looking into the British Admiralty's pilot-books and nautical charts. I had collected them for years so that I was able to dream of sailing on practically every ocean around the world. In the pilot-books you could read about winds and currents, harbours and anchorages, sailing routes and jagged reefs, all described in the light of experience garnered over several centuries.

I took out the pilot-book for Northern Scotland, the NP 52, and read about the whirlpools in the Pentland Firth. How Pekka could have survived them was beyond my understanding. An island named Stroma lay in the strongest current. It had no natural harbour, not so much as a creek where you could anchor. The tide swept past its cliffs at up to ten knots, faster than most sailing-boats would ever be able to sail. It came to me vividly: the seething water, breakers crashing everywhere, vertical waves several metres high, in all shapes and forms, that rose swiftly out of nothing and then disappeared just as quickly into nowhere, but which during their brief lives could easily cause a boat to founder and lives to be lost.

It must have been nearly one o'clock when I heard a clattering outboard-motor. The wind had abated somewhat. Between shreds of cloud I could see an occasional star and the moon which cast a glittering light over the water. Dragør still lay in darkness, but for the faint light from the moon.

The clattering came closer and grew louder. I got up and looked through the porthole. Some sports fishermen in Dragør had outboard-motors, but I had never seen them go out so late or in such weather. No navigation lights could be seen above the pier and I remember thinking that it was neither a sailing-boat nor a fishing-vessel that was approaching.

The nocturnal visitor came out of the dark at the end of the pier into a sudden moonbeam that seemed to have been rayed momentarily over the water as a leading light for the boat's entry into the harbour. That is the moment I discovered what it was. A catamaran.

My immediate impulse was to blow out the paraffin-lamp, in order to see better, or in order not to be seen.

Both wishes were equally strong. If it was Pekka, I would feel compelled to tell him about MacDuff. But something told me that this was exactly what I should not do.

On the other hand, Pekka had been out in foul weather and would certainly be grateful for a little aid in making fast and for a cup of hot coffee in the warmth of *Rustica*'s cabin. Presumably, from MacDuff's account, he had been beating down through the Sound against a strong gale from the south, with gusts of storm-force, and must be frozen stiff and worn out. Only to reach a harbour lying in darkness and a town without a light.

Perhaps that was why, as I soon discovered, he steered towards *Rustica*. The light streaming from her portholes provided the only mark to head for when the moon at times disappeared behind the stacks of cloud.

He stopped astern of *Rustica* which was moored to two wooden posts aft. The catamaran was caught by a side-wind and driven against the posts, crashing into them without its skipper appearing to care. He stood stiffly in the cockpit, his legs wide apart, with one hand on the tiller and stared at *Rustica*. I saw his lips move, but I could hear nothing above the clatter of his engine and the shrieking of the wind in the rigging.

I looked out a last time before I opened the hatch. He wore a kind of fur-lined pilot's headgear which shadowed his face and made his eyes look like two black holes in the dark.

As the wind hit me, Pekka, because by now I was convinced it must be him, vaguely lifted an arm in greeting. I responded with a similar gesture.

'I need electricity,' he shouted in an unmistakable Finnish-swedish accent. 'Do you know where I can get electricity? I must have electricity!'

His voice was tired and cracked by exhaustion.

I pointed towards the opposite side of the harbour. Since

the quays had been flooded, I had been without electricity myself, but if he was in luck he might still find electricity on the opposite quay. He lifted a hand by way of thanks, but it didn't get higher than his waist. When he bent down to put his engine in gear, he nearly fell. He didn't bother to bear away from the posts; he just opened the throttle. There was a strident noise as his hull pressed against the wood an instant before the boat sheered off to open water.

Obviously, Pekka needed help. When I saw that he had misunderstood where I had pointed to and was putting in at the pilots' berth, I made up my mind. My misgivings weren't that important after all. And at the same time I realised that I had forgotten to let him know that there was a power failure in the whole of Dragør.

I put on my oilskins and walked round the harbour. At the car-park by the Strand Hotel, there was a car with its parking-lights on. Somebody was sitting in the car, and a man beside it talked into a walkie-talkie. If I had not been thinking of Pekka, I would certainly have wondered what they were doing there, in the middle of the night and in pitch-darkness. But for once, when most needed, my imagination didn't get the better of me.

I advanced out on the pier. Pekka was already ashore. Moving on unsteady legs, he looked for an electric point.

I went up to him and explained that he had moored at an unsuitable place. The pilot-boat would soon be back and find his boat in the way. He stared at me as if he didn't understand. I pointed at the quay further away.

Then his gaze cleared. He took hold of my arm.

'Will you help me?'

He gripped my arm more tightly, as if to emphasise his plea.

I went aboard with him. I noticed that he had to hold on to the shroud in order to keep his balance. He was like a boxer who gets up after a knock-down.

'Where have you come from?' I asked.

'Anholt,' he answered briefly.

'Tonight?'

'Yes.'

'Was it rough?'

He didn't reply at once, but after a moment he said:

'No. It wasn't too bad. No ice, for one thing.'

He was silent again, appeared to consider, then forced out: 'I've got a woman on board.'

He said this in the same way as he might have been speaking of an anchor or some other piece of loose equipment. What he really tried to tell me I don't know. Perhaps that it had been hard for her.

He bent down over his engine. So it was Pekka. And the woman aboard must be the Scotswoman that he had found on one of the islands and whose life he had risked. The same woman that he had possibly snatched from MacDuff.

I bore off from the quay.

'Would you like a beer?' Pekka shouted to be heard above the engine, which again was running at full revs.

I nodded assent, though I didn't really want one.

Pekka called something down into the cabin. A moment later, the face of a woman appeared. She looked up at me with eyes that seemed to be emptied of all life. I didn't know if I ought to say something, but her gaze frightened me into silence. I had never before seen such an abyss in a person's eyes. The face vanished, but the woman soon came back with two bottles of beer. Without a word, she placed them on the ladder and disappeared again.

'Mary,' said Pekka briefly, and glanced towards the cabin.

We sailed into the next basin of the harbour. I pointed once more, and this time he seemed to understand where I

21

wanted him to put in. He slowed down and stretched out his hand.

'Pekka,' he said. 'My name is Pekka.'

'I know,' I answered.

He gave a start.

'I have met MacDuff.'

Pekka took a step backwards. Abruptly, the tiredness was gone from his eyes. Instead I saw fear, an uncontrollable terror.

I told him quickly that I had no idea where MacDuff was at the moment, that I had met the man quite by chance and that I didn't know him, but that he was on his way north according to what he had told me.

'I don't think that MacDuff will come back here again', I added.

This appeared to calm Pekka somewhat, but I noticed that his hand shook when he let go of the tiller for a moment and closed the door down to the cabin. He took hold of my arm once again and stared into my eyes without a trace of the previous weariness in his own. Rarely, in fact, have I seen a more intensely alert gaze. It was as if he wished to etch his gaze deeply in my memory.

'It's important', he said. 'Will you help me?'

I nodded mechanically. I didn't know what I should do.

Afterwards, all went so quickly that I am no longer sure that I remember exactly what happened. At the last second, Pekka grabbed hold of the tiller and put it over to go alongside a barge. Nevertheless, *Sula* - as the catamaran was called - crashed into the barge with a loud bang. I stumbled, but managed to find a line, make fast and go astern to turn off the engine. What Pekka did meanwhile, I do not know, but when I looked up the door down to the cabin stood open. At the same time, I saw two cars coming to a halt on the quay; a police car and the one I had seen by the car-park. A moment later, four uniformed men were standing on the other side of the barge. I poked my head into the cabin-door.

'The Customs are here', I said to Pekka. 'And the police.' Pekka came rushing up, but I had already caught a glimpse of him with his arms around the woman, Mary, who sat with bowed head and wept.

First he looked back at the woman, then at me. I felt that I was being judged, evaluated. He turned round, went down to a locker whose existence no-one could have suspected and removed an object wrapped in brown paper.

'Take this!' he said to me. 'Go!'

As I hesitated, he hastily went on:

'You must! I can't stand it any longer. Go out and tell them that you have nothing to do with us. That you only wanted to help.'

Again, the same burning look. Unthinkingly, I stuffed the package into a pocket of my oilskins and turned around to leave. Once more he gripped my arm so hard that it hurt.

'The Celtic Ring', he said. 'I trust you. I have to trust somebody.'

All this couldn't have taken more than a minute. I climbed aboard the barge and was stopped by one of the policemen, while his colleagues boarded *Sula*. The policeman wanted to know who I was and I explained that I had just given a hand to moor the catamaran, that I myself lived aboard *Rustica* 'over there' and that he had only to ask the harbour-master if he wished to have this confirmed.

Just then I overheard one of the Customs officers say into his walkie-talkie:

'We have made contact. It's a Finn and a Swede.'

I sensed the suspicion in the policeman's examining look. Nothing was more natural considering my situation. I regretted having said that I 'lived' on a boat. That was scarcely something that would make me more credible. So many other people had difficulty in believing just that. But perhaps I became more believable when I gave him my former official address in Denmark: Oehlenschlaegersgade 77, 2nd door left. A Swede wouldn't be able to make up an address like that on the spot.

When I was given permission to leave, the policeman declared that they were summoned because the boat had been sailing without lights.

'You are not allowed to do that', he told me and asked me to leave.

So I did, but I looked back in time to see Pekka standing in his cockpit with three uniformed men round him. For the third time that night, he lifted his arm, but this time he raised it higher, as if it were no longer so heavy.

That was the last I would ever see of Pekka.

Chapter 3

I didn't light the lamp when I got back to *Rustica*. It was enough with the faint shimmer on the cabin roof from the flickering flames down in the stove. The boat rocked gently, although she gave a jerk in the gusts. I could tell from the way she moved that the wind had backed to west-northwest. I tried to recall the weather forecast, but I realised that I must have forgotten to listen. Such a thing seldom happened. The weather report was my favourite radio programme. I usually listened to the late Danish forecast at ten to eleven. The Swedish one, an hour earlier, I always skipped since it was preceded by the evening prayers that neither had the same entertainment value, nor the same reliability, as the weather forecast. In Scotland and England, at least, you were treated to 'The Archers' in the day and to the soothing 'Sailing By' in the evening. When you think about it, it is a strange sort of general culture you get from wanting to listen to the weather forecast in different countries. In Ireland, for example, you get to know all about the latest pig prices in 'Farm News'.

For some time, I remained standing in the middle of the saloon and listened. I tried to catch sounds from the other side of the harbour, perhaps a car moving off or footsteps approaching on the quay. I felt sure that the police would pay me a visit. Why should they believe my story if, as I supposed, they suspected Pekka of smuggling?

I felt for the package and I realised all of a sudden that there might well be narcotics in it, for all I knew. The longer I thought about it, the more beset I was by the idea. What if the police should search through *Rustica* and find narcotics on board? That would certainly put an end to my hopes of leading a free and unhampered life, free from punch-clocks and ties. I was on the point of dropping the package into the harbour when some good sense returned to me. If Pekka had contraband on board he would scarcely sail about with a engine that could be heard several nautical miles away. Nor would he have entered a port frequented by pilots and ferries, one that was full of officials.

On the other hand, the package must contain something that was not to fall into the hands of the authorities since it was handed over to me when they appeared on the quay. I thought of Pekka, his plea for help, the terror in his eyes when I mentioned MacDuff, his decision to trust me, the woman's lifeless gaze, 'the Celtic ring'. If this was a drama of jealousy, then it had ominous aspects well beyond my imagination.

If it hadn't been for the fear that I had seen in Pekka's eyes, I would never have taken the package. Compared with Pekka, MacDuff seemed to be a very calm and well-balanced man. He emanated purposefulness and human warmth. From Pekka there came only helpless weariness and panic.

Finally, I took the package out of my coat pocket. I noticed that the object within was hard but insignificant. I placed it in my secret compartment where I kept the originals of *Rustica*'s papers, an extra passport and some ship's funds in various currencies. With that taken care of, I felt more at peace and went on waiting for something to occur.

A whole hour passed without my hearing anything except

the ship's bell marking the hours. The wind had dropped considerably by then and all was still. So I am completely certain that it was a woman I heard shrieking a moment before two cars started up and drove away along past the ferry-terminal. Silence again; as if nothing had happened. But what *had* happened?

Would anything have been different if I had gone back to *Sula* to find out what had happened? Probably not. It is, after all, of so little use to look back. And if, in spite of this, I am now writing down what has happened, and how it happened, it is only because it is still happening. Take it as a warning. I still recall MacDuff's words that there are certain stories that must not be told, and I realise that he could be right. But to gain certainty, there is no other way but to tell the story.

I also confess that I did not have the courage to go back to *Sula*. Not because of some general cowardice. I believe that I possess a kind of courage that makes me stay dispassionate and collected in situations where others may panic. But then it is not a question of dealing with people, in any case not with people who need my help.

I waited another quarter of an hour after the cry. Gradually I felt certain that nothing more would be heard that night from the northern pier, whether from the police or anyone else.

I closed the curtains and lighted two candles. I had stared out into the dark so long that even their glow almost dazzled me. I made some strong coffee, poured myself a glass of Old Fettercairn and took the brown package from its hiding-place.

I pulled off the paper and found myself holding a bulging, much-thumbed blue logbook. I opened the first page and read: 'S/Y *Sula*. Helsinki, Finland.'

The letters, written in black ink, sprawled across the paper. I licked a finger and rubbed the letters. The ink was waterproof. Someone who used ordinary ink in a logbook must be someone who couldn't tell the consequences of an entry blurred out by water drops from the sou'wester. MacDuff had suggested that Pekka was a foolhardy madman who knew nothing about seagoing. Yet Pekka kept his logbook in waterproof ink. Pekka had crossed the North Sea twice in a catamaran and he had survived a passage through Pentland Firth. Had MacDuff lied about him, for the same reason as he concealed the real purpose of his stay in Scandinavia? Were there other reasons than ignorance and foolhardiness that explained why Pekka had sailed through Pentland Firth? But what had driven him to do it in that case?

I turned over urgently to the first page and began to read.

Chapter 4

THE first entries were not very illuminating. Pekka had set out from Helsinki on the 16th of September, and his passage down across the Baltic had apparently been without incident. He had sailed directly to Visby, on the island of Gotland, and left next day for Hanö, a little island off the coast of southeast Sweden. He stayed no more than overnight before hastening on to Kåseberga, further south on the mainland. Here he had paused and visited the ship tumulus, Ales Stenar.

On the opposite page, Pekka had pasted a newspaper cutting about the English equivalent to Ales Stenar, Stonehenge. The article told of present-day Druids who annually celebrate the summer solstice at Stonehenge. Several different Druidic orders had competed for the right to hold ceremonies at the monument. However, many groups had withdrawn to more isolated holy sites because of the tourist invasion. One of their new places was an old Celtic earth fortress near Northampton. The writer described the Druids and their rituals with evident irony. Verses were declaimed and banners with strange symbols were carried around. A fire was lighted in a globe of copper.

A photograph showed some twenty men, all wearing

white cloaks, gathered round a Druidic priest as he officiated beside the globe. To my eye they looked rather ridiculous. Could this really have anything to do with the so-called 'Celtic Ring'? I thought of Pekka's terror which was all but ridiculous.

From Kåseberga, Pekka had sailed on to Gileleje, on northern Zealand. He must have had a particular fondness for sailing at night. Most people would have avoided sailing alone through the Sound, which has the heaviest traffic of all waterways in the world, in the middle of the night. The logbook did, in fact, contain many notes about encounters with ships, written in a careless hand that spread out over the paper, a sure sign of weariness.

On the day after Pekka's arrival in Zealand, he sailed at 07.00, on a course of 275 degrees, for the entrance to the Mariager Fiord in Jutland. On the way, he had sighted the island of Hässelö in a haze, and he commented that the island seemed to be 'shrouded in mystery'.

From Hässelö, *Sula* had picked up a fresh southerly wind and made good speed. The Mariager Fiord was reached at twilight, and Pekka had written some lyrical words about how the sun set, and cows bellowed on either side of the twisting channel as he sailed into the fiord. At 22.30 he moored in the fishing-port of Hadsund.

He stayed in Hadsund for a few days and made excursions to various places in Jutland. New cuttings, taken from different brochures for tourists were pasted in. One was about a gravestone, regarded as being of Celtic origin, in Tømmerly Church. Another of them described the so-called 'Tollund Man', the two-thousand-year-old but very well-preserved remains of a man, found in the bog of Borremose in 1946. The man had been ritually sacrificed by hanging: the hemp rope used was still around his neck. His well-kept fingernails indicated that he was of noble birth. I had already heard of 'The Tollund Man', but according to the cutting in Pekka's logbook new theories sought to prove that the man had in actual fact been a Druid. It was claimed that the remains of a man sacrificed in similar fashion had been found in England. Evidently, Pekka had taken an interest in Celts and Druids even before he arrived in Scotland. Could that have been why he set out on his journey in the first place? There were no further commentaries to the cuttings. I read on with wonder.

From Hadsund he sailed to Skagen, at the northern tip of Jutland, and the next morning he was out on the North Sea. 'Finally on my way', he wrote, 'over a sea with unbroken horizon'. *Sula* steered a course of 271°, straight towards Rattray Head, and the wind was favourable, east to southeast. Notes in the logbook were sparse now. Only when *Sula* approached land had Pekka a little more to record. He observed the birds and wondered how far they flew out to sea; if there existed an absolute limit beyond which they dared not fly, and if so how they knew when they had reached it. He made a reflection on our conception of limits as endless lines. The idea was false; nothing was endless. It was always possible to go to the limit, all the way, turn off and follow parallel to it until you could go around it where it stopped. 'This applies also to history', he had added a little further down the page, 'Everything goes on living and can rise again.'

After three days and 340 nautical miles, he moored in the fishing-port of Fraserburgh. 'Mist and drizzle' he wrote, '*Sula* and I are in Scotland.' Clearly, however, the goal was not yet reached. The next day he headed for Inverness. He was caught by violent squalls at Mary Head and took two reefs in the mainsail. To judge from all the sail-changes, he concentrated on arriving as quickly as possible. In the margin, he worked out how soon he would get to the Caledonian Canal when sailing at different average speeds. Why such haste? I thought.

31

It looked very much as if he wanted to arrive in time for something special. This was confirmed on the next page:

'15 M to Urquhart Castle on Loch Ness, where the trail may begin. There is a new Golden Road, I am sure of it. I must get there before *Samain*. Then I will find out.'

I put the book aside. First Druids, then ritual sacrifice in prehistoric times and now something called 'Samain'. None of this accorded with the impression I had received of Pekka. Where did MacDuff come into it all? And the woman, Mary? I poured myself more coffee and read on.

Sula anchored in Loch Ness, in a cove northeast of Urquhart Castle. Here Pekka remained for a slightly longer stay, his first since leaving Hadsund in Jutland. But two days later, without indication of what had happened, he weighed anchor and covered the ten nautical miles to Fort Augustus, at the opposite end of Loch Ness. His sole comment on the legendary lake was that its water was black. At Fort Augustus he had passed through the locks and then motored. He went through two more locks, and the same afternoon he came out into Loch Lochy, the smallest of the three lakes joined together by the Caledonian Canal.

Here something evidently occurred. Pekka had moored at the foot of a castle called Invergarry. There was mention of an 'opening to the underworld, of 'the present which buries itself to hide its roots and its future', of 'hidden preparations for a new era in an old form'. Further down the page, I read: 'In King Arthur's time it was the ordinary people, the heathen and mysterious ones, who lived without being seen. Now the leaders, the Kings, have gone underground and live among us like ordinary people. But soon they will come forward, exactly as was prophesied. The King exists in the underworld. The Golden Road is restored.'

I stared incredulously at the page. It wasn't that I suffer from any lack of imagination. I can at any time tell a good story and believe in it. But my stories remained within the bounds of possibility. That was clearly something that did not bother Pekka.

After leaving Invergarry Castle, he didn't stop before he reached Oban, the largest town on the west coast of Scotland. Using Oban as his base, he sailed to the islands round about, often making only day-trips, but sometimes spending a night or two away.

I took out a map and tried to find the places he visited. I found some of them without difficulty: Kerrera, opposite Oban, the Garvellachs south of Mull, Duart Bay on the east side of Mull and Loch Breachacha on the island of Coll. Others I couldn't find no matter how hard I tried. But I wasn't even sure that the names I looked for were geographical names written on maps. This suspicion was borne out some pages further on. Pekka had drawn a primitive map of Scotland and Ireland where he had marked and named a number of castles and historical relics. Between these he had dotted out or drawn lines that joined the places together in a curious pattern. I followed the lines with a finger, and it struck me that they extended without a break across Scotland and to Ireland.

The logbook's pages teemed with brief historical comments. Most of these conveyed nothing to me. I had never been particularly interested in history, and in spite of my many visits to Brittany, I knew very little about Celtic history. Even in the company of my close friend Torben, who had devoted a good deal of his life to European history, among other things, I had felt no desire to share his knowledge. Possibly, Torben would have been able to understand, or at least guess, what Pekka had in mind when making his notations. To me, much of the text in the logbook was incomprehensible, disconnected fragments of aimless narrative.

'I must get to Staffa', Pekka wrote in one place. 'Fingal's Cave must be part of the pattern. But where can I land? The sea is too heavy. A fisherman said that months can go by, sometimes a year, without it being possible to land. Just for that reason I must get there'.

A little further down on the same page: '*Sula* and I sailed past the Garvellachs, Isles of the Sea, on the way to Iona. Saw a fire on Eileach an Naoimh, the island farthest south. Must be investigated!' Pekka had underlined this. 'The island is not inhabited, but it was a great religious centre in Saint Columba's time. And now the fire.'

Who was Columba? I wondered with irritation. A saint, since he was called *just that*. But beyond that? What did he represent?

Pekka never seemed to have had time to land on the Garvellachs Islands. Then the logbook abruptly changed in character, at the very moment I came on a name with which by now I'd become too well acquainted: '*MacDuff*'. It was as if Pekka had started to keep a diary instead of a logbook; as if he no longer wrote for his own sake or to navigate, but because an unknown reader *ought to be told*.

'Today I finally met somebody who did not believe that I am crazy and talk nonsense. His name is MacDuff, and he listened with interest to my theories. He questioned me all evening, asked me how I had come to my conclusions, if there were other people who thought the way I do, and a lot of other things like that. When I left him he promised to help me with my investigations.'

'*15 October*

Met MacDuff again. When he found out that I had intended to sail to Sligo, he was very pleased and said that he knew a number of people there who might help me. He was kind enough to call them up at once. When he came back he said that his friends were prepared to meet me. And he wondered if in return I would do him a service by taking two cases of books with me. He said that he does a little publishing on the side, and it would save him the freight if I helped him. He was honest enough to add that some of the papers were aimed for the illegal organisations, hoping that I didn't mind. It might be a bit against the law, he said, but smuggling words can hardly be regarded as criminal. Naturally I said yes, that was the least I could do for him. At about two o'clock he came back with some wooden cases, and we stowed them on board together. I intended to sail at four o'clock so as to arrive by daylight in the morning, but MacDuff took me to a pub and I did not get away until 19.30. MacDuff telephoned to his friends and said I was delayed. He told me to sail into Lough Swilly, where they would meet me at Fahan, south of the town Buncrana. The entrance was easy to find. Just steer for the lighthouse at Malin Head. His friends would show me a safe anchorage to lie for the night, before I sailed on to Sligo. But when MacDuff asked me to put out the lights before sailing in, I did not like it. Not because I was smuggling his books, but because it is not seamanlike. MacDuff was so insistent, that I finally promised to do what he wanted. I was going to flash a light when I had passed Buncrana.'

I jumped over what Pekka wrote about his crossing, but I noticed that he really had arrived under cover of darkness. His last observation for the day was made when he rounded Malin Head. He probably had lots of things on his mind other than to write his logbook when he had to grope his way into the long and narrow fiord. The next note was written early the following morning:

'What have I done? I ought never to have sailed in here. I kept my word and came into Lough Swilly with lights turned off. It was hell to find the way in here. The only thing I had to go after was the light from Buncrana. But I managed. It was past midnight when I flashed my torch. Five minutes later a fast motorboat with three men on board turned up in the darkness. They told me to follow them, but they had no lights either. Instead, they towed me. As soon as I had anchored, they came on board and asked me about the cases. They seemed to be nervous and worked quickly. I put on the deck light to help, but one of them shouted at me to put it out. At the same time, he dropped one of the cases and the lid came off. But I do not believe they noticed that I saw anything. Before they went away they said they were coming back today so we could talk in peace and quiet.

I do not dare stay here. How could I have been so naive that I believed there were books in the cases? The Celtic Ring is something different from what I thought. The Golden Road is too. The worst of all is that MacDuff must have known what was in the cases. He is one of them. And now he knows that I know what it's all about. I told him everything. MacDuff did not send me here without a reason. I have not much time. It will soon be *Samain*'.

What was it that Pekka had discovered? Arms? In that case the weapons must have been meant for the IRA. On my chart I saw that Lough Swilly actually forms a natural border between Eire and Northern Ireland. And once more Pekka had mentioned Samain.

But Pekka sailed further along the Irish coast, whatever it was that he had seen and discovered. Yet again he resembled an amateur historian on an exploratory expedition. Such names as Grianán of Aileach, Dún Aengus, Dunluce Castle, Kilmacduagh Abbey and Creevykeel revealed Celtic origins. But Pekka's comments were trivial and indicated that whatever he looked for, it was not the sites as such. He was looking for something because of or beyond what he saw. This was confirmed by what he wrote on the 21st of October, when he lay at anchor in an inlet just south of Galway.

'I have seen what I need to see. Everything fits together.

But I must have proof. Today I decided to sail back to the lion's den. It will be full moon in three days. I must keep on to the bitter end. Anything else would be immoral.'

That evening Pekka turned back northwards and entries in the logbook dealt only with wind, weather, navigation and setting sails. On the 24th of October he rode again at anchor south of Buncrana, not far from Fahen where he had been previously, but this time he lay west of a little island in the middle of the fiord. He had drawn a map with two crosses on its eastern side. 'Fahen big cross' and 'Grianán of Aileach' were written in the margin. Both places were clearly in Northern Ireland, while the *Sula* lay on the other side of the boundary.

'All preparations are complete here', he had written. 'But still I do not believe that this is the place. It is done to mislead such people as me. But where? I must decide. There is not much time left.'

Obviously he made up his mind, for the next day he was riding at anchor in Loch Spelve, on the southern side of Mull, in Scotland. That was, I thought, the advantage of a shallow-draught and swift-sailing catamaran. It could cover the eighty nautical miles between Ireland and Scotland in a night. Moreover, Pekka was able to sail in and conceal himself anywhere. At low tide he could remain where he was, dried out, until the next flood tide. Not even a fishing-boat could have gone into some of the anchorages used by *Sula*. With *Rustica* it was altogether out of the question; she drew nearly six feet and couldn't stand upright without legs. In Pekka's situation I wouldn't have been able to play hide-and-seek.

The peculiar thing was that while reading his logbook, I started to identify myself more and more with Pekka. Without my reflecting on the matter, it was myself I saw on his wanderings; it was I who stood at the helm, who glimpsed the fire on the Garvellachs, who felt just as sure as Pekka when he wrote: 'Now I am sure of it. With binoculars I have seen the fire. And tomorrow is 1st November. But how am I to get across the sound? I must see with my own eyes.'

He mentioned no name, but everything suggested that he meant one of the Garvellachs, which lay on the opposite side of the Firth of Lorn. It was there that earlier, on sailing by without having time to go ashore, he had seen a fire. I understood very well that he wondered how he was to get across if he intended to take his dinghy instead of *Sula*. On the chart I had before me while I read, I measured the distance as five miles, depending on where he started from. Into the bargain, the Firth of Lorn lay open to the full force of the Atlantic.

The next day he wrote:

'Tonight I'll finally see. I am afraid, but now I cannot turn back. I know too much already.'

Thereafter came the last normal logbook entry to be found in several pages: '23.00, SW 3-4. Clear sky. Full moon. Leave *Sula* and take dinghy.' What followed was a chaotic jumble written in a strained and deformed hand. The notations had the effect of outbursts.

'We are running away. They will find us soon.'

This was the first entry after the nocturnal excursion. It was partly explained on the next page:

'I saved her from a disgusting death. But she does not seem to be at all grateful. It can be the shock of discovering that she is alive. She was dead.'

'She' could be no-one else but Mary. What had Pekka saved her from? Clearly, he was far beyond giving explanations. However, he wrote two days later:

'I believe that I am in love with her but I can't tell her. Then she would think that is why I saved her. She cries a lot.'

On the 28th of October he appeared finally to have found some peace, and for the first time there was mention of the

Celtic Ring.

'Lying at anchor in Loch Na Droma Buidhe, completely alone. Nobody comes here at this time of year. Today I asked Mary about the Celtic Ring. She did not cry, but she refused to answer. I asked why she should die, but she did not answer that either. At last I asked her if she wanted to die. She shook her head. Then I asked if she wanted to come with me to Finland. 'It doesn't matter. I have failed everyone', she answered. Tomorrow I will sail to Oban. I'm going to talk with MacDuff. He may be one of them, but he is no murderer. The head cult and the sacrifices must be stopped. What do they want? The Celtic Ring is no ring. It is broken. It is a fringe, a sickle.'

I quickly turned the page. The explanation must come soon. But the two following pages were empty. And on the third was only this, written in straggling letters:

'We sailed to Oban, but I did not catch MacDuff. For once, I had luck. The harbour-master said that MacDuff had sailed out. But he also told me that MacDuff had asked him to be notified if we showed up. I asked where I could find MacDuff. It was a sad story, the harbour-master said. MacDuff was searching for a woman who had left him. 'Mary', was her name. I said that I would look for MacDuff, and we sailed out at once. MacDuff is more dangerous than all the rest. He loves Mary.'

I turned another page, but there were only notations on courses and positions. Pekka sailed northward, not by the shortest route - by one much like that of a fox pursued by hounds. I had great trouble in following him on my charts and in finding *Sula*'s anchorages. They were all in lonely, remote and often hazardous bays without any buildings or houses close by. Pekka took great risks in order to remain unseen. The least change of the wind could have turned some of his anchoring-places into death-traps. Not before reaching the next-to-last page of the logbook did I find something more, and it was almost illegible. Pekka had first written down the forecast:

'Gale 9 with gusts of storm force.'

It took me some time to decipher the rest, but I finally succeeded. Since I still have the logbook in my possession, I am able to copy it word for word:

'Storm. We are saved if we survive it. MacDuff will never dare to follow us through Pentland Firth. Mary does not know what is ahead of us. I really do not know myself, either. A wind of gale 9 meeting a current of 8 knots. Must expect we will go under. But we may have a twenty-five per cent chance of coming through. To me it does not matter either way. She does not love me. But she must not die. MacDuff lies four miles behind us now, but *Sula* goes faster than his disguised fishing-boat. We surf on the waves at 15 knots which he cannot do with all his horsepower. I must write this. Mary does not know that it is MacDuff who follows us. I have not dared to tell her.

Stroma in sight. The water is boiling. This is hell. The tide is carrying us towards the Pentland Skerries. If it does not turn in time we are lost. The waves are as high as the mast. MacDuff has turned back. My only satisfaction is that he must believe he drove Mary to her death. But I will take us through. For Mary's sake. And so I can tell about the Celtic Ring.'

That was the last page in the logbook. I could only guess what happened afterwards from what MacDuff had told me. But I would have given a great deal to read the continuation which might still be found aboard *Sula*.

All that could be heard was the lapping of water against *Rustica*'s port side and a sigh from the heater when a gust of wind ebbed away. The ship's clock ticked hollowly, but I had no idea of the time. Before me I saw the *Sula* on its way, with Pekka at the helm into a seething chaos of overfalls several metres high. MacDuff had lied to me as barefacedly as he had lied to Pekka. It wasn't Pekka who had willfully exposed himself and Mary to mortal peril; MacDuff was responsible. But why? And why was MacDuff 'dangerous'? Why should Mary die? What did it all mean? The Celtic Ring, the Golden Road, the King in the underworld and all the rest? The human sacrifices? The head cult? The questions piled up in my head until finally I felt unable to think. When at last I fell asleep, I knew only one thing for certain. I would go over to *Sula* and find out what it was all about. Or else simply return the logbook and then forget that I had ever met Pekka, MacDuff and Mary.

Chapter 5

WAKING up next day, not long before noon, was not exactly a pleasant experience. I had dreamt that *Rustica*, disabled, was drifting with the tide towards the cliffs of Stroma. I was struggling frantically with the tiller to make her change course, but the current was too strong. Finally, I realised that she was about to be wrecked. The crack when her stem splintered against the vertical wall of rock was doubtless what brought me half way to consciousness. Before I quite realised that I was awake and still alive, I looked up and saw blue sky through the hatch-cover. Later it struck me that it is perhaps not possible to dream that you die. Perhaps even in sleep, the brain short-circuits at the idea of its failing to function at all. One does not awake from a dream in order to rise from the dead, but to escape from fear and anguish at the prospect of being about to die.

It didn't take long until all the unanswered questions of the day before started whirling around in my head. I tried to think about something else, about the seagulls out on the mooring-posts with their heads against the wind. I thought about the fact that I had never seen one turn its tail towards the wind. I had also discovered that they could distinguish between different boats and between different people. Nowadays, when I put my head up through the hatch, they might glance at me nervously, but they didn't move away. With time, they had come to know me, in the same way as they always seemed to be able to tell a fishing-boat from another boat.

Under normal circumstances, I could observe the gulls indefinitely, study their flights and squabbles, but today I was too restless. The events of the previous evening didn't leave any place in my mind for anything else. It made matters no better that *Sula*'s logbook still lay on the cabin table and reminded me that something had to be done.

Pekka's story had upset me. But it had also fascinated me. What was the Celtic Ring? A group of political conspirators? A secret priesthood? The more I pondered, the greater my curiosity became. But it still remained a manageable curiosity, more or less as if I were reading a novel in which some chapters were missing. I only wanted to know what it was all about. I had no thought then of doing anything to find out, other than perhaps asking Pekka. I finally decided to give the logbook back to him, and along with it the responsibility and the trust he had placed in me.

The unsettled weather had passed and been followed in the night and morning by a light northerly wind that brought clear, cold air from the Arctic Ocean. The temperature had dropped to a few degrees below zero. There was hoar-frost on *Rustica*'s deck and on the quays.

I got dressed and walked round to the western harbour-basin. But before I was half way, I saw what had happened. *Sula* was gone. I asked the harbour-master, but he didn't even know that a boat had entered in the night. Naturally, he wondered what sort of boat it was, but I answered evasively. For if the Customs had moved *Sula*, he would certainly have been informed. That meant that Pekka and Mary must have sailed out of their own accord.

For a time, I stood on the quay and stared at the spot where *Sula* had been. If I hadn't felt the logbook in my inner pocket, I might have been able to say to myself that this had only been another episode among many others that lead nowhere. But I had accepted the logbook. I had allowed Pekka to believe that I assumed responsibility for what he entrusted to me.

And now what? Had Pekka sailed north or south? Actually, it didn't matter which. Either way, it could take me weeks to find him, even if I took leave from my work and spent all my time looking for him. But why should I? I wasn't involved.

I walked back to *Rustica* and sat down again with the logbook and the charts. But after going through everything once more, I was absolutely none the wiser. I even considered going to the police. But to use the police out of laziness or indifference is something I can't stand. Pekka hadn't wanted his logbook to be seen either by the Customs or the police. Why, I didn't know. Perhaps for some reason that had to do with Mary. Perhaps Mary's life might again be in danger if the police made investigations. Perhaps the police might give MacDuff clues, if they talked to him, about where to find Pekka and Mary. Of course these were only guesses. But the least I could do for Pekka was to keep the logbook to myself.

I don't remember exactly when the idea occurred to me of sailing to Scotland. It began as a question: What's stopping me? And after that: What have I got to lose? The answer to both questions was the same: 'Nothing. Absolutely nothing'.

Rustica had been fully equipped for long-distance cruising for quite some time already. I had devoted years, and thousands of pounds, to making her an ocean-going vessel. But the loans were repaid; and I had more than eight thousand pounds in the bank, reserved for long-distance cruising. In actual fact, the sole reason why I hadn't already set off was simply me, myself. I had been waiting for what I called 'the right moment', but there were times when I had begun to dread that it might never arrive. Why not now? I had got a reason to cast off, although I was perfectly conscious of the fact that my reason was nothing but a pretext. I say this to emphasise that I did not sail to live up to Pekka's confidence, even if I had not forgotten the look he gave me when he put the brown package in my hands. Nor Mary's tears.

But I realise that the major factor was my feeling that I had nothing to lose. For several years I had worn a tie, clocked in and clocked out at work in order to realise my dream, and I know of nothing as degrading as having to shove a register card into a punch-clock, only to make money. Those years had taken their toll. The joy of living had been draining away for quite some time and I didn't want to leave without some of it intact. I had not wanted to sail away as a way to escape a tedious everyday existence. That way out was also a sure way to become disappointed. In the end, it had become a vicious circle and the sole reason why I had been able to hold out was my living in *Rustica*. The sparkling winter mornings with ice piling up in the Sound, the cries from seagulls and wild ducks, the wind and weather, the sea and sky and the perpetual change was a necessary contrast to a sluggish and predictable life on land where still nothing could be taken for granted.

But living on *Rustica* had not been enough. My fears that I should live and die just like everybody else were both real and well-founded. It was so easy, and at times tempting, to sink into a delusive comfort and security ashore. In spite of all that has happened since my encounter with Pekka, I am in a way grateful to him and his logbook for shaking me abruptly out of my inertia. When I left Dragør I was thirty-six years old, and time seemed to be running faster and faster with each minute that passed. Temporarily at least, I have now managed to bring it to a standstill.

An element behind my decision should not be passed over, for it has its significance. Repeatedly, what Pekka wrote about the Celts in his logbook brought my friend Torben to mind. When I had given up my apartment and moved into the boat, I had left him all my books. I was certain that he had already read - thoroughly and reflectively - not skimmed through like me - those I possessed about Brittany, which was after all a Celtic country. I also knew that he had for some time taken an interest in the Druids, the spiritual and intellectual leaders of the Celts. Torben even regarded them as some kind of ideal. He had told me that their mission and vocation consisted in keeping all knowledge alive. Which was very much what he himself devoted his life to. If anybody could have understood Pekka's logbook, it would have been Torben.

Should I ask him to sail with me to Scotland? The idea was not altogether unreasonable. I had known Torben for many years and had always considered his friendship as an indispensable part of my life. So I felt no apprehension at the prospect of spending months with him in a confined sailing-boat, as I would have with so many others. Another great quality of Torben's was that he could - and would - throw all his plans overboard at a moment's notice. Providing that he had any plans stretching beyond the next day, which was rare.

Torben was now forty-two, and as yet he had never had to subject himself to the yoke of full-time work. He frequented assiduously the antiquarian booksellers of Copenhagen; when he needed money, he made a tour of obscure auction-rooms and second-hand dealers, found a few interesting first editions which he promptly sold at the more exclusive shops in the centre of town. His profits were enough to cover his immediate needs. Torben's other source of income was less profitable no doubt, but more pleasurable. Being a connoisseur of wines with a highly sensitive palate, he was employed by wine-importers as a consultant at wine-tastings. Although sometimes paid in ready money, as a rule he preferred to be paid in wine. Money was in his eyes too abstract and the product of the kind of collective declarations of faith that he detested and only upheld to the extent that they were absolutely necessary.

Partly to satisfy the authorities' desire for social tidiness, but also from interest, Torben studied Russian at the university. That meant that he could call himself a student if need be. However, the studies in organised form proceeded at a slow and uneven pace. In his view, the university had turned knowledge into a question of technology rather than into a way of living. He himself read or studied practically everything at his own rate and following his own lines. I have never known anyone else with such a thirst for knowledge, and with less wish to have his erudition confirmed or turned to account. Words like career, ambitions, future prospects, advancement, prestige, were foreign to him. When any one of our common acquaintances asked me what Torben actually did, there was really no answer, but that he stayed mentally and physically able, free and ready to make use of any great and interesting opportunity that came in his way.

Now and then, we had spoken of his accompanying me a bit on my way when I cast off for good. The fact that he was no sailor was under the circumstances both an advantage and a disadvantage. It was an advantage since he might not realise what sailing over the North Sea in January entailed, at least not until there could be no turning back. The disadvantage was of course that I should have preferred to have an experienced mate.

I had soon made up my mind. I went up to the harbour

call-box and dialled Torben's number. He answered immediately and sounded as if he had been waiting for me, and no other, to ring up. The person he spoke to always received his complete attention at once which gave you a pleasant feeling of privileged status.

'I'm sailing this evening, to Scotland', I said simply. 'What would you say to coming with me?'

'Has the time come for your long voyage?' he wondered.

'Yes, it has.'

There was a brief silence at the other end of the line. Neither of us liked telephone conversations, and we had them only to arrange where and when we'd meet. The fact that I detected a touch of surprise in his voice certainly did not come from my question as such, but only from my putting the matter to him over the telephone.

'What will I need to have with me?' Torben asked after a moment.

'Just take what you think you'll need. I've got the rest.'

'Anything particular you'd like to have along?'

I considered.

'Well, you might bring the books you have on Celtic history. Or ones I've left with you.'

'Is that your latest passion?' he asked.

He knew that I often cast myself headlong into a new subject, which would absorb all my interest for some weeks and then vanish without leaving much trace in my mind.

'Something of that kind, yes,'

'When do you want me to come?'

'As soon as you can. This evening, in fact. I have some preparations to make, but they won't take me more than a couple of hours.'

'Are you really in such a hurry?'

'Yes,' I told him, 'I am. I have waited long enough as it is.'

'All right - I'll be there!'

As I left the call-box, I thought that there was a hint of genuine puzzlement in the way he had said this.

What would I answer if Torben pressed the question of why we were sailing so quickly? The more I pondered on the matter, the less inclined I felt to speak about Pekka before we were well out on the North Sea. Some elements in what Pekka related might too easily arouse Torben's scepticism to the full. Torben had a complex relationship to theories and symbols, to everything that did not leave the inexplicable unexplained. In that sense, he was pedantically matter-of-fact. He accepted mystery, but refused to believe in it. He meant on the contrary that the best way of destroying mystery was to place belief in it, to decide whether it was true or not. Getting straight to the point was always the important thing; what was left was mystery. And that should not be tampered with unnecessarily. 'A hypothesis is a hypothesis,' he commonly declared. 'Nothing more.' The trouble was that a lot of people started to take them for the truth as soon as they had been formulated. 'We don't need to believe' was another of his oft-repeated maxims. So I had reason to fear that he might not take Pekka and his logbook seriously and that he would dismiss it all as pure fantasy.

I looked about *Rustica*'s cabin. All was prepared. I had for example already completed lists of the provisions needed for different cruises. It took me only a few minutes to choose the most appropriate list: 'Ten days of continuous sailing and stores for three weeks'. As I didn't know how often we would be able to go ashore, or how many days we would be in harbour, it was best to take sufficient supplies from the beginning.

From my lists I also took one giving all that must be done before *Rustica* could leave, mostly in order to have the satisfaction of seeing that very few measures remained to be taken. Most yachtsmen who are planning to go long-distance cruising decide a date of departure far in advance. They then make a so-many-days-left-before-Christmas count-down, and the closer they get to the day, the more they find left to do. I once met a crew on a boat in Denmark the day before they were due to leave for a cruise in the Mediterranean of a couple of years. They were completely exhausted and did not look forward to the big day. The only thing they wanted was to sleep. And sleep was exactly what they did when I met them in the next harbour after their departure. In my view, fixing a certain date of departure is a sign of deficient foresight. The essential thing is not to determine a time to leave, scarcely even to make a voyage at all; it is being able to leave when the right time for departure comes. But the preparations must be carefully made.

I had already more or less disposed of a major difficulty: breaking off relations with the so-called authorities, a word that makes me jump, since I have always had difficulties in understanding in virtue of what higher power they can exercise this authority. One would have thought that the simplest thing was to tell the truth, that you wanted to go sailing for a couple of years, but that is when the serious problems began. My solution was first of all to live officially in a postal box, something which for some reason was permitted. The second remedy was simply to pay an accountant who filled up my tax-return forms and took care of all official enquiries using sheets of paper with my signature in blanco.

I had tried the system for two years already and it functioned well. It meant that I could sail without being reported missing and without creating any problems for anybody. If I so wished, I would vanish from the earth as if I no longer existed. Except as in blanco. That was probably, I thought on my way up to the supermarket, a suitable point of departure for this trip. Whatever happened, nobody would miss us. And no one would know where we were.

At the supermarket, more practical matters occupied my mind. With the list in my hand, I hastened about and filled several shopping wagons which I pushed down to the boat. It was no problem to stow everything quickly away since my list clearly indicated where all was to go.

When Torben appeared, *Rustica* was shipshape. The boom-cover had been removed, and the jib lay ready on the foredeck. I was sitting with a cup of coffee and looking through Pekka's logbook.

'What are you reading?' Torben promptly asked as he climbed down into the cabin with his luggage.

'A logbook,' I answered, feigning indifference.

It was, of course, Torben's passion for books and the written word in general that made him ask. If he saw someone reading a book, he could never help wondering what the book was, why you read just that book and wanted to have a look in it himself.

'Really!' he said. 'I've read a lot of logbooks in my time. Magellan wrote one which wasn't too bad. Who wrote that one?'

'Somebody I know who has been in Scotland.'

'It's a manuscript, in other words.'

'Yes. Not especially interesting. Not even as logbooks go. I borrowed it to get a few hints as to where we might sail.'

I put the volume aside, beyond reach of Torben's curiosity and reading-thirst. I would let him have it in due time. When I had prepared him for its contents.

'I can read it later,' he said.

He opened his suitcase, which seemed to be filled with nothing but books.

'I brought along a couple of books from my shelves, about Scotland and the Celts.'

He put them on the table. I looked at the titles. As I

expected, many of the books were about Druids: The Druids by Piggot and Les Druides by Le Roux and Guyonvarc'h, The Life and Death of a Druid Prince by Ross and Robins. Some dealt with Celtic history in general: The Celts by Delaney and The Celts by Chadwick, also La Civilisation celtique by Le Roux and Guyonvarc'h in the same series as their book on the Druids. Then, there were books to do with Scotland and Ireland in a general way; and two volumes about the Irish Republican Army, The IRA by Coogan, The Provisional IRA. by Bishop and Mallie and The Battle for Scotland by Andrew Marr. I recognized a book I owned but had never read, Jean Markale's La Bretagne Secrète.

I gazed at Torben in wonderment.

'Where did you get hold of all these?' I asked.

'I had some of them already,' he answered. The ones about the Druids, for example. And on the IRA. Some years ago I read everything I could lay my hands on about terrorists. But I got quite a few of the books at a bookshop on the way here. Aren't they what you wanted me to bring?'

'Yes, of course they are.'

I ought to have understood that, at a word from me, he would come hauling along half a library. I looked about for a place to put so many books. They certainly weren't foreseen in my list of where things should be stowed. True, I had reserved the port side of the cabin for Torben, but the books required more space than that.

'What else have you brought?' I asked with some misgivings.

'Don't worry', he grinned. 'That's about it.'

From his not especially capacious shoulder-bag, he produced a toilet-case, some nicely bound notebooks of a type he bought in Germany, a change of clothes and, finally, a clarinet.

'Is that all?' I asked.

'Well, you did say that you had all the rest.'

No doubt I had made a mistake. I should never have told Torben to bring what he thought he needed. That was almost nothing, except for the books.

'We can use the clarinet as a fog-horn', I said.

'Dolphins like the sound of a clarinet,' Torben assured me, and he blew two or three bars on it. 'I have read somewhere that they do.'

For all I knew, dolphins might well like clarinets. That was their problem. But I didn't.

'You can try to put everything into the locker on the port side,' I told him. 'That's your bunk, as the mate.'

'Port side?' asked Torben, perhaps joking and perhaps not.

'Right or left?'

'Left when you're looking for'ard. I'll give you a book where it's all explained.'

'Good. When do we sail?'

'Now.'

He looked up.

'In the dark?'

'Yes.'

'What should I do?'

'Nothing special. Just enjoy being at sea. At least to start with.'

'And after that?'

'Then I'll teach you to sail.'

'Wouldn't it have been better to wait until summer?'

'Yes, but I've waited altogether too long as it is. I was afraid that it would never come off.'

Happily, Torben appeared to be satisfied with this explanation; of course he knew what I felt about having to work just to save money.

I searched through my own locker and took out woollen

sweaters and a set of thermal underwear for Torben.

'Put all these on', I told him.

Sailing in January would certainly be very cold. If *Rustica* heeled more than fifteen degrees the stove wouldn't function. Actually, it wasn't until now that I really realised that we were about to sail across the North Sea in the middle of winter. We would have to listen to the ice-reports for one thing, at least until we were out on the North Sea. A gale-warning was in fact a mere trifle compared to the risk of being covered with ice. As a matter of fact, we ought to have an ice-pick on board. I made a mental note that we should get hold of one in the first port.

I looked covertly at Torben. He appeared to be full of confidence, and he whistled a little as he put on sweaters and oilskins. But how well could he cope with the hardships which we would certainly have to face? How much was he able to take? Even if he was a master at 'making the best of the situation', and though he didn't easily lose his self-possession, could he withstand the cold? Was he going to be seasick?

For a moment, I considered breaking off the last preparations, sitting down with Torben, pouring us a whisky and explaining what we were in for. Not only sailing-wise, but also everything I knew or suspected about Pekka and MacDuff and the Celtic Ring. What deterred me was a nagging doubt that Torben wouldn't take me seriously and in the end I decided despotically that we would sail, that we would do it as soon as possible and that I wouldn't tell Torben anything until we were at least half-way across the North Sea. I regret this now, but such was my decision.

Chapter 6

WE cast off on the 19th of January 1990, at 21.00 hours, in darkness, with snow-heavy clouds somewhere above our heads. Torben huddled by the companionway while I manoeuvred. He observed all my actions and wondered why I was doing what I did. One of his early questions was whether it mattered which mooring line was cast off first. This gave me the opportunity of explaining that you must always think wind when sailing: unless there was a strong current, the mooring line to leeward was to be cast off before the windward one. Torben nodded. He never neglected an occasion to learn something new.

When we were gliding ghost-like past the heads of the piers, Torben had already put on the head lamp he always had with him and begun to read one of my handbooks on sailing. The lamp was of an expensive kind intended for champion orienteerers, but Torben had acquired it so he could read in all situations, wherever he happened to find himself.

I let him do as he wished, even if light from the lamp diminished my night vision, much needed to identify light characteristics and perceive approaching ships. But I knew the Sound in and out, and we were to sail up the Danish coast, which was free of shoals and sandbanks.

We didn't say much to each other that first night. I headed for the island of Ven in a light northwesterly wind and was absorbed in thoughts about the Celts, about Pekka, about Mary and my own foolhardiness. Torben had already turned in when I lashed the helm and listened to our first weather report at sea. It seemed strange to hear about the ice situation in the Baltic and realise that we might encounter ice even in the Kattegatt, although thus far it had been ice free. For the time being, I was sure of only one thing: that we must get out on the North Sea as soon as possible.

So I was almost glad that the weather report gave a warning of near-gale for the Kattegatt the next day: 'SW, 7'. But we could happily have been spared the '*Risk of light ice forming*' and the forecasted '*precipitation in form of snow*'. I recall, however, my thinking that it was just as well for us to be put on our mettle. We needed to be hardened and get our sea legs as soon as we could.

After having been cosy in the warmth from the cabin's heater, and listening to the radio as if we weren't out sailing at all, I noticed for example that I felt a certain reluctance towards climbing up into the cold, dark cockpit. That was a bad habit I had to get rid of. Even if it might be some degrees milder when we came out on the North Sea and felt the Gulf Stream, we would certainly be very cold with the heater turned off. The paraffin-lamps gave a bit of heat, but not nearly enough to relieve the effect of a raw, damp North Sea wind.

When I came up, I saw the light from Helsingborg, in Sweden, glowing together with that from Elsinore as if the two towns formed a single narrow urban strip. At 04.30 hours we stole past Kronborg Castle, and then our course led us away from shore. The thermometer showed 3°, the wind was still light and following, and the darkness just as impenetrable as before. It would be hours until sunrise.

I began to steer standing up, in order to fight the treacherous tiredness which always attacked me not long before dawn. To keep myself occupied, I took bearings on the blinking eye of Kullen lighthouse. The chart lay in its plastic cover, under the red light of the compass, and I practised laying out bearings without a protractor. After a little practice you could measure them by the eye to as close as five degrees.

At about eight o'clock, the dawn came just as imperceptibly as always. You can never tell exactly when the darkness begins to disappear and the light is creeping forth. Suddenly you seem to sense, rather than see, a grey hue in the darkness, or in what a fleeting instant before was darkness. The beams from lighthouses and the glimmer of stars fade until you are no longer certain where they are in the greyness. You stare feverishly and you believe for some more vanishing instants that you actually see, but only because you persuade yourself that it is already light, wishing it to be light. In actual fact, you see nothing at all during the transition from dark to light; everything blurs together. That is, I think, why the dawn brings a certain apprehension. The night is a safe cocoon; the dawn is a no man's land without sky or sea. In a storm one dreads to see, as the light comes, foaming, towering waves. In calm weather, you fear that you will see the first signs of an approaching storm. At dawn no one ever believes that the morning will be calm, beautiful, clear. Why this is so I cannot say.

But when Torben drowsily put his head up through the hatch, my anxiety was over and only my weariness was left.

'Aren't you going to bed?' he asked.

'We'll see.'

I explained how he should pre-heat the paraffin stove with the Tilley wick, which always lay soaking in methylated spirits. And before long we both sat holding steaming mugs of coffee. The wind had increased a little, sufficiently for the wind pilot to be connected. It was now steering *Rustica* without my help.

A thin layer of frozen condensation lay on the deck, and there was rime on the portholes. Now and then, I looked covertly for ice floes. *Rustica*'s plastic hull was strong, but it wasn't certain that sailing into a rough block of ice wouldn't be too much for her.

Torben suddenly raised his gaze from his coffee, looked me directly in the eye and asked:

'Where, actually, are we on the way to? I admit that I don't know as much as you do about sailing, but is it really sensible to sail away like this in the middle of winter? And to Scotland, of all places!'

'I have always wanted to sail to Scotland, you know.'

'I do know. But might it not be a damned nasty trip?'

'Well, yes.'

'I read the other day that they are going to raise the oil rigs by three feet or so. Do you know why?'

'No.'

'Because they have sunk below the level of the highest possible waves in the North Sea. And do you know how high that is?'

I shook my head. I neither knew nor wished to know.

'Eighty feet', Torben said triumphantly. 'And winter storms on the North Sea can last for up to two days.'

'You don't need to come with me if you don't want to. In a few hours we'll be on Anholt, and from there you can take a ferry to Grenå.'

'That's not what I meant you to say. I simply want to know what we can expect. How fiendish is it likely to be?'

'Pretty bad, I suppose. If we're lucky. It could be complete and absolute hell too.'

'In that case I'll stay on board.'

I looked at him with surprise.

'What do you mean by that?' I asked.

'Well,' he said 'I hope you don't believe that I'd let you

sail alone across the North Sea in such conditions. You need to have a level-headed person with you if you're to get home again safe and sound.'

'Somebody who has a clarinet,' I said with a warmth intended to show what I felt.

'As a matter of fact', he said, 'I'd rather like to see an eighty-foot wave. It must be quite an experience.'

'You don't know what you are talking about.'

During the last half hour, I had noticed that the sky in the southwest was changing colour. I looked up and saw from the ragged clouds that there was already a hard wind blowing higher up.

'You'll soon get a foretaste of whatever is coming', I told Torben. 'Look over there!'

Heavy, steel blue clouds were rapidly approaching.

'We have to take in a reef. Reduce sail', I added and turned the vane on the wind pilot so that *Rustica* would come into the wind. 'Go down and turn off the heater. Stow away all cups and clarinets, and I'll take care of the rest up here.'

Torben disappeared but soon came back to see and learn.

At the same time as the *Rustica* came into the wind, I ran up on deck, pulled down the mainsail, made fast the reefing loop, took in the reef-line, then hoisted the sail again. I lowered the head sail and lashed it along the deck.

'Four minutes,' said Torben, when I came aft and set the wind pilot on course again. 'Don't you think that your hero Hornblower would have been pleased with you?'

Torben was aware of my partiality for English sea-stories; he had read several of them himself, for friendship's sake. Presumably that was where he had learned the little he knew about storm winds and sail-handling. Unfortunately, *Rustica*, with her two man crew, was not the same as a frigate or a ship of the line with hundreds of sailors on board.

'Here comes the wind', I said, pointing again. 'And snow. We're going to have a snowstorm.'

Within seconds, sea and sky both vanished, and there was nothing but a white and flickering that whipped at us. It didn't take long for the snow to cover the cockpit and to bleach Torben's bushy black beard pure white. This, I thought to myself, is a kind of madness and I wondered in complete earnest if we shouldn't have brought a snow shovel. Foam from the waves froze to ice on the foredeck and hung on the guard-rails. If the storm continued for long we'd be forced to hack away the ice. Ships have been known to founder under the weight of ice.

Meanwhile, however, we were making good speed. The log pointed at eight knots and remained there.

'How can we catch sight of Anholt now?' Torben called through the wind.

'When we get there', I shouted back.

There was no other answer. True, I had a simple radio direction finder, but that could only help us to find the island, not the narrow entry to a harbour. I had always been against having too much electronic equipment on board. My concessions were a short wave radio, to get time signals for the astro navigation, and the radio direction finder. Now, I was forced to admit that my principle would not be worth much if we went under at Anholt. On the other hand, there was almost always a safe course, away from reefs and shallows.

'If it comes to the worst, we'll just sail past,' I told Torben.

He nodded without visible disappointment. He trusted my judgement, which was more than I did myself right there and then.

'We may just as well go and lie down', I said.

I looked at the compass. The wind was strong and stable. It was the ideal conditions for the wind pilot, christened Sten after one of my favourite mates. For some strange reason almost all sailors give names to their auto-pilots. Even Slocum, who sailed around the world single-handed without fancy steering-aids, believed now and then that he had a human helper at the tiller.

There were 20 miles left to Anholt, with nothing to be done on deck. For that matter, the deck had become slippery as glass and it was dangerous to move about.

I took the thermos flask and poured out two scalding cups of coffee. Both Torben and I sank down on the starboard berth, so that we didn't have to brace ourselves because we were heeling over. We held our steaming cups with both hands, not wishing to waste their valuable warmth.

A sudden blast of wind made *Rustica* heel over an extra five degrees down to the gunwale, and a few drops of coffee spilled from Torben's cup. I got up and put my head through the hatch. But all was as before. The reefed mainsail was drawing hard. The wind vane swung to and fro, snow whipped down, foam blew from the tops of waves and spurted up on the lashed head-sail where it froze into icicles which now and then were blown to pieces and fell down on the deck with a tinkling sound. I drew the hatch cover shut. A sense of unreality, which I was not used to when sailing, came over me. Actually, I should have lain down and rested, but I felt as if we lacked time. I turned to Torben where he sat trying to rock in rhythm with the roll.

'What do you know about the Celts', I asked him, partly to distract our thoughts from the near-gale howling in the rigging, but also because I wanted to know.

He looked at me with curiosity .

'What do you know yourself? There is no point in telling you what you know already.'

'Not very much. They were a powerful people who dominated Northern Europe a few centuries before Christ. The

Druids, who were the Celts' priests, judges, walking libraries and teachers, all at the same time, had great influence on people's lives. What more? Caesar put an end to their supremacy when he defeated Vercingetorix at Alésia. The Celtic tradition has survived in Brittany, and Ireland, in Wales and Scotland. And I know that many people have begun to interest themselves in their Celtic heritage. I read something about the Celts recently in the National Geographic. Then it's the music of course, Van Morrison, the Chieftains and others. And then I've heard of the King Arthur legends in their different versions. And I've read some Irish folk tales.'

'All of them written down and probably distorted by Christian monks,' Torben said in a tone of condemnation, as if the monks had deprived him, personally, of being able to read Irish folk tales in the original version.

'There of course we have the problem,' he went on. 'Most of what we really know about the early Celts comes from the Romans, especially Caesar. And, naturally, he regarded his enemies as uneducated barbarians.

The second source isn't much better: Celtic tales retold by Christian monks who did everything they could to make the old traditions fit into Christian doctrine. At the same time, it's a fact that one of the Celts' many interesting traits was a refusal ever to write down anything of importance. They had a written language, but everything of significance was related orally. The only things preserved in writing are disconnected fragments of words, either on coins or inscribed on stones. Above all, they never wrote anything about their rites and cults, or about what nowadays we'd call religion. According to many people, the Celts believed that what was written down died. And in a way the Celts were right. Because if all knowledge is to have room in the memory of one man and to be conveyable orally, it must be kept alive. The fact that the Druids did keep it alive was certainly one of the reasons why they exercised such a great influence - why they were the equals of kings. The Druids quite simply possessed all the Celts' collected knowledge of their time. It's reckoned that twenty years of learning were required to produce a Druid. And what did they learn? ... Well, presumably they had to remember everything worth preserving. They were actually living libraries and universities at the same time.'

Torben fell silent and I saw a yearning look in his eyes. No doubt that the idea of all knowledge being constantly available, always infused with life, exerted a great attraction on him. So it wasn't difficult to understand why he had developed such an interest in the Druids.

After some reflection, he went on.

'It may have been for that same reason that they didn't build temples or churches. They were satisfied with holy woods and wells. Then, too, they never succeeded in forming a state or a nation. Unlike most other people, they lived in federations with many equally important kings. Jean Markale - one of the authorities on Celtic, and especially Breton history - thinks that Celtic culture is opposed to fixed and established borders, whether geographic of other kind. And that the idea of a state or nation is entirely foreign to Celts. It is typical, for instance, that Bretons had only a duke as their leader as late as 1532, when they lost their independence. Nobody dared to proclaim himself king and thereby draw on himself the displeasure of the common people. In early Celtic there isn't even a word for 'native land', not as the French use *patrie* and the Germans *Vaterland*.'

'And what about the Druids?'

'First of all, they placed spiritual powers before secular ones. They were not merely the equals of kings; they stood above them. No king would take any action without first consulting the Druids. That may have been why Celts were conquered by the Romans, in spite of the fact that

Vercingetorix had half a million men under arms. But the Celts had soldiers who fought naked because that had received the Druids' blessing and they believed they were invulnerable. But they believed, too, in a life after this one, in *Sid*, a paradise lying somewhere to the west of Ireland where all was peace, youth and love, and where time stood still. Caesar thought that *Sid* was the reason why Celts went so willingly to war and what made them formidable soldiers. Strangely enough, there are still some that profess this idea. Jean Markale is one of them. But both he and Caesar must have got hold of the wrong end of the stick. The Celts couldn't have fought for their lives. On the contrary, it must have been tempting for them to be a bit incautious, so as to die and get to *Sid*. Not to escape from the life they lived, they had no sense of sin, but only because *Sid* was so attractive in itself. There was no better place to be, quite simply.'

'Have you read anything about a head cult and human sacrifices?' I interrupted, thinking about Pekka's logbook.

'Oh yes. Many of the Celtomaniacs hold that reports of those things are slanderous lies. But I don't believe it. So many people have idealized the Druids and made them peaceful men in white robes. But there are other testimonies besides Caesar's word that the Celts sacrificed human beings, their enemies or themselves, and that they were fond of keeping the heads on public view. But nobody knows how common it was, who they sacrificed or why. Was it just about anybody, first come first served so to speak, criminals, or was being sacrificed to the gods a mark of honour for those in power? Nobody knows. One of the latest theories is that the Druids sacrificed one another when they were in the mood. Two archaeologists who investigated the so called 'Lindow Man', a two thousand year old fellow they found in England, maintain that the man was a prominent Druid sacrificed by his colleagues to three different gods. Each god was privileged with the right to a special method of execution. So the Lindow Man was knocked unconscious by three blows on the back of his head. Then strangled with a garrotte, and finally drowned. None of the three gods could feel neglected.'

'But how can all that be known?' I wondered.

'Well, an Irish folk tale relates how the person to be sacrificed was chosen. A round piece of bread was broken up and the bits of it were laid in a basket. One of the bits was burned, and the person who took it out was sacrificed. And they happened to find traces of burnt bread in the Lindow Man's stomach. A case of Celtic Russian roulette you might say. But the most interesting thing may be that remains of bodies sacrificed in the same way have been found in Denmark the 'Tollunda Man', for example. You've heard of him? Well, it could indicate that the spiritual sway of the Celts extended over all northern Europe.'

The Tollunda Man, Pekka had written about him. I was just going to question Torben on the subject when we heard a loud thud from the hull.

'What was that?' said Torben.

'Probably ice,' I answered in as calm a voice as possible.

I dashed up on deck with Torben after me. Quite right. A small clump of ice, which could have done no damage, was disappearing in the wake of the ship.

'We'll have to start keeping watch, instead of telling stories,' I said.

Torben looked at me thoughtfully.

'Why are you so interested in the Celts? You even forgot that you were sailing.'

'I'll explain later,' I told him, but somewhat brusquely.

Until the North Sea, I thought, when it will be too late to turn back. I stared through the snow with screwed up eyes, attempting to catch sight of any large block of ice before it would be too late. Torben asked nothing more, but he didn't help me to keep a look out. He had known me long enough to suspect that I was keeping something from him. But at the same time he also knew that I would never do anything that could be of harm to him. If I had dragged him out to sea in the middle of winter, he took it for granted that I had good reasons for doing so. I reflected that neither of us had ever questioned the other's good intentions. In a way that was the very basis of our friendship. As it should be of all friendships.

But now, in the midst of a snowstorm, I began to realise that sailing to Scotland and Ireland in full winter could very well be disastrous for him. Whatever might happen when we got to the other side, crossing the North Sea in the winter certainly had its dangers. The thought dejected me. But there was still something that stopped me from telling Torben the whole story. But I only stared more and more obstinately through the snowstorm.

At 15.45 hours we sighted Anholt. Actually it was not an island that we saw, only something massively white beyond the dotted and flickering whiteness of the falling snow. We were about half a nautical mile from the southern point of the island, and when we drew closer we saw that the high cliffs were topped with snow. From a distance, the island resembled a monumental iceberg, newly sliced out of Greenland's inland ice.

The sea was still rough, and I understood that the entrance to the harbour open to the southwest would be a maelstrom. Under normal conditions, I suppose that I would have sailed on, or hove to on the leeward side of the island, or waited for the wind to shift. But the disturbing silence between Torben and me had to be broken. And I was so exhausted that I ached. Moreover, it was just as well that we accustomed ourselves to taking some risks. I had no reason to believe that things would become easier in the immediate future.

We were fast approaching the harbour entrance, which

was sixty feet across. I saw to it that *Rustica* arrived at the opening with the wind on the quarter. That was her fastest position and we needed speed to get steerage way. The log showed nine knots when *Rustica*'s stern was lifted up on the summit of a huge wave which pitched her into the outer harbour. It was all over in a couple of seconds, and the peace that fell over the boat seemed unnatural, something which no longer exists in this world. Many people who sail live just for that instant. I do myself. But I prefer to have sailed some hundreds of miles beforehand, the better to feel how tension is relieved and replaced by deep satisfaction.

We lowered the sails in the big outer harbour, started the motor, an old Norwegian SABB that sounded like a tractor, and chugged into the inner harbour. We berthed at a quay astern of a fishing boat; this was the AN 29, belonging to the island, and now the only other boat in that large harbour, which in the summer sheltered hundreds of yachts. To see it as we did, in the light of only an occasional lamp, of fragmented flashes from the lighthouse on top of the cliffs and of the leading lights, with snow on the quays, was both uplifting and uncanny. A harbour without boats always makes me think of graveyards, which I have never much cared for.

Two fishermen came up on the deck of the fishing boat; they stared at us as if *Rustica* were a Scandinavian Flying Dutchman.

'I'm going to go below and sleep.' I said to Torben. 'We'll talk things over later.'

'All right, Captain. I'll take a look at the town.'

'There isn't one. A hundred and-sixty lonely souls live here in the winter, most of them in a village at the middle of the island. But there is a tavern.'

'Then I'll go there and have a beer.'

Torben pulled on his old skipper's jacket and disappeared up the steep hillside, between wind tormented pines and juniper bushes. I waved in greeting to the two fishermen, climbed down into the cabin, lighted the heater and turned in. I was awakened by somebody knocking on the pulpit. Who..? Torben wouldn't have bothered to knock. I opened the deck hatch, put up my head, and saw the shadowy form of somebody standing on the quay.

'Can I come on board?' asked a raucous Danish voice.

'Of course!' I answered without giving it much thought.

I quickly reclosed the hatch. There was a cold and biting wind outside.

I got up, put on trousers, lighted the paraffin lamp and opened. A man in wellingtons and blue overalls stood in the cockpit. He had thick knitted headgear and, in one hand, two bottles of beer. I recognized him as a fisherman from the fishing-vessel.

'May I offer you a beer?' he said. 'We don't often have visitors in the harbour at this time of year.'

'Come in!'

He stepped down and looked about. I was slowly returning to life, and I wondered why I had invited him on board. But it was too late for regrets. I saw from the ship's clock that I had slept for two hours. Not much. But I had a whole night before me.

'Nice and warm here,' the man said and opened two bottles of beer, one with the help of the other.

From my years in Denmark I had learned never to be surprised by the ways a Dane can open a beer bottle. A lighter, the heel of a wooden shoe, a key, anything did the trick.

'Rough weather, though. We measured a good seven.'

'It could have been worse,' I told him.

He pushed a bottle over to me.

'Easy to say that, when you have come into harbour. Skål!'

We clinked our bottles.

'Where are you heading?' he asked.

I had no cause to be secretive about the matter. Torben had doubtless told everybody willing to listen that we were sailing northwards across the North Sea, which was what I said.

Carsten, as his name was, shook his head.

'Have all the yachties gone crazy this year?' he said half to himself after a moment.

I must have looked at him in surprise.

'Well, the day before yesterday,' he explained, 'a Finn arrived here directly from Scotland.'

Just then I heard a footstep on deck. Torben was coming back at the worst possible moment, for I had not yet managed to give him my version of what lay behind our voyage. I feared that he would now put two and two together, but make it five, and abandon *Rustica* and me. How could I quickly get Carsten on to another subject?

But at the next minute Torben's bearded face appeared in the hatchway.

'You won't believe it's true,' he said. 'Here we have been out in a snowstorm talking about Celts, and then I hear in the tavern that the island has recently been invaded by people with Scottish connections. One of them was a mad Finn who came straight from Scotland in a catamaran. And in his wake a real Scotsman turned up and wanted to get hold of the Finn. Then I came happily in and proudly declared that we are going to sail to Scotland. Hardly surprising that they looked a bit peculiarly at me. And I couldn't even explain why we are going to Scotland just now! I couldn't really tell them the truth, could I, that I too sailed with a crazy skipper who has a lot of weird ideas in his head. Or perhaps you have a better explanation? A credible one, the sort that could be believed in?'

I heard from Torben's voice that there was no way out of it. I'd be forced to make everything clear. Meanwhile, he finished shaking off snow, came down into the cabin and saw Carsten.

'Oh, excuse me,' Torben said, 'I didn't know you had a guest.'

Chapter 7

'This,' I explained to Carsten, 'is Torben, my crew.'

The fisherman looked with a certain awe at the still snowy creature with a head lamp on its brow.

Torben brushed off a little more snow and put the lamp down on the table.

'You ought to set up street lights on the island,' he said to Carsten, sat down at the navigation table and put his feet up on the engine-box.

'So what are you two talking about?' he asked.

'We had scarcely begun to have a conversation when you arrived' I said.

'You must admit,' Torben said and turned to Carsten, 'that it's strange that so many people who are interested in Scotland happen to turn up here at about the same time.'

'It is,' said Carsten.

'Did you meet that Finn, Pekka I think he was called?' Torben wondered.

'No, not really,' Carsten replied evasively.

'How was he?'

'Who?'

It was quite clear that Carsten tried to avoid the subject,

but Torben didn't give up.

'Pekka, the Finn,' he said. 'From what I heard at the tavern, he's an odd customer.'

'He talked a lot.'

'About what?'

'Everything possible. Mostly nonsense. He drank.'

'Was he alone on board?'

Carsten raised his eyebrows.

'I don't know. I was never on board.'

'There was somebody up at the tavern who thought he saw an unfamiliar woman down here in the port. And, apparently, someone at the radar station had seen a fire on the cliff south of the port. With his binoculars, he saw a woman standing in front of a fire with her arms stretched towards the sky and the sea. Mysterious, eh?'

Carsten didn't answer.

'Didn't you see the fire from your boat?'

'At night I sleep.'

'And the Scotsman?' Torben asked with an obstinacy that surprised me.

'The fellow named MacDuff? What did you make of him?'

'He asked too many questions. Just like you.'

It was obvious that Carsten didn't like Torben's stubborn manner. 'Are you from the police?' he burst out in an aggressive voice.

Torben's amazement was comical. That anyone could mistake him for a policeman must have been completely beyond his comprehension.

'Pekka was a sailor,' Carsten added. 'Nothing else.'

'Do you really believe,' I asked him, 'that we would have come here through a snowstorm in a sailing boat if we were policemen?'

'Maybe not,' Carsten admitted after a moment.

'I'd never heard of Pekka before today,' Torben said when he had found his voice again.

He took his feet down from the engine-box.

'Somebody at the tavern said that he was headed for the Sound, when he sailed from here. For Dragør, to be precise. And I have just come from there.'

He turned and looked at me.

'A strange coincidence, isn't it?'

The whole thing had got out of hand. Now I'd be compelled to tell Torben all I knew before we had left the Kattegatt. But perhaps I could keep the important part until I was alone with Torben.

'It's my fault from beginning to end,' I told both him and Carsten. 'I have met Pekka.'

Torben didn't show any surprise. But there was no mistaking Carsten's curiosity. I realised that he had talked more with Pekka than he had allowed to show.

'When was that?' he asked.

'The day before yesterday'

'Where?'

'In the old harbour at Dragør. Pekka sailed in at about eleven o'clock.'

'Was he alone? '

'No, he wasn't.'

I waited for a moment, then added:

'He had a woman on board.'

'Where are they now?' Carsten asked.

'I haven't the faintest idea.'

'And MacDuff?'

Without realizing it, Carsten asked me almost the same questions as Torben. I already knew that the next question would be if I had met MacDuff.

'They never met,' I said to forestall him.

Carsten seemed to understand immediately what I meant.

73

Relief appeared on his face. He spun his beer bottle on the table.

'What happened?' he asked.

I related briefly what had occurred at Dragør, without revealing how much I knew, or mentioning Pekka's logbook. I wanted to learn more of what Carsten had heard.

'I was sorry for Pekka!' he suddenly said.

'Why?' Torben broke in. 'I know nothing, absolutely nothing about the affair, other than what I heard at the tavern and what came out just now. But it seems as if everyone else knows quite a lot. How about sharing some of your knowledge, in the name of democracy, so to speak?'

'Why are you sailing to Scotland?' Carsten asked me abruptly, exactly the question I wanted to avoid answering just then before I had talked privately with Torben.

'To help Pekka,' I replied, startled by my own frankness.

'Shouldn't we be sailing in the opposite direction in that case?' Torben wondered.

'No.' I answered, without giving any reason.

'I don't understand,' Torben said. 'Listening to you, it sounds as if MacDuff were the Devil in person.'

Torben looked at me, and I tried to pass on the question by looking at Carsten, and Carsten looked down at the table. When he raised his eyes, he had evidently decided to entrust us with what he knew.

'I don't know much more than you do,' he began. 'MacDuff arrived here on the same day as Pekka had sailed off. As soon as he came ashore, he began to go about the port and ask us fishermen if we had seen a Finn with a catamaran. I think he went aboard all the boats here. There were five or six of us at the time. None of us was willing to say anything. We're not much for getting ourselves involved. Besides, his coming to Anholt just to look for Pekka seemed peculiar. Some people thought he was an English policeman, and that didn't make things any better. We haven't normally any police on the island, and we don't need them either.'

Carsten gave Torben a meaningful look.

'When MacDuff didn't get anywhere with us, he went up to the tavern. And there he must have met somebody who was drunk, and who told him that Pekka had been on the island and had sailed just that morning. It wasn't long before MacDuff came running back. Now he had to get to Zealand at any price, and he wanted one of us to sail him there. He offered to pay a lot, but none of us wanted to have anything to do with his money. The more he offered, the less we cared. When he understood that we weren't going to raise a finger to help him, he started talking about how he was a fisherman himself, and fishermen should help one another. Nobody believed him. I don't know what he did after that. In any case, he wasn't at the tavern. The ferry didn't sail until next morning, but I suppose he either took that or got a taxi plane to come. If he reached Dragør that same evening, as you say he did, he must have got a plane.'

'Did he say anything about why he was so anxious to get hold of Pekka?' I asked.

'He said that Pekka had stolen something from him.'

'What?'

'At first I thought it was just a lie, but afterwards I wondered if it couldn't have something to do with the woman.'

There was a silence after that.

'Why did you feel sorry for Pekka?' Torben asked. 'I mean, there is no shortage of people to feel sorry for. Why pick on him?'

Carsten drank up the last of his beer.

'Pekka was afraid,' he said. 'I have never seen anybody else that scared in all my life.'

'What was he afraid of?' Torben asked.

'MacDuff. But not only MacDuff. There was something else as well. Something I didn't really understand. Pekka drank a lot while he was here. Something had happened to him when he was in Scotland, something horrible. He didn't say straight out what it was, but when he got drunk he rambled on about murderers and people being sacrificed alive. When he had sobered up, I asked him what he'd talked about, but then he didn't utter a word and looked as if he wanted to get rid of me as fast as possible. He said that he had seen too much. That was the only thing I could get out of him.'

'And the woman?' asked Torben, who had listened attentively to what Carsten related.

I couldn't help noticing to my satisfaction that Torben seemed to be fascinated by the story.

'Pekka kept her hidden in the boat,' Carsten said. 'I'm sure of that. Or she hid herself. Both one way and the other, I expect. I never saw her. But who would she have come here with if not with Pekka?'

The question was rhetorical, but Carsten would doubtless have been grateful to have his suspicions confirmed. But I didn't wish to share what I knew with him; Pekka had placed his trust in me. He had given his logbook to me. Not to Carsten.

'What are you planning to do?' Carsten asked. 'If MacDuff gets hold of Pekka, I'm afraid anything can happen. Absolutely anything.'

Torben didn't answer but instead looked at me with curiosity.

'We intend to sail to Scotland and find out why MacDuff wants to get his hands on Pekka,' I said.

'Somebody should help him,' said Carsten. 'Here on the island, nobody took him seriously. They all thought he was mad. But Pekka was right in the head,
I'm sure of that.'

Carsten got up.

'When are you leaving?' he asked.

'Tomorrow.'

'I would like to go with you.'

He gave Torben a fleeting glance.

'You ought to have another man with you. It's no picnic to be sailing on the North Sea in the winter.'

'We know that,' I replied. 'We'll manage.'

'I hope so,' said Carsten.

He climbed up the ladder, and we heard his heavy footsteps on the deck before he jumped ashore. Then the snow must have muffled them completely, for we didn't hear him go further.

'Why did he look at me like that?' Torben asked. 'Just because he is an old salt doesn't mean everybody else is a useless land-lubber.'

I wasn't certain that I had heard him aright.

'We'll see what I'm capable of when we get out there,' he added, with something like wounded pride.

'Then you are coming with me?'

'Why didn't you tell me the truth from the beginning?'

'I was afraid that you would dismiss it all as wild fantasy.'

Without waiting for an answer, I crept into the quarter-berth, thrust a hand into the secret compartment and took out Pekka's logbook.

'Before you say anything more, read this! It's the famous Pekka's logbook.'

Torben took the volume with a voracious look in his eye. It was very clear that nothing could be gained from speaking to him for some time. He always immersed himself completely in what he read. It made no difference if he read a document, which perhaps was the case with Pekka's logbook, or a novel. To Torben, there was no decisive difference between fiction and reality, and if anything was real, it was rather the fiction and the words.

I left him to himself and took a walk along the shore. It had stopped snowing, but the sky was without stars and the darkness was dense. It took time for my eyes to adjust, but just as often I used my hearing to avoid wading out in the waves that exploded on the wet sand. Behind me, a feeble glow came from the port, and short red flashes from the radar station up on the hill. You could only see the outlines of the island because you already knew that they had to be there. But if somebody had asked me to identify the silhouettes of the high cliffs, and then been able to check the result, my attempt would have been nothing more than a groping about in the dark on shifting sands. Like so much else.

I tried not to think of MacDuff and Pekka. Instead, I concentrated on locating the last bay before the large Packhus one where ships anchored to discharge their cargoes in the old days. That was before the new harbour had been built. During heavy storms, merchant vessels still lay in the bay waiting for better weather. I was hoping to see some anchor lights or deck-lights to lessen the sense of emptiness. But when I should have arrived according to my calculations, the darkness was just as dense and hostile as before. Behind me, the light from the harbour had disappeared, but I was never worried. It was my firm conviction that you cannot get lost on an island. And in principle I would still maintain this, had it not been for the Garvellachs islands off Scotland's west coast.

When I paused on the shore, certain thoughts returned to me. Who was Mary? And why had she joined Pekka? Was she a victim, a fugitive, or merely in love with him? I had glimpsed her for only two brief moments. I tried to imagine what MacDuff would do if he found Pekka and Mary. I pictured everything imaginable, but nothing that came close to the truth.

Then I strode quickly back towards the harbour. I could suddenly wait no longer to talk with Torben of what I knew.

A cosy light was shining from the *Rustica*'s portholes when I got back. Snow and ice on the deck had melted. The hatch screeched as usual when I opened it. I had tried everything available, oil, fat, vaseline, paraffin, but nothing helped.

Torben sat immobile on the port side berth, with a pipe in his mouth. Before him lay a number of his books on the Celts, Pekka's logbook and some charts. I sat down opposite him and waited.

'If I hadn't listened to Carsten,' Torben said finally, 'I expect that I'd have found it pretty difficult to believe Pekka's stories. He might as well have been doing Crowhurst's thing. You know, the sailor who was supposed to be sailing around the world alone in a race but who only circled about in the Atlantic, while sending wireless messages giving invented positions and distances he was supposed to have sailed. Until it became too much for him, and he committed suicide. But I have heard what Carsten had to say. And I have verified every syllable in the logbook which can be checked. So far as I can tell, it's accurate.'

Torben noticed my glance at the title of a book on the table: Ancient Mysteries of Britain.

'A lot of historical monuments and remains are described in that, with drawings and pictures. And Pekka's descriptions of quite a few of them accord exactly, without having been copied. He must have been in those places. But there is one thing I don't understand.'

'What's that?'

'How the Celts could have caused Pekka to write what he does. The Celts are not a people. Let alone a nation. Their language is on a fair way to disappearing. Not even Northern Ireland will be Celtic if it becomes independent. The idea of a

Celtic resurrection is no more than a beautiful dream. It doesn't help even if they give Irish students credits if they use Erse instead of English in their examinations. That merely shows that they are fighting a hopeless battle.'

I objected that his own attitude towards symbols and myths might not be shared by others, that at times it might prevent him from perceiving the force of myths and symbols shared and honoured by real people.

'Well, it's possible,' Torben admitted. 'But Pekka seems rather to be talking of some kind of conspiracy. But why would the Celts want to establish nations now when they never wished to before? And in Pekka's logbook it mostly appears to be a question of sudden violent death. It makes you think of political terrorism in some sort of disguise. Or perhaps Pekka has come into contact with a fanatical sect. If they can exist in the United States, causing collective suicides by the dozen, why not in Scotland.'

Torben pushed a little book over to my side of the table. Teachings of the Druids it was called, and had the subtitle: Light of the Occident. The author was named Coarer Kalondan. I saw with surprise that it had been published in French in 1971, and that a Danish translation had come out the following year.

'Where did you find this?' I asked.

'In a second-hand bookshop. It looked like a curiosity, so I had to buy it.'

I turned the leaves at random and came to an epilogue. A passage caught my eye:

'And we shall succeed in restoring our people's culture, a culture that will enable our people to understand profoundly the secrets of the Celtic intellectual world and its wisdom. We shall make it possible for them to collaborate again in spreading the thought and wisdom of Man. We shall achieve that goal, for we are, as has already been stated, patient, stubborn and impossible to eradicate.'

I read this aloud to Torben. He merely shook his head.

'The fellow is mad. He calls himself a Druid and he is a committee member of the Order of druids, bards and ovates of Brittany. It says so in the book. He calls himself a pacifist. He devotes many pages to proving that the Celts didn't cut off people's heads or go in for human sacrifice. His argument is fantastic in its very simplicity. Of course, he writes, people were sacrificed at times. But only if they had already been sentenced to death. As if that made any difference to those who were sacrificed. He says, too, that the blood of those condemned to death was never shed at the lawful executions. Why not? Because they were burned to death!'

I pointed out that, all the same, Pekka wrote about human sacrifice and the head cult as things he had seen with his own eyes.

'Yes,' said Torben. 'No doubt about it. And that's what is so alarming. Do you remember what I told you about The Lindow Man? He's thought to have been an influential Druid who allowed himself to be sacrificed of his own free will. One would almost believe that Pekka had read the book by Ross and Robins which appeared last year in England. The authors believe that the man let himself be sacrificed in order to halt the Roman invasion which threatened the Celts' foremost trade route, used for transporting gold from Ireland to the Continent. The theory is that the Druids were in control of the gold trade, and that was why, in England, the Romans opposed them and their teachings, as they had never done with the Druids or other religions in Gaul. In fact, the Druids seem to have shipped gold from Ireland to Anglesey, which the Romans razed to the ground in 60 AD. From Anglesey it was transported along a route lined with sacred places of the Celts. The high civilization achieved by the Celts was founded on the gold trade, and 'gold from Ireland' was a proverbial term during the Roman period.'

Torben looked into the logbook.

'But now we come to the curious thing,' he said. 'Pekka writes that 'the Golden Road is restored', exactly as if Ross and Robins theories had acquired some real equivalent in our day. One could interpret his remark as meaning that people are successfully attempting to recreate the basis for a new Celtic realm. Now that is very difficult to believe. And Pekka writes of 'the King in the underworld' as if there actually existed a Celtic leader who had gone underground to await the moment of liberation for the Celts. Precisely what happens in so many Celtic legends. That is altogether too fantastic to be true.'

'But could it be at all possible?' I asked.

Torben made no answer. Instead he wondered if the reason I had decided to sail to Scotland was to learn more about all this.

'Not only because of that. I really didn't understand much of what Pekka wrote.'

I told Torben all about my ponderings. Perhaps I laid a little extra emphasis on a desire to gain knowledge, on my wish to solve a mystery and to satisfy my curiosity; all motives, of course, to which Torben would be sensitive. But otherwise I was completely frank.

'I'll come with you,' Torben said after a while. 'On condition that you don't withhold any important information from me in the future. If we're to find ourselves in the same boat, we must do the thing properly. You can always start by telling me what happened in Dragør, without omitting the slightest detail. I want to know everything.'

When I had finished telling my story, the ship's clock sounded eight bells and it was midnight. I stuck my head up through the hatch to get an idea of the weather. The wind had abated to a light westerly breeze and it was a starry night. The harbour basin was calm and shining. In *Rustica*'s cabin nothing indicated that we were on our way.

Torben stared reflectively before him.

'I believe that the woman, Mary, is one clue to the riddle,' he said after a little while. 'Why did she sail with Pekka across the North Sea in mid winter? What sort of woman was she exactly?'

I answered evasively.

'She seems to be quite particular,' Torben insisted.

'How should I know? I hardly saw her.'

'But you did see her, didn't you?'

I didn't know what to say. How could I have seen her when her eyes lacked all human life?

Torben didn't insist. But I too felt that Mary was a key figure. Suddenly I regretted not having gone back to *Sula* when I heard the cars drive off. Now we were moving away from both *Sula* and Mary. Perhaps everything was wrong from the beginning. Maybe it had been a mistake to let Pekka and Mary out of sight.

On that singular night at Anholt I could in no way guess how justified my feeling was. But the first indication of it would soon come.

Torben and I sat over a glass of whisky for another half hour and talked of nothing in particular, and least of all about our impending voyage. It was as if we'd had enough of mysteries and forebodings. We wanted to be simply two sailors enjoying the satisfaction of being in a safe harbour after a rough crossing. One of the greatest joys of sailing is the feeling that all problems are solved once you are securely tied up in port. But for us it was the contrary. It was in port our problems began.

Chapter 8

WHEN we woke up next morning, I realised how changeable the weather can be in winter. We put out from Anholt in crystal clear air, a light easterly wind, and with a temperature of two degrees below zero. The sea had a sharp glitter that made the eyes smart. It was as if we were sailing on splinters of glass. The visibility seemed limitless; one had the impression of seeing through the objects one looked at.

We headed for the Hals Barre lighthouse, which lies outside the entrance to Limfjorden, but I still didn't know if we should sail on northwards and round Skagen, or pass through Limfjorden and come out on the North Sea at Thyborøn.

When finally, after hearing the ice report at twelve o'clock, I decided on the Limfjorden route, it was partly because of the favourable ice situation in the fiord. But I also considered the fact that no-one would expect us to take it. In winter, the normal thing would have been to sail to Skagen, and from there on out to sea. That was where somebody would think first of looking for us.

I wouldn't want to give the impression that I really believed that someone was after us. MacDuff couldn't know where we had gone, or even that I'd sailed away and still less know of my having met Pekka and been given the logbook. Unless MacDuff, for some reason, had returned to Dragør and there got hold of Pekka. Or had observed that *Rustica* was no longer in the harbour and begun to make inquiries. Consciously, what troubled me was the risk of ice, the cold and the wind. But in another part of my mind the treacherous word *unless* was working away. It took a long time before I realised how much that word influenced my actions; and later Torben's as well.

At about one o'clock the characteristic silhouette of Hals Barre, fat and broad bellied like a goose, rose up before us. In that clear light it appeared to hover just above the water.

Then came the two lighthouses, stern and lankily tall, that marked out the entrance. I had heard stories about sailing into Limfjorden when the current met a strong east wind. But in our light breeze it couldn't touch us, even if it gurgled and seethed just under the surface.

The little port in Hals was deserted. Some flags were flapping outside a ship's chandler, but it was closed for the winter. The pilot boats lay idle alongside the quay. The yachts were left deserted under covers until spring. The quays were white with rime frost, which sparkled in the sun. Not a soul was to be seen and no one was there to see us sail by.

We didn't meet a single vessel on our way to Ålborg. Torben, who had never been in the area before, complained about the flat and vaguely formed landscape. Yet, he assured me, people in Denmark always talked about the beauty of Limfjorden.

But the sun was beautiful in the winter twilight. Its light sank slowly over *Rustica*'s bow; like a lump of molten steel, it lowered itself down along the forestay. There is something special about the twilight in winter. Even on clear and sunny days, the sky has shrill, naked hues not seen in summer.

Then, when Ålborg was in sight, spreading cranes etched themselves against a grey black sky, pierced at the horizon by the lights of the town. The old suspension bridge towered up above our heads. We had to wait a long time for the bridge master to discover us. As we were unable to communicate with him by radio, we were reduced to signalling in morse code with a searchlight.

After twenty minutes, traffic was stopped and we glided through using only the head sail. I hadn't turned on the engine so that Torben could practise manoeuvering the boat, and we sailed about making haphazard geometric diagrams on the water. The bridge master had opened a window, and he stared at us as if we were creatures from outer space. I waved our thanks, without any response.

On the other side of the bridge, we moored alongside an empty industrial quay, thus avoiding the two small boat harbours further to the west. I was glad that my supply lists had made us independent. Having promised Torben to do our cooking, I made an honest attempt at what was listed as 'chili con carne'; this I filled with garlic in order to conceal the culinary deficiencies. Torben, an unrivalled cook himself, shovelled it down out of pure and rabid hunger without any comment, either for or against. But when we had finished our meal he wondered if it might not be best in future if he became the cook and I, the dish washing machine.

Although I found washing up at least as tiresome and soul destroying as cooking, I very much appreciated good food; so the matter was settled as he suggested. After that, Torben took up an essential problem to which I had not given enough attention, although I should have known better.

'Where is the wine cellar?' he asked.

I pointed to the locker for bottles, confessed that it was empty, and excused the omission on the grounds that good wines are destroyed by the rolling of ships.

'There are wines that can stand it and wines that become undrinkable. Tomorrow I'll go into town and provide us with what's absolutely indispensable.'

I would have preferred to sail at dawn, before too many people had noticed our presence. But to protest would have been as if the captain of a cruise ship tried to tell the chef how to fry a beefsteak.

When I awoke, at half past eight, Torben had already left. I took pleasure in sitting alone with my breakfast. All the stir of recent days had caused me to forget that *Rustica* was my home. Under normal conditions, during regular summer cruises for example, I was constantly reminded that I actually lived on board. On deck and in the cockpit, close to the sea and the waves, all was as before when the boat had served as a temporary holiday dwelling place. But as soon as I arrived in harbour and went down into the cabin, I had the curious sensation of being at home wherever I happened to find myself. It was a feeling that I had never become altogether reconciled to: that of being at one moment as much away from home as is possible only when sailing; at the next moment, feeling more at home than I might do anywhere else.

At about ten o'clock, a taxi stopped on the quay. Torben jumped out and unloaded four cases, each containing six bottles of wine.

'I was in luck,' he called. 'I found exactly what we needed. Take hold of this, will you?'

Not very willingly, I helped to get the cases on board. Since *Rustica* was both my home and my boat, she already lay about two inches below her waterline. And Torben's books and bottles were making her suffer further from overweight. My consolation was that wine, with Torben in the boat, would not be permanent ballast.

'Are we ready to leave?' he wondered, when we had

stored some of the wine, for want of a better place, under one of the berths.

The easterly wind continued to blow. We hoisted the genoa and set off directly by sail from the quay. A number of passers by observed us and looked after us for some time as we sailed on. Was it really so strange to see a sailing boat in Limfjorden in January?

After Ålborg the landscape became even flatter. The river banks were overgrown with brown reeds, made stiff by the cold, and it was impossible to take one's bearing from the lie of the land. We sailed on compass-course and distance made good, because we couldn't trust buoys to be were where they should be according to the chart. In winter the Danish information to seafarers always began with the same message: 'It cannot be expected that buoyage in Danish waterways is in place and in good order.'

Before coming to Løgstør we were allowed immediately under the bridge, as if the bridge master knew in advance that we were approaching. We sailed past Løgstør, which had fallen into a torpor in 1945, with the excavation of a new sailing channel which by passed the town itself. After Løgstør, both the landscape and the fiord became more open as we came out on Løgstør Bredning. This is notorious for its choppy water. But in the light easterly wind it came as a relief to us winter sailors. We made three knots with mainsail and poled out genoa, and we enjoyed the run.

But when we drew near the Oddesund bridge, I began to feel restless and wanted to advance more quickly. We put on the engine in order to arrive at the bridge before five o'clock, when the bridge master would leave. But at the same instant we blew our first signal with the fog horn, I saw through my binoculars that he demonstratively locked the door to his little cage and went his way.

We cursed him and sailed into the abandoned harbour by

the northern foot of the bridge. We shared the harbour basin with the wrecks of two ships and a fishing vessel that remained afloat against all odds. In spite of its loneliness and the cold, the place stank of fish. We looked at each other, climbed down into the cabin and went to bed.

It was still a light easterly next morning when I gazed out over the wretched harbour. But, even if we had luck now with the weather, I started to fear that the high pressure might move away and thus force us to sail to windward or even beat the four hundred nautical miles to Scotland. The bridge master let us through with a listless gesture of greeting. The channel opened wider again after the bridge, and we sailed out on to Nissum Bredning. The lines of the shores disappeared into a bluish mist. There was a smell of the sea.

We were both exhilarated by the fair wind and adjusted the sheets as if we were competing in a regatta. I let Torben take over the navigation, laying out courses and measuring distances. Before long he had become so adept that I only checked what he did as a matter of principle, more precisely the principle that we should check each other as often as possible. In that sense we didn't trust each other, but only because we didn't trust ourselves. Or simply because nobody can be infallible.

After a few hours we sighted the expected row of buoys in Thyborøn Canal. They lay low in the strong outflowing current. We rushed past them on our way towards the entrance of the vast fishing port. I told Torben to steer directly towards the southern pierhead, as if we intended to ram into it, and he wasn't to budge an inch from that course. He looked at me wonderingly, but he understood my advice when the current turned us towards the mole opposite with such force and speed that, in the end, we had only a couple of yards to spare when we swept into the outer harbour. I noticed that there were drops of sweat on Torben's brow, but that relief appeared on his face when we were in safety.

I had the same feeling as we glided past fishing boat after fishing boat, all painted the same light blue colour. But for me it came more from having escaped the ice during our passage to the sea. The water in the Thyborøn Canal was too rapid flowing and temperate to freeze over. Now we could sail as we wished. Nothing could hinder us.

We moored in the western basin. There was a pause in activity on some of the fishing boats about, but only for a brief moment, and we only received a few covert glances. There could be nothing odd here about sailing in winter. The fishermen were probably only curious to see if we were seamen enough.

When we had made fast the boat, furled the sails and lighted the heater, we walked across the sandy beach west of the harbour, then out on the gigantic moles to have a look at what the Danes call 'The Western Sea'. But we learned nothing of value from inspecting it; in the off shore wind, it resembled any other water. Waves rose too far out to give an impression of what they were like. The North Sea, 'the world's largest ships' graveyard', looked more inviting than dangerous.

We walked back, and then into the town. It consisted of two main streets, one leading to the port, the other along the harbour. There were some shops, a couple of taverns and hot dog stands; and also a 'Seamen's Home', a three storey house, with a pale yellow stucco facade. It contained a restaurant and an austere lounge with a television set. The restaurant looked like a rather good milk bar. It had an ice cream stand, and chairs of dark wood, shiny where most sat on. On the walls there were posters and amateurish paintings. One might wonder if anyone really noticed them. But I recall a picture with two weather beaten old salts standing in front of a windswept sea. On shelves, trade journals like *Dansk fiskeri*, the daily papers and some periodicals of an edifying and religious nature, were offered to guests. Much as fishermen doubtless appreciated the establishment, just so little they seemed to have read the still immaculate and encouraging pamphlets about God's excellence. But northern Jutland, I knew, was the strongest bastion of the nonconformist church in Denmark.

Torben pulled a face when I ordered for myself a national Danish dish: fillet of plaice, coated in egg and bread crumbs, fried, and served with chipped potatoes and remoulade sauce. When he himself wanted to test the quality of the wines provided, he discovered to his dismay that the only beverage to be had in the name of God was the local light lager.

'I think,' said Torben, 'that I'll have a shower instead of lunch.'

He bought a counter for the purpose. It cost him thirty kroner, which seemed rather much. The physical cleansing was dearly bought in contrast to the spiritual, which was given away for free.

The plaice arrived, but in spite of its having been slaughtered uniquely for my sake, it tasted of little more than what coated it. The absence of taste was not compensated by the huge portions served.

I didn't read during my meal, which is as unusual for me when eating alone as drinking coffee without smoking a cigarette. Or the other way about. But afterwards I borrowed a copy of Jyllandsposten, named the 'Jutland's Pest' in Copenhagen, a thing that didn't make it any better or worse than other papers.

First I gave a cursory look at the news. Having observed that nothing radical had been accomplished to make the world an easier place to live in, I hunted up the weather forecast. I tried to interpret the general situation. The high pressure and easterly wind would remain but weaken. An area of deep low pressure lay just south of Cape Farewell on Greenland, but everything indicated that it would take a northeastern course over to northern Norway. That might produce southeasterly winds. The five day forecast prophesied strong winds from southeast to southwest. But in the Danish weather reports a 'strong' wind was a moderate force 6. Out on the North Sea, that was quite a lot of wind, but it was not anything like a gale. So, with a bit of luck, we should escape too much windward sailing. On the whole, all was more encouraging than I had dared hope. With a feeling of relief, I was about to lay down the paper when a brief notice, tucked away at the bottom of a page, caught my eye.

BESTIAL MURDER IN SAILBOAT

The Swedish Coast Guard reports that at five o'clock yesterday afternoon a sailboat was found adrift off Falsterbo, in southern Scania. The dead body of a man about forty years of age was discovered on board. His head had been severed and removed from the boat. His identity has not yet been established. At the time of going to press, the police have found no trace of those responsible or of what lies behind the murder. All who have seen the boat, whether in Denmark or Sweden, are asked to contact their local police authority. The sailboat is a catamaran bearing the name *Sula*.

Chapter 9

'Are you feeling ill?' Torben asked on returning from his shower. 'You should never have ordered that plaice.'

I passed the newspaper over to him and pointed at the notice. I had difficulty in keeping my hand steady.

'Well,' Torben said in a flat voice when he had read the notice, 'that's that. We'll just have to find the nearest call box and call the Swedish police.'

The calm and dejected finality in his voice brought me out of my stupor.

'Wait a bit,' I told him. 'We must first think the matter through.'

'There can scarcely be anything to think through. It's not a matter for us any longer.'

I didn't know what to answer. For the last half hour I had been trying to find out what the news could mean. But more and more questions seemed to mount up like a house of cards, only to topple over.

'Let's go back to the boat,' I said, in the hope that the walk would give me time to think.

We passed the big fish storehouses. At the last of these, a trawler was discharging its catch of unsorted fish. It was so heavily loaded that water ran in through the scuppers when it heeled ever so little. As we went by, I heard one of the fishermen say something about Scotland, but I didn't catch what.

'That it can manage to float at all!' Torben commented at the sight of the fishing-boat.

He didn't know that fishing boats had gone down with all hands because they were so heavily loaded that the bow didn't bear when it pressed into a steep wave. A fisherman had told me that one boat came in so over loaded that it couldn't be moored. They had been forced to keep up its speed so that the bow-wave would help keep it afloat. When they were finally berthing the boat, they had only seconds to get enough fish ashore to prevent the boat from sinking. All to make a profit of some extra thousand kroner.

I had more respect for those who risked their lives only for the adventure of it. That was more honest.

Further on I saw a rather small fishing boat with a black hull. It looked abandoned. No lights were visible, either in the wheelhouse or in the cabin. I suddenly recollected from brochures and pilot-books that many Scottish trawlers had black hulls. *F 154* was painted on the prow; but I could see no name or home port. I made a mental note that I should come back and have a better look later. The skipper could certainly give me good advice about safe harbours on the east coast of Scotland.

This made me realise that I hadn't given up my intention of sailing across the North Sea to find out what Pekka had seen and what had brought about his death. Now when I had finally cast off, turning back would have seemed my life's greatest defeat.

But there remained the difficulty of convincing Torben. And that, I knew, was only possible using common sense and rational arguments.

'Well, what do you want to talk about?' he asked as soon as we sat down in *Rustica*'s saloon.

I didn't answer but instead took out the British Admiralty chart of the North Sea, one of the few charts of the North Sea which showed both Thyborøn and Rattray Head at the easternmost point of Scotland, and our natural land-fall before we sailed on into Inverness Firth.

'About how we should plan our crossing of the North Sea,' I said, when I had laid out the chart between us on the cabin table.

'You are out of your mind,' Torben slowly told me. 'I can accept that we should sail to Scotland, and look for Celtic Freemasons and Rotarians, and find out what they do in their spare time. If they grill sheep alive on stone altars, or merely utter invocations and pick oak leaves. I can even accept that we do it in the middle of winter. Then in any case we won't be crammed into over filled harbours. But a murder has been committed. And that must put the whole basis of our detective work in a different light.'

I took out the long rule and drew a pencil line from Thyborøn to Rattray Head. I didn't need to use a protractor. Measurement by the eye sufficed to show that our course was almost directly westward, 275°. To this, westerly variation had to be added in order to derive the course we could steer by compass. The problem was only that, while variation was 3° at the coast of Jutland, it was 8° close to Scotland; after some extrapolations I arrived at a mean value. The next operation was to take a pair of compasses, measure out a distance on the scale of latitude at the level of our intended course, and then work out the distance. It came to 340 nautical miles. Of course this was wishful thinking. At least occasionally, we would probably meet westerly winds and be compelled to beat and alter our course. But the preparations were important, and I made them more conscientiously than usual in the hope that if

I took my time Torben's frame of mind might change. And perhaps it did.

His tone was more conciliatory when he asked once more why I didn't just go and telephone to the police, tell them all I knew and then forget all about Celts and Scotland. As for himself, he could very well consider spending the rest of the winter in my cosy boat right there in Thyborøn. He was sure, he said, that it could be just as rewarding to spend a winter there as elsewhere. There was much to be learned about fishing and the fishermen. And one never got tired of looking at the sea.

But I had made my decision. And I had an argument which even Torben would need to take seriously.

'What happens if we do get in touch with the police?' I asked finally. 'We'll be called in for questioning. Worse than that, if they get hold of MacDuff we might be called as witnesses. And even if they don't get hold of him, very possibly he'll find out that we have been questioned which means that he'll know that we know that Pekka was murdered. Perhaps he'll find out as well that we have Pekka's logbook. What happens then? Is there any reason why we wouldn't be his next victims? The best thing for us to do is sail to Scotland, pay MacDuff a visit, after all I was invited to come, and then ask him as innocently as we can if he found Pekka. That, at least, could convince him that we don't know anything. As long as we are in Scotland, we can perfectly well be ignorant of a murder somewhere in Sweden. MacDuff is dangerous. How dangerous we know now. You remember what Pekka wrote in his logbook. As I see it, we would be safer in Scotland than we are here.'

I could tell that this argument made a certain impression on Torben.

'But what would we do in Scotland?' he objected.

'We don't need to do anything in particular. Read books

here in the saloon. Look at the sheep. Drink Guinness and whisky at the pubs.'

'Not whisky,' said Torben.

'Well, you can certainly get wines instead, if that's what worries you.'

'Is it possible to get good wines in Scotland?'

I was clearly on the right tack.

'Why shouldn't it be? At least by the bottle.'

Torben went so far as to smile. But then he became serious again.

'I do see,' he said, 'that there's a point in our paying a friendly visit to MacDuff so he won't get the idea of killing us, too. But after all he seems to have cut the head off one of our fellow human beings. Shouldn't there be some punishment for that sort of thing?'

'Of course.'

'Yes, yes,' said Torben. 'But I suspect that you have something else in mind. You probably believe that we could inflict just retribution, or at least that we could uncover a great conspiracy and be acclaimed as heroes. You, Ulf Berntson, the Captain Hornblower of our time, with a shot of James Bond put in for good measure. But the world has changed since his days. People like us are hopeless cases. We can't do anything. We can't shoot. Can't give karate kicks. Can't pilot a plane. We haven't gone in for body building. Have you a driving licence?'

'No.'

'There, you see! We can't even hire a car if we should need one in Scotland.'

Torben was right. We lacked all the requirements for heroism. What were we capable of? Well, I could sail a boat. I could skin dive and had even been an instructor in the art. But what more? I could express myself, I could tell stories in other words, in several languages for that matter. But what good would it do to be able to express oneself when confronted with a man of MacDuff's calibre? Not much. As for Torben, he had a good and clear head. He was widely read. He could draw logical conclusions. That was always something.

'My only heroic will be to take us safely across the North Sea,' I told him.

'Is that a promise?'

'Yes.'

I regretted my reply a moment later. At sea, in a small boat, it is wiser not to be so presumptuous as to give promises about anything.

At 10:20, delayed by more than a day, we left Thyborøn in a light southeasterly breeze, clear weather, and with a temperature of two degrees above zero.

Against all predictions, we had had a howling westerly gale during the previous twenty-four hours, and the sea had hammered mercilessly against the low lying coast. We had passed the time reading sailing descriptions and books on Scotland, talking to the fishermen at the Seamen's Home and watching the sea as it raged insanely at the shore. On one occasion I went out alone to the furthest tip of the mole. I remained there for a long time trying to inure myself to the fury of the wind.

I returned chilled to the bone and with hearing temporarily impaired, but I was no longer as apprehensive as before of stormy weather. The most important thing when the wind picks up to a gale or worse is to accustom yourself to it as quickly as possible. Many people make the mistake of sitting tight and hoping that it won't get worse, or, when it has got worse, that it will very soon be over.

Before our departure, we had walked round the harbour and looked at the fishing boats being unloaded and loaded in spite of the wind. We exchanged some words with members of the crews. They were amiable but not easy to talk to. In general, people in Thyborøn were both friendlier and more hospitable than is usually the case. One afternoon when we had sat at a tavern, each with a glass of beer, we decided that it might be pleasant to pass the time looking at television. Neither of us possessed a set and I at least hadn't seen a programme for at least six months. The tavern had a TV, but the proprietress said that unfortunately they were closed just that evening. We had scarcely left the place when she came running after us and asked us to come back later by a rear door. She hadn't wanted the regulars to stay on because they needed to sleep off the effects of what they had drunk already. Of course we could look at her telly! We were so surprised by such good will that we politely refused her invitation. Afterwards, I was ashamed that we hadn't accepted it.

I never managed to talk to anyone on board the Scottish *F 154*. I passed by several times without seeing a soul. Once, I even went aboard and knocked at the door to the cabin, but all remained silent. Fishermen in the trawlers close by knew nothing about the *F 154*. It had arrived about a week earlier, but no one had been seen on board.

I had, a few times and in a general sort of way, taken up with Torben the possible reason for Pekka's death. I tried to get his ideas on the subject, but he wasn't inclined to speculate. He was anxious not to encourage any foolhardy behaviour on my part. At the same time, I am quite sure that he had his own ideas and was more disturbed than he revealed. So it must have been a relief for us both when the gale finally subsided, and we could set out.

As we emerged from the Thyborøn Canal, the 'Western Sea' met us with an irregular swell that made *Rustica* roll, unable to catch the rhythm. The mainsail and the blocks banged and rattled. Torben looked as if he had apprehensions, but I was elated at being on our way out to sea. Only towards three o'clock did Thyborøn disappear from sight. As Torben didn't seem particularly disposed to do galley duty, I went down and prepared a meal, something with creamed potatoes, if I remember rightly. We had it in the cockpit, where we enjoyed watching the descending sun rather more than my food, of which Torben swallowed only some mouthfuls. He wasn't hungry, he said. I blamed my cooking, but the fact of the matter was that he would get nothing more down during the next three days. He was seasick, but he was very slow to admit it.

At about six o'clock, there was a cracking noise, and *Rustica* came up into the wind with flapping sails. I thought that the steering lines to the wind pilot had come loose. But it was something much worse. The transmission from the vane was broken. We could do nothing else than take the helm ourselves for the rest of the trip.

We decided on having three hour watches, day and night. I insisted on taking the first one so that Torben could rest and escape having the dog-watch. He still seemed able to overcome his seasickness sufficiently for his turn at the helm: that and no more.

Shortly after he had taken over, he woke me up to tell me that we were 'being followed by a fishing boat'. In normal circumstances, I'd have shrugged the matter off. Fishing boats are inclined to behave unaccountably, changing course when you least expect it, as if bent on forcing you to change course yourself. But now I took Torben seriously and went up to the cockpit with binoculars. True enough, a couple of miles astern of us, I saw the lights of a fishing-boat, green over white, and it was following the course we were on.

'And I've changed our course twice,' said Torben. 'But each time it seemed to change, too.'

'How many degrees did you change?'

'I don't know. Thirty to forty perhaps.'

'That can't be seen from the other boat. You have to make it at least sixty seven and a half degrees for the side lights to be visible. Alter the course by seventy five degrees, and we'll see what happens.'

Rustica willingly turned over to the new course. I kept the binoculars directed on the fishing boat. At first nothing happened, but then she slowly turned to port. So it did actually look as if she were trying to overtake us.

'I don't know,' I told Torben. 'It can be an accident. But we'd better make sure. As far as we can.'

I switched off the lights and took down the radar reflector, which hung under the starboard spreader halfway up the mast.

'Now we can do no more. Wake me if anything happens,' I said.

An hour later, Torben woke me up again.

'I don't see the boat any longer. Its lights disappeared just after you had gone back to bed. But the wind has started to pick up. Shouldn't we do something?'

I put on a jacket and went up on deck. The wind hadn't freshened to more than a strongish breeze, but it was as well to reef in case worse was coming. Then we wouldn't need to worry in the night. With a reef in the mainsail and the small jib, *Rustica* could take a strong breeze if required.

'Is it good seamanship to reef in nothing but long underwear?' Torben asked.

'Captain Hornblower wouldn't have given it a thought. He even did it naked once. As long as the right thing was done.'

'I am sorry I needed to wake you up again.'

'That's all right.'

But when, only twenty minutes later, I was awakened a third time to take my watch, I admit that I did feel somewhat sorry for myself. The coffee in the thermos flask was no more than lukewarm. The cigarettes were damp and tasteless. On top of that it was cold, damp, raw and pitch dark, and I was dead tired. But after half an hour I had got into the particular state of night sailing, the singular sensation that you are in an emotional vacuum; yet with all your senses, except that of sight, directed outwards and intensely alive. My gaze was directed only at the steering compass, illuminated by a faint red light which didn't affect night vision. I felt the wind on my face and on the hand that grasped the tiller. I felt the waves, too, in my body as it followed the movements of the boat. Sometimes I tried to look ahead, to see through the darkness. I don't know why. There could be no point in doing this unless it was a starry night or the moon was up.

I didn't observe the fishing boat during my watch. But if, in spite of my precautions, we appeared on its radar screen, the boat could perfectly well be lurking near us in the darkness. At three o'clock, I awakened Torben and lighted a lamp in the saloon. I could see that the seasickness had hardened its grip.

'Can you manage to steer?' I wondered, even though I was too frozen and painfully tired to think about taking another watch.

My fingers were numb, and I had steered standing up during the last half hour, from fear of falling asleep.

'Why shouldn't I be able to steer?' Torben said while he was doggedly piling on all his layers of clothes before coming up into the cold air.

'Steer 250 degrees,' I told him, 'until I have worked out a new course.'

The wind had risen to about force 6, and it had backed to the northwest so that we couldn't keep a straight course towards Rattray Head. We were 60 nautical miles out, at a position of 6° 30' E 56°40° N, just north of Monkey Bank, heading towards the Ekofisk oil field.

I gave Torben a course with slack sheets, so that we

wouldn't need to sail too close to the wind or have to change course again. Thereafter, I went below and fell into a heavy sleep.

I awoke to a brilliant morning at sea. I wasn't completely rested, but refreshed. With a certain effort, I got up and made coffee, enough to fill two thermos-flasks. I ate some bread and butter, and I rolled a number of cigarettes. *Rustica* heeled over to the gunwale, but she didn't complain and sailed on, steadily, harmoniously and even majestically through the huge waves which I saw mounting up outside the portholes. Torben looked worn out when he gave me the tiller. Each time I took over, I hoped that sleep would improve his seasickness, but each time he woke up he was in a worse state than before.

'Oh, all's well,' was all he said, and disappeared.

Although the sea was high and heavy, *Rustica* advanced all day with dream-like ease. She made from five to six knots as she pressed on through the masses of intensely green and translucent water. Snow white foam spurted up round her.

Next day at dawn, I sighted a fishing boat to port on a parallel course. Of course it was impossible to tell if it was our previous nocturnal companion. But even when she was still at a considerable distance, I could see that her hull was painted black. When she got close enough for me to make out her registration number, there could be no doubt; it was the same boat that had been moored at Thyborøn. When she sailed laboriously by, only about two hundred yards to leeward, I waved. But there was no response. Probably the automatic pilot was switched on, and the crew had gone below.

After the boat had passed out of sight, I began to feel an inexplicable uneasiness creep over me. But what was more natural than that we should encounter a Scottish fishing boat when we were on our way to Scotland? I knew that the catches of Danish and Scottish fishermen were often unloaded abroad in order to get higher prices. Even so, I remained uneasy. It seemed to me that the boat was too small to be fishing out in the open sea. And why didn't it have a name or a home port. Even after she had disappeared over the horizon, I stared at her wake, cursing myself that I hadn't questioned the fishermen at Thyborøn more closely about her skipper and crew. But it was too late now.

That was the last ship we saw for two hundred nautical miles. All was unchanged during the day and night that followed: hard wind, clear sky, the sparkling cold and close-hauled. But I recall two things vividly: *Rustica*'s heedless progress through the green water and Torben's struggle with his seasickness. Each time he got up for his watch, it looked as if he had just been brought to life after a visit to Hell. He neither ate nor drank. He simply slept and steered, steered and slept. He suffered, but he endured it.

In the morning of the third day, the wind started to abate. We had sailed past the Ekofisk oil rig without seeing it. Torben's seasickness was somewhat better, mostly, I think, because he at last admitted to himself that he was seasick and nothing else. When I took over around noon, he swallowed his pride and threw up several times, took two pills and went to bed. When he woke up the worst was over, even if he was tired and sluggish from the pills. But as he remarked, to be tired is paradise compared to being seasick. Later, when Torben must have thought that I was asleep, I overheard him say both to himself and to all the powers that rule the sea: 'You have to be a masochist to like sailing!' I took that as a sign of his return to health.

I, who had never known the awful scourge of seasickness, felt much relieved. Now I had come to understand what the long distance sailor Ian Nicholson, who was always seasick himself, meant when he wrote that there are two stages in seasickness. The first one is when you think you are about to die. The second one, and the worst, is when you begin realising that you are not going to die.

At 19:00 local time, we were sailing over a shiny sea with a light northeasterly wind behind us. And we began already to speak of sighting land, even if my dead reckoning showed that we still had ninety nautical miles to go. But we had made a dozen or so changes in course without Torben having been able to double-check my navigation.

It was an agitated night. For the first time since his first watch, Torben woke me up.

'What is it?' I asked from a sleeping bag which I was most reluctant to leave.

'You had better come up.'

I put on all the layers of clothes. That is one of the greatest drawbacks of sailing in the winter: ordinary underwear, thermal underwear, a ski suit and lined oilskins, woollen headgear, gloves and mittens, two pairs of socks and a pair of boots way too large just to have room for my feet. Everything had to be put on in the right order. I hoped that Torben hadn't got me up without good reason.

When I came up on deck, I saw at once points of light lying ahead, lined up as if they marked out a landing strip. In the midst of this strange runway, there was a configuration of lights looking more like the decorations on a Christmas tree.

'There must be a strong current here,' said Torben. 'I've tried to sail round the thing, but nothing helps. It just gets closer and closer no matter what I do.'

I understood nothing and didn't believe what I saw. There was no tidal stream out here to talk about and no bore holes were marked on the chart. I was so bewildered that I didn't think of taking a look with binoculars. After a time, when the horrendous beast seemed to be drawing us forward with the intention of sucking us down, Torben produced the magical solution.

'Perhaps *it* is moving. Not us?'

Roused from paralysed inaction, I took out the binoculars. And I saw what it was: two large tugs pulling an oil rig fifty metres high straight across our course. I supposed that the other lights were from fishing boats. The atmosphere on board *Rustica* changed in an instant, but it was difficult for me to go back to sleep, the more so because the mild breeze wasn't enough to steady the mainsail, which again made an enervating creak and rattle. When I took over the helm at four o'clock, the fishing boats had disappeared. We had passed Greenwich meridian without noticing it. The wind had shifted and freshened, so that we were running almost directly before it. I said to myself that I'd had enough sleep and decided to steer for more than my three hours.

Morning arrived bringing sunlight and still more wind. There was a hissing noise from round *Rustica*'s bow when she threw herself down each wave. She stopped with a sigh until the stern started climbing and before she picked up speed again. I felt like cheering her on, hoping that we would see land the faster. I half lay across the cockpit and tried to refrain from rising and peering about in search of a shore. Strangely enough, it is a chronic infirmity with many sailors that they start looking out to see land far too early, as if they didn't trust their ability to navigate, or as if they wished for nothing better than to be ashore. I belong to those for whom it is necessary to sail. The sea awakes in me something which seems to be as deeply rooted as the sense of self-preservation. But perhaps it is that same sense of self-preservation that stops me from spending more than twenty four hours at sea without beginning to wish that I'd already arrived in port.

When Torben finally awoke, I had steered for six hours and the wind had risen to the upper limit for trouble free and enjoyable sailing. It quickly increased still more, and we were soon forced to lower the head-sail. The waves mounted higher and higher behind us. By ten o'clock, I estimated the wind as force 7 or 8 and the highest waves as twelve feet. In spite of *Rustica* being long keeled and displacing seven tons, she surfed down the waves. Now and then the bow wave would come all the way aft to the cockpit. The log often hit the limit and remained glued at ten knots. The tiller vibrated in my hand. The pressure on the rudder was so strong that I felt unsure about how much I dared counter it. I had never before seen such steep and chaotic waves. Had I known then what I know now, that the waters off Rattray Head are notorious and have swallowed two lifeboats from Fraserburgh with their crews, I would certainly have taken a more northerly route.

Torben was standing in the companion-way, watching the mountainous waves that came rolling along, and to keep him occupied I told him to take photographs. For my own part, I avoided looking astern. It was actually worse for Torben than for me. I saw him recoil now and then when the crest of a particularly high wave broke and fell towards us. But each time *Rustica*'s stern was lifted by an invisible hand, allowing great masses of water to rush by. Except once. I saw on Torben's face that something was wrong and I glanced back. Three gigantic waves had mounted in close succession. I succeeded in parrying the first one and the second, but the third sent cascades of foam into the cockpit and splashed against the plexiglass hatch. When the water ran off, Torben's stiffened features were revealed. I made a gesture to him meaning that there was no danger, but I was no longer wholly convinced that there wasn't.

Perched on the top of a wave, I suddenly caught a first glimpse of land only a couple of miles away. *Rustica*'s stem pointed straight towards the lighthouse at Rattray Head. We had hit our goal spot on after sailing 380 nautical miles and making twelve course-changes, as if we had simply crossed the eight miles between Limhamn and Dragør. My satisfaction lasted no more than a fleeting moment, for with the lighthouse as landmark, I discovered that the strong current was carrying us quickly southward. We would have to gybe, to take the mainsail over, with a following wind, if we were to round the headland. With the mainsail unreefed in a force 7, the manoeuvre was not without risk, and I tried to conceal my anxiety from Torben. He was already elated at the prospect of having firm ground beneath his feet.

I waited until *Rustica* had picked up speed on a giant wave so that the speed reduced the pressure of the wind on the sails. I then warily put over the helm. The mainsail swung with a report like that of a pistol shot, but not as badly as I had feared. The situation was immediately under control again.

However, when I told Torben that we probably wouldn't be able to stand in for Fraserburgh's harbour with such seas and an offshore wind, his face fell. At the thought of another night at sea and of it being sixty miles to the next safe harbour, all the joy disappeared from his eyes. If Torben had been sailing alone, I am certain that he would have risked his life to enter the harbour.

Happily, when we had got round Rattray Head the sea was sheltered from the wind, and at 14:30 we were able to sail in between the twelve foot high piers at Fraserburgh. As if by order, a heavy mist descended and at the same time it began to drizzle. There could hardly be any doubt that we were in Scotland.

I had steered continuously since three o'clock in the morning, and everything seemed to flicker before my eyes. Now when all tension was released, I had to draw on my last reserve of energy to get us to the northern harbour basin, which lies furthest in. We moored alongside the first boat we came to, one of the many fishing boats that didn't look as if it would sail out next morning.

When we were about to furl the sails, my legs shook with exhaustion. But we had arrived. Just at that moment, nothing else mattered. It took us a good half hour to put the sails in order, and it was another half an hour before we were out of our oilskins. After that, we made coffee, shook hands and without a word sat down in the cockpit to look at Fraserburgh's grey and gloomy houses, which in our tired eyes was more like a colourful idyll. I felt an unconstrained fulfilment, and gratitude for experiencing it. I am sure that we both felt exactly the same thing at that moment, and that we, for the same reason, overcame and bridged the solitude which too often is the only thing that we know for certain is uniting us all. That too, sailing can accomplish.

How long we sat there enjoying this sensation, I do not know. But I do know when it ended. It was when Torben pointed over my shoulder at a fishing boat with a black hull. I read the registration number: *F 154*.

Chapter 10

PERHAPS I only imagined it, but I did think that the Customs officers treated us with suspicion. They were surly and wanted to examine every document we had on board. They peered into all the lockers, lifted floor boards and even opened the lids to the water tanks. They were searching too systematically, it seemed to me, for their inspection to be of a routine order. The situation became critical when one of them began to rummage in the quarter-berth. But my secret compartment was hidden under the insulation and almost impossible to find if you didn't know where to look. The Customs officers discovered nothing, but before they left they took the opportunity of telling us that it would have been illegal to go ashore without having cleared. Of course their suspicious attitude might have derived from mere scepticism. Sailing across The North Sea in the middle of winter could hardly be for pure pleasure and required a bit of explanation.

Unless. Once again that word came to my mind. Could MacDuff have found out where we had gone? No. *Unless* Pekka had been forced to tell him about me and the logbook. But would Pekka really have told him, even under threat? No, surely not. *Unless* the threat had involved Mary. That wasn't impossible. But was it likely? No. *Unless* that was precisely what happened. After all, it could not be ruled out that the conscientiousness of the Customs officials also had other motives than purely professional ones.

On the other hand, they had not been standing on the quay waiting for us. Shortly after our arrival, we had run up the yellow quarantine flag which indicated that we wished to be cleared, and we had waited an hour. As no one had appeared, we went ashore on unsteady legs, inquired after the Customs office and left a piece of paper announcing our arrival and requesting clearance. After that, we found ourselves in a poky pub down by the harbour. We sat on stools covered with black plastic and I ordered a whisky, well-deserved, and Torben a glass of wine, equally well deserved, but of less certain quality. On either side of us sat two rough fellows who talked to each other above our heads, as if we weren't there at all. Being so tired, it took some time before I suddenly realised that I understood only a single word of what they said. The word was 'fuck', which seemed to recur in every other sentence. The rest was totally incomprehensible and sounded like nothing I had heard before.

'Are they speaking Celtic?' I asked Torben.

He listened attentively.

'You mean Gaelic,' he said after a moment. 'Yes, it probably is, but in that case they are visitors. Gaelic isn't spoken on the east coast. It only exists as a mother tongue in the far west of Scotland. Here, people very often speak a Scottish variant of English which can be almost as incomprehensible as Gaelic, come to that.'

I couldn't refrain from looking discreetly at the two men, as if there would be something specially Celtic about them besides their language. But the only thing that seemed peculiar was how little notice they took of us foreigners sitting in their local pub. It seemed as if they were well aware of possessing a language that no outsider understood. How many foreigners had actually ever learned to speak a Celtic language? There couldn't be very many.

Torben's seasickness had vanished at the same moment we entered the smooth water in the port of Fraserburgh. He didn't say much over his first glass of wine, a certain sign that he was hungry. I had already decided that we should have a sumptuous meal financed by the ship's funds. Torben deserved it. He had achieved a feat by struggling through every other watch for three and a half days, of which he had been unable to eat at all for two.

After leaving the bar, we went into the first restaurant we came to in the main street and found ourselves in a dining-room with dusty chandeliers, flowery wallpaper and elderly ladies who had come there for 'high tea', something between afternoon tea with cakes and a real dinner, which we later learned was a rather recently revived Scottish custom. I don't recall much about the dinner beyond that I drank a pint of beer and became so tired that we had to leave before the dessert. No matter how I strove against my sleepiness, I couldn't prevent my head from descending in slow motion towards my plate.

Torben accompanied me back to *Rustica*, where I fell into a profound sleep after the Customs' visit. I woke up to a lovely smell of coffee and newly baked bread. Torben told me that I must have slept soundly, for if I looked out I would notice that we were now berthed alongside a rusty steel boat. Torben himself had been awakened at about four o'clock by peculiar noises on deck and he had rushed up from his bunk in the belief that it was his turn at the helm. But when he reached the deck he saw that the crew of the fishing boat on the inside wanted to take her out and were re-berthing *Rustica*. When Torben wanted to help, the fishermen had waved him away. 'Go back to sleep!' they simply told him, and looked displeased with themselves for not having been quiet enough. In Denmark or in Sweden, the fishermen would have begun the operation by waking us up properly and then given us hell because we were in their way.

Torben gave me further news: he had made a morning prowl round the *F 154*. He asked me if I was certain that it was the same boat which had sailed past us out on the North Sea.

'Look in the logbook and you'll see!'

I had told him about the *F 154*, but I hadn't been sure that he, seasick as he was, had taken it in. I had told him nothing about my uneasiness, however, because of course it could be unfounded.

'The fact is that the boat looks as if it hadn't been out fishing for years,' Torben said. 'And there isn't a soul on board.'

'How do you know?' I asked with surprise.

'I knocked.'

He made this sound like the most natural thing to do in the world.

'Why did you do that?' I asked.

'Why shouldn't I have?'

'Hadn't we decided that we would keep out of the way?'

'Yes. But of what? You surely don't think that the fishing-boat has something to do with MacDuff?'

I didn't have time to answer because at that instant we heard knocking on the roof of the cabin.

'It's probably someone who wants to return your visit,' I remarked and opened the hatch.

On the rusty boat alongside was a man of about forty. He said 'Good morning', and introduced himself as 'John', owner of the boat.

'Just wanted to welcome you here to Fraserburgh,' he said. 'I am the diver here, but there isn't much for me to do at this time of the year. So you are welcome to stay where you are for a couple of days. If you don't mind the rust.'

This was good news. We could remain alongside John's

boat, so that we didn't have to keep adjusting our mooring ropes with the tide. John gave a look at the flag at *Rustica*'s stem.

'You haven't sailed here from Sweden now, have you?'

'Yes, we have,' I replied. 'From Sweden by way of Denmark.'

'At this time of year!'

He looked at me scrutinizingly but in a friendly fashion.

'Tell you what,' he said. 'I'm in a bit of a hurry just now. But if you like, we could go out and have a beer later in the afternoon. All right?'

I nodded agreeing that it was all right.

'Fine. I'll fetch you at about five.'

He lifted a hand to his forehead in a casual salute, then climbed up the slippery, algae covered steps of the iron ladder. It was around low tide, and the quay was fifteen feet above deck level. Coming from the tideless Baltic, the tide was something we had to get used to. The fishing boats were moored by long ropes that slackened a good deal at high tide which in turn meant that they drifted around all over the place if there was any wind. And we were the smallest boat of the lot.

'We're invited out,' I said to Torben when I came back below. 'By somebody called John.'

'I heard that.'

'He looks like a pleasant fellow.'

'Why shouldn't he?' demanded Torben. 'The Scots are well known for their hospitality. At least if they have no score to settle. And if you don't belong to the wrong clan. Did he ask how many we are on board?'

'No. Why?'

'Well,' Torben remarked, 'he might have liked to know how many people he was inviting. We could just as well have been six on board.'

I hadn't thought of that. And I realised that Torben too had an *unless* working inside him. We were in the same boat, just as we'd agreed to be, but not quite in the way we had imagined.

Shortly before five, John came back in a car. He drove us about in the town and showed us what there was to see. Meanwhile, he told us that for some years he had taught at a High School in America, but he had discovered that money could not outweigh the pleasure of having a beer in a Scottish pub or of taking a misty autumn walk along the North Sea. Then he took us to 'The Oyster Bar'. The proprietor, Robert, had also recently returned to Scotland, after spending three years in Australia.

'There are Scotsmen all over the world,' said Robert. 'We Scots are a travelling people.'

'Who tend to be chronically homesick,' John added.

Torben wondered what it was that made them sick for home.

'It's got something to do with roots,' said John. 'You lose something when you leave Scotland, something you can't get anywhere else. During my four years away, I was never really myself.'

I asked them casually if the Celtic tradition meant anything to them. But they seemed to evade my question.

'I have spent some time in Brittany,' I said by way of explanation.

'And there appears to be a Celtic revival there. They even have a Celtic television station.'

'Television can't pass on any sort of Celtic tradition,' said Robert, without suggesting what could.

John gave him a look which I interpreted as a reprimand. They then began to ask us about our voyage. For the most part I was quiet and let Torben reply. He sounded like an old salt who had crossed oceans by the dozen. He was cautious, however, when questions touched on our reasons for sailing in mid-winter.

On the little round table before us, glasses seemed always to be full, without our knowing when drinks were ordered or by whom. It was not easy to drink only moderately, to keep our heads clear and to order rounds ourselves. We failed miserably on all three counts. Later we discovered that Scottish hospitality, whatever other motives or conflicts might be involved, is unconditional. Just to get the chance to buy a Scotsman a pint means you have to be cunning. Such an opportunity as the absence of one's host in the Gents must be instantly seized. Or else you had to order a new round long before the first one was emptied. Just take a look at any table in a Scottish pub and you'll find it full of filled glasses. Strangely, this was the case even with people whom we came to regard as our enemies.

When John left us on the quay above *Rustica*, he urged us to be careful when climbing down the ladder. We were again at low water, and only the top of *Rustica*'s mast showed above the quay. It would be a long descent.

John also invited us to visit the lifeboat station in the morning. The Duke of Kent was to launch Fraserburgh's new lifeboat. Twenty years earlier one of the former lifeboats had gone down with all on board during an attempt to aid the Russian ship *Inian*. That was the second time a disaster of that kind befell Fraserburgh, which is why it had taken so long to get a replacement.

'It will be a lovely ceremony,' John assured us. 'You must come!'

'A lovely ceremony!' Torben said to himself while climbing down the ladder. 'Typically English.'

'We are in Scotland,' I objected.

'It evidently makes no difference. Some bagpipers and a duke on a red carpet. And that's enough to make a whole crew of volunteers go out to grapple with death. It's crazy!'

Torben was so upset that he forgot about where he put his feet. Luckily, I was able to catch hold of him and push him on board when he stumbled. But he didn't so much as notice my aid.

'You don't have to come,' I said.

'Of course I'm going! You can always learn something you didn't know before.'

'And what will you do with what you learn?'

'Nothing,' Torben answered characteristically. 'Knowledge is useful even if it's to no purpose. In fact, useless knowledge is the best kind.'

He hastened below and took out some of the books he had brought with him. I assumed that he wanted to confirm statements John and Robert had made about Scottish history.

I myself remained in the cockpit, and I took a sweeping look round the now vague forms of hulls and masts in the harbour. The pale glow from lights on the quay fell on the decks of ships. I tried to make out the *F 154* among them. In vain. Finally, I took out my binoculars and found that she had gone. And her mooring ropes were gone as well.

I went down to Torben and gave him the news. But he was too absorbed in his book to hear what I said. I opened the drawer of the starboard navigation table to make an entry for the day in the logbook. But the drawer was empty.

'Do you know where the logbook is?' I asked Torben.

'No,' he said, still reading. 'I haven't touched it. That's your department.'

'Are you sure that you haven't taken out the logbook?'

'Certainly,' Torben replied and gave me a look of irritation at being disturbed.

'Somebody has been on board,' I told him.

His vexation turned to puzzlement.

'What do you mean?'

'Exactly what I am saying. Somebody has been aboard. The logbook isn't in its place.'

'Have you looked for it properly?'

'There's no looking for it. It's gone!'

Torben got up and opened a number of drawers.

'Here it is!' he announced triumphantly.

He had found it on top of the charts in the navigation table.

'You had just put it in the wrong place,' he told me and went back to his book.

I made no reply, but I knew that Torben was wrong. For as long as I had owned *Rustica*, the logbook had always been in the same drawer. It was the only way of having it constantly at hand. And I had never forgotten to put it back in its place. Someone had been on board while Torben and I were drinking at The Oyster Bar. I looked about. What had they been after? Except for the logbook everything seemed to be where it usually was. Of course they had seen Torben's books on the Celts. And it didn't matter if they had read the logbook. I'd been careful not to write anything there which might bring Pekka to mind. Pekka's logbook! I threw myself into the quarter-berth, pulled out all the sails and pushed a hand into the space between the inner and outer decks. The lock to my secret compartment had been broken open. But Pekka's logbook was still there. The things that had disappeared were money, the equivalent of a hundred pounds in various currencies, and my extra passport. What did that mean? That it was a piece of simple burglary? But how had they found my hiding place?

When I re-appeared, Torben regarded me with surprise.

'We've had a visit,' I told him. Of specialists. I didn't think it was possible for anyone to find my secret compartment if you didn't know where to look. They can't have been ordinary thieves. If so, why didn't they take my radio direction finder? But then, why didn't they take Pekka's logbook, if that's what they were after? What do you think?'

Torben scratched his beard, as was his custom when he didn't know what to believe or say.

'A possible explanation,' he suggested, 'is that they only needed to know if we had read Pekka's logbook. But they left it where it was to put us off the track. They read *Rustica*'s logbook to find out what we are likely to know and intend to do. They took the money to make it look like an ordinary burglary. They can hardly have been professionals. If they were, they would have turned the whole boat inside out and taken everything they could sell.'

'And the passport?' I wanted to know.

'They needed it to make a false one. Or they believed it was your only passport. In that case, we can expect the visit of a Customs officer, genuine or disguised, before long.'

'But we have cleared the customs.'

'In Fraserburgh,' Torben agreed. 'But the Customs in Inverness, for example, wouldn't necessarily be aware of the inspection.'

All that Torben said was possible. But it gave no answers and solved no problems. It merely raised new questions which we couldn't answer. How had they got into *Rustica*? What part had John and Robert played in the matter? Was it of any significance that the *F 154* had sailed the same evening? What was it, exactly, that made us embarrassing, if that was what we were?

Late into the night, we sat discussing various alternatives, among them that of turning around and going home. But even Torben no longer seemed inclined to go back. I suspect that the mere thought and possibility of three more days of seasickness was sufficient to make him consider seriously all other possibilities rather than just that one. But we came to no decision except that we would report the theft to the police without mentioning the passport.

'Whatever happens,' Torben said when we had gone to bed, 'we must act as if we didn't know that they know about it. And at the same time we must behave as if they knew that we know. My hypotheses may not tally at all - they seldom do - but it would be dangerous not to put some trust in them until we know better.'

Chapter 11

We awoke to a clear and windless morning. But the calm was torn to pieces by the shrill blast of bagpipes.

'I think I'm going to be seasick again,' said Torben, sitting up with a start.

I looked out through a porthole. I could see that there were lots of people down on the quay, all wearing their Sunday best. And in their midst a dozen kilted pipers stood blowing away.

'It's the ceremony,' I said.

We had a quick breakfast, put on our ordinary, shabby seamen's clothes, went out and mingled with the multitude. After half an hour, two policemen cleared a path through the crowd and they were followed by the eminent persons of Fraserburgh, the ladies in flowery skirts, tweed jackets and jaunty hats with silk bands, the men in dark suits with ribboned medals on their chests. They must have been cold, for there was a wind and a biting one at that. But the decorations of the men could not have been appreciated under winter coats. A scent of perfume and after shave lotion was left in their wake. They stood at attention, each before his particular chair facing a platform, while God Save the Queen was played. They all joined in singing the anthem, but some people standing where we were remained almost demonstratively silent. At the next moment, the Duke of Kent, chairman of the RNLI, appeared from nowhere. He spoke of all those who had contributed funds for the purchase of the new lifeboat, Fraserburgh's third, the two others having been lost with all hands. The Duke also spoke a few words about the firm solidarity shown by the people of Great Britain with the residents of Fraserburgh. It was, he said, 'the sort of generosity which binds a people together.'

'Bullshit!' I heard a voice behind me say. 'The oil belongs to Scotland!'

This, I remembered, was at one time the slogan of the Scottish Nationalist Party. During the Seventies, Nationalists, if not exactly party members, had carried out a number of attacks against oil installations and pipelines. I recalled some alleged connection between the more radical nationalists and the IRA. At the middle of the decade, the SNP as a perfectly respectable and legitimate party had actually received thirty per cent of the popular vote in Scotland. Many people had then believed that it was only a matter of time before Great Britain broke up. The Labour Party made some concessions. But when the Conservatives came into power led by Mrs Thatcher, she declared that any form of real self government in Scotland was out of the question.

This was part of the same attitude which had made Northern Ireland one of the last militarised states in Europe. It was obvious that England would take the same stand against Wales if ideas concerning self government should gain more support there. I imagined that the Conservatives' policy must have sharpened opposition and fomented bitterness. Surely, in Celtic eyes, Great Britain could seem as unmotivated a union of states as the old Soviet Union or Yugoslavia.

I turned round to see who had made the protest. One of

the fishermen I had seen in the harbour was standing behind me. And beside him stood John. When he saw Torben and me, he gave us a broad smile.

'Good of you to come out with me yesterday evening,' he said somewhat overwhelmingly although it was we who should have thanked him for a nice evening. 'You got down to your boat without any trouble, I hope?'

'More or less,' I replied, and I decided to put matters bluntly. 'Torben was on the point of falling into the water. And when we had got aboard we found that we'd had a little burglary. So we'll have to make a report to the police.'

'Burglary?' said John.

'Yes. Somebody had broken in.'

He seemed very surprised.

'There must have been a misunderstanding,' he said enigmatically. 'You were my guests. I'll look into it immediately. Don't do anything until I come back. And don't contact the police.'

He disappeared with speed.

'Did you see?' Torben wondered.

'See what?'

'The fellow who laid claim to Scottish oil vanished as soon as you said 'the police'. We must have been shadowed. Perhaps he was trying to find out if we had been fooled into thinking it was an ordinary theft. So now they probably believe they have made mugs of us. Well, that puts us one up.'

The ceremony ended a few minutes later. With cheering from the crowd, the new lifeboat was launched. I wondered how many of those present actually considered that members of the crew would voluntarily, time after time, year in and year out, risk their own lives to save those of others. Well, perhaps they did get a fleeting thought, mixed with mild astonishment that men should deliberately, expecting little honour and receiving no payment, expose themselves to such risks.

How many people, sitting in front of their television sets and hearing that there will be a gale during the night, picture a pilot boat going out from harbour, or fishermen lying at sea and trying to save their catch, or lifeboat crews awaiting with dread distress signals from their radios? A high jumper who jumps an inch or two higher than all other high-jumpers becomes a hero. But a pilot who in a snowstorm jumps from his boat to a rope ladder on a tanker and then climbs up thirty feet over its hull - who gives him a thought? If the Duke of Kent hadn't come to Fraserburgh, the red carpet would certainly have remained somewhere in the town hall. It wouldn't have been rolled out merely for the lifeboat crew.

Torben and I lingered while it was being rolled up. The principal spectators in their best clothes had quickly dispersed and walked off in the direction of the pubs and bars.

'What shall we do now?' asked Torben.

'Sail,' I said spontaneously. 'As a way of getting solid ground under our feet.'

'What do you mean?'

'I don't like the atmosphere here. If you have troubles at sea, at least you know what causes them. You can never be sure when you are dealing with people ashore.'

'But isn't that why it's so fascinating?' Torben asked. 'If everybody was predictable and plain, our existence wouldn't be exactly thrilling.'

'It can be too thrilling,' I said.

We walked back to *Rustica* and stowed everything away in preparation for sailing; not only the logbook had its special place. When we had all in order, we heard a knock and found that John had returned. He handed over an envelope.

'Here is your money. It was some young rascals who didn't know any better. It would be a pity to get them into trouble with the police. In Scotland we respect our guests. Now they know that. I hope you can let the matter pass this time.'

'Of course,' Torben and I answered together.

'Can I invite you to lunch by way of consolation?'

Had we accepted, the lunch would doubtless have been sumptuous. But something in his tone suggested that he would like to get out of it.

'Thank you very much,' said Torben. 'But we're putting out to sea in half an hour. When the tide turns.'

'Oh, really?' John said with interest. 'And where will your Odyssey take you next?'

'We don't really know,' I admitted frankly.

But then I had an inspiration:

'We've thought of sailing through Pentland Firth.'

John gave a start.

'That would be foolish!' he said. 'If you want to play around with life and death, the Pentland Firth is a good place to start.'

'That's exactly why we want to do it,' I assured him and began to take the gaskets off the mainsail.

Torben looked at me curiously, and John was silent. Finally, he took out a pen and a bit of paper, on which he wrote down some words.

'Before you do something too rash,' he said in a low voice, 'you must put in at John O'Groats' harbour, south of the isle of Stroma. Find Brian Murray and ask him for advice. He's an old fisherman, and he knows all there is to know about the Pentland Firth. But don't tell him that I sent you to him. I want you to promise that!'

'Certainly,' I replied, although I rather wondered afterwards if John really believed that my promise was seriously meant.

He hurried off.

'Are you serious?' Torben asked when we were alone again.

'No. I wanted to see how he would react. I still think we should go on to Inverness, as we planned to do. But it won't do any harm if we sail northwards until we are out of sight.'

A quarter of an hour later, when we had cast off and were leaving between piers twelve feet high on either side, we met a large fishing boat coming in. I cursed our ill luck and prophesied to Torben that we'd get a proper dressing down for being in the way. But instead the captain and the entire crew waved to us and wished us good sailing - and meanwhile left so much room for us that their boat couldn't have more than a few inches to spare on the opposite side. Their cordiality warmed us, and once again I thought how different it was in Scandinavian waters, where bulkheads were, so to speak, watertight between fishermen and those who sailed for pleasure.

At 14.00 hours we put up the mainsail, and just before reaching the entrance to the port of Fraserburgh, the light wind genoa went up as well. With a gentle to moderate offshore breeze from the south, Torben didn't need to fear the torment of seasickness. During the first hour we simply enjoyed the sun and the glitter of the sea. Our only worry was the too good visibility. The weather report placed it at over 30 nautical miles, as if that were an everyday occurrence. At a speed of five knots, we would have to sail northwards for six hours before we were out of sight from Fraserburgh's heights.

But two hours later the outline of land faded imperceptibly into a luminous, silver blue haze, and soon thereafter twilight fell. We discussed whether we should sail without lights. But after brief consideration, I decided that we shouldn't make any compromise with proper seamanship. Besides, I knew that our manoeuvre to mislead must be seen on the coastguard's radar screen, so that we could only hope that 'they', whoever they were, didn't keep in contact with the coastguard.

126

The twilight was beautiful, and soon we were sailing about shielded from the rest of the world. At times, I felt a desire to change our course northwards again. Up to the Orkneys and then vanish without trace out onto the Atlantic.

Our discussion about the lights had broken the spell, and we started to talk about John. We opened the envelope he had brought to us and there was my money, right enough. But not my passport. I concentrated on our sailing and left Torben to draw conclusions.

'They kept your passport in order to have a hold on us,' he suggested after a time. 'If they had your only passport, it would be easy for them to get you expelled from the country, if that should be necessary. Meanwhile, they evidently don't want us to make a report to the police. That may indicate that they don't wish to attract attention. Not yet, in any case.'

'And how about John?' I asked.

'John had been instructed to keep us away from the boat, but perhaps without having been told why. His well-intentioned advice about Pentland Firth probably shows that he doesn't feel any particular desire for us to be drowned. Something which his employer might regard with more approval.'

'Perhaps we're imagining the whole thing,' I said.

'Pekka's logbook isn't imaginary,' Torben pointed out. 'Nor Pekka's death either.'

A thought struck me.

'But ...! What have we done with the newspaper notice?'

'Did you keep it?' Torben asked. 'Wasn't that a bit rash of you?'

That was the least one could call it.

'Take the helm!' I told him.

I went down to the cabin and opened the locker on the starboard side. The newspaper lay innocently rolled up where I had left it. The next minute I laughed with relief.

'What's so funny?' Torben called from the cockpit.

I climbed back up.

'How many Scots can read Danish, do you think?'

'Not very many, I suppose,' Torben admitted, taking the paper from me and browsing through it rapidly. 'But 'polis' and '*Sula*' are certainly comprehensible even for a Scotsman. For safety's sake, we'll have to assume that they know that we know.'

'Isn't it rather unlikely that they do?'

'Perhaps, but unfortunately it is possible.'

At dawn we sighted the church spire of Lossiemouth. All was still in the port, although seven large North Sea fishing boats had crowded into the eastern harbour basin where we moored. As the tide was out, Torben had to climb up twelve feet on a rusty ladder in order to make fast. We locked up *Rustica* and took a walk in the town to stretch our legs. It would have been useless to labour on against the tide.

The first person we met was an elderly man washing his car. He greeted us with a cheerful 'Hello!' and asked us at once where we came from. And how did we like Scotland? He was proud, we felt, of our making such efforts to visit his country. It turned out that he was a fisherman, and he was extremely interested in our crossing. Then, a bit further down the same street, we met a couple with a pram. When we were still a little distance from them, they called to us and commented on the weather. Before our conversation was over, they had almost married off their elder daughter to Torben, and they wanted us to have lunch with them so that he could meet her. We had difficulty in declining.

Light of foot, we returned to the harbour. Encountering such simple friendliness was a healthful antidote to all we had experienced since leaving Dragør. We would meet with it again and again in Scotland. Perhaps that was why we didn't lose heart.

Everything seemed easier when we were back on board. We put out at the turn of the tide, and helped by the current, we covered 22 miles in three hours. Soon, Burghead, Findhorn and Nairn, inviting little coastal towns that clung to bright green slopes, were behind us. After Nairn, the sunlit haze returned and we could only trust that log and compass would keep us off the two shallows in Murray Firth. After some uncertainty, we found the buoy which marks out the most easterly point there, Riff Bank. Before long, we divined that there was land on both sides of us, and without much delay we sighted Chanonry Point and the entrance to Inverness Firth. While Torben was down making coffee, I sat wondering at the singular green light that covered the sky. To either side of the boat, a strip of sand lost itself in green. Then I looked higher up and saw with astonishment the tree-covered mountains which, only two cable lengths or so away, rose many hundreds of feet high. In the mist I had not realised that they were mountains and not sky. A moment later my eye was caught by a round grey object ahead of us.

'Come up!' I called to Torben. 'There's something odd in the water.'

When we got closer, we saw that it was a seal; we and the seal stared wide eyed as we glided past. And just afterwards, a half dozen dolphins appeared and began to play around *Rustica*. Torben gripped my arm.

'Believe it or not,' he said, 'I think I am beginning to understand why it is necessary to sail.'

The dolphins soon left us for an on coming freighter. After a few minutes, we saw them surfing on the bow-wave of the other ship. And we fully realised the limited possibility of *Rustica* competing for their favour. Soon, we sighted Kersoch Bridge, portal to the Highlands.

We argued as to whether we should moor in the town itself or pass at once through the locks of the Caledonian

Canal. We finally decided on the canal. At exactly 16:00 hours the lock gates moved smoothly aside, and we were admitted to Muirtown Basin. Neither of us had uttered a word all day long about the Celts, MacDuff or Pekka, but we were both aware that our reason for avoiding the harbour at Inverness was to gain further respite from the matter of MacDuff while it was still possible.

Chapter 12

WE overslept, but it was still cold when we woke up. The thermometer showed -6°, and a strong northerly wind swept over the deck, taking with it part of the warmth from the heater. I stuffed a rag into the air vent, turned up the heat and placed the paraffin lamp at the entry, where cold air sank down to the floor.

We had breakfast in silence. Torben read a book about the IRA with a bright green shamrock leaf on the cover. Meanwhile, I tried to make some sense of the recent happenings. But nothing became any clearer. Rather the contrary. When, with considerable effort, I had taken away everything we didn't know *for certain*, very little remained.

I left Torben to his book, went ashore and looked first at Muirtown's staircase of locks. Some of them had warped and tumble-down wooden gates. It wasn't difficult to understand why on occasion gates had given way; the canal was more than a hundred years old, and it showed its age.

There was a little grocer's shop at the foot of the locks. I bought cigarettes and a can of Tennant's lager. This was decorated with a picture of a girl wearing a bikini, as if that would give a more interesting taste to the beer. I also bought a map of Inverness. With the map in one hand and the beer in the other, I sat down on an out of the way bench above the locks, opposite the now deserted quays, where boats could be chartered at other seasons. After some searching, I found Anderson Street on the map. Apparently MacDuff lived on the west side of the River Ness, not far from the harbour.

When I got up and began to walk towards the town, I had far from decided if I would pay a visit to MacDuff. I was, rather, provoking myself to see how far I might be prepared to go. After a half hour's walk, I came to Waterloo Bridge, which divided the town into two parts. MacDuff lived in a somewhat shabby neighbourhood of sooty, two-storey, red brick houses. Anderson Street contained two pubs, a laundry, and a grocer's. The shop had yellowed posters advertising sun bleached foods and also some tins in the window. The street itself seemed lifeless.

Number 15 looked neither better nor worse than the rest of the houses. I hesitated. What I saw didn't agree with my image of MacDuff; I had imagined that he lived in a stately house with a view over the sea.

A passerby stared at me curiously and made me cross the street to enter the house. In the half light at the bottom of the stairs I looked for MacDuff's name. There was no mistake: he lived on the second floor, to the left. At the landing, I found a single door, painted in flaked-off green, and without a name. Once more, I hesitated. But anyone at home would have heard my steps echoing on the bare stairs and wondered why they became silent. And the door might be opened at any instant, possibly making me into a suspicious character merely because I was loitering on the landing.

I knocked. All was silent, except for the lingering sound of my knocking. After a bit, however, shuffling footsteps could faintly be heard. The door was cautiously opened, little more than a chink. But I could see that an old woman with snow white hair was scrutinizing me from top to toe. She had an intense, bright blue gaze that I had some difficulty in meeting.

'What do you want?' the woman asked in a muffled voice, at the same time gentle and sharp.

It seemed to be the voice of a much younger woman.

'I am looking for MacDuff.'

'He doesn't live here,' she said quickly. 'Not any more.'

She seemed to say this because it was what she *should* say.

'You don't by any chance know where I can find him?' I asked, although I felt sure that I would receive a negative answer.

'No,' she answered, exactly as I had expected.

Well, that's that, I thought and felt in a way relieved. MacDuff was out of view. There was no getting in touch with him. And I was about to go when the old woman stretched out a hand as if to keep me there.

'Forget MacDuff!' she said beseechingly before banging the door shut.

I knocked again several times, but the door remained closed. I went down to the street and looked up at the windows, but they showed no hint of life. After some time, I turned on my heel and walked back to Muirtown and *Rustica*. Who was she? I wondered. His housekeeper? I couldn't imagine his having servants. His mother, then? They didn't resemble each other. But if I hadn't known better, I would have thought that I had already met her somewhere.

Torben was lying on his bunk when I arrived. He had read a few hundred pages more and didn't seem to have noticed my absence. But when I had sat down and opened a bottle of beer, he put his book aside and said:

'We've had a visit.'

'From whom? From MacDuff?'

Torben looked at me with curiosity and, I thought, amusement.

'Why do you think so?' he wanted to know.

'Just an idea I had.'

'No. Our visitor was a zealous Customs officer. I took out our landing card from Fraserburgh, but it didn't appear to interest him in the least. It was our passports he insisted on seeing. I may be mistaken, we all can be, but I'm practically certain that he was surprised or disappointed when I produced them both. I told him to stamp them, but he only got out a few incomprehensible words and disappeared. So my hypothesis and my prophesy weren't so wide of the mark, were they?'

Torben looked pleased with himself and with his morning. He appeared to be developing a taste for all the unsolved questions which whirled about in the otherwise crystal clear air around *Rustica*.

'Where have you been?' he asked.

'I thought I'd say hello to MacDuff,' I told him casually and actually succeeded in dumbfounding him. 'He wasn't at home,' I added.

I related briefly what I had done and seen.

'You shouldn't have gone there alone,' he said.

'Why not?'

'You know that as well as I do.'

Did I know? Hadn't I gone just because I did not know. But before I could work this out, the lock keeper came by and offered to lock us through with Scot II, the converted tugboat which takes tourists to Loch Ness in the summer and in winter serves as an ice breaker. Half an hour later, we were motoring our way through the canal. Now and then, we caught sight of the River Ness, gleaming beyond conifers, parallel with the canal. The closer we got to Loch Ness the thicker the woods became. Then the sun broke through. It was pleasant to be without any need to think of tides and weather conditions and courses to follow. We seemed to be in action, not simply allowing suspicions to close in around us. However, I couldn't stop casting occasional glances in among the trunks of trees, perhaps looking for reflections from binoculars or the shape of a shadowy figure following our progress.

That was also the first time I noticed a singular feeling which would never leave me for the whole trip. The certainty, or the mere suspicion, that we might be watched made it difficult to be oneself. Simply the thought that we could at any time be observed, without being able to see the observer, forced us to make a constant and conscious effort to make sure that we remained what we were. We could never properly relax.

One of the few times when we forgot all watchfulness was on seeing the landscape open and Loch Ness spread out before our eyes: a long and narrow water, bordered by mountains with green slopes, then steeps which, half-way up, lost their vegetation and mounted to bald and barren summits and crests covered with snow. We were overwhelmed by the sight and distinctly awed by the oil black water of the loch. I have never, before or since, seen water with that particular shade. It actually called forth images of mysterious monsters and drew our thoughts to the bottom of the lake instead of staying on the surface.

In the distance, we clearly saw Urquhart Castle, sharply outlined just south of an inlet where we intended to anchor for the night. But an hour later the bay in question still seemed to be no closer, and we realised that we had grossly misjudged the distance. It would take long before we learned to estimate distances in Scotland's high and transparent air on cloudless days.

It wasn't until six o'clock that we dropped anchor in the calm inlet, where the water was like a mirror. On the opposite side, high up the mountain, we saw a lighted window, but otherwise the darkness was soon complete. We lit a candle and drank a bottle of wine with our dinner, in a devout silence broken only by Torben's comments on the bouquet, the colour and the taste of the beverage. I listened with interest and, as usual, was carried away by his enthusiasm. When we had finished the bottle, he began to rummage among his few possessions on board and then produced an empty, corked bottle.

'Smell this!' he said, drew out the cork and moved the bottle back and forth under my nostrils.

From the bottle there emerged a deep and rich aroma left by some Portuguese wine.

I never ceased to wonder at Torben's thoroughness, although we had known each other so long that it should have ceased to surprise me. In his flat, empty but corked bottles stood in rows. It was his way of prolonging the enjoyment he had known when drinking the finest wines he had tasted. From time to time, he would pull out a cork and inhale the fleeting emanations that lingered on within the bottle. To begin with, I thought that he was having me on. But in due course he had taught even me to catch the scent of some great experience. So it was perfectly natural that he had taken an empty bottle with him across the North Sea.

'Bairrada, Louis Pato, 1978', he said, smelled himself, and then put the bottle back in the locker.

A little later, the moon came up and laid a silver stripe across the little bay.

'I think I'll row ashore and take a look at the castle,' Torben said.

I helped him to lower *Rustica*'s dinghy, an old Optimist named *Sussi* that I had bought cheap second hand from a Danish yacht club who sold it because none of the children wanted to race in such a heavy old thing. I kept an eye on Torben as he rowed into the moonlight. After that he was swallowed up by the darkness nearer land.

I lay down and fell asleep, only to be awakened a couple of hours later by the sound of splashing. I rushed up to the cockpit, and from there I discovered that Torben was wading with the dinghy, close to land and in water up to his knees. What could have happened? Nothing was visible behind him except the black shapes of trees and that of the ruined castle. I had no means of giving him aid. Without the dinghy I was as helpless as he seemed to be. Then he vanished into the dark, and waiting for him to reappear made me very anxious. But soon there came the creaking of oars, and he could be seen rowing frenetically along the edge of the moonlight.

Thereafter, *Sussi* bumped with a bang into *Rustica*. Torben stood up too soon, and if I hadn't caught hold of his arm, he would have fallen overboard. When I got him back into *Rustica*, I sat him down forcibly and fetched some whisky, which he swallowed before discovering what it was.

'What the hell are you trying to get into me?' he asked.

His voice was still strained, but he had begun to sound like himself.

'What happened?' I asked, attempting to conceal my anxiety.

He shook his shoulders dejectedly and looked up at me as if he wished to beg for pardon.

'I was pursued,' he said quietly.

'Pursued? By whom?'

'Not by whom,' he corrected. 'By *what*. It was by a ram. A furious ram that went wild.'

At first I didn't think that I had heard aright.

'When I went up to the castle everything was peaceful enough,' Torben explained. 'It's beautiful, come to that. But no trace of Pekka or any Celts.'

So that was what he'd been after! But that could wait.

'On the way back, I came to a fence. I followed it for a

bit to find a path down to the water. Instead, I stumbled upon a sign with the head of a big, furious ram, and 'WARNING! DANGER!' painted on it. So I went back to the castle and took another path down to the water. But I must have passed the fence without noticing it because suddenly I heard snorting and the stamping of hoofs. I ran out into the water, but the ram came after me. I thought my last moment had come!'

Torben looked up at me with a tired smile.

'But as you see, I'm still alive.'

'How could you be so frightened of a sheep?'

'Because I am afraid of sheep. Should that be regarded as a moral failing of some kind?'

I regretted my tone.

'Just forget the whole thing.'

But it wasn't so easy to ignore his reason for going up to Urquhart Castle, sitting ghost-like at the foot of the bald pated mountain, sharply silhouetted against the moonlit sky. A strong wind from the north east was blowing next morning. With only her storm-jib set, *Rustica* seemed to fly forward between the mountain sides. At Fort Augustus, the lowest lock gate opened as if on previous order and three quarters of an hour later we had left all five lock gates behind us. We were so pleased with our speed that we moored at one of the wooden jetties and went down to the only pub at Fort Augustus, naturally enough called the Loch Inn.

When Torben and I walked into the pub, reality seemed to be transformed into a still photograph, with every face turned toward us. Everything stopped. We did too, for no other reason than that the others did the same. Silence prevailed. Then the man behind the bar nodded briefly in greeting, and it came to us that we ought to order what we wanted to drink. But not before I had asked for a glass of the house's best single malted whisky did the still picture come into life.

Even so, it never seemed completely real during the short

time we remained in the pub. The atmosphere was strained, and people seemed withdrawn, although without animosity. I looked discreetly from face to face. Before I had got half way round the room, Torben whispered:

'Have you seen the big fellow in the corner by the window? Surely he's our friend the fisherman from Fraserburgh? Who didn't like the Duke of Kent.'

I had a better look. The man was sitting with his back to us, but I could see the reflection of his face in the dark window.

'You are right,' I told Torben. 'It's the same man. Let's get away from here.'

'Why?'

'Later.'

I drank up my whisky, and Torben the wine in his glass. We were forced to pass the man's table on our way to the door. I stopped behind him, put a hand on his shoulder and said 'hello'

'Haven't we met somewhere?' I added quickly.

He turned brusquely, but stopped when he saw me and Torben.

'No,' he said calmly. 'I don't think so.'

'Sorry! I must have mistaken you for somebody else.'

I moved on.

'What got into you?' Torben asked when we were outside.

'And why did you go up to Urquhart Castle last night?' I asked in return and added: 'I simply wanted to see how the fellow looks. No harm in that, is there?'

We walked silently back to *Rustica*. Then, without a word, we cast off and continued on our westward journey.

'We need to get a few things sorted out,' Torben said after he had lighted his pipe.

'Yes, I agree.'

'In the first place, it might be better if we acted together, not each by himself. And stopped pretending that nothing is up.'

'Even if it means taking risks?'

'It's hardly a crime to be curious. Besides, we know too little to be dangerous.'

He was, I thought, forgetting that there might be people who took another view about what we knew and did not know.

'That's the strange thing about it all,' he went on. 'We know nothing, and nothing has actually happened to us, except for the burglary. But at the same time it seems to get worse and worse. And I think the time has come for us to do something.'

I refrained from reminding him of what he had said and meant in Thyborøn about our heroic prospects.

'Have you a suggestion?' I wondered.

'Well, to begin with, as I said, we should stop pretending. No matter how we behave, when we are sailing about in a boat with a Swedish flag in the middle of winter, we'll not be taken for ordinary tourists. We may just as well show openly that we are interested in Celtic history. Of course there's nothing strange about that, is there? If we are to get any answers, we must start asking questions. And then, I suggest that we follow Pekka's route in the future. What he found, we can find.'

'In other words, you mean we should sail to Ireland?' I asked.

'Yes. For instance.'

'And also through Pentland Firth?'

'Well, not if we can help it,' he said. 'I don't think that Pekka had intended to sail through Pentland Firth. He was forced to if he hoped to save his skin. It was his only chance.'

'But it might be ours, as well.'

'In that case I suppose we too will have to sail through Pentland Firth.'

140

In spite of his crossing the North Sea and his seasickness, it was clear that Torben had still not acquired enough respect for the sea. His tone was far too easy-going and he took the sailing for granted. Already, I had begun to worry about the exposed anchorages on Ireland's northwest coast where the swell and the storms swept in with invincible force from the Atlantic. I had also to consider ways of avoiding the Corryvreckan, a sound almost as feared and notorious as Pentland Firth. Torben, of course, was sure to leave all such worries airily to me.

'I have been thinking about Ireland', Torben said as we neared Invergarry Loch and the last loch before Loch Oich. 'The smuggling of arms that Pekka wrote about reeks of the IRA. That's the reason why I was reading Coogan's book the other day. I wanted to investigate possible connections between the IRA and Celtic nationalism.'

'And what was the result?'

'It doesn't say that there are any clear connections between the IRA and pan-celticism. But it doesn't say the contrary either. One of the IRA'S best known slogans is: 'Not only to be free but also Celtic, not only to be Celtic but also free.' Moreover, there is concrete evidence of co-operation between the different Celtic national movements. At the beginning of the Sixties, for instance, the IRA had scarcely any weapons left. Do you know why? Because the IRA had sold what they'd had to the Welsh nationalists! And of course Wales is Celtic to the highest degree. Coogan thinks that the main reason why the English don't dare let go of Northern Ireland is because it would encourage the movement for independence in Scotland and Wales. If there's truth in that, and there very well might be, then it wouldn't be very strange if the Scottish and Welsh Celts supported the IRA. After all, it is still stated in the IRA's Green Book where they set forth their tactics and platform that they wish to have a Celtic

Ireland.'

'Yes,' I said. 'But how do you explain 'the King in the Underworld', 'The Golden Road', the head cult, and the rest of it? The IRA doesn't seem very inclined to mysticism, does it?'

'I don't explain anything as yet. I simply draw a few parallels.'

While listening attentively to Torben, I failed to notice how close we were to Invergarry Loch. Suddenly, its lock gates were alarmingly near. I threw myself onto the reversing gear for the propeller, and nervous minutes passed before we were sure that the boat would not crash violently against the gates. Afterwards, I understood more fully the large sign at every lock: *Don't trust your reverse*!

But before we lost all momentum, the gates had glided apart. We could only assume that the lock keepers kept one another informed about approaching boats. Nevertheless, we now saw no lock keeper at all, only a black Labrador retriever that ran back and forth along the edge of the quay above us, barking cheerfully.

'What do we do now?' Torben asked.

We had no way of getting up to the bollards.

'Throw up the ropes,' I told him, 'and we'll see what happens. Of course somebody must come.'

Torben coiled up our long mooring ropes and managed to throw them, one by one, onto the quay. To our surprise, the labrador took the end of the first one with his teeth and placed the loop over a bollard. He accomplished the same service with the second rope. After that, the lock keeper came strolling into view and closed the gates behind us. As water flooded in, *Rustica* began to rise. The dog waited expectantly, with wagging tail, for us to reach the same level or at least high enough for a reward. He got the best we could find. There's no resisting a labrador's eyes.

The lock keeper, on the other hand, couldn't possibly

think of accepting a tip. We expressed our gratitude, and I remarked that whenever we arrived at a lock, the gates seemed to open immediately.

'Is that always the way?' I asked.

'Not in summer, it isn't,' he replied. 'But my colleagues have rung up and told me you were coming. Just now, I believe you are the only boat in the canal. Except for *Scot II*, the passenger boat, you know, she's always here. And yesterday there was a fishing boat from Fraserburgh. But we haven't a lot of work, my dog and I, at this time of year. Worse for him. He gets so many sweets in the summer that they've become a bad habit with him. But I'm the postmaster here, so I always have something to do.'

Torben was first with questions:

'A fishing boat from Fraserburgh? You don't by any chance remember the number? Some pleasant fishermen we met in Fraserburgh said they'd be coming this way.'

'Hundred and fifty four, I think that was the number,' the lock keeper answered.

'Did they say where they are off to next?'

'No. There seemed to be only one man on board, and he wasn't especially talkative. But if you'll wait a couple of seconds I'll ring to Corpach and see if he has gone through.'

He was soon back.

'It's odd. The boat hasn't passed there. So I got onto the keeper at the other side of Loch Oich. No sign of the boat there, either. She must be still lying somewhere in the loch. Whatever a fishing boat would be doing that for in the middle of winter.'

'Thanks again for your help,' I called back as we were putting out. 'We're sure to find them!'

'If that's what we want to do,' Torben said more or less to himself.

Of the three lakes connected by the Caledonian Canal,

Loch Oich lies highest up and is both smaller and shallower than the others. Like Loch Ness and Loch Lochy, it is surrounded by mountains, but not as high and mighty as the others. It is the narrowest of the lakes, being only five hundred yards wide, and its shores are much more luxuriant. To me, there was something Scandinavian about Loch Oich.

According to our chart, we needed to keep well to starboard of the islet, no bigger than half of a tennis court, in the middle of the lake. Otherwise, we might run into submerged rocks. Behind the islet we discovered the *F 154*, lying at anchor. Neither Torben nor I saw any sign of life on board; we were certain nobody was there. For one thing, the thumping of *Rustica*'s old motor must have been distinctly heard from so short a distance, and would have aroused the curiosity of someone on board.

Further on, we glimpsed among trees the ruins of Invergarry Castle where we planned to moor for the night. Our chart indicated that we would find a jetty there. It might have been the place where Pekka tied up his *Sula*. But of course, with a shallow draught catamaran, he could have gone in anywhere.

It was almost dark when we drew near, and we had to feel our way forward to what was little more than a pontoon with a few fingers. Torben stood at the stem shouting out commands as if he were an expert in soundings. The silence that fell when the engine was shut off was intense and a trifle uncanny. The only sound came from a distant waterfall. The indistinct silhouette of the ruined castle shot up over the tops of trees. I remember asking myself what was so special about just that castle. Pekka had made his comment about Kings in the underworld at Invergarry Castle. The castle had been burnt down in the eighteenth century during one of the innumerable raids made by contending clans. Since then it had never been inhabited.

After a brief but excellent dinner, Torben went out to get a breath of air. With the heater and two paraffin lamps all burning, it was often too hot in the cabin, at least up at head level. In winter, and with a below zero temperature outside, there was always a difference of some twenty degrees between the floor and the roof of the cabin.

Torben hadn't been gone long when I heard the splash of oars. Then came voices. And Torben's face appeared at the hatch.

'One of the locals is here,' he announced. 'A young fellow who wonders if he can borrow a spinner. He wants to go fishing and has forgotten his own.'

'Sure,' I said and took out a plastic box containing a miscellaneous collection of spinners that were seldom used.

'And he wonders if I'd like to go with him.'

Torben must have noticed my misgivings.

'He seems a decent sort,' Torben added.

'Be careful all the same. You never know.'

'Do you have a whistle somewhere?' Torben asked.

'There's one in the drawer with the binoculars. What do you want it for?'

'I'll whistle if I want anything.'

I wasn't altogether easy about the matter. But after an hour I again heard the sound of oars.

'Not a bite,' reported Torben on entering. 'Not of any kind. We rowed past *F 154*, but I saw no light. What would you say to our asking my fishing friend down here for a glass of something.'

'Go ahead!'

Torben came back with a gangling youth, about twenty years-old, wearing a duffle coat and a cap. He looked curiously about and without more ado sat down beside the heater. He was not shy.

He began straight away to relate the story of his life. He

lived in a little village not far away and often fished in the lake. At night for the most part, became he couldn't afford to buy a fishing licence. He was without work, so he had plenty of time to fish and drink beer with his friends at the pub. The only difficulty was with his wife, a girl he had got pregnant the previous year and therefore married. She scolded him practically all the time because he never came home when he had agreed to. She had locked him out three times. But that was nothing to worry about. Otherwise he got along pretty well. Scotland was a lovely country. A fine country to live in.

He then narrated with enthusiasm, and sometimes fervour, the history of the region during a number of centuries. I asked him how he could be so knowledgeable on the subject. Did he read a great deal?

'Read?' said he. 'I never open a book.'

'Then where did you learn everything?'

'I don't know. People tell you about it I guess. Everyone knows about history. Ask anybody at all.'

A little later, when we were talking about Invergarry Castle, Torben happened to remark: 'A pity it was burnt down.'

'It's not a pity at all!' said Tom, as he was called, with evident contempt. 'The MacLeods built it. They had no business being here - they're not one of our clans. The castle should have been levelled to the ground!'

Torben and I found it difficult to understand his indignation about something that happened so long ago. But his suppressed rage was so great that we didn't dare suggest that the crime could now be barred by the statute of limitations.

To change the subject, I asked if many tourists came to the area.

'Oh, in the summer it's full of foreigners here. Mostly Americans. They shouldn't be allowed into the country. A terrible lot. Almost as bad as the French and all those other Southerners. I was in Paris once for football - what a country! We'd set them straight if they came here!

Tom passed from one to another of peoples he couldn't abide. His condemnation of them was touched by violent humour and some irony, but underneath he was completely in earnest. After the Southerners he turned to the Germans, of course everybody knew what to think of them. Then came the English, for whom his abomination was beyond all joking. His hate of Mrs Thatcher was especially strong. Did we know that she had sent Scottish regiments to Northern Ireland? But she wasn't going to escape much longer. Think of the attempt on her life in Brighton! He wept when he heard that she had survived it.

After the English, it was the turn of the Lowlanders: they who had sold Scotland to the English. And finally, when he had dealt with some Highland clans who had forfeited their right to existence, he came to the neighbouring village, which needed to be given a lesson from time to time. An occasional fight was all to the good, for it kept the laddies in condition. At the end, it boiled down to Tom's own village. His was a case of unequalled patriotism, but it didn't really seem to be a matter of national frontiers. When he had finished with his harangue, I asked him if there was any other people he accepted.

'The Irish,' he answered at once.

They were genuine, he explained, exactly like the Scots. I never understood what he actually meant by 'genuine'. Nor, for that matter, what he thought about Scandinavians, whom he was considerate enough to pass over.

'And the Celts?' Torben asked. 'Are you a Celt?'

For the first time, Tom looked a trifle hesitant: not, it seemed, because he disliked the question, but because he didn't know how to answer it.

'I am a Scot,' he finally replied. 'But there's a man in the village who holds that we are Celts first and Scots afterwards.'

'Why so?' Torben inquired.

'Why?'

Tom had a wondering look.

'Isn't it enough just to be a Scot?' Torben asked.

'I thought it was,' said Tom. 'And the man in the village says we ought to be an independent country. But we should have a federation with Ireland, Wales, Brittany and I think it was Galicia. I don't know why he wants Southerners in it. There's nobody down there who speaks a Celtic language any more, is there?'

'But it's all right with the rest, Tom?' Torben asked.

'Oh yes, why not? As long as long as we're allowed to take care of ourselves. I don't want a lot of foreigners telling us what we should and should not do. Not even Irishmen.'

'Are there others who talk about a Celtic federation? Your man in the village surely hasn't thought of it by himself? Is there a political party involved?'

'I don't believe so,' said Tom. 'There have been some meetings, but I don't know who is behind them. Not the Nationalists, in any case. We've had them for a long time, but they talk mostly about oil and don't do a thing. No, it's some others. They say that we should do exactly like the countries in Eastern Europe. Break free.'

'You haven't met somebody called MacDuff?' I asked on sudden impulse.

Tom shook his head.

'He's a good friend of mine,' I explained. 'I thought that perhaps he has been at one of the meetings.'

'Not that I know of,' Tom replied. 'But I haven't been to them all. I'd rather be out on the lake fishing.'

He looked at his watch and got up.

'My wife will lock me out if I don't go home now.

Thanks a lot for the spinner and the whisky. If you come by another time, I'll show you some fine spots to fish in. Just ask for Tom. Everybody here knows me.'

'Do we dare show ourselves in your village as foreigners?' Torben asked with a smile.

'Why not? You'd be my guests. Anyhow, it just a matter of people behaving properly.'

'What does that mean?' said Torben.

'To start with, calling a Scot a Scot and not an Englishman, as so many foreigners do. That goes a long way. And let me give you a bit of advice. If you're in a pub, don't talk politics, or religion, or about what's right and wrong. They're delicate subjects.'

When Tom had gone, we both felt puzzled. How could the boy's evident good nature, sense of humour and hospitality be mingled with so much hatred?

'What do you make of what he said?' I asked Torben.

'It sounds incredible. But there seem to be people who believe that what has happened in Eastern Europe could also happen here.'

'Why not? If Lithuania can declare itself independent of the big and despotic Soviet Union, why shouldn't Wales, Scotland or Brittany be able to do the same thing with England and France?'

'I am not saying that it would be impossible. It might even be desirable, for that matter. The smaller nations are, the less harm they can do. But I refuse to believe that the Celts feel that they are one people. I wonder what attitude the Western democracies would take if the Celtic peoples really did lay claim to their independence. Or if they set up their own parliaments and refused to have any military connections beyond their own borders. For instance, how would Mitterrand react if Brittany suddenly announced itself to be a sovereign state? After all the support which we in the West gave to

Eastern Europe in the name of democracy, we'd be in a difficult position. But that the Celts should be ready for such a thing no, I refuse to believe it. Quite simply, they don't see themselves as Celts. Not yet. You heard yourself, Tom goes fishing rather than to the meetings.'

'Making them all Celts is perhaps the mission of the Celtic Ring,' I suggested.

'Perhaps. But at least from what we think we know, the Celtic Ring is a mystical society with rites and ceremonies. How could it make the Celts into a people? That the need for freedom could do it and at the same time undermine armies, that's one thing. But I won't accept that myths and traditions can accomplish the same.'

I didn't try to argue, but I pointed out that an explosive force might lie behind Tom's feeling for history.

'Think of how violently he reacted when we asked about the castle.'

'Yes,' Torben admitted. 'But that's Scottish, not Celtic, history. As for the castle, maybe we should have a look at it. Just as well to begin our investigations straight away.'

'This evening?'

'Why not? If we're to reach Corpach tomorrow we'll have to sail pretty early, won't we? And at this hour we'll certainly have the place to ourselves. Nobody could very well suspect that we're interested enough in an old castle to search through it in the middle of the night.'

I was not much attracted by the idea of trailing round an old ruin in the dark, even if Torben was right that we would be undisturbed. With the *F 154* so near, I wasn't very willing to leave *Rustica*. However, I didn't want Torben to go up alone to the castle. It wasn't an easy decision, but finally I went with Torben and left *Rustica* to her fate.

Invergarry Castle looked more spectral than before when we

stood underneath it and allowed the beams from our torches to play over the outside of the tower. The place was enclosed and the gate padlocked. But, illogically, there was a sign which declared that persons who entered did so at their own risk. We took the risk and climbed over the fence. When we went into the ruin, we saw that only the walls remained. It cannot have been a large castle, as castles go. The hall where we stood measured perhaps ninety feet each way, and, to judge from the gaping holes left by cross beams, the tower had been four storeys high. Nothing rose any higher except an outer tower facing over Loch Oich.

We went out again, and turned to the right, down dilapidated steps which stretched along a kind of built out extension at the foot of the tower. We came out on the loch side and stopped short. The tower stood on the edge of a precipice that descended sheer to the water. *Rustica* lay somewhere below us, but we couldn't see the light from her portholes because of the large trees which somehow clung fast to the cliff.

'We can't get any further,' I said to Torben. 'It's too steep.'

'I'll look,' he answered, squeezing past me.

He moved the light from his torch back and forth along the foot of the tower.

'No problem. We can go on,' he said, failing to conceal his eagerness. 'If we just steady our feet against the trees.'

And without waiting for my response, he started the descent. Reluctantly, I followed him. Holding on to branches and roots, we slowly investigated the wall. *What imbecility*! I remember thinking. Pekka couldn't have come this way. But after some minutes Torben pointed a little further on.

'There's a passage,' he said. 'It seems to lead down to a cellar.'

We had to creep into a hole, but we could soon stand up

again. And we found ourselves in a tunnel, under the tower which didn't look so disintegrated as the rest of the castle. The tunnel slanted sharply downwards, but after some twenty yards it levelled out and then ended at a door. This was a heavy iron affair that could very well have known a number of centuries.

'It must be the dungeon,' said Torben. 'Every Highland chief with an ounce of self-respect kept a dungeon for prisoners from other clans. Presumably, there's a trap door to it up in the castle.'

He pushed down the handle and the door glided open without a sound. We cautiously took a couple of steps into the room beyond. The beam of my torch caught a table and two chairs. Two half emptied glasses on the table beside a couple of bottles of beer gave the impression that the room had been left in all haste.

'This must be used for something,' Torben remarked, taking a few steps forward.

As he did so, the iron door slammed shut behind us. A metallic echo reverberated between the stone wall, then died away under the ground. Almost at once, the room was flooded with light. I turned round. MacDuff stood to the left of the door. Beside him, just beyond the light that came from the ceiling, there were two heavily built men. One of them was our acquaintance from Fraserburgh and Fort Augustus. I had never seen the other man before. I didn't care for the sight of either of them, if only because of the sub-machine gun hanging from the shoulder of the man we had already seen.

'Welcome to Invergarry Castle,' said MacDuff. 'It's a small world, Captain!'

Chapter 13

I stared dumbfounded at MacDuff and his two companions.

'Fancy meeting you here!' he went on with blunt cordiality, as if we were two old friends who chanced to meet in a pub. 'It really is a small world. And always has been. I never thought you'd take up my invitation so quickly. Or that we should see so captivating a lady as your *Rustica* on these waters.'

I sought frantically for something to say. I hoped that Torben would let me go on talking, while he listened and worked things out in order to come to my rescue when I got into straits, as sooner or later I was certain to do.

After a silence which to me seemed endless, but which probably lasted no more than seconds, I was able to speak.

'It must be your fishing boat lying at anchor behind the islet,' I said, possibly hoping that this might take MacDuff by surprise.

'Yes,' he calmly replied, 'it's my boat. I thought you knew that already. Didn't you inquire on the subject at the Invergarry lock?'

I didn't answer.

'Why?'

Did he ask this because he hadn't guessed why? Or to find out if were trying to hide something? That was more likely. As he knew of our inquiry about the *F 154*, it would be stupid to suppose that he didn't know other things as well.

'We felt that we were pursued.' I told him. 'Your boat was in our wake all the way across the North Sea. Then we saw her again in Fraserburgh. So when the lock keeper said that a fishing boat had gone through before us, it was surely not very odd that we thought of the *F 154*.'

'Why?' insisted MacDuff. 'A fishing boat happens to sail from Thyborøn to Fraserburgh, from a large port on one side of the North Sea to a large port on the other. It stops for two days and then passes through the Caledonian Canal to new fishing waters. What's odd about that?'

I'd made a blunder. Of course, on the face of it, there was nothing very strange involved, unless you had preconceived ideas.

I lamely pointed out that the boat had no name.

'Anybody can find a boat if it has a registration number,' MacDuff replied.

I couldn't deny that. Happily Torben entered the conversation.

'But admit,' he said with ironical ambiguity typical of him, 'that we had some reason for our suspicions. After all, the boat was yours.'

MacDuff's gaze moved hastily over to Torben, but then back to me.

'Is that your opinion as well, Skipper?'

I didn't know why he made a point of talking only to me. Either he underestimated Torben, or else he believed that I took charge in my capacity as 'captain'. This was, I thought, the usual attitude of people who exercised power; they would speak only to others in command. I wanted to believe that this was a weakness of MacDuff's and a strength of our own. The question of who made decisions had never arisen with Torben and me. And I allowed myself to suppose that it might be to our advantage if MacDuff imagined otherwise.

'In a way,' I answered, feigning to have thought it over. 'We were obviously right in believing that the *F 154* wasn't just a fishing boat. Perhaps you were on board it yourself out on the North Sea?'

'Perhaps I was.'

'And in Fraserburgh?'

'It is possible.'

'But you were not at home in your flat?'

'No.'

So MacDuff knew that I had made a visit to Anderson Street. I was pleased to have got him to reveal the fact, and I thought this might put me in a better position. But it wasn't that easy.

'It was my housekeeper you spoke to,' he said, unperturbed.

'She said that you didn't live there any longer.'

'Neither do I. The flats hers now. But she takes care of my letters and my visitors.'

'She's not particularly good with visitors,' I remarked. 'She told me to forget you, whatever she can have meant by that.'

For the first time I sensed something like uncertainty, or perhaps surprise, in MacDuff. He gave his two companions oblique looks, as if to see whether they had taken in what I said.

'That was not the right thing to do,' he answered. 'I must speak to her about it. You don't simply forget MacDuff.'

'She's a lovely old lady!' I added spontaneously. 'She seems young for her age.'

Now, without knowing for what reason, I was sure that I had got MacDuff into an awkward corner.

'And one thing was very strange,' I went on in the same vein. 'I thought that I'd seen her before.'

For one brief instant, it seemed that MacDuff would lose all self restraint, but he recovered himself without my guessing what was involved.

'What are you trying to tell me?' he asked. 'What do you want?'

'As a matter of fact, that is exactly the question we are asking ourselves. We are tourists. But other people seem to want us to be something else.'

'Why are you inspecting Invergarry Castle? Not many tourists would climb round on the side of the loch in the middle of the night, not without a good reason. It could be dangerous.'

'Perhaps, but it's nothing compared to a tommy gun.'

'Why did you say that you intended to sail through Pentland Firth?'

'Probably because we didn't know any better. We did later. So we changed our minds.'

John, or somebody else in what seemed to be MacDuff's staff of informants, must have delivered a report. Presumably, MacDuff knew everything and held us in his grasp. But I thought that I was managing rather well.

Torben had told me that the ancient Celts, like the Greenlanders, competed in poetry. They challenged one another, tried to outdo each other, drove themselves to desperation and tears, with words as their only weapons. It was no game; they were in bloody earnest, and the loser could very well commit suicide. For he was scorned and humiliated. But the winner gained power and glory. It occurred to me that MacDuff and I were engaged in such a combat. But it was difficult to forget the sub-machine gun at my back. Torben and I just had to win. It wasn't fair play.

What was MacDuff's weak point? Everybody has a weak

point. Ours was that we knew too little at the same time as we were accused of knowing too much. Soon MacDuff would put questions about Pekka. While I was evasively answering his first ones, I tried to think out my reply when he would ask if I had met Pekka. But it seemed as if MacDuff wanted us to reveal what we knew without naming Pekka.

'Is this some kind of cross-examination?' I asked.

MacDuff appeared to be considering his next step. He evidently hesitated to threaten us with the violent end which might await us. That gave me the opportunity of seeming abused, if that is not too mild a word when you were threatened with death.

'Why does your friend stand there fingering his trigger?' I said. 'I thought that the Scots were known for their hospitality.'

'We are hospitable,' said MacDuff. 'But not with people who poke their noses in where they shouldn't.'

'In other words, we are supposed to have pried into things that don't concern us. But what things? You can't very well *pry* into things you don't know anything about.'

'No,' MacDuff admitted and regained something of his first cordiality. 'Assuming that you *are* truly ignorant. And refrain from trying to find out what you don't know. Or forget what you have already learned.'

'But in that case,' I said, 'you must know what to forget. Not so?'

'There are things which are none of your business. For your own sake. Or even anyone else's. You don't seem to be the type of man who lives at another's expense.'

It was strange to hear those words from MacDuff. For never living at another's expense was the only important moral principle I tried to uphold.

'Don't you think so, too?' MacDuff asked and turned abruptly to Torben.

'Oh, certainly,' said Torben. 'But what do you do with people who don't agree?'

'You crush them,' MacDuff answered curtly.

'How?' Torben wondered, as if the answer really didn't interest him.

'Once and for all,' said MacDuff.

'Then its lucky that we think the same way,' I threw in, and cast a furtive glance at the two men behind me.

They hadn't moved, and their faces didn't reveal that our conversation had made the slightest impression on them.

'Listen,' MacDuff said to me. 'I like you. You and I are the same kind. If I'd been in your shoes, I'd have done exactly like you. In actual fact, I envy you. You can still pretend that life is some sort of adventure. A hundred years from now, there may be somebody who will think that MacDuff's life was an exciting adventure, a life worth living. Perhaps somebody thinks so already. But it's not true. That's why I envy you. And I'd like to go on envying you.'

'What's stopping you?' I asked. 'If it means that much to you.'

'Nothing but you yourself. It's up to you.'

When MacDuff went on his voice sharpened:

'Everyone should have the right to decide their own destiny. You're too intelligent not to realise that if Dick goes about with a tommy gun, it's hardly for the sake of appearances. And that it's not to amuse ourselves that we've been sitting here in this old dungeon drinking beer. That's our cause and our destiny. Nothing to do with you. Absolutely nothing. Which is the only thing you need to remember. What I personally think or believe is irrelevant. That's precisely why I hope you'll listen to me now and try to understand fully what I'm saying. It's a pity you two are so curious. It would have been easier if you hadn't seen us here. Now you have something more definite to forget, not merely something further to abstain from finding out about.'

I began to breathe freely again. It looked as if nothing would happen for the moment. But I still wondered why he didn't ask about Pekka. Of course that was the simplest way to find us out. Could it be that he was afraid of revealing something we didn't know on the subject? In view of how extremely little we actually did know, such wariness might well be justified.

I couldn't help thinking of how he'd said that he liked me. Even that we resembled each other. Yet he had, more or less certainly, killed one man. Perhaps he had killed others as well. In what sense could we be at all alike? But I could not deny that it was very easy to be fascinated by MacDuff. Even now, at this very moment, I couldn't help feeling attracted to him, no matter how much I told myself that he was nothing but a murderer.

'And Pekka?' I suddenly asked. 'Had he also something that he should forget? Is that why you were so anxious to get hold of him? To say the same to him t hat you have said to us?'

'Pekka is dead,' MacDuff said in a flat voice. 'He couldn't forget.'

Was this a confession? To my consternation, I realised that I didn't want to know for certain if he had killed Pekka. I couldn't get myself to ask the logical question of how Pekka died. I said nothing at all, although this could be interpreted as meaning that I already knew of Pekka's death. I had stopped thinking tactically. Instead it was Torben who broke the long silence.

'And Mary?' he asked. 'What became of her? Couldn't she forget either?'

Torben's question remained hanging in the empty air until it was torn apart by MacDuff's voice, which reverberated between the walls.

'Who?' he said slowly. 'Who are you talking about?'

'Mary,' Torben repeated with unnatural calm. 'The woman who sailed away with Pekka.'

Torben hadn't been led astray. He had listened closely and found MacDuff's weak point. But was it well considered to make use of his discovery just now? MacDuff's large body stiffened like that of a big cat before it makes a lethal bound. It lasted only an instant, but long enough to put the two men behind us on the alert. Without daring to turn round, I was aware that the sub-machine gun pointed directly at us, ready to be fired. Torben had taken a great risk.

'She no longer exists,' MacDuff said when he had recovered.

His tone was final. Not even Torben was sufficiently bold to say anything more. MacDuff made a gesture warding off his henchmen.

'Wait outside!' he ordered in the tone of one who is accustomed to being obeyed.

The two men muttered, but they were silenced by a look from MacDuff. The iron door slammed shut behind them; the sound echoed abysmally as before, before it seemed to be absorbed deeply into the thick stone walls that dripped with moisture.

'You probably don't realise it,' MacDuff told us when silence returned, 'but today I have saved your lives. If I hadn't happened to be here when you came, you would now be dead men.'

'Happened to be!' Torben broke in. 'Are you saying it was by pure luck that we met here this evening?'

'Luck?' repeated MacDuff. 'Hardly that. Rather unfortunate circumstances. I wasn't here for your sake this evening. I might perhaps have expected you tomorrow. Or looked you up. Alone. But how could I have guessed that you would go in for cliff climbing at this time of night? Happily, we heard you in time. Otherwise, I assure you that things might not have ended like this. But now you've been given a reprieve. For how long I don't know. Long enough, however, for you to vanish from these waters. Sail to Corpach tomorrow, and head for England, the Isle of Man or anywhere you like. But away from Scotland. And not to Ireland.'

He turned to Torben.

'You'll excuse me if I speak only to the captain of *Rustica*.'

'Oh, that doesn't matter,' said Torben sincerely. 'Not at all. In any case, I wouldn't be willing to set my foot in a sailing-boat with you two on board at the same time.'

'No,' said MacDuff amicably. 'But then what would a solitary anchorage in Pentland Firth mean to you? Nothing, probably. Nor sailing in places of such magnificent beauty that you can be another person when you leave them. But I understand the skipper is your friend, and for his sake I hope you'll think of what I've told you both. You know nothing about life and death. I do. And I trust that you will be spared that knowledge. Do you understand what I am telling you?'

Neither of us answered.

'Well, you'll understand soon enough if you continue to pry,' he added.

He stood up.

'Well, I'm letting you go now.'

He opened a concealed door behind him.

'There is no reason why you should risk your lives by leaving the way you came. You must be careful with your life if you've been given a second one. How many have that privilege, do you think?'

We hesitated, and he smiled.

'Don't be surprised. You'll come up in a shed outside our neighbours, Glengarry Castle. It's always full of hotel guests, so nobody will notice you.'

We crossed to the door. MacDuff stopped us there.

'Just one more thing,' he said quietly. 'I'm telling you this for my own sake. But it has to be said. Never mention Mary again by name.' He looked especially at Torben.

'Absolutely never. If I ever learn that you have spoken about her, even if you've only mentioned her name, I'll immediately give orders that you are to be got rid of, once and for all. If necessary, I'll take care of the matter personally.'

He stepped aside, indicated with a gesture that we could go.

'Gentlemen ...!'

We hastened away through a long passage. After a time, the sound of loudly quarrelling voices reached us, one of them was MacDuff's. A sign surely that he had told us the truth; that, both possibly and plausibly, he had not expected us to turn up: that, no less possibly, no less plausibly, he had in fact saved our lives. We still didn't know what it was that we were not to find out. But now we had, precisely as MacDuff said, something to forget. If we were able to.

Chapter 14

IT was past one o'clock when we got back to *Rustica*. The light from the paraffin-lamp glowed cosily in the darkness, and I thought of what MacDuff had said in Dragør about *Rustica* being a boat that breathed security. She still did, for both Torben and me. But I wondered how much longer it would last. The fact that I drew the curtains, which I otherwise never did, was an unmistakable sign of something being wrong.

'That was a close one,' I said, when we had sat down.

I had sweat under the arms, and my muscles were taut as the shrouds and stays in *Rustica*'s rigging. I did my best to breathe normally, but it took time to regain some degree of self possession. To my astonishment Torben appeared to be almost his usual self, even in fact somewhat exhilarated. It seemed that he hadn't quite realised what might have happened to us.

'Well,' I remarked, 'now we know one thing. The Celtic Ring isn't made up of peaceful Druids in white draperies and with golden sickles in their belts. They have exchanged those for machine guns.'

'I wonder,' said Torben, as if this were an abstract

intellectual problem like any other, 'why MacDuff let us go.'

'He's simply a decent fellow at heart,' I suggested, wishing to bring Torben down to earth.

'You know,' he replied, in the same tone of cool analysis, 'to some extent you might in fact be right. Everything indicates that he shouldn't have saved our lives.'

'What was the alternative? To have us shot?'

'Yes. Why not? He doesn't seem to have any scruples otherwise in such matters. We have no longer the slightest reason to doubt that MacDuff was a party to Pekka's death.'

'He doesn't need to have done the thing himself,' I said lamely.

Torben looked at me.

'Are you defending him?' he inquired with surprise.

'No,' I answered half-heartedly, and heard instantly how unconvincing I sounded.

But I said no more. It was precisely as if the image of that sub-machine gun had deprived me of words. As long as we had needed words in order to stay alive, I hadn't had too many problems getting them past my lips. But now? What was there to be said when the answer might come from the barrel of a tommy gun?

'Is there any point in our going on?' I asked finally.

Torben looked at me, wonderingly, as if he hadn't quite understood the question.

'MacDuff isn't going to touch a hair of our heads,' he told me confidently. 'If we only do as he said and don't mention Mary by name.'

'MacDuff, yes. But the others?'

'Oh, they seem to obey him, don't they? So what is the problem? Moreover, we are pretty well forced to follow Pekka's route until we come to Oban on the coast. If I have understood the matter rightly, there are no turning-off places for boats on this canal. Much can happen in these few days.'

This was exactly what I feared. I left Torben and turned in much irritated by the remote way he treated our difficulties. It was as if they didn't concern *us*.

After a hasty breakfast next morning, we left Invergarry Castle and then Loch Oich behind us. I could tell that Torben had come to some conclusions the previous evening, and, in spite of everything, I awaited them with a certain curiosity. Some of my irritation had disappeared and been replaced more or less by fatalism. As Torben had said, whatever decision we might come to, we were obliged to take the route which we were in fact following. True, at the start we could have sailed round the little island and seen if MacDuff's boat still lay there, but neither of us had thought of doing so, and it was now too late.

After Loch Oich, we had only a short stretch of canal to cover before we came out through the Loggan Locks into Loch Lochy. In the distance, Ben Nevis raised its snow covered crown, and the lake stretched out for ten nautical miles in front of *Rustica*'s stem. On the steep-to sides, clear felling in narrow strips had scarred the woods up to the tree-line.

We made excellent speed in the fresh wind. Distractedly, Torben began to throw crumbs to the gulls that circled above our wake. Soon their acrobatics made us forget all else. To see them hover suspended, then dive, take the bread, lift again, without losing speed or balance, was to witness a matchless spectacle. Torben threw the bits higher and higher, and each of them disappeared down a gullet before it had even begun to fall. Ultimately, he didn't bother to throw them up at all, but held each between thumb and forefinger. And very soon the gulls were taking crumbs from his hand. I managed to take a photograph of a gull just as it snapped up a large bit. I have pasted the picture in *Rustica*'s logbook to remind me that we also had some brighter and more joyful moments, in spite of everything else.

The game ended at the same time as we reached the western end of Loch Lochy. We had no more bread. And the sails had to come down on deck and be furled before we entered the last section of the Caledonian Canal.

'Well, that's that,' I said when this was done. 'Within two hours we'll be out on the Atlantic. With open water before us all the way to the Caribbean.'

This was a veiled proposal, but I was convinced that Torben would not take up the gauntlet. Nor did he.

'Last night,' he said, as if he hadn't heard, 'I started by asking myself why MacDuff sent away his two henchmen when the subject of Mary came up. MacDuff seemed to be in the habit of commanding the two. Yet it was clear that he concealed something from them. Didn't he say that he had intended to meet us alone? Well, I believe there's something he is *compelled* to hide. And it must be possible for us to discover what it is, since it seems that MacDuff believes that we might reveal his secret, voluntarily or not. In other words, we should be able to gain a hold on him.'

'That may be,' I countered. 'But we haven't grasped yet what it is or what it's worth. And in any case, hasn't he got a pretty substantial hold on us, too? He saved your life. And, come to that, mine as well.'

'Why should that matter?' Torben asked.

'From a moral point of view, you can ignore a threat. It's without weight. But disregarding the fact that somebody has saved your life is another matter.'

Torben filled his pipe with care and lit it. He did this with the same thoroughness as he read a book or tasted a wine. Nothing was left to chance.

'You obviously mean that we should feel grateful to MacDuff,' he said when he had finished. 'I don't understand you there. It was damned well his duty to save our lives. If it hadn't been for him, we would never have found ourselves in a situation where our lives needed saving.'

'True. But he didn't have to let us go.'

'Exactly,' said Torben. 'Now you're thinking along the same line as I have. MacDuff did take a risk when he let us go.'

'Why do you think so?'

'The quarrel we heard when we left, if nothing else.'

'But not only that?' I persisted.

'What was it you said about his housekeeper? That she looked young for her age? Though you didn't know how old she was. And you had the impression that you had seen her before?'

'Something of that kind, yes.'

'I believe,' said Torben, 'that you had seen her before.'

His words to sank into my consciousness, but caught hold of nothing there.

Casually, as if he had given up hoping that he wouldn't need to be so precise to me explain everything in complete detail, Torben said:

'Mary.'

My first impulse was to wave this idea aside. But Torben was not given to foolish fancies. And before I was able to say anything, I saw once more Mary's empty stare when she was aboard the *Sula*. Then, the almost unbearably intense gaze of MacDuff's housekeeper fastened on me again. The eyes were the same, but with the utter void replaced by life.

'Yes. You are right,' I said.

'I have a theory ...' Torben began, but he was interrupted by our reaching Moy Bridge.

We moored temporarily beside the groyne, but we didn't need to wait long before the bridge slowly glided to one side. We scarcely noticed the lock, which lay shortly beyond the bridge, and when the gates opened, Torben continued as if he had never broken off.

'I believe,' he said, 'that we have stared ourselves blind at Pekka and MacDuff. I had taken for granted that Pekka was put out of the way because he knew too much. But about what? The IRA? Probably. The smuggling of arms suggests that. Lough Swilly is not far from the border of Northern Ireland. Or about the Celtic Ring? But what is the Celtic Ring? A collection of fanatical neo-Druids? A cover name for the IRA, thought up by Pekka himself? Or a new and unknown branch in the terrorists' tree? There are many possibilities. And it would certainly be a risky business to investigate most of them. We can hardly doubt that Pekka took the matter too lightly. The question is whether he was murdered for some other reason as well. How much can he really have found out? Perhaps he got his most important information - and for him the most dangerous part - from Mary. But at the same time I'm convinced that Pekka would have been killed even if he hadn't learned a thing about the Celtic Ring or anything else, whether from Mary or by his own efforts.'

'Surely.' I said, 'you don't think that MacDuff killed him out of jealousy? I refuse to swallow that. It wouldn't be like MacDuff.'

'I don't believe it, either,' Torben agreed. 'But if we can credit what Pekka writes in his logbook, Mary was to die. She was condemned. Why and by whom, we don't know. But very likely it had to do with betrayal. Yet ... if she too was killed, why did nothing about it appear in the papers? What became of her? Was her body thrown into the sea? Don't forget that according to what Pekka wrote, MacDuff loved Mary. I feel sure that MacDuff has saved her life, too. There's beginning to be inflation in MacDuff's heroic lifesaving.'

'Well,' I remarked, 'as he loves Mary, there's nothing very strange about his sparing her life.'

'But,' answered Torben, 'I believe that MacDuff saved her in spite of the orders he had received.'

'What do you mean by that?'

'MacDuff can have had orders to dispose of both Pekka and Mary. But he couldn't bring himself to kill Mary. He is strong and courageous, but perhaps not in the way some people might think. Because he loves Mary, he is jeopardizing his own life and maybe damaging the cause he has fought for over many years. He is brave, but presumably he is clinging to a weak branch which we can cut off if we wish to.'

'How?'

I felt slow witted, as if I somehow didn't want to understand.

'By revealing that Mary is alive. And that MacDuff is keeping her hidden. Because of course, that's what he is doing. Sooner or later, the organisation, or whatever it may be, will find out. And MacDuff will belong to a closed chapter. Along with Mary.'

'What happens to us if we begin to tell what we know?'

'That,' said Torben, 'depends on who first reaches whom. If MacDuff gets hold of us, or the IRA gets hold of him before he does. Anyhow, he must make haste to protect himself. The IRA is efficient. Coogan writes in his book that, when he asked a leader of the IRA why they kneecapped and executed their own members for failure or treachery, he got the reply: 'It's good for discipline.' Coogan tells also about two sons who remained faithful to the IRA although their father, whom they knew to be innocent, was executed for treason.'

'You speak now about the IRA.'

'Well, the IRA must be involved in some way. I can't imagine that there is room for two unconnected organisations of the same type. The IRA would never tolerate a rival. Not nowadays. So as I said: MacDuff is brave. Because he knows who he is defying.'

'But do we know?' I asked and once more I couldn't help feeling an irritation with Torben's way of dealing with the whole enigma.

We were not, as he made it sound, mere pawns in someone else's game.

'No, no,' he answered. 'We don't. That is perhaps another matter to which we must give a little thought.'

'Do you want to die?' I asked.

'That's an impossible question to answer.'

'Why not? Ask me and I'll tell you: I don't want to die.'

'What you mean,' said Torben, 'is that you wish to live. Who doesn't? Of course the real question is really what one wants to live for.'

He pointed beyond the stem.

'If you don't happen to have more practical matters to think about, that is.'

I looked ahead. Torben had been steering while he talked, and I had scarcely noticed the shores gliding past us. After all, navigating a boat through a canal is simpler than driving a car. There isn't a single side turning. We had just rounded a bend, and I saw that Neptune's Staircase, a flight of eight locks with a swing bridge at the end, lay a few cable-lengths further on.

As my eye followed Torben's pointing finger, I caught sight of a man who turned round and dashed away when he saw us approaching.

'Did you see him?' I asked.

'Who?'

'The man who disappeared behind the bushes there.'

'No. I simply meant that we must start through the locks.'

I soon forgot the man and concentrated on ropes and fenders. From Neptune's Staircase it is only half a mile to Corpach and the two last locks before Loch Linnhe and the Atlantic Ocean. There was a smell of the sea in the moist west wind that came sweeping to meet us. It brought heavy grey clouds that stuck fast to the mountain sides. Of the highest mountain, Ben Nevis, nothing more could now be seen apart from its broad and massive foot, which seemed to sink from sight into the primary rock. Our luck with the weather had evidently run out.

'The gates are open,' Torben announced.

'Splendid. The faster we come out the better. Then at least we'll be able to sail where we feel inclined.'

I was tired of being enclosed on the motionless water of the canals. Not to have to follow predetermined and already marked out routes was after all one of the most important reasons why I sailed.

Now I sprang about on deck to get our mooring ropes ready. They were more than ten fathoms long, made of polyester nearly an inch thick, and each had a breaking strength of seven tons. We could, if we wished, lift *Rustica* in them. Having heard many horror stories about the strong currents and rapids in all sorts of locks, I took no risks.

But thus far all had gone so peacefully that we could have held the boat in place with a flag halyard twisted round our fingers. Passing through locks had become a routine matter for us; we no longer thought much about it, not even in a staircase like this.

We stood on top of the lock, each one holding a rope. *Rustica* lay by herself beneath us, well fendered off with old tyres. When the gates opened, we hauled her by hand into the next lock where the same procedure was repeated. I had started to believe that the horror stories about locks must be highly exaggerated or only concerned the Panama Canal.

The gates were the sole worry. Many of them were new; that is, they had been installed when the canal was automated in the sixties. But others had remained in place since the canal was built; they creaked, grated and screeched before they moved together with great reluctance.

In Neptune's Staircase there were two pairs of gates of the old kind: at the second lock and at the next to last one. But we were probably already hardened by earlier moaning and groaning from other gates. In any case, I no longer gave them much attention.

In the last lock, we went aboard again, put a loop of rope round bollards so that we could easily adjust their length as the water lowered. For a moment, while Torben was below getting a cup of coffee for the both of us, I held both lines in my hand. He returned with mugs just as the gates ahead began to glide apart and I was bending down to start the engine. I had already taken the warps on board by then and was keeping *Rustica* in place by holding on to a ladder.

When I looked up, I saw that Torben had dropped the mugs and was pointing at the gates behind me.

'The gates!' He said in a scarcely audible voice. 'They're giving way!'

I too looked back. And I shall never forget the sight. Slowly, inch by inch, the unwieldy gates were being forced apart by the masses of water behind them. They still remained in place, but how much longer would they hold out? The more they were forced open, the less resistance they would make, until finally they would doubtless be torn apart in one single instant.

A lock keeper came running down from the lock above. He gestured wildly and shouted:

'Get away from here! I have to release the gates. Or everything will break up!'

Then came the longest moment I have experienced in my life. *Rustica* has a variable pitch propeller instead of a reverse gear, and it takes her a little time to get under way. When she did move, she went so slowly that we felt as if our feet were caught in quicksand. I remember deciding that I must install a bigger engine while fully realising that this decision was wholly idiotic. In the first place, we had the engine we had, and in the second, it was far from certain that I would have a boat to put a new engine into.

After that, nearly everything happened at the same time. We were right between the opening gates ahead when we heard the crash, the sound of splintering wood and the roar of water.

'Close the hatch!' I shouted to Torben.

I could at least be thankful for the measures I'd taken to make *Rustica* seaworthy. If she was going to be pooped, I knew that she was watertight. A gallon or two of water might get in through the air intake to the engine. But that was all.

Torben slammed the hatch shut. When he turned back, I saw hopelessness in his eyes.

'The bridge,' he said only. 'We haven't a chance.'

In fact, some fifty yards before us, our way was blocked by a pivoted bridge. It was so low that, even without her mast, *Rustica* couldn't have passed under. The lock keeper had pressed the button for the bridge to swing open, but it couldn't possibly manage to open enough for us pass in time. Unless ... there was only one thing to do: full speed ahead!

'Are you mad!' shouted Torben.

'It's our only chance!' I shouted back. 'We must be able to steer.'

The water came down on us then in a violent, bubbling, whirling torrent. *Rustica* took in something like fifty gallons, but then she raised herself onto the crest of a wave and gained speed. It was our luck that most of the water came from above. The wall of water never became so steep that it made us surf like a surfboard, and I felt immediately that *Rustica* was still answering the helm. But what good did that do?

The space between us and the bridge seemed to diminish far more quickly than the width increased between the end of the pivoting bridge and the brink of the canal. But the bridge was opening away from us. If it had opened towards us, we would already have been lost and could just as well have given up and been trying to save our lives instead. But I saw that we had a chance, one in a thousand, of saving both ourselves and the boat. I put the tiller over so that *Rustica*'s stem pointed to the middle of the bridge instead of the opening now about two feet wide at the end of the bridge.

'What the hell are you doing?' Torben yelled.

'We must make her heel!' I shouted back.

I couldn't explain more. A few seconds later, when we were perhaps fifteen yards from the bridge itself, I put the helm over again and waited for *Rustica* to come round. She did. It probably took only a few seconds although it felt much longer. In the midst of everything, I remember thinking that all the hackneyed old clichés about seconds that lasted an eternity were not dead just because they were used, and that the time we measure by watches and clocks was perfectly meaningless.

Rustica's bow pointed once more at the opposite side of the canal: the side where the bridge was opening and which we were approaching at full speed parallel to the bridge. Thus, it was impossible to see if the opening had become wide enough for us to come through. Not that knowing could have helped. We were doing the one thing possible.

'Hang on!' I shouted to Torben who didn't hear me.

He stared spellbound ahead. When the stem came level with the end of the bridge, I violently put the helm over a last time. And *Rustica* heeled! Not much. Not like a motor boat in a fast turn, but enough for us to gain the inches we lacked.

The next instant, all was over. Two stanchions were torn out, but with our speed and weight that couldn't stop the boat or make her turn around. I don't dare consider how much space we had to spare between our starboard side and the edge of the canal. I had only had one single thought in my mind: to steer as close to the bridge as possible. I didn't even notice that the road-bridge, which crossed the canal before the railway bridge, had been open from the beginning.

I freely admit that we were close to weeping, the two of us, with joy and from pure relief. Torben hugged me so hard that our newly gained happiness nearly came to a lamentable end. For I suffer from a chronic bad habit shared by some helmsmen: I can't hold a course and do something else at the same time. If I try, then the boat takes large swerving turns in one direction, then the other. But I straightened our course just in time.

We were still moving at far too great a speed. The water level had lowered by now and a good deal of water had evidently flowed over the banks of the canal. But there was yet another lock at Corpach, only half a mile downstream. It would be preferable not to crash into the gates there.

I managed by letting the propeller remain in reverse and opened throttle in short bursts. A long keeled boat like *Rustica* can't really be steered backwards in a straight line; either she goes to port or else she goes up into the wind, if one is blowing. This behaviour is so predictable that I always let go of the tiller when reversing.

On the other hand, in situations where *Rustica* wants to go in the same direction as I do, I can stop steering and think of something else. Such was the case when were approaching the next lock. I saw a red-haired man who waved at us from a sailing boat made of steel and with a carrot-coloured hull. Already at some distance, we had caught sight of both hull and hair.

'We'll go alongside that boat,' I said to Torben. 'Can you take care of the lines?'

'After what we've been through, I can manage anything,' Torben replied. 'Just let me know what I should do.'

We were just abreast of the red-haired man and his steel boat, a typical Maurice Griffiths design, when I revved up again. *Rustica*'s stern drew as usual to port, and Torben, without so much as stretching, could lay a rope over the bollard on our neighbouring boat.

'Well done!' said the red-haired man, who, viewed at close quarters, seemed to embody all the characteristics attributed to the Scots, except for the kilt.

'A living prototype,' Torben said in Swedish, 'with freckles and all. I'm sure he has a bagpipe on board.'

'What was well done?' I asked our neigbour.

'Your berthing like that. Was it chance or skill?'

'It's the boat. Sometimes she handles beautifully.'

Just then, I felt an extreme tenderness for *Rustica*. I realised with awful force how close I had been to losing her. Never, during the five years I'd devoted to her, had I so nearly failed her.

'My boat would never do that', the red-haired man told me. 'But then I'm not much of a sailor.'

He pointed up towards Neptune's Staircase.

'A piece of bad luck, that was,' he said sympathetically.

'You call it bad luck!' Torben broke in, 'Two lock gates breaking apart over our heads! I call that a catastrophe.'

'Then I don't suppose you'll say no to a wee dram?'

'To a what?' Torben asked.

'I won't say no to a shot of whisky,' I intervened. 'On the contrary. But you must excuse my friend.'

'For what?'

'He doesn't like whisky.'

Our neighbour looked a Torben as if he doubted this information.

'I know very well that whisky saves people's lives,' said Torben. 'But I have a preference for wine.'

'I'm sorry but I've none on board,' our neighbour replied.

He looked sincerely distressed, presumably because he had lost an opportunity of being as hospitable as he would have liked to be.

'Don't worry!' Torben said in a friendly tone. 'I have

always my own wine with me. If you like, you can give me a glass of something this evening up at the pub.'

He went below and fetched a bottle of some German white wine, whereupon we changed decks and cockpits.

'The name's Junior,' said our host.

Torben introduced himself and me, then asked if Junior had been really christened 'Junior.'

'No, I was given the same name as my father, Hugh McNair. But to tell us apart I was called 'Junior'. And it's stuck ever since. When I've become an old age pensioner, I'll still be known as 'Junior' when I'm collecting my pension, I expect.'

He filled two ordinary drinking glasses to the brim with what seemed to be a somewhat inferior whisky. Torben poured wine into the wine glass which he had also brought along. Junior watched with wide eyed wonder while Torben behaved as if he were both sommelier and guest in an excellent Paris restaurant.

On adjudging that the performance must at last be over, Junior raised his own glass.

'Skål - that's what you say in Scandinavia, isn't it? Well, if it wasn't bad luck the lock gates collapsed, it's certainly good luck that you managed to survive.'

'Oh no,' said Torben, 'that wasn't luck either. It was entirely due to the skipper here. He steered *Rustica* as if she were a rally car.'

It wasn't until then that my reaction came. Perhaps it can best be described as quiet, delayed panic. I tried to get up, but my legs shook, and I swayed forward.

'Are you sick?' Torben asked.

'Something like that. It will soon pass.'

I sat down again, and my whisky spilled when I put down my glass. 'It's only a kind of reflex, I think.'

'I am sorry,' said Junior, as if it were his fault.

In a bounding stride, a man was approaching from Neptune's Staircase. I tried to pull myself together, but I had difficulty in focusing my eyes.

'It's the lock keeper,' Torben told me.

When he arrived at the boat, I recognized him as the man who had been in charge of the hapless gates.

'I am sorry,' he too said.

Torben shook his head despairingly.

'Is that all you can say? We might have died.'

'But I am sorry,' repeated the lock keeper. 'And very glad that you got out of it.'

He looked at me with what I took to be admiration.

'It wasn't meant that way, I'm afraid,' he added.

'What?' Torben asked. 'What do you mean?'

'You shouldn't be sitting here now, safe and sound. I don't know why or how. But it was sabotage. Somebody had made sure that the gates would break.'

'Sabotage?' Junior looked incredulously first at the lock keeper and then at us. 'Who would want to do such a thing to you?'

Chapter 15

THAT was just the question. It seemed unlikely that MacDuff had suddenly changed his mind. Consequently, his assistants must be responsible. Had they acted on their own initiative? In that case they must have had strong reason for disregarding MacDuff's order that we were not to be touched. Or had they received orders directly from higher up, orders which not even MacDuff could oppose?

To Junior we said merely that we didn't understand a thing, and that the sabotage must have been directed against whatever company owned the canal.

The lock keeper stayed only for a moment, to ascertain that we had not been injured in any way. It was impossible to know whether he had hoped for the contrary, but he appeared to be sincerely relieved. Although I normally had no expectations of any kind where unknown people were concerned, I'd begun to feel uncomfortably suspicious of people who came our way.

It was reassuring that Junior had also been exposed to great danger; he was freed of my mistrust. He told us about his luck in having been on board and on deck when he heard the violent noise and saw the flood arriving. Like us, he had reacted instinctively and managed to get his doors closed before the deluge reached his boat.

'As for myself, I just held tight to the mast,' he said, and indicated the state of his trousers, which were wet up to the knees. 'I was convinced the mooring lines would part, but they didn't. However, the boat was forced down until half the deck lay under water. It was an ordeal. But it must have been much worse for you. What you went through doesn't bear thinking about.'

'It all happened so quickly.' I said. 'I hadn't time to reflect.'

'But I had.' said Torben, 'Time for that and to be terrified! And I was.'

We began to talk about the fears and anxieties of sailing. Torben spoke about his seasickness on the North Sea. He explained that he hadn't been frightened then because nothing could be worse than being seasick. It was entirely different when we were making the landfall in Scotland, and he had nothing to do but look on.

'Fear is no problem for me,' Junior said and laughed unabashedly. 'I worry about everything when I am at sea.'

He told us that he hadn't sailed very much, had actually made only one proper cruise: alone from Nairn, where he had built his boat, the sixty nautical miles across to Wick, and then back again. I asked him where he was heading now. He didn't really know. Perhaps to Portugal. However, if he succeeded in making it to Glasgow unscathed, where he had a good friend, that would be good enough. He had worked for a year as a welder on an oil rig, and after that the only thing of any importance was to escape, travel freely, come and go as he liked. He developed claustrophobia while on the rig. It was beyond his understanding that there were people who would rather be on a rig than ashore. But then, he added, there were dogs that ran and fetched their leashes when they were about to be taken for a walk.

Half an hour later, the lock keeper came back and asked us if we would please pass through the next lock and down into the harbour basin of Corpach.

'Have you made sure that the gates will hold?' Torben demanded.

'Surely you don't suppose ...?' the lock keeper began.

He disappeared at once down towards the lock, the last one before the sea-lock opening up the way to Loch Linnhe and the Atlantic.

Junior asked us if we really believed that the sabotage was directed against us. Not that he had ever heard of somebody having a grudge against Scandinavians. On the contrary.

'Against the English perhaps. But not people like you.'

'Scandinavians or not,' said Torben. 'Either it was only a coincidence that we happened to be in the right place at the wrong moment, or the other way about. Otherwise, there must really be someone who has it in for us. Providing of course, that they weren't out to get you.'

'Me!' exclaimed Junior with astonishment.

'Yes. You were in a pretty bad situation for a time.'

'That's out of the question,' Junior declared firmly.

The lock keeper returned with the assurance that he had personally inspected the gates and they would hold. Torben muttered inaudible misgivings, but we cast off. With Junior in our wake, we entered the lock. A quarter of an hour later we were snugly berthed at Corpach, the only truly safe port north of Kintyre and south of Ullapool. We had heard that even fishing-boats on the Scottish west coast would pass through the sea-lock of the Caledonian Canal and moor in the basin at Corpach during the worst winter storms.

As long as we had been in the canal, we hadn't taken an interest in the weather. We noticed now, almost with surprise, that there was a strong wind blowing, perhaps a near gale.

'Shall we go through the last lock at once?' Torben asked.

'Let's wait a bit,' I replied undecidedly. 'It might be a good thing to discuss where we'll go next.'

Junior came up alongside and told me that he intended to leave immediately. We helped him with his lines as he passed through the last lock, then wished him a good sail and watched him set course towards Fort William. He had hoisted up an altogether too small mainsail and a jib, which didn't appear to have been sewn for his boat.

'A pity that he has gone,' said Torben, as we went back to *Rustica*. 'He's the first person we've met who has given me a feeling of confidence.'

'Same with me.'

Another half hour passed without our doing anything in particular. We simply cleaned up a bit and stowed everything away before our encounter with the Atlantic. The wind howled no louder in the rigging than did a stiff winter breeze at Dragør, but merely the knowledge that it came all the way from Nova Scotia, without let or hindrance, made an impression on us.

Just when I had take out the chart of Loch Linnhe, there was a knock on the pulpit.

'Will we never get any peace?' Torben wondered.

I opened the hatch. Junior stood on the quay. His freckled face bore a slightly self-depreciating grin.

'Too much wind,' he said simply. 'Am I disturbing you?'

'Not at all,' called Torben. 'Come aboard!'

The evening was consecrated to sailors' tales. I told the stories of my cruises to Saint Malo, in Brittany, on board my previous Marieholm Folkboat, *Moana*. Torben recounted stories he had read about seafaring, everything from Ove Allanson's descriptions of life in modern freighters to that in

Conrad's dark holds. And he gave us selected excerpts from the logbook of the Spanish pilot, Juan Sebastián Elcano, who returned with nineteen men in the Victoria to give the news that Magellan was dead, but that it was possible to sail around the world. Junior told a true story, heard from a Norwegian, about a ship that had overturned in the North Sea and been abandoned by her crew after a man was washed away. A week later, it was found drifting like a ghost ship off the coast of northern Norway.

'And do you know where they found her?' Junior concluded rhetorically.

'Just off an island with the same name as the boat. She still lies in the port of Bergen. But nobody who knows her past and everyone does - will have anything to do with her.'

'That's not an amusing story,' said Torben.

'No,' Junior agreed. 'But unfortunately a true one.'

'Perhaps you shouldn't have told it,' I said. 'We have to go back across the North Sea to get home.'

'I am sorry,' said Junior, looking contrite.

'We'll always make it back home, in one way or the other,' Torben remarked comfortingly. 'We can sail the other way. Around the world.'

Go home? I thought. For the first time, I began to wonder if we would be able to return at all. Perhaps it would be more a matter of simply staying alive.

No doubt it was Junior's story that sharpened my imagination and made me realise the seriousness of the sabotage in Neptune's Staircase. In the best of cases it was a warning. In the worst, an unsuccessful attempt on our lives.

There was too much wind next day for us, as well as Junior, to leave Corpach. Moreover, we woke up late. Torben and I had breakfast in our unsociable manner: each with his book, and not a word spoken. At one o'clock, Junior appeared and informed us that he preferred to wait until next day. He asked if we were in a great hurry to get out on the Atlantic. Actually, it was pretty windy, he added, and it was clear that he very much wished to have our company.

I looked at Torben.

'I've got nothing against staying another day,' said he.

The afternoon passed uneventfully. No further boats came down from the canal, as it had been closed while awaiting repairs. I went about hoping that MacDuff was still in his boat on Loch Oich, unable to follow us. But that would have been too good to be true. And my doubts were confirmed a little later by the lock keeper. The *F 154* had, in fact, passed through two hours before we came down. Torben and I quickly made the round of Corpach where a butcher's shop, a pub, two grocers and hairdressers tried in vain to look like a shopping centre.

At about two o'clock, I went to the harbour master's office to pay our canal fees, but in view of what had happened, the lock-keeper wouldn't hear of it. I asked if they had learned anything more about what caused the incident.

'No, we haven't.' he answered, 'but we are now sure that it was sabotage. The bolts in the leverage cannot simply come loose by themselves. The gates were old, that's true. But the mechanism was new. We have informed the police. It is very possible that you will have a visit from them. They would certainly like to ask you some questions.'

'But we have nothing to do with the gates,' I replied.

The police were the last people I wanted to have on board. If MacDuff found out that we had talked to the police, he might believe that we had talked about other things than those gates. I wasn't willing to take the risk.

I thanked the lock keeper and told him that we intended to pass through the last lock in about an hour, if that was possible.

'If the police need to talk to us, tell them that we're sailing north through the Sound of Mull. And we count on being at Ullapool within a few days.'

'Right you are, sir. We'll be opening for you in an hour.'

On the way back, I realised how aimlessly we acted. Torben and I had not yet talked things over, and now we were suddenly about to sail southwards. Simply to avoid the police! A momentary impulse had made me lie to the lock keeper. But I didn't have the slightest idea of where that lie would lead us. And our manoeuvring space was increasingly reduced.

When I arrived at *Rustica*, I found her empty with the hatch unlocked. After a quarter hour without any sign of Torben, I went over to Junior, but he hadn't seen Torben either. When I said that I intended to leave at once, he looked very disappointed. So I felt forced once again to alter my plans.

'I can't stand the canal any longer,' I explained. 'I'll anchor behind the island on the other side of the loch. We'll sail on tomorrow when the gale has blown over. If Torben doesn't turn up before the lock opens, can you tell him I'll come back and fetch him with the dinghy.'

'Oh, certainly,' said Junior, who had already recovered his good humour.

'Tell him that we'll meet at the pub. I'll come back after dark.'

Junior looked surprised.

'Wouldn't it be better to come back while it's still light? There's a strong current in the fiord.'

'That's exactly the point,' I lied. 'I want to wait until the tide turns, so I can be certain that the anchor holds.'

'But I thought ...' Junior began.

I didn't give him time to finish, but hastened back to *Rustica*. I hoped that he wouldn't check the tide in the almanac. On leaving the harbour master's office, I had in fact noticed that the tide had just turned.

It was four o'clock when the lock gates opened for the last time without Torben having returned. I was worried, but meanwhile I had other matters on my mind. It would soon get dark, and I hoped to be behind the island just when twilight fell. It wasn't much of a hiding place: *Rustica*'s mast would be clearly discernible from Corpach in the morning. But with a bit of luck the lock keeper, at least, would believe that I'd sailed off for good.

Beyond the lock, to starboard, there were some boats on two trots of moorings, mostly sailing-boats, but I wasn't in the least surprised to discover MacDuff's fishing-boat among them. It had just been hidden behind a few other boats when I had looked for it from Corpach. MacDuff must have sailed from Invergarry Castle at dawn. I sincerely hoped that no one was on board because there was nothing I could do to conceal myself and *Rustica* just then.

Ten minutes later I was across the fiord. I sailed as close in under land as I dared, the current being always weaker there. But the tide still won over the wind, for when the anchor chain rattled out *Rustica* still lay with her stern to the wind. I took some bearings by eye, but I didn't bother to back the engine to make the anchor hold. The current did that job with at least the same efficiency. But it was a new and uneasy sensation to hear the water purling along the hull and see the log move although the boat lay still.

Ahead, three miles away, I saw the lights of Fort William at the foot of Ben Nevis. Astern, all was darkness. To starboard, there was a slope covered with woods, and this provided shelter from the wind. To port, I could dimly see the outline of the bare and low lying island that spread out between *Rustica* and Corpach. I was alone again for the first time since Torben had disappeared to buy wine in Ålborg. The thought came to me ... I went down to the cabin and opened the wine box. It was empty.

Very likely, Torben had simply taken a bus to Fort William to stock up. And Junior would tell Torben where I was as soon as he was back. I tried to say to myself that there was nothing to worry about. In an hour or two he would be back at Corpach, and by that time I would have rigged *Sussi* and would be on my way to the other side of the fiord.

Half an hour later, the dinghy was ready. It was pitch dark when I got on board with a torch and a hand-bearing compass which I tied to the foot of the mast. I then lay down on the bottom of the boat where I wouldn't have to duck each time I wanted to tack or gybe. The Optimist is designed for twelve year olds, and there is very little space under the boom. But I had accustomed myself to navigating while I lay on the floor with my head just above the surface of the water.

There was still quite a strong wind and I stretched out on the starboard side as counterweight. If there was one thing I wished to avoid, it was to capsize in two knots of current and ice cold water.

I steered by keeping the same angle between the wind and the heading of the boat. I wanted to avoid using my torch to look at the compass since it shone with a white light instead of red. I didn't need to worry about the navigation, however. I would always hit the other shore, somewhere or other.

And I did get there, but only much later. Suddenly, the outline of a dark hull loomed up before *Sussi*'s stem. I turned sharply, but too late, and *Sussi* collided with black painted side planks. A dull thump, then total silence. I cursed my imprudence. Naturally, it was the *F 154*, MacDuff's fishing boat, I had rammed.

My first impulse was to push off and make myself invisible in the darkness. But at the same time I realised that I wasn't likely to get very far if there was someone on board. The searchlight to be found on all fishing boats would soon discover me. Cautiously, I hauled myself round to the stern, took down *Sussi*'s sail and mast, then waited. Nobody came up on deck. No light was switched on. All was quiet. I finally felt that I was safe. So I made *Sussi* fast at the stern, took my torch and climbed on board.

On reaching the deck, I paused hesitantly and listened again. The wheelhouse was before me, and I went round to its starboard side. The door opened without a creak. I didn't put on my torch at once, but felt my way to the navigation table, where I counted on finding the logbook. Or notations. Or I didn't know quite what. I stopped several times and listened. Once I heard something that sounded like footsteps, and I crept back to the door. But the sound died away. And the deck was empty.

I continued my investigation, and at last I found the logbook. I sat down on the floor, where the light of my torch wouldn't be seen from outside the wheelhouse. The logbook recorded nearly half a year's sailing: too much for it to contain more than entries on positions, courses, distances and weather conditions. I took down the uppermost charts lying at hand and concentrated on the positions given to see if they formed some sort of pattern.

I soon noticed that *F 154* sailed for the most part between Scotland and Ireland, and that the Irish ports where she put in were seldom far from the border of Northern Ireland. It was carefully stated how many cases of fish had been discharged in each port. But when had the fish actually been caught? MacDuff must have had fabulous luck if he could haul up such quantities, sometimes in a single day. The explanation appeared on a number of separate pages where someone, presumably MacDuff himself, had noted how many cases were taken on board. This would give the impression that the *F 154* functioned as a small refrigerated carrier. Something struck me. All the fish taken aboard were loaded in countries with

Celtic languages: Scotland, Wales, Brittany and Ireland. Some trips had been made to the Basque country, and to Galicia, far out to the west in Spain.

I thought of what Tom had heard about a Celtic federation, and what he had said on the subject of Galicia. It was, according to Torben, a matter of dispute in the modern druidical orders which were spread over all Europe whether people who did not speak a Celtic language could be initiated as Druids, or if they could be regarded as Celts at all. This must certainly apply to the Galicians. And what about the Basques? Their language wasn't Celtic. But Torben declared that basque terrorists, or revolutionaries, depending on which side you were on, had collaborated with the IRA.

Suddenly, I thought I heard the sound of steps. I put the logbook and the charts back in their places, slipped out of the wheelhouse and hid myself aft. But all was silence. It had been only my imagination.

After some minutes with my senses sharpened to the utmost, I summoned enough courage to go for'ard. The entrance to the cabin was at the stem: a door with a half roof sloping behind it, typical of fishing boats. I pressed down the door handle. The door was locked. That ought to mean that no one was on board, but also that something aboard warranted the precaution. But I didn't know how to pick locks. The closest I had been to thieves was when I went to prison for refusing to do my military service. But I hadn't learned any useful tricks from my fellow-prisoners. Then I remembered that I had seen, or felt rather, a bunch of keys when I was groping about in the wheelhouse. I went back and found them. The third key fitted the lock, and the door slid open as easily and as quietly as the door of the wheelhouse.

I hesitated and looked around. How long had I before the crew returned? Curiosity got the better of me. I had a golden opportunity to find out as much as possible. I quickly descended the stepladder.

Chapter 16

I had scarcely managed to set my foot at the bottom when I heard a voice behind me.

'If you turn round, I'll shoot.'

But I had already turned around before I realised what the words meant, perhaps because I had recognized the voice as Mary's. She was sitting on a chair behind a table. And a pistol lay on the table.

'You have to hold the pistol if you want to shoot.'

She took it up, but pointed it towards herself.

'Not another step.' she said quietly. 'Or I will shoot.'

At first, I understood nothing. Was she actually threatening to shoot herself if I came closer? This was so absurd that I took a step forward. Her finger curled implacably round the trigger. I backed as far away as I could.

'No, no,' I said. 'Don't shoot! I didn't come here for your sake. I didn't think there was anyone on board.'

Her finger lightened its pressure a trifle, or so I imagined. But she continued to look at me very coldly, and her hand appeared to be steady.

'It's the truth,' I quickly went on. 'I'd never have dared

come aboard if I'd known that someone was here. I know very well what can happen to people who poke their noses into things.'

'What do you want?' she demanded. 'Why are you here?'

'I don't know,' I answered honestly. 'Really, I don't know. I never guessed that you might be here.'

'What do you mean? Haven't you been pursuing me and MacDuff ever since Dragør?'

'What!' was all I could say.

Had MacDuff given her such an idea? Or was it her own? 'There must be some misunderstanding ...' I began.

'A misunderstanding!' Mary broke off disdainfully. 'Would you be here if it was a misunderstanding?'

'Why not?' I asked. 'I met MacDuff a few days ago. He didn't seem to think we were after him. Or you.'

'Where did you meet MacDuff?' Mary inquired.

'At Loch Oich,' I said without giving any details.

If she wanted to test my truthfulness, she could ask the questions.

'What did he say to you?'

'Hasn't he told you?'

'What did he say?' she repeated sharply.

I tried to work out the situation quickly. Did she ask to find out if I told the truth? Or did she want to find out what MacDuff had said? Intuitively, I decided that the last alternative, the most difficult one, was also the right one. Which meant taking an additional factor into consideration. Why had MacDuff not wanted to tell Mary about our meeting? Was it because he didn't wish to alarm her? If so, I should try to reassure her.

'He said that he was happy to meet us. Or at least me. My friend Torben seemed to be too much of a landlubber to his taste. He also said that he liked my boat, *Rustica*, and that he hoped that he and I could sail together one day.'

'That doesn't mean a thing,' Mary cut me off again.

'To me it does' I replied, 'I would never suggest to anybody out of pure politeness that we should sail together. I don't think MacDuff would either.'

'He said that you should stop pursuing us!' Mary declared.

'No, he did not.'

And in fact he hadn't said that.

'He told us that we should sail home *for our own safety.*'

Mary still looked sceptical.

'It wasn't a threat on his part,' I added in explanation. 'He merely pointed out that it could be dangerous for us to remain here. That was all. If you think that MacDuff is afraid of Torben and me, you are wrong. That would be a misunderstanding if anything is.'

'MacDuff is never afraid,' said Mary.

'Not for himself perhaps. But he might be for others.'

Mary at last put the pistol aside. My impression was that she had started to believe me and wished to hear more. This calmed me.

'Before we left,' I went on, 'he said that he would personally kill us if we ever mentioned to anyone that you are alive.'

Any idea that this might take Mary by surprise was wide of the mark. In fact, I caught the ghost of a smile on her face. Then she became as serious as before.

'Why did he say that?' she wondered. 'How could you know that I was alive? Or that I was dead?'

'We didn't know. Not with certainty. I thought that I recognised you when I saw you in Inverness. But it wasn't until later that I realised it had been you. Because of your eyes.'

Mary looked directly into my eyes. I tried to meet her gaze, but it was as if I began to lose my foothold or as if I were drowning. How long can two people look into each other's eyes? Ten seconds? Before long, in any case, you begin feeling anguish. You fear what you see, the reflected image of your own eyes which suddenly appears in the eyes of the other. You dread being completely absorbed by the other's gaze. Or you become confused about your own identity and that of the other. Identity is not to be found like they say in the gaze of other people. That's where you lose it. You only regain it when you look away.

But there is also a boundless temptation and fascination in abandoning oneself to another's gaze, disappearing into it, being devoured by it. That's how I felt when I looked at Mary. But that made me waver between self esteem and self effacement. When she spoke, I vainly tried to turn my eyes away, just in order to concentrate on what she was saying. I must have made an impression of being very insecure and confused, but either she was used to arousing such a reaction and hardly noticed it, or else she didn't really see me as I was at all.

'MacDuff is right,' she said after a time. 'Sail home! Why should you expose yourself to the same risks as Pekka did?'

'That's exactly my view,' I countered. 'But then why should a person like me need to worry at all about his own survival?'

'There are those who believe that they can make themselves free by killing others,' Mary replied. 'Even MacDuff can do nothing about it. If you stay, there will be more who die. Is that what you want?'

I didn't reply. There was only one answer to such a question. But why shouldn't I ask other questions? That I and Torben were powerless was one thing. But why couldn't a man like MacDuff do something about the killings? It seemed as if Mary and MacDuff deliberately courted mortal danger. I'd like to have asked a hundred different questions. But time was short. MacDuff might come back at any minute, and I was by no means certain that I'd be able to explain what I was doing on board.

'How can a person be both alive and dead?' I asked. 'Pekka wrote that you were dead.'

'Don't ask any more.'

'Oh,' I said, 'but I do ask. I am tired of not knowing what it is I already know that is so dangerous.'

'You should trust MacDuff,' Mary told me in an almost friendly tone. 'The less you know the better.'

'Can't I be allowed to decide that for myself?'

'Would it matter if you did?'

'Perhaps,' I said, 'you don't realise that somebody has already tried to take my life and Torben's. MacDuff couldn't prevent that, either.'

I briefly described what had happened in Neptune's Staircase.

'Is it so strange that I'd like to know why someone wants to kill me?' I said and for once looked straight at Mary.

All of a sudden, her eyes seemed as lifeless as they had been at Dragør.

'Then our respite has run out,' she said.

'What respite?'

She didn't answer.

'Why are you locked in?' I demanded. 'I can help you to get away from here. I have a boat alongside.'

She gave a start.

'No,' she said. 'It's impossible.'

'Was Pekka the first who tried to help you?' I asked. 'Is that why he died?'

She made no reply, but I was sure that I had guessed aright.

'And is it MacDuff next?' I inquired. 'Must he die as

well? Or is he the one who kills?'

It seemed that she was about to take up the pistol again. And I got ready to throw myself forward and kick it aside. I had forgotten the pistol too soon. But it had been only a tentative sort of movement on her part.

'MacDuff saved my life,' she said.

'You mean that he refrained from taking it?'

'No, he saved it. I was to die. I am still condemned. MacDuff saves my life every day, every hour, every second.'

'Why didn't he save Pekka's? Are you aware that Pekka was murdered?'

'Yes,' she said calmly, 'I was there.'

'But why?' I asked. 'There must have been another way out.'

'MacDuff was forced to choose. My life or Pekka's. He chose mine. And if he hadn't chosen, there would have been three dead instead of one. What would you have done? Taken one life and spared two, or let all three die?'

'Who forces him to choose?'

Yet again, Mary didn't answer. She seemed to realise that she had said too much. At the same time, I felt that she was listening for something.

'The Celtic Ring?' I tossed out. 'Is that what you are all afraid of? Is that what kills?'

'You already know too much,' she said absently.

'No,' I protested. 'I know too little. When Pekka came to Dragør he was frightened. He feared for his life. And for the lives of others. When he entrusted his logbook to me, instead of handing it over to the police, he said that he had to rely on me. I believed him. It may have been naive of me, but I believed that I could do something by finding out what he was afraid of!'

Mary was listening, but not to me.

'But I couldn't save Pekka's life. And now I want to

195

know why he had to die. And why you should die.'

'I can't tell you anything,' Mary replied, looking at me with a pity that I didn't understand.

'Why can't you? What have you to lose if you could just as well be dead?'

'MacDuff,' was her answer. 'Nothing else.'

At that instant, I thought I heard an indefinite sound that might come from oars. Mary had heard it, too.

'But the head?' I asked.

She looked at me uncomprehendingly.

'Why was Pekka's head cut off?'

'That was the proof.'

'Proof of what?'

Mary shook her head. The measured splashing of oars came more distinctly.

'Go now!' she said, and I was sure that she really wanted me to get away before it was too late.

I looked at her a last time, hastened up the ladder, hurried astern and let myself slide down into *Sussi*. I cast off, laid myself on the bottom and let her drift off with the wind. I hadn't got far when I heard a boat draw up alongside the *F 154*. It had been a narrow escape. Then a dreadful thought struck me. I felt in my trouser pocket. There they were: MacDuff's keys, including the one to the cabin and Mary.

Chapter 17

I rarely have regrets or ask myself what would have happened if I had done something other than what I actually did. There are those who say that no one can live a life without having something to regret. People have often said this to me as a reproach, which in essence is the same thing as saying that I ought to regret some things that I have done. And true, it does sound presumptuous to pretend not to suffer from a bad conscience. But what you really *suffer* from the most, that is, exactly, a bad conscience.

In that sense Torben and I were alike. He never said one word of reproach about my nocturnal excursion, even if we both were to suffer the ultimate consequences of it. And, for my part, I did my best to conceal how anxious I had been about his unexplained absence.

When I entered the pub in Corpach, he and Junior were sitting with glasses of beer before them. Torben gave me a relieved but questioning look. But I couldn't tell him what had happened with Junior around. Nor had I the slightest wish to take *Sussi* again and sail out with him, past MacDuff and Mary, just to give him a report.

If MacDuff had discovered *Rustica*, we were sure to

have a visit. But if he hadn't, or believed that we'd sailed off, we might, with luck, remain unseen. MacDuff would certainly have made inquiries as to why we were no longer moored in the canal. And if he believed that we were gone, then he might well have weighed anchor immediately on his return to the *F 154*. In that case, I counted on his having sailed east of the island, as that was a short cut, and he could thus have failed to catch sight of *Rustica* in the dark. But what would we do if the *F 154* had not left by morning?

In a casual tone, Torben wondered why I hadn't waited for him to come back.

'Oh, you were gone so long,' I said in the same manner. 'Where did you go?'

I could see that he already understood that something must have happened.

'I went to Fort William,' he said, as I had guessed he would. 'Our wine had run out, you know. And I had to arrange a couple of things.'

'What things?' I couldn't help asking.

'Two air tickets home.'

Junior reacted first:

'Are you going home?'

He looked disappointed. I didn't know what to believe. Was Torben joking?

'Do you want to go back?' I asked him.

'Not yet. But it never does any harm to buy plane tickets. They are hard currency. Just as good as traveller's cheques, actually.'

'Then couldn't you have kept your traveller's cheques?' Junior objected.

'I didn't have any traveller's cheques. Only cash.'

'But why air tickets?' I asked again.

Torben gave me a look that clearly told me not to ask anything more.

'They sort of make a good impression,' he said. 'For example, when you go into a travel agency, somebody almost always turns around and wonders where you are off to. Sometimes I get the impression that there are people who actually want to see you leave.'

Junior looked at Torben with bewilderment. Torben, too, must have received a warning that it would be better for us to disappear. By whom?

'What shall we do now?' he wanted to know.

'When does the plane leave?' I asked teasingly.

'But shouldn't we be sailing?' Junior protested mildly. 'I thought that we'd decided that I would get some psychological towing from you, so to speak. Till I'd learned to stand on my own legs.'

He looked at us.

'We'll sail together,' I said, reluctantly but sincerely. 'We'll sail at dawn. If you don't mind, that is.'

'The sooner, the better,' said Junior.

I cast a glance at Torben to see if he had objections, but he looked somewhat absent-minded.

At the same time, I got an idea.

'What would you say,' I asked Junior, 'to our sleeping tonight on board your *Fortuna*? Then we can help you through the lock. And we won't have to row out to *Rustica* in the dark.'

Torben gave me a telling look. He knew that I wouldn't leave *Rustica* alone at anchor without good reason.

'Fine!' said Junior. 'That way I'll be sure of getting away.'

Corpach lay empty and forsaken when we walked to Junior's boat after a few more pints of lager. Some flakes of snow circled aimlessly about in the night air, as if to remind us that it was still winter. All was peace. At dawn, we passed through the lock, with *Sussi* in our wake.

The lock keeper wished us a pleasant voyage, but at the same time he was surprised to see us on board Junior's boat.

He turned to Junior.

'See you again in twenty minutes,' he said jestingly.

'No,' said Junior, smiling broadly back, 'in a couple of years perhaps.'

When we approached the spot where MacDuff's fishing boat might still lie at anchor, I asked Torben below in the cabin on some pretext. Through one of the portholes, I observed that MacDuff's boat was no longer there. So much the better.

'What do you want down here?' Torben demanded.

'To avoid somebody seeing us. That's all.'

'Who?'

'Three guesses. But there's no danger now. He has already sailed off.'

'What's become of you two?' Junior called down.

'We're coming up,' I called back.

Rustica lay precisely as I had left her. Junior went alongside, and we made her fast temporarily, while we transferred to *Sussi*. The padlock on the hatch had not been broken open. I had a feeling of having won a small victory. For the first time since we left Thyborøn MacDuff didn't know where we were. He was doubtless searching now and the west coast of Scotland is full of inlets, deep or small, where we could anchor without being seen from the main channels. But would that suffice? And what, really, was the use of our hiding? Simply to make ourselves invisible was pointless. We might just as well find seats in an aeroplane and disappear for good. I looked at Torben, who was casting off Junior's lines. Had he actually bought air tickets?

'Everything ready?' I shouted to be heard above Junior's old diesel engine.

'I'll follow after you,' he shouted back.

'Lismore Island!' I shouted even louder. 'There's a good anchorage on the west side!'

Junior raised a thumb and put *Fortuna* in reverse. I started our engine and motored slowly against the tide to make heaving up the anchor less heavy work. Meanwhile, I realised that I had forgotten to look in the tide tables. Corran Narrows further south was a narrow passage where the current could run at six knots, more than the engine of *Rustica* could stem. If the tide was against us, we would never be able to get through.

Torben lashed down the anchor, and I increased the revs. We slowly began to make way.

'We've got the tide against us,' said Torben and laughed. 'You must have had other things than the tide to think about lately. Shall we run up the sails?'

We had a westerly wind, with some north in it. In the Scottish lochs, the wind comes from two directions only: it's following or it's on your nose. Loch Linnhe runs north south, and with luck we would get a fair wind.

'Go ahead and hoist,' I told Torben. 'But take a reef in the mainsail. We mustn't sail away from *Fortuna*.'

I looked astern. Junior had run up his ill matched sails. Money was in short supply on board Junior's boat. His only luxuries were a black and white television set and an autopilot. He was standing on the foredeck waving happily. Two ropes trailed from his stern, both attached to the autopilot. He intended to catch hold of these if he should happen to fall overboard. 'I worry about everything,' he had said. Not a bad principle at sea, if you can bear it.

Torben waved back to Junior in a rather preoccupied way and sat down in the cockpit.

'And now,' he ordered. 'Tell me everything. Why did you pass through the lock without waiting for me to come back?'

'Would you bring me the tide table first?'

'No,' he said in a tone that allowed no objections. 'That

can wait. Now when we finally have time to talk.'

I didn't insist. Sooner or later we would notice if the tide was pushing us backwards. And however curious he might be to hear what I had to tell, I was at least as curious to have a report from him.

I began by explaining why I had wished to avoid the police, and of what I had said to the lock keeper about our future plans.

'You didn't need to worry about the police.' Torben assured me.

'Why not?'

'I had already talked to them,' he said. 'Yes, yes, I know. You don't have to give me a lecture on the subject. It's always suspicious to associate with the police, even with the best of intentions. But I had no choice. They were headed directly for *Rustica* when I ran into them.'

'What did you tell them?'

'Well,' said Torben, 'they wanted to know if I had any idea about who was behind the sabotage. Of course I had no idea. But I impressed on them that it was not a decent way to treat foreign visitors. I had heard so much good about Scotland! But we had now decided to go back to Sweden. They asked if I believed that the sabotage was directed against us. Naturally, I didn't think so. But the result was the same, and I was on my way to Fort William in order to buy plane tickets home. Could they possibly give me a lift there? We'd be able to talk on the way. So they drove me to a travel agency, and it aroused a certain amount of attention that I arrived there in a police car. It would be easy for somebody to discover what I had done: bought two plane tickets from Glasgow to Copenhagen, by way of London.'

He showed me two tickets.

'What do you say?' he asked. 'Shall we fly home? We have the tickets.'

His tone was too deliberately casual for the question to be seriously meant.

'Do you want to go home?' I asked him.

'No,' he said. 'Not now when it's becoming really exciting.'

'Hasn't it been all the time? If I recall correctly, in Thyborøn it was you who wanted to ring up the police and leave it all to them.'

'I know it was. But we knew nothing then. We had only speculations. And since we hadn't learned anything, we had nothing to lose. But now, I think we've started to understand what might be involved. As a matter of fact, I have recently discovered some interesting things, if I may say so myself.'

'In Fort William?' I asked.

'Yes, I made a round of the bookshops.'

'What else would you do?'

'We are not Druids,' Torben asserted. 'You are quite as dependent on books as I am. If you had no almanac how would you know when the tide turns? But not a word more from me until I have heard what you were up to while Junior and I sat in the pub!'

'I had a chat with Mary,' I said bluntly, to have the satisfaction of seeing him taken aback, to the point, in fact, where his pipe dropped from his mouth.

Until I had related everything, as precisely and completely as I could, he didn't bother to retrieve it. By the time I was finished, Fort William lay behind us, and we were rapidly approaching Corran Narrows. To starboard, there was a ferry berth, and on the tip of a flat headland a lonely white lighthouse. Not a soul could be seen. The wind had fallen, but we didn't need to run the engine. The tide having turned after all, it carried us at five knots towards the narrow sound ahead.

The land masses seemed to liberate themselves from a frozen state and stick out their tongues at us as we got closer.

We could only keep going straight on in the strong current. To turn around would have been impossible, no matter what would, or could, possibly happen on the other side of the Narrows.

It struck me once again how much I worried about what might happen. Present realities retreated more and more into the background and finally became unreal, while the things that might happen, a possible danger, a hidden threat or simply what might lie beyond the next headland became the true reality. It was what we didn't know that mattered most. Torben was right. If fiction was everything that was possible, then fiction could be much more real and significant than reality itself.

But beyond the promontory nothing appeared except open water. With Junior still faithfully in our wake, we slipped quietly out onto Loch Linnhe, which was smooth as glass. A faint bluish haze enshrouded everything: water, sky and land. Even the mountains had a steel blue edge. We sat reverently and regarded the scene. I felt a lightness rising within me and we almost seemed to be hovering in the air. There was a quality of unreality even about the scenery. The water reflected the mountains with such clarity that one could not tell the image from reality. The only way of making sure was to look astern and see how, in our wake, the reflection was cut in two and how it shivered before it smoothly came together again, but only until the sharp stem of Junior's *Fortuna* knifed into it.

Not before we had the cape of Rubha Mors abeam did we speak again. A mild westerly wind began to fill our sails. We kept our voices low, but for once this wasn't because we were afraid of being overheard or of attracting attention; it was simply what the atmosphere of the place demanded.

In due course, Torben questioned me closely about Mary and concerning MacDuff's logbook. I tried to recall MacDuff's different catches and the names of the various ports where he had put in. Torben kept nodding as if much of this could be taken for granted, and he wrote down what I told him in a little notebook.

'Well,' I asked, 'what do you make of it?'

'It would surprise me if what MacDuff loaded and discharged was fish.'

'I worked that out too, as a matter of fact. But the question is: What are the fish? Arms?'

'Oh certainly. But the weapons have a thought behind them.'

'A thought?'

'Yes, a thought. The grandiose idea of establishing the first Celtic national state that has ever existed. Or perhaps the idea of a Celtic Ring: a federation of Celtic countries united by a cultural heritage that goes back thousands of years and has never died out. Or possibly the idea of Druids taking the offensive to restore their spiritual dominion over all the countries they controlled so long. Until Caesar forced them to go underground. Where they have been active ever since.'

Torben looked as if he meant every word of this.

'Druids?' I said. 'You surely don't mean that the Celtic Ring is just a bunch of neo-Druids? Could they accomplish anything?'

'Not necessarily. But at least they have the will.'

Torben went down into the cabin and, as might be expected, came up with a book. I hadn't seen it before.

'I found this in Fort William, in a second hand bookshop. Not that it's of any antiquarian interest. On the contrary. It appeared as recently as 1983. The shop has a special section for such books.'

He was enchanted by his find.

'It's not open to the general public,' he confided. 'It's totally reserved for what I take to be an exclusive group of the chosen few.'

'And you belong to them?' I asked. 'Since you got in?'

'For a short time, yes. For less than a quarter of an hour I was a member of the presumably very exclusive Celtic Ring.'

Now it was my turn to be taken aback. He was only joking, wasn't he? His sense of humour was of the sort which doesn't reveal itself until it was too late to laugh. But no ... if he wasn't in earnest, I would have caught the glint in his eye perceptible to those who knew him well.

'So you've got even with me,' I said. 'I met Mary. And now you have been a member of The Celtic Ring.'

'Well, almost. After I'd been at the travel agency, I walked about the town looking for bookshops. It came to me that, in actual fact, I hadn't been in a single bookshop since I left Copenhagen. The mere idea of it gave me an abstinence syndrome. And I supposed I'd find lots of books about the Celts that aren't available in Denmark. Which was more or less the case in the first two shops I visited. But at the third, a poky little second hand place in a back street, they hadn't a single one. Not one! I was on the point of asking why not, when I happened to recall a book-shop I know on the Rådhus Square in Copenhagen. They have a special section reserved for people who belong to the Masonic lodges. You have to prove that you are a member before you can see the books. Show a card or give a password, I don't really know. Well, I wondered if it mightn't be the same thing in that shop. Strange, you must admit, that they had no books about Celts on their shelves.'

'The question,' continued Torben, 'was what I should do, supposing that you had to be a member of some order to see the books on Celts. If there were any to see, that is. Believe it or not, the whole thing was solved when the assistant came up and asked if I was looking for anything special. 'Yes,' I answered, 'I'm looking for The Celtic Ring'. Of course it must have been one of those chances in a thousand. I was taken into a back room filled with 'Celtiana'. Impossible to find it by yourself. The door was a whole bookcase that moved aside. The room was long and narrow, and I saw at once any number of books by Celtic authors. Then I was left alone, with the bookcase door closed.'

I abruptly discovered that yet again I had been sailing *Rustica* without sufficient attention to what I was about. This showed signs of becoming a dangerous habit. I glanced at the chart while Torben kept quiet, as if the navigation was none of his affair.

Before turning in the previous evening, we had looked at Junior's charts and agreed on several different plans. The idea behind them all was that we should remain out of sight until we had decided on our next step. Lismore Island possessed a number of anchorages on its west side. But *Rustica* and *Fortuna* would be clearly seen from the main channel between Fort William and Oban. The east side also offered anchorages, but even there the channel was rather too much used. Loch Creran, in spite of nasty whirlpools and gushing streams at its entrance, had ideal anchorages hidden further in. However, if MacDuff thought of looking for us there, we'd be in a cul de sac. And what would Junior say? After much hesitation, I decided that we should sail to Kerrera and anchor on the west side of Oban Bay. True, it was opposite the town. But we would be far enough away to prevent immediate identification. In any case, I assured myself that MacDuff would be looking for us up to the north, where there was an abundance of inlets, small or long and narrow, which we could reach in a day's sail. It would take him quite some time to have a look in them all. But if he suspected that we had sailed northward only to turn back south ...? Well, then we could catch sight of him if we anchored at Kerrera. A short walk up to the top of the island, and we could look out over the Sound of Mull, the natural channel for all boats coming from the north. And

Ardentraive Bay at Kerrera was not a blind alley. There were two ways of escape.

'We'll sail to Kerrera,' I told Torben and pointed to the place on the chart.

He scarcely looked at it.

'Through Shuna Sound.' I added.

'Oh, I see,' he remarked indifferently.

So I would have to take all the responsibility for him, for *Rustica* and for Junior. I had noticed that the handbook described the passage of Shuna Sound as 'just difficult enough to be interesting', a typical British understatement that you would never find in a Swedish pilot-book. But the most important thing was that it was an inner channel more tucked away than the route west of Lismore Island. The decision became definite when we were passing to the west of the little island called Eilean Balngowan. Thereafter I felt more at ease and could give my attention to Torben for a while.

'Of course,' he went on, as if he hadn't been interrupted at all, 'I wasn't altogether unflurried about finding myself in that room. The door would have to be opened from the other side, and how was I to notify the assistant that I wanted to come out? Another thing: I didn't know if the books were for sale. But in many cases there were several copies of them. So I picked out a couple, almost at random. I didn't dare stay as long as I'd like to have done. I might suddenly be joined by a fellow member of the illustrious association. But I looked in vain for some means of making known that I wished to leave. I began to think that I was caught in a trap. I assumed that there had to be a silent signal that wouldn't arouse the curiosity of casual customers. Actually, the whole system was damned well conceived. A code to get in and a code to get out. All accidental entries eliminated. I'd got in by luck. To get out that way was beyond all probability.'

'But you did get out,' I observed.

'I knocked,' Torben confessed. 'And loudly. What else could I do? I pretended that I was completely absorbed by one of the books. Which of course wasn't very difficult to feign. But I was reprimanded for not having done what I ought to have done, whatever that was. I took the rebuke as further proof that it was no ordinary bookshop.'

'Were there any books about the IRA?' I asked, thinking of possible connections to the Celtic Ring.

Torben looked crestfallen.

'I forgot to look. I should have thought of that myself.'

We had just reached the Sound of Shuna. And I forgot Torben while piloting us through. He, meanwhile, seemed to forget that he was aboard a sailing boat at all. He lost himself in his newly acquired books and let me do the navigating.

Shuna being very shallow, it was wisest to reduce our speed, and I had to dash up to the foredeck myself and take down the jib. I made signs to Junior that he should follow in our wake, which he seemed more than willing to do. '*Just difficult enough to be interesting*'! I could see the bottom distinctly through the clear water. I became impatient with Torben and finally I told him a bit sharply that he should sit in the bow and watch for rocks. Not that I was worried about *Rustica* if we should run aground. The risk was that we might require help if we got stuck in the mud. Should that happen, it would soon be generally known where we were. It reassured me to know that the tide was rising. To run aground on a falling tide would have been particularly idiotic, that much I had understood in spite of being a non-tidal sailor.

My anxiety proved unfounded. We did touch the bottom at one moment, but only enough for Torben, still absently keeping watch, to lose his balance and be on the point of falling overboard. But then we were through.

To port, Castle Stalker appeared, a massive square castle of the same type as Invergarry. At high tide, it stood on an islet, but at low-water it was at the tip of a tongue of land. The castle was by no means a mouldering ruin and I read not long ago that it had been bought and restored by an unknown Scotsman.

Navigation became much easier when we had left the Sound of Shuna. I called Torben back.

'Didn't you say that you have made some interesting discoveries?' I asked.

'I have.'

He handed me the book which he had brought up from the cabin. 'According to this, there are at present about a million members in the various druidic orders of Europe! It does sound incredible. Yet nothing indicates that it isn't so.'

I let Torben take over the helm, and I looked at the book. It was in French: a doctoral thesis submitted at the University of Rennes, in Brittany. As well as being a Doctor of Philosophy, the author, Michel Raoult by name, was himself a Druid. The Doctor of Philosophy part of it didn't impress me much, being one myself, and the combination of science and mysticism struck me as even more dubious. The book's title indicated its contents clearly enough: *Les Druides: Les sociétés iniatiques celtiques contemporaines*.

'Is this thing to be taken seriously?' I inquired. 'Or is it the same twaddle as that *Light of the Orient* you showed me earlier?'

'There's no comparison,' Torben assured me. 'Raoult's is a scholarly work, his evidence and reasoning are all up to scientific standards. He doesn't try to defend any theory or personal prejudices of his own. In fact, it's hard to tell which druidic society he must belong to himself, even if I think he has a certain preference for non-Christian Druids who speak a Celtic language. In any case, he is most reticent about those. So he may be respecting the vow of silence he would have given when he was initiated as a Druid.'

'But what does he say? Could there be a million Druids today?'

'There may be, yes,' said Torben. 'At least if membership in a druidic association confers the status of being a Druid. Raoult takes up more than fifty such societies, of the most varying kind. He describes their rites, symbols, origins, their requirements for membership, ceremonies on admission of members. He gives the number of members each association possesses, even the address of its secretariat, if it has one. There are druidic societies all over the world. Sweden, for example, has one with four thousand adherents and a head office in Malmö. However, Raoult regards the Swedish body as being, for the most part, merely a variant of a Masonic lodge. And of course the majority of druidic societies, and the largest ones, are in Celtic countries.'

Torben gave the helm back to me, took the book and opened it at the end.

'Listen to this! There's the *Ancient Order of Druids* with several thousand members. The *International Great Lodge of Druids* has two hundred thousand members with sections in various countries. There are the druidic monks of Avalon. That was the Celts' holy island, you know - where King Arthur waited before he liberated the Celts from the Anglo Saxons. The *Isis Society* in Ireland has about a thousand members. In Wales, Brittany and Ireland, there's *Gorsedd*, a loose combination of Druids and bards who go in for the old Celtic poets. And so on. But the most remarkable society of all is certainly *Les Communautés druidiques et celtiques*. The communities in question are spread over all France and, taken together, they are said to have something like 540,000 members. Each member voluntarily contributes two per cent of his earnings as membership fee. The headquarters of the association are in Reims, where a hundred and seventy four secretaries are employed along with other staff. *Les*

Communautés allege that their history extends back to the first Druids. They celebrate all the old festivals: *Samain* on the first of November, *Beltaine* on the fourth of May, and also the solstices. Traditions are passed on orally, precisely as with the ancient Druids. But there are so called 'writing witnesses', whose works are found hidden in secret places. And if that weren't enough, the society carried on its work in secret until only a few years ago.'

Torben looked silently and reflectively into the book he was holding. And after a time he assured me:

'The movement is much greater than we could ever have imagined it to be. Of course it contains many different tendencies. Some associations have sections in various Celtic countries; others are active in only one country. Sometimes they cooperate; sometimes they can't abide one another. Naturally, there are groups which regard themselves as more orthodox than the rest. They are pronounced non-Christians whose ceremonies are held in Celtic languages and they require that those applying for membership should at least have Celtic ancestors. A line of division exists between pacifists and those who accept the use of violence, or of 'force' as the IRA would say, to promote their cause, even if they themselves would not bear arms. But there are also many common features. Meetings are generally held in the open air, in groves and in glades, or beside a historic monument like Stonehenge. All give highest place to knowledge, peace, art. Many hold the same great festivals as did the ancient Celts. And the most important thing; nearly all dream of a new Celtic realm. It's not at all a matter of keeping some few traditions alive, of preserving the little that's left of a dying culture. When you put together all that is written, both quite openly and between the lines, there can be no doubt that powerful forces are at work to bring about a rebirth of independent Celtic nations. Make fun of Druids if you like, of their rituals and symbols and ceremonies. But you can't leave them out of account. Not after you have read this book.'

Torben left no room for objection. I didn't know what I ought to say. If he, in spite of his aversion to symbols and myths, had been persuaded, it must be because he admitted the reality behind the symbols. He must have thought that they were signs, as smoke is a sign of fire, and not more or less distorted representations of the fire.

'Of course it's difficult to swallow everything.' Torben admitted. 'But take the myth about King Arthur. That's kept very much alive. He is Pekka's 'King in the underworld', nothing else. And he isn't only a symbol for the Celts' coming nations. There are people who, in deadly earnest, believe that he will come again in one guise or another, and liberate the Celtic countries from their occupying powers. The myth of King Arthur and his sword Excalibur is particularly potent in Cornwall. And each time a Druid from Brittany meets a colleague in Wales, they perform the Ceremony of the Broken Sword. It symbolizes the essential unity of the Celtic peoples, and King Arthur's sovereignty over both Brittany and Britain. Druids from the two countries always recite the same hymn. It goes like this:

'Let us strive for the rebirth
Of our language and our culture,
In order to prepare the way for Arthur's return
Heart against heart
Although each on his side of our mutual sea.'

Torben declaimed the incantation in a voice so loud and clear that for a moment I was afraid Junior would hear him. It struck me that for Torben our own situation was reduced to a tiny episode by his new found knowledge about the Celts' history and their possible future.

'Moreover,' he continued, 'all the druidic societies in the various Celtic countries have a national anthem, each sung to the same tune and with pretty much the same words. The difference comes at the end: in Brittany it's La Bretagne à jamais! in Wales it's Wales for ever!, and so on. Oh, and something else ... First, Raoult distinguishes between, on the one hand, such secret *organisation*s as the Bretons 'Freedom Front' and the IRA, and on the other hand, initiatory societies, like the druidic orders where a member is admitted at a ceremony, makes a vow of fidelity, all that. But nothing prevents the secret societies from being initiatory ones as well, in which case their political activities can be taken as merely an outer expression of the same kind of religious or philosophic convictions as are to be found in the orthodox druidic bodies. An example ... Raoult mentions that the 'Gallic Freedom Front', formed as recently as 1979 in Wales, adheres to tenets of the orthodox 'Gallic Druids' Society', and their activities run parallel. So you see ... It may well be that the druidic spirit and tenets direct such organisations as the IRA and other Celtic national movements, or create a basis for them.'

'That sounds insane!' I said spontaneously, not a little alarmed by the perspective Torben opened to view.

'Yes, it does,' he admitted. 'But I still can't see anything that prevents it from being possible. If the druidic associations have more than a million members, or let's say just half of that number for good measure, then there must be people among them who believe that they can be united. It would be strange, if there weren't. Resistance movements, like the IRA or the FLB in Brittany support one another and want to liberate the Celtic countries. The druidic orders also strive for independence. And nationalist parties in the various Celtic countries do the same. Their combined efforts may, against all odds, be powerful enough to mobilise the Celts as a whole.'

'That must have been part of what Pekka discovered,' I said.

'Oh, certainly. And he may, who knows, have got hold of Raoult's book, made some investigations himself, and reached the same conclusions we have come to now.'

'What about the head cult and human sacrifice?' I wondered. 'Does Raoult write anything about them?'

'Yes,' Torben said. 'But he tries to explain away all that. Unlike most other writers on the subject, he holds that only one Irish folk-tale, of the more than a thousand that survive, mentions human sacrifice. And the matter isn't crystal clear there either. But then he ignores what the Roman sources say. I don't know where Pekka got his information from. In any case, we must accept that he saw something gruesome, appalling in fact. For it now appears that other ideas of his were not pure imagination. Let's suppose that, somehow, he happened to witness one of IRA's secret trials and the execution of a traitor. With all the rest in his head, he may have believed it was a ritual sacrifice.'

'And how about MacDuff?' I demanded. 'And Mary? After all, they are our closest concern just now.'

'Oh, I don't know about them,' Torben answered lightly.

'In any case,' I affirmed, 'MacDuff does not resemble a Druid.'

'Oh, don't say that! Historically speaking, at least, no principles have prevented Druids from taking up arms, although they probably let the kings risk their lives in their stead. People in power, as the Druids were, seldom care to risk their own lives. Now, when you consider the matter, there's an armed liberation movement in all the Celtic countries. Not only Northern Ireland. There's the *Front de Libération de la Bretagne*. Wales has one, as well. And the IRA sold weapons to it at the end of the Sixties. Oh, and not so long ago, in 1979, a new branch appeared on the same tree: the Gallic Liberation

Front I talked about.'

'But there's none in Scotland?' I inquired.

'Well, there scarcely needs to be a special liberation movement here. That was pretty evident from what we were told by the young man who took me out fishing. And the SNP, being a respectable democratic party, has come close to gaining a majority of the votes without having to resort to secret organisations or terrorism. But there have been some strange organisations even here. MacDiarmid, the poet, started one called Clann Albain, the Children of Scotland, which was supposed to foster the Celtic Idea and to rescue Scotland from England. As late as 1979, Siol Naan Gaidheal, or Seed of the Gael, was founded as a more extremist, mystical and military organisation that actually carried out some bombings and other attacks. The Scots might be Scots first and Celts second, but they can't be all indifferent to the power inherent in the ancient Celtic symbols. Just one example. According to Irish folk tales, there's a stone called Lia Fâl which every Irish King had to sit upon for his sovereignty to be acknowledged. The stone is said to have been taken to Ireland by descendants of the goddess Dana. During the Irish migration, the stone was brought over to Iona - not far from here, is it? And Saint Columba used it when he crowned kings there. Later it was kept in a monastery at Scone. But in 1291, the English King Edward I took it over and incorporated it in England's coronation chair so it would legitimise future monarchs of England and Great Britain. It remained under the chair until 1950, when it was carried off on Christmas Eve by a group of Scottish Nationalist commandos! Imagine what that stone must represent when it caused Westminster Abbey to be burgled - quite aside from its weighing three hundred pounds. Quite possibly, the stone was taken with the coronation of a new Celtic king in mind.'

'Do you *believe* that?' I asked.

'Believe what? The stone exists. It's a true story.'

'That may be. But about the Celts taking over power, led by a procession of Druids - do you believe that?'

'I no longer know what to believe. But why should we suppose that the western democracies will always have their present boundaries? After what has happened in Eastern Europe, we should be aware of how quickly frontiers can change. Even if, after having waited nearly a millennium, it can hardly matter to the Celts if they must wait another ten, or hundred, years. Did you know that there's a castle on Skye, Dunvegan, where the MacLeods have lived without interruption for seven hundred years? In such a country, people don't easily forget.'

'Yes, yes. But now? Why was it so important to get rid of Pekka just now? And of us?'

'That's what we must try to find out. It will be easier if my principal hypothesis is correct.'

Torben said this as if it were obvious thing. He had changed. It was he who pressed us forward and I who hesitated. I watched the sound between Kerrera and the mainland open slowly ahead of *Rustica*. We rounded Maiden Island, turned to port, then to starboard, and soon we lay in the calm water of Ardentraive Bay. The anchor chain rattled down, and we furled our sails. Junior arrived just after us, and he repeated the same manoeuvre. All was peace. It looked as if we were alone.

Chapter 18

Two days later, we parted from Junior. *Fortuna* hoisted her ill-matched and sun-bleached sails; then she set off southward. But first, Junior made a last turn round *Rustica* and waved lamely. We all three smiled, though we were sad. When sailing, you sometimes meet people like Junior in foreign waters, people you would like always to have near you. But at the same time there is the urge to sail on, and that urge is stronger than new friendships. Presumably it is just this conflict that makes such fleeting encounters so precious. You know from the beginning that parting will soon come, that probably you will never see each other again, not for an entire life.

It was on the fifteenth of February that *Fortuna* disappeared from sight. As soon as we were alone again, Torben faced me.

'Now it's our turn,' he said. 'MacDuff hasn't shown up yet. We still have time.'

'For what?'

'To find out what the Celtic Ring really is.'

Just then I didn't bother to argue. I didn't want to destroy Torben's mood of high spirited expectation. If I had known

218

what I do now, I wouldn't have been so considerate. For it wasn't long before it became perfectly clear that we no longer had any choice about what to do and not to do.

'And how are we to find out about The Ring?' was all I asked, in the vain hope of discouraging Torben. 'If a Celtic Ring exists, we must know where. And the only clue we have is a bookshop in Fort William. You can hardly go back there, can you? Should we creep about under windows and peep in? Put in hidden microphones? Ring up the police and ask them to send a patrol? Or shall we apply for membership and infiltrate?'

'I want to show you something!' Torben said and took me firmly down into the cabin.

He produced the Imray's chart of Scotland and Northern Ireland.

'Thus far,' he explained, 'we have kept mostly to Pekka's route. That's why we went through the Caledonian Canal and moored beside Urquhart Castle and Invergarry. It was in Oban that Pekka loaded the 'cases of books' on board. Unfortunately, we don't know at which places Pekka found something interesting. But take a look here!'

Torben pointed at the chart. Here and there he had drawn little rings and crosses. Certain inlets and other places were marked with both a cross and a ring.

'What do they mean?' I asked.

'The crosses are for places that Pekka visited. The rings are for the places you found in the logbook aboard MacDuff's fishing boat. If we're to begin somewhere, it surely ought to be where there is both a cross and a ring. Here at Oban, for instance. Or here?'

Torben pointed at the southern tip of Kerrera.

'What is there?' I wondered.

'Yet another castle. Gylen Castle, it's called. The name comes from the Gaelic for 'spring'. Apparently, the tower is built above two springs. Like the other castles we've seen, it had a violent early history, and it was set on fire in 1647. Now it's a ruin, like Invergarry.'

'Do you think we'll find anything there?' I asked.

'I suppose we'll have to go and have a look.'

But before we had time to do anything at all, we heard the sound of a powerful diesel engine approaching at high speed.

'It might not be necessary,' I said. 'We'll be picked up instead.'

We had no means of escape. Two people can't hide themselves in a sailing boat thirty-one feet long. I looked out.

'It's the harbour master's boat,' I told Torben with relief.

'*Rustica* ahoy!' a voice shouted.

I climbed out and was greeted in friendly fashion by the man at the wheel of the boat.

'I'm coming up alongside,' he said and did so with a neat manoeuvre.

'My name is Campbell,' he told me. 'I'm the harbour master here. Is there anything I can do for you?'

I began automatically to search for money in order to pay harbour dues. He made a dismissive gesture.

'Consider yourselves as our guests. It isn't often that we receive visitors from so far away at this time of year. I have a message to you from the Commodore of the Lorn Yacht Club. He very much wants you to be the club's guest at dinner this evening, and wonders if you would care to tell members something about your voyage across the North Sea.'

'Just a minute! I'll ask my crew.'

I put my head down through the hatch.

'What do you say about it, Torben? We're invited to dinner.'

'You decide,' he told me.

Personally, I couldn't resist the temptation of being the Yacht Club's guest of honour and doubtless hearing our winter

sail described as a considerable feat. There are few sailors who
don't suffer from a certain vanity. To boast yourself of having
survived a storm is meaningless and presumptuous. The sea is
too mighty and man too insignificant to delude yourself into
believing that you can conquer it. But to hear others suggest
that one has shown courage or seamanship, that is a different
matter.

'We're coming!' I told the harbour-master. 'Our best
regards in return and thanks for the invitation!'

'You are both coming?'

'Naturally.'

'Good. The Commodore was anxious to have an
opportunity of meeting the whole crew.'

'And where shall we meet?' I inquired.

'He will come and pick you up in his boat. Can I be of
service, otherwise?'

Torben put his head up through the hatch.

'Hello!' he said. 'Could you perhaps help us with a bit of
information? We met some nice Scotsmen with a fishing boat
in Fraserburgh. MacDuff, I think the captain was called. Have
you possibly seen his boat? Oban is his home port, if I
remember rightly.'

'MacDuff, the pilot? Do you know him?'

'Not so well as we'd like to,' lied Torben.

'He's one of the best! They don't make his kind any
more. If there's anything you need to know about the waters
around here, or anywhere round Scotland or Ireland for that
matter, then you have only to ask MacDuff. There isn't a
whirlpool or an anchorage he doesn't know about. I haven't
seen him for some time. But one of the ferry captains has been
in touch with him by radio. He was on his way northward then.
Come to think about it, he asked about a Swedish boat. Funny
coincidence, isn't it? I'll tell the ferry captain to notify him
about where you are. No, I don't mind at all. Everybody wants

to do MacDuff a favour.'

'Thank you,' said Torben. 'It's good of you.'

'Don't mention it!'

The harbour master raised two fingers to the peak of his captain's cap and disappeared in the direction of Oban.

'A decent fellow,' Torben remarked. 'Obliging.'

'But why should you think it necessary to ask about MacDuff?'

'To find out if he could possibly have something to do with MacDuff. He evidently hasn't. And then we learned that MacDuff has sailed northward, so we can enjoy our dinner in peace. We've also discovered that we must be on our guard. MacDuff has such a large network of useful contacts at sea and on land that it won't be easy to find a hiding place in his home waters. Especially not with a mast ten metres high. Couldn't we possibly cut it off a bit?'

'Are you out of your mind?'

'I was only joking,' said Torben. 'But it won't be easy for us to hide *Rustica* if we should need to.'

That made me think of an article I had saved which had appeared in some yachting magazine. It was about Corryvreckan, the treacherous sound between the isles of Jura and Scarba. The article described not only the currents and overfalls which made it impossible to pass through the sound, but also a tucked away anchorage which could be reached only in certain favourable circumstances. Now that could be a hiding place for us. MacDuff would never believe that we dared sail into Corryvreckan and, still less, anchor there. Just as he hadn't believed that Pekka would survive Pentland Firth. I thought of the despair MacDuff must have felt when he couldn't overtake the *Sula* with Mary on board. Scarcely what he would feel for me and Torben in the same situation. Not any longer, not after my visit to his boat.

At about seven o'clock, we heard an engine still at a distance. Darkness had fallen two hours earlier, and we had put on riding lights so that the Commodore could find us. Before sunset, it had looked as if a storm was coming in from the west. Tattered clouds swept over the mountains on Mull and into the long and steep valleys of the mainland. The weather had been mild for some days, but now the narrow column of mercury was just above zero. As yet, there was no more than a fresh breeze, but if it was a cold front running in from the Atlantic, there could be a gale in less than an hour. I worried about Junior and his *Fortuna*. True, he was in sheltered waters, and it wasn't very far to the Crinan Canal, but there were several rather tricky passages on the way. I missed him already. Before he had cast off, he left us two addresses: one of his yacht club in Findhorn, the other of his good friend in Glasgow. But I had no address of my own to give him in return and, for once, I felt this to be a disadvantage. My postal-box, where I lived officially, wasn't of much use since the mail couldn't be forwarded. That, of course, made it difficult to keep in touch with people like Junior.

My dream had always been to have, as well as a boat, a small house on an island somewhere along the western coast of Ireland or Scotland. I would rarely live there of course. The house would be a single large letter box. That would make me feel secure: owning a habitable letter box, and a fixed postal address, where I didn't need to live. Now, while lying at anchor in Ardentraive Bay, I realised that I had needed that form of security: a place to which I could have withdrawn.

The thump of the engine came very close. Torben and I went out to help the boat draw alongside. An elderly man stood at its helm, and his very white beard seemed to be luminous in the dark. We soon saw that he had all the necessary attributes of an old salt: orange-coloured oilskins, captain's cap, and a pipe.

'Hello there!' he called. 'I'm Duncan MacDougall. And I'd like to wish you welcome to Oban. On behalf of myself and that of the Lorn Yacht Club.'

We thanked him and introduced ourselves.

'Are you ready? Then hop aboard!'

I locked *Rustica* and gave a last look about. Each time we left her now, I felt it might be the last time I saw her. I had hidden away both our own logbook and Pekka's in a place that I deemed impossible to find without tearing up the whole deck. I jumped aboard MacDougall's launch.

We cast off immediately and headed southward, but not in the direction of Oban, as could be expected. Torben and I exchanged a glance which was perceived by our host.

'Ah yes. You wonder where we are off to. Well, I'll tell you. We are going to what I hope will be our new clubhouse. And you are in for a surprise! Actually, you'll be present the first time it's used and be our first guests on the premises!'

Even if we couldn't clearly see his expression, we heard that he was proud of the acquisition.

'It won't be any ordinary sort of clubhouse,' he assured us. 'Perhaps we're going to have a whole castle to ourselves. Gylen Castle, it's called. I don't know if you've been able to see it yet. It's not far from the south point of Kerrera.'

I grasped Torben's arm. It was the castle he had hoped to look at. Certainly, neither of us then suspected that MacDougall could be anything other than the Commodore of the Lorn Yacht Club. He talked casually and blithely on.

'Yes indeed, an entire castle that goes back to the Middle Ages. I've been making excursions there for a long time. But we had no idea that some of our members had actually bought the place and started to make premises for us there. Not until a recent meeting when they offered it to the club. And of course we were delighted to accept. We haven't yet the got the run of the whole castle, but the setting couldn't be better. For me there's something altogether special involved. The castle was built by the clan MacDougall in 1587. But General Leslie set fire to it sixty years later, and since then it has been in ruins. Originally, there were two towers, but only one is still standing. But the club has pledged its help to restore the rest. At the moment, the place is a bit primitive. But what does that matter? It's only the beginning.'

The compass light was much too weak to light up the interior of the wheelhouse. But now and then the glow from MacDougall's pipe would grow brighter and cast formless and fleeting shadows on the walls. The island of Kerrera lay in complete darkness; not even its silhouette could be discerned against the sky. Behind us the lights of Oban glimmered vaguely, uncertainly, as if they were shrinking away from us. What our host used as navigation marks and leading marks I do not know. Abruptly, he slowed down.

'One has to take it a little bit carefully here,' he told us. 'There's a nasty rock in the middle when you come into the bay. At ebb tide it sticks up, and you can see the thing. But otherwise you can't, and it's perfidious as the devil. A lot of people have gone hard aground.'

I had in my mind an image of the island from the chart. We must have come into Little Horseshoe Bay. But I couldn't be sure of anything in the darkness. MacDougall opened the wheelhouse door and went out. At the next instant he dropped anchor. Then he came back and switched on a searchlight. This swept over a short stretch of beach with cliffs to either side.

'To announce that we have arrived,' he explained.

'Announce to whom?' Torben wondered.

'Members of the club - those on the committee and some others. Including the people who have offered us the castle as a clubhouse. We have already had a committee meeting here.'

'How have they got here?' Torben asked. 'I don't see any

other boats.'

'No,' our host replied. 'We usually take this launch when we're just going back and forth.'

That meant that we were cut off from the mainland if something happened and dependent on the good will of others to get there. We couldn't even get out to *Rustica*, although she lay at anchor only a cable length from Kerrera. The water was too cold for a swim, and *Sussi* was as usual securely tied down to the cabin top. If this was a trap, it was fool-proof. Only naive amateur heroes like us could have stuck their heads into it.

After a few minutes, a large dinghy glided into the beam of the searchlight. It reminded me of the spectral arrival of Pekka's catamaran on a glimmering streak of moonlight, at Dragør. Now Pekka was dead; for the first time, I truly grasped what this meant. A once-living person was dead. One more among so many people in the world who have died because some people think they have the right to kill for some cause or the other. One more who would never be resurrected because of promises of future happiness in this world.

The dinghy was close to us now. It was steered by a man of about MacDougall's age.

'Good evening, Sir,' he said. 'You have the guests with you?'

'I have indeed,' said MacDougall and introduced us. 'Bill is our bosun.'

'A pleasure to have you at Gylen Castle,' Bill said. 'I hope you'll enjoy being here.'

'Is everything ready?' MacDougall asked.

'No troubles at all,' Bill replied and bade us join him in the dinghy.

I stepped down with certain misgivings. But Torben simply looked about with curiosity and either didn't notice, or didn't wish to notice, my uneasiness.

But when we had got ashore, he turned to MacDougall and asked:

'Isn't MacDuff here?'

'No,' MacDougall said without hesitation. 'He couldn't come tonight. He's at sea.'

'What a pity!' said Torben. 'We'd hoped to meet him again.'

MacDouga l halted.

'For that matter,' he said, almost as if he had suddenly realised this was the thing he ought to ask, 'how do you two know MacDuff?'

It wasn't clear to me whether he wondered where and when we'd become acquainted with MacDuff, or he was merely puzzled by our actually knowing him.

'I met him some time ago,' I answered. 'In Denmark.'

'In Denmark?' MacDougall repeated, but without further comment.

Our nocturnal stroll to the castle took perhaps twenty minutes. Bill guided us along with a torch and lighted a path that wound up and down between hillocks and steep cliffs.

'Who uses this path?' Torben asked.

'Nobody, in the winter,' MacDougall told him. 'There are some houses on the island, but most of them are empty.'

We arrived at the top of a hill and abruptly the ghostly single tower stood out against the black sky. Bill turned into a narrow track that led downwards. The wind had already turned into a near gale, and everything indicated that it would become worse. I recall thinking that, if nothing else, it might provide a kind of security. Not even MacDuff would sail back to Oban in the midst of a winter storm.

'Filthy weather!' burst out Bill, the boatswain, as if he had caught my reflection.

Neither he nor MacDougall said anything further until we suddenly stood before a stone wall that loomed high over our heads.

'This is the rear wall of the castle,' our host explained, and he began to pilot us around it to the right. 'It faces in towards the island. There are no windows, only two or three slits. That side of the castle was hardest to defend. From the sea it was practically impregnable.'

On rounding the corner, we were met by the full force of the wind, an icy blast that penetrated to the skin in spite of our having put on heavy woollen sweaters and oilskins. We walked along a kind of ledge and only a few yards to our right the cliffs descended straight down to the sea.

'Is the weather often like this?' I asked Bill.

'Yes,' he grunted. 'Or worse. We always have a lot of weather in Scotland.'

It was difficult to catch his words because of the wind and the sound of waves crashing against the cliffs below us. We went round another corner and saw light streaming out into the night from two slits. The effect was eerie, but when a door opened we looked into a cosy, but rather primitive and barren sort of meeting-place. There were some nautical charts on the walls and posters from the RNLI. At one end a door doubtless led to the cloak room; there were a couple of shelves with a few magazines and also a pantry-kitchen. A kind of gallery ran along the length of the room on one side. Part of this was curtained off and lay in shadow. In the centre of the room, a simple wooden table had been laid for eight people.

'How nice of you to join us here at the Lorn Yacht Club,' said a woman's voice that came from somewhat behind me.

We turned round. Our host introduced us to the club secretary, Margret Hathwood I think she was called. She was tall and blonde, and didn't fit in. With her high heeled red shoes, black nylon stockings, tight fitting skirt, her silken blouse in colours that matched her lipstick and eye shadow, she looked more like a photographer's model than the secretary of a yacht club.

'Bill, our bosun, you know already,' MacDougall continued. 'Then we have Mike O'Connell, our treasurer. It's thanks to him we're here.'

A weather beaten and middle-aged man stepped forward from the half shadow up in the gallery. We exchanged greetings.

'Mike takes care of our international contacts,' our host explained. 'He's an Irishman originally, but as so many Irishmen are more or less Scots, and the other way about, that doesn't matter at all. It's worse with our Englishman, the only one in the club. He doesn't always have an easy time of it, I fear.'

'That's me,' said a good natured voice that came from a gentleman neatly attired in a double breasted blue blazer.

He told us that his name was Tim Johnson.

'It's not my fault that I was born on the Isle of Wight. My parents didn't consult me about the matter. Or know that I would spend my life in Scotland.'

'No,' said MacDougall indulgently. 'It wasn't your fault. That's why we show such tolerance about it.'

This was evidently a standing joke. Our host, the secretary and Tim all laughed. Bill and O'Connell smiled a trifle, but mostly out of courtesy to their Commodore.

'Tim is even our vice-commodore,' said MacDougall. 'A great mark of favour for an Englishman. But they are capable fellows at sea, Englishmen, that must be said in their defence. Just like you Scandinavians. One has to be a true seaman to sail across the North Sea in the middle of winter.'

'Not a bit of it,' Torben put in. 'It's quite enough to be stupid or ignorant. Like me. I was seasick, terrified and frozen through nearly the whole way.'

I saw that the others didn't really believe him.

'Well, shouldn't we think of our dinner?' MacDougall

said and began to take off his sailing gear.

I scarcely believed my eyes when I saw what he wore beneath: a blazer of the club, grey flannel trousers, a white shirt and a tie.

'Where is Dick?' he demanded, looking about as we sat down.

'He was here a minute or two ago,' said Tim.

I noticed that Bill and Mike O'Connell cast stealthy glances towards the gallery. I looked, too, and was almost certain that I caught sight of a rather too familiar face disappearing behind the curtain. It was the man at the ceremony in Fraserburgh, at the pub in Fort Augustus, the man with a machine gun down under Invergarry Castle and perhaps the one I glimpsed at the top of Neptune's Staircase. What was he doing here? Was he merely a member of the yacht club? Or had his presence something to do with Torben's crosses and rings on the chart? For Gylen Castle had both a cross and a ring. Had it also a dungeon?

Torben hadn't noticed anything. He was exchanging polite phrases or deep thoughts with Margret.

'Dick is our storekeeper and general custodian,' MacDougall explained. 'He and Mike have both helped with the premises. And with much else, for that matter.'

'And we truly need a custodian here,' Margret said. 'There's an awful lot of valuable equipment in the club.'

'What kind?' asked Torben.

'Radio equipment, for example. And two fast motor boats with ninety horse power outboard motors. I don't know what's happened to us, but we used to be completely dependent on membership fees. But now one large company after another seems to present us with sophisticated equipment. Mostly, thanks to Mike. As our treasurer, he handles marketing. I believe that we could almost compete with the lifeboat service or the coastguard.'

'Or with smugglers?' Torben suggested.

'That, too,' answered the secretary.

She gave him a captivating smile.

'Not much to compete with,' O'Connell said. 'The competition can scarcely be described as cut throat. There isn't any shady business to do. There's no abroad around here. Trying to smuggle whisky to Scotland would hardly be worth-while. Nobody here is going to touch Bourbon or faked Scotch from Bulgaria.'

'Where has Dick got to?' MacDougall demanded with a touch of irritation. 'He knew perfectly well that we had guests.'

Bill looked uncertainly at O'Connell, as if he knew something that he didn't dare say.

'Perhaps he was worried about the launch in this weather,' O'Connell said after a moment's silence. 'I suggest that we start without him. We know how he can be when there's a wind like this. He wants to make sure that all is in shelter. And there's nothing he likes better than gales and dirty weather.'

He turned to Torben and me:

'Dick would happily cross the North Sea in mid winter. He's that kind. Nothing impresses him.'

'Yes, let's start,' Tim agreed. 'Dick is an excellent storekeeper, the very best. But he's not sociable. At least, not till you've known him for a couple of years.'

'It's not impossible that he's taken a turn to the boatyard,' Bill suggested, in a relieved tone. 'He has quite a lot to see to there. I believe he has a boat in the water just now.'

'Dick has a little boatyard for doing repairs here on Kerrera,' MacDougall explained. 'You must have seen it. It's on the south side of Ardentraive Bay, near where you are lying at anchor.'

Once again, Bill and O'Connell exchanged a glance.

'Is that a boatyard?' said Torben. 'We walked by, but it looked as if it had been abandoned. Except for the barbed wire, that is. That was new.'

'He has had trouble with thieves,' MacDougall said. 'And he is seldom there in the winter, as he hasn't much to do then.'

'Well, well,' said Torben humorously. 'After all, you too have some shady business going on, here as elsewhere. We don't need to be afraid of something happening to our boat, I hope? She has already been broken into. A shame, because it happened in our first port in Scotland, at Fraserburgh. But it turned out to be a mistake.'

'A mistake!' said Tim. 'How can a break-in be a mistake?'

All looked questioningly at Torben, all except O'Connell, who simply stared at him.

'Well, it must have been. Because what we'd had stolen was returned to us. The thief was evidently somebody who hadn't realised that we were visitors.'

'I do regret that you should have had such trouble,' said MacDougall. 'Scotland is not quite what it used to be, I'm afraid. In the old days a guest was safer than in his own home. But it's a different matter nowadays. There are too many who don't respect our traditions.'

'Such as me,' said Tim, with a glint in his eye.

'We have met lots of friendly and obliging people,' I put in. 'More, I expect, than we would have done at home.'

'That sounds reassuring,' MacDougall said. 'And now, do tell us all about your sail across the North Sea in the month of January. Begin at the beginning. We have plenty of time.'

During dinner, I tried to give as vivid and precise an account as I could of our trip. Now and then, Torben chimed in with reflections on the hardships and general wretchedness of life under sail, especially in his case. He spoke about the difficulty of storing wine, of how fishing boats seemed to pursue peaceful yachtsmen, of oil rigs towed directly across the paths of ships out in the open sea. All listened attentively to us both. Questions were asked and answers were given. Then our host proposed a toast to us; everyone else rose, and glasses were lifted.

'If you don't mind my asking,' MacDougall said when the glasses had been put down, 'I still don't quite understand why you decided to sail to Scotland at this time of year.'

The question sounded innocent enough, but the gaze of all present fastened upon me.

'I had heard so many good things about Scotland,' I began, without having to lie, 'not least about Scottish hospitality.'

'That's very pleasant to hear,' said MacDougall. 'But was that really enough to send you off in the middle of winter?'

It seemed to me that his voice had a note in it of calling me to order. I glanced at Torben, but he didn't seem to have noticed anything unusual.

'Don't look at me!' Torben said and looked around the table. 'I came along simply because I was stupid. Ask the Skipper why we came. He ought to know. Even if I've had my doubts in the matter. He and your storekeeper, Dick I think it was, they would get on well together. As it seems that he also lacks an instinct of self-preservation.'

All eyes were again fixed on me.

'Sailing in winter has its advantages,' I said, for want of anything better to say. 'You avoid all the tourists and are more warmly received. For instance, would you have invited us here if we had come in the summer?'

No one answered at once.

'Why not?' Tim finally said. 'Even in summer, not very many Scandinavians come here after sailing across the North Sea.'

'By the way,' Torben unexpectedly broke in. 'How did you know that we had sailed over the North Sea? Do you use bagpipes as jungle drums?'

'Oh, that's not very odd,' MacDougall said, unperturbed. 'You have met MacDuff, you know. It was he who suggested that we should invite you. He told us that you had much of interest to relate, and of course he was right. But I still think that you ought to tell us why you are sailing in the middle of winter. We are certainly accustomed to rough sailing, but I don't believe that any of us would be willing to cross the North Sea in January. But I seem to recall that MacDuff said something to the effect that you were interested in Celtic history. Is there some particular aspect that interests you?'

It's coming now! I remember thinking. I looked about at the people present, but nothing in their faces gave them away. Yet I was already fully and firmly convinced that it was not merely the committee members of a yacht club I saw before me. How incredibly guileless I had been when I accepted their invitation! I felt the panic rising within me and tried to tell myself that it was, once more, nothing but my imagination running amok. In view of what MacDuff must have told him, it was natural that MacDougall should be curious about our motive for coming to Scotland.

'The fact is ...,' I began, without really knowing what I intended to say, 'that it's MacDuff's fault, or maybe you should say that it is thanks to him that we are here this evening. I met him in Denmark very nearly a month ago, and ...'

'In Denmark?' Mike O'Connell broke in, as surprised as MacDougall had been when I told him the same thing.

'Yes,' I said in a cheerful tone. 'He invited me to come to Scotland. And very soon afterwards, I met a sailor who had arrived directly from Scotland in his boat, and he had many fine things to say about your country. If he could sail across the North Sea in winter, I supposed that I could too. Come to think of it, perhaps you met him. He was also here in Oban, if I remember correctly. A Finn called Pekka.'

There was absolute silence in the room.

Chapter 19

'WHEN was that?' O'Connell asked after a long moment, as if I were a witness being interrogated in a court room.

'I don't remember exactly,' I told him. 'But in any case it was after I'd met MacDuff. It must have been at some time in the middle of January.'

'And Mary?' continued O'Connell, as dogged as before.

Everybody, except Torben naturally, seemed to be avoiding one another's gaze.

'Who is Mary?' I asked ingenuously.

'I am sorry this came up,' MacDougall said. 'There is a rather unpleasant story involved, which naturally you couldn't know about.'

He hesitated.

'We believed that Pekka was dead.'

'He wasn't dead when I met him, I assure you. Although he looked worn out.'

'Did you talk to Pekka?' Mike O'Connell asked. 'Did he say anything about MacDuff and Mary?'

'Easy now, Mike,' MacDougall admonished. 'Our guests have nothing to do with the affair.'

'Oh, I have nothing against answering questions,' I said.

'Pekka came to Dragør in Denmark in his catamaran. We spent a pleasant evening together and talked about everything possible. But I don't think that he mentioned MacDuff. At that time, I had no idea that they were acquainted.'

'Was Pekka alone?' O'Connell wanted to know.

'I suppose so. In any case, I didn't see anyone else on board. But we sat mostly down in my cabin.'

MacDougall cleared his throat.

'I believe,' he said, 'that we owe our Scandinavian guests an explanation.'

'No,' O'Connell protested flatly.

'Why not tell them?' Margret wondered. 'It's common knowledge already in Oban. And scarcely something that needs to be kept secret.'

She took over the role of story-teller from MacDougall.

'Mary,' she explained, 'had been MacDuff's woman for many years. One day, she suddenly disappeared. Nobody knew where she was, and we all believed that something serious must have happened to her. MacDuff was in despair, but, if I may say so, not always in the way that could be expected. For example, he didn't join in the search for her. Though he knows the waters around like the back of his hand! It wasn't at all like him. Particularly as I am certain that Mary didn't leave him of her own accord. I'm quite sure she didn't, because I talked to her the day before she disappeared. But then one day MacDuff came and said that he had found her, and that Pekka, the Finn, had kidnapped her. We had met Pekka, and it's true that he seemed a bit mad, he wasn't my type in any case, but all the same it did seem unlikely that he had kidnapped Mary. Well, MacDuff took his boat and followed Pekka. It wasn't hard for MacDuff, with his contacts at sea and in all the ports, to trace them. He wouldn't have anything to do with the police. He said that the police would never believe that Mary had been forced to leave with Pekka against her will. And he was certainly right about that. I didn't know myself what to think. Three days later MacDuff came back. And now nobody could doubt that he was desperate. He had caught up with them, he said. But too late. Pekka had sailed into Pentland Firth, wind against tide, in a full gale. He hadn't a chance. Neither he nor Mary. Later, MacDuff declared that Pekka's body was washed ashore on one of the Orkney Islands and that Mary's was never found.'

Margret was silent.

'So you see,' she then said, 'it came as a surprise to us when we heard that Pekka is alive. And that his catamaran is still afloat.'

I glanced at Torben. Ought we to reveal that Pekka should be spoken of in the past tense. Something in Torben's expression made it clear to me that it would be best to say no more.

'Are you quite sure there wasn't a woman on board?' MacDougall asked Torben.

'I know nothing,' said Torben. 'Ulf was alone when he met Pekka.'

'I was aboard Pekka's boat for at least ten minutes,' I said. 'And I saw no woman.'

'I knew Mary well,' Margret said.

'And MacDuff?' O'Connell broke in. 'What did he do?'

'Do? I don't know. We happened to meet on a ferry between Malmö and Copenhagen. And then we passed the evening together on board my boat.'

I described our strange crossing as the only two passengers, and gave something of our conversation in *Rustica*'s cabin.

'But now,' I concluded, 'when I've heard what you say, I realise that he might have been looking for Pekka. He did question me a bit about people who sailed in the winter. Perhaps he'd learned that Pekka could have survived. How should I know?'

'Dick must hear about this,' O'Connell said, half to himself but threateningly.

Our eyes met briefly, but it was as if he looked through me. All of a sudden, Torben and I seemed to have become of minor importance. If O'Connell had believed that Pekka and Mary were dead, but now discovered that they might be alive, the object of his evident wrath could be only one person: MacDuff. But that didn't fit the situation. For Mary had said that Pekka's severed head was the proof. Had MacDuff after all been incautious enough to lie about Pekka's death? In such case, I could unintentionally have revealed that Mary might be alive and done precisely what MacDuff had threatened to kill us for.

'As you will understand,' Margret said, 'it's something of a shock for us to hear that Pekka survived Pentland Firth. Then Mary too may still be alive.'

This came casually, too casually for it to sound quite natural. Not that naturalness was a reliable criterion, for in this game there seemed to be no natural rules at all.

'This is a rather sad story, I am afraid,' MacDougall said to Torben and me.

He turned to the others.

'Perhaps we should shelve the matter now for the sake of our guests, who can scarcely be interested in our local love-affairs. How would it be if we helped them with good advice and some suggestions about the waters in the area?'

But no one showed real interest in this, not even Tim and Margret, who otherwise seemed to be full of good will.

'I'll go and find Dick,' said O'Connell.

MacDougall's eyes followed him as he left. He was evidently displeased; whether because of Dick's inhospitable behaviour or for some other reason I could not know.

'I'd gladly be of help,' said Tim, 'But I am afraid I must

239

get back to Oban now. Can you come and see me at home tomorrow instead? And bring your charts ... Bill, would you sail me back over before it gets too late?'

'Certainly. Whenever you wish.'

'Then I'll come with you,' Margret said. 'The launch can't take us all, in any case.'

MacDougall looked from Tim to Margret.

'Very well. I'll stay here and take care of our guests until you get back, Bill.'

'It may take a bit longer than usual,' Bill observed. 'The wind has freshened and veered. So it will be against us on the way back.'

'Yes, yes,' said MacDougall, 'You must take the time that's needed.'

Bill, Tim and Margret hastened away without taking leave of us.

'South-west now!' Bill called back as the wind swept into the room before he closed it with his shoulder.

The wind was indeed more southerly. At our arrival, the door had been on the lee side. It struck me that there must be another way out. For there had been no draught when O'Connell left.

'Well, well,' said MacDougall. 'I am sorry they couldn't stay longer. They ought to have stayed. To think that the story about MacDuff should crop up again! I am sorry that you should have been subjected to it. The affair has been gone over and over, backwards and forwards, without anyone made the wiser. MacDuff is an excellent person. Why not leave him in peace? We can all make a mistake.'

'What was MacDuff's mistake?' said Torben. 'If you don't mind my asking.'

'Falling in love with the wrong woman,' MacDougall answered. 'Not very original, I'm afraid. Who hasn't made that mistake?'

'Wrong woman?' said Torben, feigning disinterest, as if he were asking only to be polite. 'In what way?'

'She was too mystical, too enigmatic. Or at least, she chose to give the impression of being like that. I don't know if she really was. She liked to talk about old Celtic rites and ceremonies as if they provided solutions to all our problems. I've heard that she belonged to some sort of druidistic society. One wouldn't believe that such groups exist in our day, but as a matter of fact they do.'

'And of course MacDuff is altogether the opposite to mystical and enigmatic?' Torben asked.

'Not in everything, perhaps. Is anybody? But he is not enigmatic. He is straightforward and sincere. He has, it's true, a number of political opinions one may not necessarily be in accord with. But above all he is an excellent fellow.'

Although MacDougall seemed to wish us well, I'd have liked to be left alone with Torben for a few minutes, so that I could tell him about my glimpse of Dick in the gallery. But it is no easy matter for a properly invited guest to dispose courteously of a benign host. Torben extracted me from the predicament.

'Didn't I hear that Dick, wasn't that his name, has a shipyard on Ardentraive Bay, where our boat is lying?' he asked MacDougall.

'Yes, quite so. He does a lot of repairs for fishermen in the neighbourhood.'

'Then I suppose he must have a dinghy?'

'I'm sure he has. Why do you ask?'

'Well,' said Torben, 'I thought that perhaps we might get him to row us out to *Rustica*. Then Bill wouldn't have to bother sailing into the bay and could go directly to Oban.'

'It's no bother. Absolutely none.'

But I saw that he would like to return to Oban as quickly as possible. I sensed again that Torben and I had become mere pawns in the game being played round about us and of which we understood nothing. We were not intentionally being left behind. Simply, it didn't seem to matter as much any longer what Torben and me thought or did. Not since the instant when O'Connell and perhaps also Dick, had heard that Pekka, and possibly Mary as well, were still alive. And it was all my fault.

'I am convinced that Bill would sail us to the end of the world if we asked him to,' Torben said. 'The helpfulness of the Scots has no limits, we know that well.'

MacDougall brightened up.

'The thing is,' Torben continued, 'that it would be an experience for us to walk round an island like Kerrera in a gale on a February night. To appreciate the fury of the sea, you should see it from land. It's a bit more difficult in a boat that may sink at any moment.'

'I understand,' MacDougall politely told him.

'If you will excuse me,' Torben replied, 'I am not certain that you do. For people like you and Ulf, it means nothing to have land under your feet.'

We got into a rather too long discussion about the differences between landlubbers and sea-lovers. After that, it was decided that we would wait until Bill returned before we walked across the island to the bay.

'If you don't get hold of Dick,' said MacDougall, 'you can always come back here and sleep on the sofas.'

He showed us where we could find the key.

After that, MacDougall took some charts and pointed out some excellent anchorages which were not to be found in the Clyde Cruising Association's handbook, the sailing bible of all who cruise on the west coast of Scotland. He placed a finger, finally, just west of the sound between two islands, Jura and Scarba. And I knew what was coming.

'This is the Gulf of Corryvreckan. Shun it like the plague! If hell has a special department for dead seamen, I'm certain it looks exactly like Corryvreckan. When there's a hard west wind, such as the one blowing this evening, no sane man would try to sail through the sound.'

'I've read about the place,' I said. 'But I have also seen somewhere that there should be an anchorage right inside the sound.'

'I know there are people who say that. I have even met a man who once anchored there for a night. But in my opinion it's a death trap. If the wind shifts, you must leave at once. And where are you to go? That's the question. Out into Corryvreckan?'

His words were emphasised by the howl of the wind outside. It blew still harder now, presumably at storm force. Nevertheless, a kind of peace prevailed in the castle. Its stone walls, two feet thick, mitigated the clamour.

'I suppose that I had better go down to the inlet,' MacDougall said. 'So Bill won't have to anchor. With a southwester like this, the sea can be unpleasantly rough even in the bay.'

He prepared to leave. His immaculate attire disappeared under orange coloured oilskins.

'Well, I hope you have had a worth-while evening,' he said at the door. 'In spite of everything.'

'Very much so,' Torben replied.

'I wouldn't want to give advice to experienced North Sea sailors like you, but even so I would ask you to be careful'

'About anything especially?'

Did MacDougall hesitate?

'No,' he said after a moment. 'Nothing special. But the terrain is difficult, and you don't always know what lies hidden behind a jutting cliff.'

He left us. And as he went out, the room was filled again with icy air. I thought of *Rustica*'s cosy cabin, where the Reflex heater diffused its warmth and the paraffin-lamps their gentle and yellowish glow.

But one glance at Torben convinced me that he did not consider for a second lying in a comfortable bunk, reading an enjoyable book and listening to the wind howling in the rigging.

'Well, what do you think?' I asked him.

'I don't know what to think. I can't make head or tail of anything. Not any longer. As soon as I believe I know something, somebody or something changes everything. We'd be wiser to look round here, instead of trying to form hypotheses and find explanations which will be just as short lived as the last ones.'

'Do you think MacDougall wanted to warn us against being nosy?'

'Perhaps,' said Torben. 'But as far as that is concerned, we know more or less what's involved.'

'There is something you aren't aware of.'

I told him that I thought I had recognised Dick.

'So much the better!'

Torben rubbed his hands together. I didn't at all feel as reassured or expectant.

'What do you mean?' I asked.

'We have been given a stay of execution. Not a bad idea on your part to mention Pekka. He and his catamaran must have aroused a lot of attention when he came here. But what interested O'Connell most was Mary and the possibility that she may still be alive. It would be nice to know why she is so important. Why must MacDuff keep her hidden? Or keep her prisoner? Perhaps she meant it literally when she said that she should die. Can she have been condemned to death for treason, exactly like Pekka? At all events, MacDuff hasn't been able to present proof of her death, that's quite certain. But, in view of what MacDougall indicated about her interest in Celtic rites and ceremonies, why exactly should she have been condemned to death? If only I could work out a neat hypothesis where everything falls into place!'

'At least we know one thing now,' I said. 'O'Connell and Dick are out after MacDuff because of me. We ought to warn him.'

'Ought to?'

There was, I thought, a hint of irony in Torben's voice, and it surprised me.

'Yes,' I told him. 'In spite of everything, MacDuff has already compromised himself. First with Mary, then with us. His threat held only if we revealed that Mary is alive. We haven't done that. But we have sowed suspicions.'

'Do you really believe that MacDuff cares a damn about such delicate differences? I thought we were supposed to give him a very wide berth.'

'Only as long as he thought we were endangering Mary.'

'Why should he suddenly change his opinion about us now?' Torben inquired.

'If we warn him against Dick and O'Connell, he must understand that we don't want to do him and Mary any harm.'

'Perhaps,' Torben said after a silence. 'But what's the good of it if he does understand? Have you changed your attitude towards MacDuff? Or just possibly to Mary?'

Was he being ironical again?

'No,' I told him, 'I have not changed my mind. But in the first place, I don't want MacDuff and Mary to be decapitated because of us. And in the second, we might at last get to know what the whole thing is about. Who else would possibly tell us?'

I didn't say what I really thought. What would we do with the knowledge we hoped to gain? Did we wish to be acclaimed as heroes who had exposed a giant conspiracy? Were we to sell the whole story to some newspaper or other for a sum on which we could live happily until the end of our days? Torben's motive was certain: simply to learn more, to increase his knowledge. But for me that was no longer sufficient, not if the stakes were ours or somebody else's lives.

'Well,' said Torben, 'I can't stop you from trying to find MacDuff. Even if it must be a case of looking for a needle in a haystack. MacDuff can be anywhere at all. But just now we are here, and I think we ought to have a look.'

We started by examining the premises, but we found nothing there. All the drawers and cupboards were completely empty; we came upon no files, no papers at all, nothing beyond the actual furnishings; it seemed that only what was needed for the dinner party had been brought to the club.

'There must be a door here somewhere,' I said. 'Dick can't have disappeared through the wall after all.'

'Or down a trap-door?' Torben wondered.

He was standing in a recess of a wall, and he looked down at the floor.

'Here it is!' he said. 'The question is only how to open the thing. Presumably we must whisper a password into a hidden microphone. That would seem to be their style.'

'Or just knock,' I suggested. 'That worked last time, didn't it? But you know, we can't be sure that Dick and O'Connell are down at the boatyard. They might as well be sitting in a dungeon here, each with his sub-machine gun. That also appears to be their style.'

'I hardly think so,' Torben said looking around everywhere for some means of opening the trap-door. 'They aren't interested in us. Not just now.' Finally, he gave up. 'We'll have to look from outside. There must be another entrance.'

'How could we find it?' I wanted to know. 'We haven't even got a torch. It's pitch dark outside.'

'Hang it all, Ulf!' Torben abruptly burst out. 'We have to try! We must find out sometime what we want to know. Pull yourself together!'

I did try, and it was I who led the way out of the castle. It was nice to be out in the fresh air again, but the wind was so strong that we had to turn our faces away to get our breath. Strange as it may sound, it is physically difficult to breathe in storm force winds. We walked bent forward to keep our balance. I stumbled a number of times and nearly fell. Then, the wind blew me over backwards when I was trying to get a new foothold. I managed to break the fall with my hands, but I hit the back of my head on something hard. Although I felt a little blood trickling down, I felt no pain. And even if I was already stiff with the cold, I forced myself on towards the next cliff-wall, where I was sheltered from the wind. For a time I heard nothing but the wind and my own panting.

Suddenly I heard the sound of a cry. I turned round. Torben was no longer behind me.

Chapter 20

CAUTIOUSLY, I groped my way back along the same path that I thought we had taken. The going was slow. At times I crept on all fours. If Torben had fallen down into a crevice, I might fall there too. I called several times without any reply. Time passed. I had to find him. If he was lying unconscious or with a broken leg, he would freeze to death. But what would I do if I found him injured? I would have to get help? But how? I was no longer sure even of the direction to the castle. And I had no idea how far we had come from it. I realised with dread that I might have to go to Dick's boatyard and ask for help. And then he would know that we had been out prowling again. But was there any other recourse?

I called once more and listened. No reply. Suddenly, I heard a voice that seemed to come from a place beneath me.

'Don't move!'

I stopped where I was and felt cold sweat breaking out. Resignedly, I waited for the muzzle of a pistol to be pushed against my back. Instead, I heard the hollow voice again.

'In other words, stand still!'

It was Torben.

'If you take two more steps,' he went on, 'you'll fall into

the hole where I am. And it hurts, believe me! Not so bad
when you get down here, though. There's hardly any wind. I
am standing on a narrow pathway. Or seem to be.'

'But where are you?' I asked out into the darkness.

'Just lie down flat on your stomach and feel about with
your hands. Carefully now!'

I obeyed. Only a few inches from me, the path was edged
by empty air.

'It's a cleft in the cliff,' said Torben. 'Down here it's
only about two feet wide. I don't know how it looks higher up.
But it can't be more than eight or nine feet deep. Otherwise,
I'd have been killed. I'm not exactly the Rambo-type. Now, if
you just slide yourself over the edge, legs first, I'll hold on to
you!'

Slowly, I let my legs glide out into empty space. At the
instant when gravity took over, I felt his hands beneath my
feet. Next, we stood beside each other.

'Do you have a cigarette?' he asked.

I had. And I needed one quite as much as Torben. It took
time to recover from the shock and breathe normally again.
My lighter revealed that the crevice was much as he had
supposed. It was surprising that he could have survived his fall
with nothing worse than blue marks, a small cut on his leg and
an awful fright.

'How did you know where I was?' I wondered. 'So that
you could warn me in time.'

'I didn't know. I hoped that you'd call. And when it
sounded as if you were near enough, I told you to stop.'

'Couldn't you have said it a little less dramatically? I
thought that it must be Dick or O'Connell far too close.'

'Exactly what I wanted. It was the only way of making
sure that you wouldn't take a single step in any direction. It
worked, didn't it?'

He was pleased. But I couldn't help feeling a bit cheated.

I was the one who should have rescued him, not the other way around.

'Left or right?' I asked, wanting to move on.

We went to the right. We felt our way to start with and bumped into the walls of the cliff. Then the cleft opened and the wind found us again. The crash of breakers against the cliffs became louder and louder. We were evidently drawing close to the southwest coast of Kerrera. In the end, the thundering was so great that we had to stand close together in order to hear each other speak. By then, we were in front of a small inlet, scarcely ten yards wide, with steep sides. Outside the entrance, we could make out the shape of a tiny island, where the waves were breaking into foam that glittered with sea-fire. The flat little islet sheltered the inlet from the worst of the waves so that only the remnants of the swell pulsated lightly where we were. It was a perfectly discreet landing place. No one could suspect that it might be possible to moor on that exposed side of Kerrera. When we came closer, we discovered that iron rings had been driven into the rock, and that a wide ledge of the cliff served as a quay.

'Well worked out,' I remarked to Torben. 'Who would ever think of putting in here?'

He nodded agreement, but I knew that he didn't fully understand what I had in mind. He couldn't appreciate either the advantages of the place or the skill required to take a boat past the islet and the Kerrera cliffs into the inlet in a rough sea. MacDuff could bring it off, to be sure, but how many others? I pictured him, standing at the helm and heading straight for Kerrera on a course that would bring him very close to port of the tiny isle. I saw him wait for the crest of just the right wave on which to make full speed ahead and then, after the islet, how he turned hard to starboard before the breaking wave hit the cliffs. It was the same manoeuvre I had made in Neptune's Staircase, only executed in cold blood.

We turned back. Walking was easier now as the darkness was less dense. We could see the outlines of the sharp and jagged cliffs. Was the wind abating? Just as with the dawn at sea, that's something one never knows with certainty until the moment when there no longer remains any doubt. In a strong wind, there is a period of transition, filled with hope and continued strain, when the strongest gusts seem to recur a little less often, when the wind's steely grip no longer makes the rigging shriek quite as piercingly as before, when the mast doesn't shake quite as rapidly, when the leech of the sail doesn't seem to flog quite so violently.

To our right, I glimpsed a gigantic block of stone that rested on a formless collection of much smaller and more irregularly shaped stones. A black spot, which I assumed to be some kind of hole, caught my eye. When I went closer, with Torben behind, I saw that the huge block constituted the roof of a grotto. The opening passed from sight as we came close, but reappeared after we had clambered over a number of rocks. We went in. I lit my cigarette lighter.

I wouldn't say that I felt surprise at what we saw. Along one side of the grotto, covered by a tarpaulin, wooden crates were piled on top of one another. The place stank of fish, and fish was what the crates contained, beneath a layer of crushed ice which didn't melt in the cold air. We lifted down a number of crates, but they all seemed to be filled with fish. I thrust a hand down through the ice and the cod, and came only half way. We removed some of the ice and the cod and, with some difficulty, the covering below.

We are no experts about weapons, Torben and I, but there couldn't be the least doubt that what we found was ammunition. We looked at each other in the flickering light - and abruptly we were both in a great hurry to get everything back as we had found it. Someone could arrive at any moment. We were not alone on Kerrera.

'We must get away from here,' I told Torben, as soon as we had climbed out.

'I want to see where the path leads in the other direction.'

'Are you out of your mind? If somebody is coming it will be from there.'

'All right then, we'll follow it from the path above. Anybody coming will have a torch. And we'll just keep quiet if somebody goes by.'

We hadn't got very far when we saw the ray of a torch directed back and forth, sometimes on the ground, sometimes on the side of the cliff. The wind *had* fallen since I could catch the murmur of two voices. We crept in behind a large stone and some bushes. This was by no means an ideal hiding place. If the person with a torch happened to direct it back towards us after passing the stone, we would have no chance of remaining invisible. The only advantage was that we could see out towards the sea if something should happen.

The ray of light and the voices drew closer. But instead of passing on by, two men stopped only a few yards in front of us and looked out to sea.

'Well, what's your guess?' asked one of them.

I recognised O'Connell's voice. 'Will he come?'

'He has always been punctual,' replied the other man, whom I took to be Dick. 'But with this wind, putting in can certainly be dangerous. Not that it's ever easy, at least for anybody except him. But I wonder if even MacDuff won't have to give up tonight.'

'Well in any case, he's one hell of a fellow.'

There was admiration in O'Connell's voice.

'Aren't we all?' said the other voice. 'What I can't understand is that he should let us down now. What's he thinking of? He must know what the outcome will be. Just as well as we do.'

'But we don't know yet whether he has failed us.'

O'Connell objected. 'He did what he should with that Finn. No question about it.'

'And Mary?' asked Dick. 'It's a pity those two Swedes didn't see her alive. If they had, we'd be certain. MacDuff is too weak. If you think that Mary would jump into the water and drown herself before his eyes, you are mistaken.'

'No, I don't think that.' O'Connell said quickly. 'Not of her. But we don't know yet. There may have been an accident. The Pentland Firth is no picnic. We must be sure before we can do anything.'

'We'll find out all right. Just as soon as he gets here.'

The two were silent. I was listening intensely, as much for any sounds from us as from them. But I couldn't even hear Torben's breathing.

'And the other ones?' asked O'Connell. 'What do we do with them?'

'A damned shame that the bridge master at Corpach thought so quickly. Worse for them actually. Next time it will have to be a more direct method.'

'It's convenient that they parked directly under our windows.'

'Not at all,' said Dick. 'It shows they knew exactly where to go. Which in fact shows how stupid they are. Otherwise, they'd have been cannier. No need to be in a hurry about them in any case. Not as long as we have them under our noses.'

'When ...' O'Connell began, but he didn't have time to finish.

We saw the single flash of a strong light out at sea. Then three short ones.

'So he's not coming,' commented Dick. 'Not now. We'll have to wait till tomorrow night.'

'And the fish?' O'Connell asked.

'It'll have to stay where it is. And you will have to stay and see that nobody gets near it. You know the stakes.'

'You don't need to tell me,' O'Connell sourly replied.

A second torch was lit, and he went off in the direction of the grotto, some fifty yards away. Dick remained where he was until the Irishman had got there. Then he went back in the opposite direction. Only when the beam of his torch had entirely disappeared did we at last dare move again.

Torben rubbed his legs to get some blood into them.

'Did you really have to sit on me?' he complained in a vehement whisper.

Now, both creeping and walking, we got ourselves up over the first summit above the cliff. I seemed to be covered with two kinds of perspiration: good old fashioned sweat and clammy cold sweat. I had never been through anything like this. Torben appeared to have been less alarmed. On land, he was always more courageous than I was.

'Do you really want to investigate where that crevice leads in the other direction?' I asked.

'I would, but I suppose it would be wiser not to. Not now.'

'Is that all you have to say?'

'Yes,' Torben replied. 'Except that probably it would be best to move *Rustica*. Playing follow my leader with that gang requires some precautions and preparations.'

'How do we get out to *Rustica* to start with?' I asked.

'We'll steal one of Dick's dinghies and set it adrift afterwards.'

'And when he wakes up we and the dinghy will be gone,' I objected. 'Dick's conclusion: those two have spent the night on Kerrera. Not a very well conceived idea, I am afraid.'

'No,' Torben admitted. 'Well ... We'll steal the dinghy but return it with the help of *Sussi*.'

'That will mean three trips across the bay, just under their noses, as Dick said. And they may not be asleep.'

'It's dark.'

'Not dark enough. And we have to think of the light from Oban on that side of Kerrera.'

'Have you a better suggestion?' Torben demanded.

'Yes,' I said. 'We'll knock, wake up Dick if necessary, and ask to borrow the dinghy. Then at least we won't run the risk of being caught red-handed. Also, MacDougall will attest that it was our intention to do just that, which gives us an alibi.'

'But now we have no alibi for several hours, have you forgotten that? Perhaps Dick will ask MacDougall at what time he left us.'

'We'll say that we stayed in the club room and waited for the weather to improve.'

'Your story isn't more credible than mine. If we are caught in the act we'll say that we didn't want to wake him up in the middle of the night. And we thought he wouldn't mind if we borrowed his nice little dinghy. Actually it makes no difference at all what we say. We are too suspect in his eyes. You heard what he said. We know too much. But apparently not enough, although it's beginning to seem that we know more than enough.'

'Even for your taste?'

He didn't answer.

'At the point we've got to,' I added, 'we may just as well steal the dinghy and let it drift off. Or, even better, sink it.'

'Now that's a good idea,' said Torben. 'An eye for an eye, and a boat for a boat.'

We were getting closer to Ardentraive Bay, providing that my dead reckoning, using the lighthouse at the entry to Oban Bay as a mark, was correct. So as not to risk meeting anyone, we walked along the shore on the west coast of Kerrera. We assumed that Dick would take the shortest way back to his boatyard. It wasn't very likely that there would be more than one smugglers' cove on the island. At the same time, I began to realise that it was still blowing force seven, even if the wind had abated somewhat, that I had no idea about the tides around Kerrera, that it would be some hours before daylight and that we wouldn't get a wink of sleep. And where should we sail to?

In low voices we tried to work out the implication of what we had heard. That Dick and O'Connell had some connection with the Celtic Ring seemed obvious. We knew, which was more than those two did, that Mary was alive and that MacDuff was playing a perilous game. Also that Pekka had to die because of Mary. Did the same end now await MacDuff? It might be only a matter of coincidence. At first I didn't dare formulate the thought, but then I could no longer ignore the possibility that it might well be Mary's task, her mission, to bring about the downfall of Pekka and MacDuff.

Finally, we came to the ammunition we had found. And the weapons naively transported to Ireland by Pekka. Of course the immediate supposition was that they were destined for the IRA. On the other hand, MacDuff's logbook had not mentioned ports in Northern Ireland more often than ports elsewhere.

Then I recalled a name that had reappeared several times in the logbook, without comment or simply with the word 'waited'. Could the place be MacDuff's own retreat? If so, that was surely the place where MacDuff would be tonight. The name was 'Bagh Gleann nam Muc'. Why I happened to remember that name among all the others is difficult to understand. But the fact that it is now engraved in my memory is easier to explain. Bagh Gleann nam Muc changed everything.

When we arrived at the top of Kerrera and looked down on Ardentraive Bay, in the lee behind the cliffs, all was peace and quiet in the shelter from the wind. *Rustica* lay motionless on what looked like calm water. Not a gleam of light could be seen from the boatyard, but it was unlikely that Dick wanted everyone to know that he was up and about at night. We slipped down to the shore and followed it until we came to the pier. Dick's dinghy had been drawn up on land because of the tide, but on our side of the pier, hidden from Dick's sight. The oars lay in it. For someone who worried about theft, Dick seemed to be imprudence itself. We carried the dinghy to the water. I took off my socks and wrapped them around the oars in the rowlocks. Torben watched this operation with surprise.

'What are you staring at?' I asked him. 'When for once I have a chance of turning what I learned in the Hornblower books to practical advantage, shouldn't I do it? This is how they always silenced their oars.'

Torben shook his head, but in actual fact the oars were soundless. Torben climbed first aboard *Rustica*. Then he stood on deck, took the oars and held on to me while I placed my feet on the side of the dinghy. Water soon filled the boat and it quickly sank being built of solid plastic. With Torben's help, I drew myself up on deck with some difficulty.

We felt something like surprise that no one had been on board in our absence. Everything seemed to be just as we had left it.

I had already decided to make an attempt at finding MacDuff. True, there was no reason why I should reproach myself. I hadn't revealed that Mary was still alive. But I couldn't escape from the thought that I had gained a reprieve for Torben and myself at MacDuff's expense. Torben said nothing. He knew that he couldn't take any responsibility for our safety when we were out at sea. So he let me make the decision. I took out the chart and looked for Bagh Gleann nam Muc. It didn't take me long to find it. Precisely as I had suspected and feared, it was the only anchorage right within the Gulf of Corryvreckan.

Where else could MacDuff feel safe and secure? None

but he would dare to go there in bad weather. Nobody else, I thought, except me, Torben and *Rustica*. I looked up Corryvreckan in the Clyde Cruising Association's sailing descriptions for the west coast. I still recall one sentence although I haven't looked at it since: 'Corryvreckan is at its most dangerous when a heavy swell from the Atlantic, built up by several days of strong westerly winds, meets the flood stream. A passage at such time would be unthinkable.'

'What do you say?' I asked Torben. 'Shall we leave?'

'Certainly. Whenever you like.'

He tried to sound cheerful, but despondency showed through. I at least thought I knew what we were in for. He only thought that we were running away, no matter where we went.

Chapter 21

WE put out under sail in order to make our departure as discreet as possible. A storm jib and two reefs in the mainsail seemed about right for the weather. As soon as we had rounded Rubh a Bhearnaig, Kerrera's northern extremity, we observed that this was not too little. The sea out in the Firth of Lorn, between Mull and the mainland, was both rough and choppy, and it was made worse by the favourable tide running against the wind. Wind over tide is among the worst things a sailor knows. The stream deepens the troughs of waves and raises the crests, so that the waves build up and finally break, as if the boat lay constantly in a surf close to the shore. There are tables where you can see that it doesn't take very much wind and tide to double or treble the size of the waves.

The Firth of Lorn is entirely open to the southwest, and we had to make short and wet tacks between Kerrera and the mainland. *Rustica* suffered, but not even here did she stamp or slam when she hit the waves that crashed down upon us. With some slack in the sheets, her weight and sharp entry made her cut her way smoothly and with dignity through the waves.

Perhaps it was worst for Torben. He was at the helm during most of the dark hours since I had to navigate. There was little to go after, but a good deal to try to keep track of, what with the tidal stream, and the leeway because of the wind. The only marks were the lighthouse at the southeast point of Mull, on Duart Point, the south cardinal buoy at Bogha Nuadh, and the lighthouses at the entry to the Sound of Luing. However, the water was deep nearly everywhere, except for a spot just north of the island called Insh, where there were two nasty sunken rocks. It was not difficult to imagine how these looked. And, in fact, we used them as navigation marks. The breaking white surf feebly lighted by sea-fire, was the only means of telling where the water ended and land began.

We had a sail of approximately fifteen nautical miles to Corryvreckan: normally about three hours' sailing time. I counted on the stream and the leeway cancelling each other out, but when I looked in the tide tables I found that we had only two hours of fair tide. This meant that we would have easterly current in Corryvreckan, which is to say wind with tide. That was at least one positive thing. We didn't have to consider from which direction we ought to enter Corryvreckan. It was quite simple, we had no choice but to continue on through the Firth of Lorn and past the Isles of the Sea, the Garvellachs as they were called in Gaelic, where Pekka had seen a fire and saved Mary. But to put in there now, in such weather, was of course out of the question.

After two hours the tide turned, and during the hour or so of slack, we had only wind and waves to struggle with. This was strenuous enough, but the worst came when the stream set against us. It was then five o'clock in the morning, and at about the same time we caught the first flashes from the lighthouse on Eileach an Naomih, the southern most island of the Garvellachs. My bearings on the lighthouse revealed how little progress we were making; the change in angle was scarcely measurable. We appeared to be standing still. But, for once, this didn't make me feel frustrated.

Tacking in a strong wind, against the stream, close to land, is one of the most unrewarding activities at sea. The slowness of the boat's advance is confirmed at every second. Out at sea, when you have no fixed mark on land to judge by, the knowledge that you barely advance is too abstract really to matter. But perhaps I am alone in disavowing that kind of theoretical knowledge, especially when water rushes past the hull and cascades of it splash on deck. Everything indicates that you are making tremendous speed through the water. That my reason tells me the opposite doesn't affect my impressions, at least not at sea.

Needless to say, all this is afterthought. There and then, when dawn came and tore asunder the cocoon of night two miles south of Eileach an Naomih, I wasn't thinking at all and merely experienced dread. I believed that I knew already what would be revealed by the washed out light of dawn, but the reality exceeded my worst apprehensions. It is said that fear of unknown dangers is greater than fear of known ones, but this is not so when night dissolves into dawn at sea. The waves I saw were very high, just how high it is difficult to say, but when the sun had come up far enough to be seen at times as a shadowed circle behind clouds on the horizon, the entire disk vanished from view when we plunged down into the trough of a wave. Tattered strips of foam ran in lines along the waves, a sign that the wind was again approaching gale force. *Rustica* heeled constantly over to her guard-rail, and water poured across the deck. But we were still sailing, and I had no thought of turning back as long as we made headway. It was bitingly cold, and I realised that I would have to take over the helm until we reached our destination; Torben had been splendid, but he looked tired, and the worst lay before us.

We heard it already. Through the howling of the wind, the flapping of sails and the hissing of breaking waves, there came a dull, powerful and shrieking rumble, like that of continuing thunder after lightning that strikes close by. It was the roaring thunder from Corryvreckan's constantly shattered and renewed wall of water, which was said to be heard tens of miles away. It was a wall, and I realised already then that we would never be able to sail over it, but that we must prepare ourselves to sail *through* it.

Before taking over from Torben, I sat at the navigation table and imprinted our route in my mind. Once inside the channel of Corryvreckan, the boat would have to be hermetically sealed. I hesitated a long time about the best route, if there was one, but finally I decided to stay well out in the Firth of Lorn, to go round the worst races marked on the chart, then steer straight in under land along the coast of Jura and slip into the bay on the north side of the island. Meanwhile, I'd better not flirt too impertinently with the cliffs when the sea was so rough.

There was also supposed to be a weak counter current close to land. Somebody had claimed that it was possible to sail through Corryvreckan against the tide by following the shore 'at a boat hook's distance'. But the risk for us was rather to run into the counter current if we sailed too near land with wind over tide as a result. So no genuine alternatives were offered. If we wished to reach the bay, we had to venture out into what the chart called 'The Great Race', with, in parenthesis, the telling commentary: 'dangerous tidal streams'.

Having determined our route, I put on my skin diving suit, retained since my days as a scuba diver for use in just such extreme circumstances. As it had quite of lot of in-built buoyancy, it relieved me from wearing a cumbersome life jacket. Also, a wet-suit is made to keep the wearer warm when wet, while oilskins try to accomplish the opposite: keeping the wearer warm by keeping him dry. But all sailors know that this is a hopeless task in certain situations.

Then I took out storm shutters, plates of stainless steel about one fifth of an inch thick, and put them over the portholes and the companionway. I closed the ventilators on deck completely, and finally I put on the harness over my skin diving suit. That being done, I felt less worried. Short of *Rustica* being broken up by waves or crushed against the cliffs, we should be able to survive practically anything.

In spite of his tiredness, which always gives you some relief and comfort in difficult conditions, I saw that Torben was anxious. While struggling with the helm, he observed my preparations.

'Will it get worse?' he asked.

I nodded. In order to be heard, we had to shout into each other's ears. Otherwise our words were lost in the roar of the waves or just blew away. Not even downwind, did our voices carry further than a couple of feet. I sat down opposite Torben in the cockpit, on the lee-side, and leaned forward to make sure that he caught what I said.

'Yes, it will probably be bloody awful. But only for a short time, half an hour at the most. Then we'll come into calm water. Go and lie down now. But you must be ready when I call. Either you come up with a lifeline, or you shut yourself in the cabin and stay there.'

'I'll come up.'

We drew swiftly closer to the cliffs of Jura, which were covered with foam and obscured by cascades of water many feet high. *Rustica* changed ahead. After the turn towards land, she had slack sheets; and with wind on the quarter, we were making eight knots on the log. We surfed several times down the steepest waves, and the log hit the limit, exactly as when we were approaching Fraserburgh. Now as then, we should have reduced sail to slow down. When you are going too fast, there is always a risk of sailing into the back of the wave in front, to be stopped and then pooped by the next high wave that comes tumbling down from astern. But it was no longer feasible to go on deck. Twice, the cockpit was filled by breaking waves, so that I sat with water up to my chest. In my wet suit, it didn't matter much, but I discovered a disadvantage that I could never have imagined beforehand. Its buoyancy made it difficult to stay put in the cockpit until the water had run out through the self-draining holes. I quite simply floated. Unfortunately, I was incapable of appreciating the comic element in my predicament as I struggled to reach down to the tiller.

Madness! I thought when this happened the second time. But by then we hadn't more than a mile left to Jura; ten minute's sailing at the most, before we had to ease out the sheet still further and then rush into the sound and the Great Race. How did the Great Race look? On the one hand, it cannot easily be described; on the other, I hadn't the time or the courage to take a closer look. All my attention was directed at staying on course and parrying waves that might throw *Rustica* sideways and overturn her. But I constantly heard the rumble and the thundering to port, and out of the corner of my eye I glimpsed giant formations of waves that seemed to be standing still with constantly breaking crests and vertical sides. The pilot-book's description of the Great Race as a long, vertical breaking wall of water was not an exaggeration.

Rustica's bow pointed now at the islet of Eilean Mor, just west of the entry to Bagh Gleann nam Muc. For a second or two I considered sailing between Eilean Mor and Jura. Then I recalled a symbol on the chart indicating another race and another for a sunken rock in the middle of the strait, which was no more than three hundred and fifty yards wide. So the only possible thing to do was to follow the original plan.

Some cable lengths' west of Eilean Mor, I slackened the sheet again, and I signalled to Torben that he should come up.

In order to have more light in the cabin on dark autumn and winter days, I had replaced the normal wooden hatches with thick Plexiglas. So normally the helmsman and the man off watch could keep an eye on each other when the entrance was closed. But with the steel storm shutters put in instead, sitting in the cabin must have been like being in a submarine or a diving bell.

When Torben came up, I told him to fasten himself with a short lifeline.

'Are you seasick?' I asked.

'No,' he said. 'Unfortunately not. Because then I wouldn't care where I was. And I care now.'

'And perhaps you think I don't?'

'No,' he said, but changed his mind as soon as he had looked into my face. 'Yes, but you chose this.'

'It will soon be over,' I answered lamely, unable to find anything better to say.

He turned away and looked to see where we were going. When he turned back again, his gaze was completely empty. I realised that at that very moment he did not believe we would survive. At the same time I knew how wrong I had been in my decision. I had decided to sail so that I might save two lives. What then if Torben and I should drown? But I didn't have time to finish the thought, or to think at all, only act. *Rustica* drove her bow into the first pillars of water and writhed with the pains from all the conflicting forces that pulled at her and tried to tear her to pieces. Whirlpools tried to throw her off her course and made her heavy on the helm. I held on to it with both hands, and at the same time I attempted to take a bearing by eye, using Eilean Mor, which already lay to port, as a fixed point. We should not come over too far to the north side. The stream set us towards the northeast, and there on the Scarba side a shoal produced a whirlpool. Once caught by this, no sailing boat could extract itself. We would stand still in the midst of it while waves unceasingly broke over us. But it was difficult to take bearings, or just to see anything at all. The foam, which whipped through the air like smoke, reduced visibility and made my eyes smart from salt. The roar was deafening.

Abruptly, without the least warning, sailing became a matter of survival. We went straight through a wall of water. I received a violent blow on the chest which threw me up on the little aft deck above the tiller. Only my lifeline saved me from being washed overboard. For some seconds, *Rustica*, Torben and I were under water. And before the fear came, a kind of peace fell in the midst of the maelstrom, merely because of the silence. But then came the need to breathe. At the next instant, I got air again, gasped for more, dragged myself down to the cockpit and caught hold of the tiller to get the boat back on course. Slowly, *Rustica* raised herself and shook off most of the water. Torben remained where he was, sheltered behind the cabin. Even if wet through, although sputtering to get air into his lungs, he was alive. But he hadn't yet been able to grasp that he was surrounded by air when enough water to fill two or three buckets came down on his head and drenched him anew. The water must have collected in the reefed folds of the mainsail, which meant that we'd had at least five feet of water over our heads.

Soon after it was all over. We had passed through the race between Eilean Mor and the other island at the entrance to the inlet, Eilean Beag. Now Eilean Beag lay a cable ahead, where it made a deterring face at us. I put the tiller over, turned hard to starboard, hauled in the sheet and let *Rustica* rush on into Bagh Gleann nam Muc.

Torben broke out in a strange laugh of exhilaration when he saw that we would make it. I too laughed, although I didn't feel the same joy of living just then. Knowing that death had not been far away could not make my life more worth living.

266

Rather the contrary. But we would soon be in calm water, and that alone counted. All else was insignificant. Even the fishing vessel with a wildly gesticulating MacDuff on her foredeck.

Chapter 22

I stared at the pistol beside him.

'You should be glad that you're still alive,' said MacDuff, when he followed my look. 'Because of Corryvreckan, I mean.'

'Oh, we are,' Torben told him. 'I have never been happier in all my life. You can put the shooting iron away. It might destroy our pleasure in being here.'

MacDuff showed no inclination to remove the pistol.

'You have lots of time,' Torben added.

'For what?' asked MacDuff.

'Until the wind drops to a mere caress, I won't leave this place of my own free will. So if you are thinking of shooting us, you can just as well wait till the blow is over. We won't disappear.'

Torben was becoming himself again. MacDuff looked at us with both suspicion and admiration. He pocketed the pistol as naturally as if it were a comb or a door-key.

'That was a first rate piece of work,' he said to me.

'I would call it stupid and rash,' Torben said. 'Or just say we were lucky.'

MacDuff almost smiled.

When we had come over to his boat in *Sussi* and asked if we might come aboard, MacDuff had a hard expression on his face that his civility didn't belie. He had taken us down into the cabin and asked us to sit down. As if by accident, the pistol had lain on the table, pointed at us. Casually, he had placed a hand on its butt. I had tried not to turn around and look about for Mary. My first words had been that I had something important to tell him. But he'd made it clear at once that this could wait. First Corryvreckan.

'That's nothing to be proud of,' Torben insisted. 'We could just as well have been on the bottom of the sea by now.'

'Yes,' replied MacDuff, 'quite easily. But you are not. It requires a great deal of a man to sail through Corryvreckan in this weather. You chose the right way nearly all the time. Your only mistake was to come in between Eilean Mor and Eilean Beag. It's worse there. It would have been better to go round Eilean Beag.'

'Then we would have been forced to tack into the inlet,' I objected.

'Yes,' he admitted, 'or motor. All means are permitted to survive in Corryvreckan. But if I may say so, Skipper, I didn't believe you'd come through. Or even dare to make a try.'

He stretched forward his rough hand and I took it without hesitation. I felt childishly proud and gave Torben a quick glance to see if he understood the significance of the praise I received. I had always admired pilots, and now what was probably one of Scotland's most skilful pilots had praised my seamanship. Although blushing is not my way, I may very well have done just that at that moment. But Torben appeared to notice nothing at all. He was far from being insensitive, but his attention was always sharply focused, and he could be wholly unaware of what lay outside it. Now his awareness was fully on himself and his pleasure simply in being alive. Under normal circumstances, he would not have allowed me to forget our real situation where MacDuff was concerned and why we had come. Foolishly, I let MacDuff take the initiative and ask questions which I was not at all prepared to answer.

'How did you know I was here?' he began.

I looked at Torben. And the look he gave me in return indicated that I would have to watch myself. I couldn't very well tell MacDuff that I had entered his wheelhouse and read the logbook there.

'We guessed,' I said.

Of course he didn't believe this.

'Try something else. Nobody has ever guessed right. Why should just you two do it? By the way, could I have my keys back? I've discovered that I ought to lock up a bit better. As a rule, it's not a matter you need worry about among seagoing people.'

His keys! I had totally forgotten them.

'Yes, certainly,' I answered automatically. 'I had no intention of keeping them.'

I still had them in a pocket, and I put them on the table.

'I can explain ...,' I began, but MacDuff broke me off.

'I'm not sure that I want an explanation. What would I do with it?'

Yet again, I cast a glance at Torben.

'When I let you leave Invergarry Castle,' MacDuff went on, 'I believed that I could trust you. Evidently I was mistaken.'

'Not entirely,' Torben at last intervened.

'What do you mean?' asked MacDuff.

'That you can trust *Rustica*'s skipper.'

'Is that so?' MacDuff said. 'In spite of the fact that he stole my keys.'

'I forgot the keys,' I protested, but neither of them paid any attention.

'Just because of that,' said Torben. 'If Ulf hadn't come

aboard your boat at Corpach, we would never have found you.'

'But I'd have found you,' MacDuff answered. 'Be sure of that!'

'Oh, we are. But then it would probably have been too late.'

'Too late?'

For the first time I sensed something like uncertainty or at least surprise in MacDuff. He had quickly put me at a loss. But Torben needed only to make a remark or two to open an emergency exit. Now he was leading the conversation. Unawares, MacDuff had begun to follow his line of thought.

'Too late?' MacDuff repeated. 'For what?'

Torben paused before answering.

'Too late to warn you against your cohorts O'Connell and Dick. They don't believe in you any longer.'

'What they believe is of no interest to me.'

'Not even if they think, or believe they know for certain, that Mary is alive, thanks to you.'

I waited for an explosion. But MacDuff's sole reaction was to clench his fist and the silence that followed.

'And to tell me that, you have risked your lives?' he finally said.

'It was Ulf's idea,' Torben answered. 'Not mine.'

'What do you want?' MacDuff demanded.

'In the first place we want to know why Pekka had to die,' I said quickly. 'Secondly, why we ourselves were evidently supposed to disappear from this world. Was it on your order that Dick tried to drown us in Neptune's Staircase?'

'Why do you ask? You know the answer already.'

'I want to hear it anyhow.'

'I let you go. That's answer enough.'

'And Pekka,' I said, 'did you let him go, too?'

MacDuff didn't reply.

'Are you afraid of the truth?' I asked.

'No,' he said at last. 'It's you who are afraid of hearing it.'

I was facing a person who, almost certainly and in cold blood, had taken the life of another human being. Oughtn't I to feel disgust or hatred? Unwillingly, I thought of what Mary had said. There were extenuating circumstances - just to think about that term sent shivers down my spine - in the form of simple sums. I kill one person so that two may live. Minus one plus two equals plus one. But two people are alive. I refrain from killing one, so that two or even three people die. Minus three. Yes, it was incontestably the case. But you can't count human lives. It's absurd; it must be absurd. Because you don't count with those who die. One dead is enough to make the sum negative. Perhaps MacDuff was right; I feared the truth because I didn't know what I should do with it.

'Why was Mary to die?' I ventured awkwardly, but realised how empty it sounded. 'And why were you to die if Mary and Pekka were allowed to live?'

'How do you know about that?'

He looked genuinely surprised, but he showed no sign of agitation. He evidently regarded the threat hanging over his life as a circumstance among other circumstances; it was something he had accepted and learned to live with.

'Mary told me.'

He knew I wasn't lying.

'Did she say anything more?'

MacDuff looked almost amused.

'She pretended that you saved her life each day.'

'Actually I do,' he replied calmly.

'But that she must die all the same.'

'It's possible. But not as long as I live.'

'That is in a way what we came here to talk with you about,' Torben began.

Abruptly, MacDuff began to laugh.

'You don't mean that you sailed through Corryvreckan in order to discuss my chances of survival?'

'I don't think that you have quite understood,' Torben went on unperturbed. 'Ulf has risked not only his own life but mine as well to tell you that you are running certain risks. For instance, it would be unwise of you to sail to Kerrera and load ammunition tonight.'

MacDuff's smile vanished.

'You know too much. I didn't believe that.'

'I'm afraid that you still don't understand what I am saying,' Torben said, as if he hadn't heard. 'We risked our two valuable lives to save yours and Mary's. We were lucky, or skilful, if you wish, it doesn't much matter. Just now the figure stands at plus four. If we'd gone under in the sound, the equation might have worked out even, but probably two lives would have been lost, one of them being yours.'

I looked at Torben. Sometimes it was as if my own thoughts echoed in his head. But, like MacDuff, I still didn't understand what he was after.

'Shouldn't that be rewarded in some way?' Torben asked.

'But I have already asked you what you want. What *do* you want?'

The question came as if MacDuff reluctantly wished to fulfil his duty.

'Ulf has already told you. We want to know more.'

'About what?'

'About the Celtic Ring.' Torben answered. 'What else?'

'No,' said MacDuff. 'It's impossible.'

His voice sounded tired, but at the same time final.

'I won't do it for a very simple reason,' he added after a moment. 'You may have saved my life. Telling you what I know about what you call the 'Celtic Ring' would be the same

273

as condemning you to death. Wouldn't that be ungrateful of me?'

'Who would need to know that you have told us?' I objected.

'I know,' said a clear voice behind us.

Torben and I turned round simultaneously. Mary was standing in half profile behind the ladder by which we had come down to the cabin. She had probably been standing there since we arrived and had heard every word we said. In her hand she held her pistol pointed at us, but, unlike MacDuff earlier, she had a finger on the trigger.

'I ought to shoot you,' she said coming closer. 'You have no right to ask such questions.'

'We're in a mad-house,' Torben remarked to me in Danish.

'If Mary had understood what you just said,' MacDuff answered Torben in broken Norwegian 'she might have shot you on the spot. The strain has been severe lately, enough to pull a trigger incautiously.'

Torben was taken completely unawares. My surprise was just as great, until I suddenly remembered my first meeting with MacDuff on board the *Ofelia* and how he had started to laugh already before the captain had finished reading his message to his two sole passengers.

'Don't look so caught out.' MacDuff said to Torben with a smile. 'I have worked several years on a Norwegian oil rig and picked up a word or two.'

I glanced obliquely at Mary, who was looking intensely at MacDuff. It struck me that I ought to have been afraid. But somehow I knew that Mary wouldn't shoot, not even when she she didn't aim her pistol at herself. For some reason, the pistol seemed unreal, just as unreal and fictitious as so much else that was happening to us. But like many other people, I wasn't able to imagine how horrible and absurd the reality can in fact be.

'What did he say?' Mary asked in a condescending voice.

'Nothing of importance,' MacDuff answered. 'I don't think we have anything to fear. Not from them.'

'I know that we have. From them like all the others.'

'You heard yourself. They believe that they have saved our lives.'

'One more respite,' said Mary. 'It must come to an end some time.'

She had moved round us and now stood, still with her pistol in her hand, close to MacDuff. It seemed to me that her words wounded him deeply.

'It's enough for me that the two have risked their lives for us,' he said. 'Just now that is enough.'

'Not for me. Not for the cause.'

'That can't be our problem,' he told her.

'Well, it's mine. It will always be mine.'

'That is possible. But as long as I go on saving your life, I am the one who decides what you do with the lives of others.'

Their exchange was charged with both inflexibility and tenderness. Certainly they loved each other. Yet I felt that they didn't accept their love, but even considered it to be a necessary and unavoidable evil. It was evident that they didn't fit together; nothing else than their love could have bound them together.

During the hours we were to spend in one another's company, I would neither hear nor see the slightest token of friendliness, or even complicity, between them. When they spoke to each other, their words were sharpened by a finely ground chisel. In words, Mary and MacDuff were complete strangers. But when they looked at each other they were so close that any attempt at separation seemed impossible. Several times, they didn't listen to what Torben or I said, and we sat like spectators in a theatre where the actors had forgotten their audience.

I didn't understand what divided them at a deeper level, and I am not sure that I know now. Mary was closely connected with the Celtic Ring; of that I was certain. She was probably a fully-fledged member, practising or initiated, if you actually could be a 'member' of the Celtic Ring. It was also likely that MacDuff remained on its outskirts and kept himself aloof, even if his actions were clearly inspired by some outward authority. But there was in him a supreme independence which not even Mary could impinge upon. It must have been typical of him that I never heard him make reference to what others had said and thought in order to uphold his own view. His personal experience was enough not to have doubts about the life he led or about the opinions he held. It was also clear that Mary was a believer and MacDuff a sceptic who lived without expectations. He hadn't planned his life in advance, whereas she appeared to know down to the last detail what would happen in hers.

How could they love each other? I would ask myself that question over and over, and I ask it still. I have no complicated theories to explain their love. I only know that love against all odds and all logic is possible. MacDuff and Mary proved it beyond all doubt.

We can probably thank MacDuff for our lives. I realise that now. The battle of wills that took place before us was fearful to behold, although I don't believe that either Torben or I was quite aware that our lives were at stake.

Suddenly, MacDuff raised his head and listened. The wind still showed no sign of abating. We could hear the anchor chain grating as the boat twisted in the blasts. Muffled by the stout planking on the cutter, we could hear the dull rumble of Corryvreckan 's breakers.

'The tide will soon turn now,' MacDuff said to me. 'There will be wind over tide, which means that nobody can sail in here any longer. Not even reckless dare devils like you two. Won't you come back and have dinner with us on board? I'd like to hear more about your travels, and Mary should get to know you better.'

The invitation was made with cordial emphasis, as if we were being asked to a friendly gathering at a safe anchorage somewhere. Meanwhile, it was a way of telling us that we would all do well to return to normal. I had risked Torben's and my own life to warn MacDuff, and perhaps to clear my conscience. Now I felt that we had got very little in return. The dinner was our only hope of gleaning some more splinters of truth, whatever purpose that might serve.

'Come back in two hours' time,' said MacDuff.

An ear splitting roar met us when we got up on deck. The tide had indeed turned and the waves from the Atlantic now met the current which was raging through Corryvreckan at from seven to eight knots. It was under such conditions that the roar could be heard at a distance of ten, or even twenty, nautical miles. And we were scarcely half a mile away. The breakers, mounting up at one and the same place, could be more than twenty feet high. As MacDuff said, nobody could reach us from the sea. And coming here by land would mean dragging a dinghy a long way over the inaccessible heights of Jura. We were safe, but also imprisoned.

Torben was in high spirits when we arrived back at *Rustica* after a wet and tiring little trip in *Sussi*.

'We brought that off pretty well,' he declared with satisfaction. 'A nice thing if we had sailed through the Hell out there only to be shot dead!'

'But we haven't learned very much more than we knew already,' I commented.

'Well, it was your idea to barter the warning for an answer, to exchange mercy for knowledge. People who don't mind killing to keep secrets hardly answer questions just because they are subjected to moral blackmail.'

'It's not over yet,' I said. 'We have dinner before us.'

'Oh, we won't get anything more today for being Good Samaritans, I'm convinced of that. I'll just give yet another account of how beastly cold it was on the North Sea and how horribly seasick I was.'

Torben would do exactly that. But neither of us could have guessed what we would get in return.

Chapter 23

I gave *Rustica* the two hours till dinner time. Too much had happened in recent days for me to take care of her as she deserved. Of course her deck had been washed clean of gravel and sand in Corryvreckan, but the sea had not removed long stripes of dirt on the freeboard and the cabin top. It didn't seem to matter where you were in the world. Soot and grime always fell from the sky. Some places were dirtier than others, but nowhere was the air as clean as it looked - not even in Scotland, where it seemed so clear that lines of the landscape appeared to be sharply etched.

I scrubbed the deck and rubbed the freeboard with a rag steeped in detergent. This was the only thing that helped - combined with manual effort. Torben manifestly felt the same need as I did to be alone. He had poured himself a glass of some red wine and lay on the starboard berth reading a book. Not one about Celts or Druids this time. From my fastidious collection he had taken *The Riddle of the Sands* by Erskine Childers.

Erskine Childers! I repeated the name mechanically to myself afterwards - and the importance of what I had overlooked became plain to me. How could I have failed to think of him during our journey? Another Celtic ring, of which I had been unconscious, now closed round me. Childers with his single book had meant more to me than any number of other writers. Perhaps a motive of which I was previously unaware had lain behind my decision to sail to Scotland. It was an alarming thought in view of what had happened to Childers.

I went down to Torben.

'Do you know about the book you're reading?' I asked.

'No, not at all,' he answered. 'I was curious when I noticed the author's name. There's an 'Erskine Childers' in Coogan's book about the IRA - he's one of its leading martyrs, according to Coogan. His writings and ideas still exert influence on the Celtic nationalists. Can't be the same person as this Childers, can it?'

'It is,' I said, 'No doubt about it.'

Torben must have seen how disturbed I was.

'What's wrong?'

'Read on and you'll understand.'

Well ... I'd have something to talk to MacDuff about. It was inconceivable that he hadn't read Erskine Childers.

Twilight had begun to fall when we placed ourselves in *Sussi*, and cast off. MacDuff had wisely put on his riding-light so that we'd have a navigation mark to steer towards. By the time we were half way there, the darkness had become dense, and we couldn't distinguish as much as the silhouette of *Rustica* behind us. The fact that Macduff had lit his anchor-light for our sake also indicated his certainty that nobody else would find him.

There was no point in either Torben or I trying to speak on the way over: the roar from Corryvreckan was too great. However, the gale no longer came with the same headlong force as before. When, in some hours, the tide would turn again, it might be possible to leave Bagh Gleann nam Muc, which so protectively imprisoned us. I wondered if MacDuff still thought of sailing to Kerrera. He was no coward, but if, with Mary on board, he sailed straight into the arms of Dick and O'Connell, more than courage would doubtless be required. True, Mary herself possessed a determination that yielded to nothing, except perhaps MacDuff's strength of will and his love for her ...

We were warmly received when we stepped on board the fishing vessel. I couldn't really comprehend how MacDuff managed to relieve all the tension that had vibrated between us only a few hours earlier.

On going down into the cabin, we saw that Mary was less at ease. Traces of her earlier agitation had not yet disappeared. But she smiled disarmingly and greeted us so hospitably that I felt embarrassed. The more so because her new attitude towards us seemed quite unfeigned. During the hours that followed, the world outside might not have existed for us. Torben sank into a state of relaxed well-being that showed all over his face and in his entire manner. At such moments he looked almost shamelessly pleased with himself and with life in general.

We avoided all sensitive topics. MacDuff and I talked a good deal about boats and seafaring. Hearing him relate his experiences at sea gave me some of my richest moments ever as a listener. I then perceived that what I had discovered myself about the sea amounted to no more than fragments of an unsuspected whole. For MacDuff the seagoing was not merely a way of life; it was the very basis of how he looked at reality. It meant learning to live with perpetual change, never taking anything for granted, being trained continually in humility and respect for what you have not mastered, for what you must safeguard at every instant. When you are at sea, you grasp the true range and worth of mere Man.

On land, according to MacDuff, people always give themselves an importance that is actually unwarranted. They try to leave traces of themselves behind, both in the minds of others and as viewed by what they think is eternity. But people of the sea understand that such efforts are useless. When a ship passes, the water closes again in its wake and all becomes precisely as it was before.

For MacDuff, the sea not only provided the guiding rules for how now a man should attack the business of life. It taught still more: the ethics which ought to govern our relations with other people.

We spoke about Erskine Childers - who, it seemed, was the sole person MacDuff looked up to. If the choice were allowed to MacDuff, he would wish to have had Erskine Childers' life.

'Including his violent end?' I wondered.

'Just because of it,' replied MacDuff. 'His death produced such a resounding echo that he still lives on.'

Meanwhile, Torben and Mary were discussing Celtic history; they talked of Druids and bards and Irish folk tales. I didn't hear them say a single word about what was round about us; their reality seemed to lie a thousand years in the past. I was far too deep in conversation with MacDuff to follow their hypotheses about that reality and how they attempted to interpret it. Now and then, however, I caught bits of what they said. As when Torben asked Mary what she thought about Caesar's description of the Celts - this being surely the source of modern ideas about Celts and Druids.

Mary answered that Caesar was doubtless the most reliable of those who wrote on the subject in ancient times.

'Even about the head cult and human sacrifice?' Torben inquired.

'Yes.' Mary replied without hesitation. 'Certainly.'

Later, I overheard Torben ask why the Druids had been

willing to pass on their spiritual authority to Christian monks. 'Especially in Ireland - exactly the country where the Celts were strongest, as they had never been obliged to live under Roman rule there.'

'It was no gift,' said Mary. 'They didn't surrender anything.'

'I'm afraid, I don't understand you,' Torben admitted.

'The Druids didn't give up overnight a legacy passed on for a thousand years. They simply realised that for all the foreseeable future Christianity would have a dominant place in their world. Such was their foresight and wisdom that they didn't wish to fight a hopeless battle. So instead they opened the way for the monks and helped them take over spiritual power. But the Druids demanded in return that the monks should pass the Celtic heritage on until the time when Christianity would decline in its turn, and disappear.'

Torben seemed to be less than convinced by what Mary told him. And she went on.

'Why else would the monks have devoted so much of their time and energy to writing down the Irish folk tales? Fiacc, consecrated by Saint Patrick as Ireland's first bishop, was a Druid. We know that. Many people maintain that the Druids discarded their wisdom and became Christians. But it wasn't that way. The Druids who became bishops were guarantors that their faith would survive in the secret hiding places of Christianity. From generation to generation. Until the day when a Celtic People could claim its return. In the Christian church there have always been priests who were at the same time Druids. In 1970, on the twenty seventh of June, the first monk was received into the Avalon Order by Iltud, archbishop of the Celtic Church who said that he was empowered to do so by virtue of the legacy transmitted by the first druidic priests in the church. But Iltud made a great mistake. He tried too soon to call the Druids back to life. Such an error will not be committed again.'

The boundless conviction in Mary's voice gave these last words a threatening incantation. I would wonder later why I didn't think of her as a kind of fanatical preacher or sectarian missionary. Perhaps it was because I grasped that she had no conception of sin or a Day of Judgement. Moreover, she never attempted to convert or save the soul of anybody. In all this she was true to the Celtic tradition.

I should have liked to see her face while she was answering Torben's questions. But I dared not risk meeting her eyes. Her gaze still alarmed me. I wasn't frightened of her, but for myself; that I might lose my foothold.

MacDuff had been absent in his own thoughts for some minutes. But he heard Mary's words about the error made, and he regarded her with evident disapproval.

'Yes,' he said, 'mistakes will be made as long as some people want to lead others. Whether they are archbishops or dictators.'

'There are people who need direction.' Mary replied with irritation.

'Oh yes,' said MacDuff ironically, 'leaders, gods and other bosses do. The rest of us get along better on our own.'

The regard of each was caught by that of the other, as when two grapnels become entangled. Without having timed them, I think that Mary and MacDuff stared into each other's eyes for two or three minutes. Torben and I looked on mutely. Of course I don't know what went on in their minds. But I was seized with panic at their need for such a long and direct gaze. Very slowly - imperceptibly, in fact - their eyes softened. The tension there had been replaced by tenderness. Finally, the compulsion lost its hold on them.

Afterwards, MacDuff was the first to speak. In an entirely natural tone, as if he was unaware of what had happened, he said to us:

'Do please excuse my behaviour earlier today. I am not usually so inhospitable to visitors. My apologies - if you can accept them.'

'We can,' Torben replied. But he looked at Mary.

MacDuff added: 'These are difficult times ...' And for once he seemed to be at a loss for words.

Soon he turned to me and asked: 'How would you like to make a little excursion to Eilean Mor? You can't get closer to Corryvreckan by land. It's worth the effort.'

'I'd like nothing better,' I answered. It was, I realised, the opportunity of a lifetime.

Torben merely shook his head and wondered. 'Haven't you two seen enough of Corryvreckan?' No further reply was needed.

MacDuff smiled and led the way up on deck - then climbed down to the dinghy. He placed himself at the oars and, with powerful strokes, rowed straight out into the sound.

Chapter 24

'THE wind has dropped,' MacDuff observed after a time in the dinghy. 'I suppose you know what that means.'

'I don't know.'

'It means that I'll have to sail tonight.' MacDuff stated this with finality.

I was about to expostulate, to say that perhaps he might get out of sailing.

But MacDuff went on at once: 'I don't intend to explain why I must go. However, you can take it as proof that I am grateful for your coming and warning me. Even if it wasn't necessary. Nothing would be more suspect than my not turning up at Kerrera tonight. And who would have tipped me off if not you? Even Dick can work that out. He must have seen that the *Rustica* was gone. A matter of returning a favour when the water is rough, so to speak.'

I guessed that he was smiling in the darkness. And I realised that, in an instinctive sort of way, he understood very well why Torben and I had acted as we did.

'About favours,' he said, 'I am thinking of asking you to do me a service of a personal kind. I'll put the question only once, and of course you have a perfect right to say no. But I have confidence in you, and that's why I make the request.'

'I never promise anything,' I replied.

'You don't need to promise me anything. It's much simpler than that. I'd like you to take care of Mary while I am off at Kerrera.'

I said nothing. I don't know whether I was surprised by the request; it was no more unexpected than all the other unexpected things that had happened to us.

'It's for her sake,' MacDuff went on, without waiting longer for an answer. 'I am not taking a risk myself. At least, no more risk than usual. Mike O'Connell and Dick are little people, very little people. They obey orders - even my orders. As you may have understood, the trouble is that I don't always obey orders. And consequently, quite a few people are after me. Having Mary on board, or even my being in love with her, are breaches of orders, the worst I could be guilty of. I can't explain why for the same reasons as I couldn't explain other things to you earlier. But so much I can tell you; if O'Connell finds out that Mary is alive and where she is, her days are numbered.'

'Like yours,' I commented.

'Yes,' MacDuff agreed. 'But my days have been numbered nearly as long as I can remember. I've lost count of the times. What really matters is simply Mary.'

'Doesn't she run as much risk with us?' I asked.

'Oh, it's only for a day or two. And I'll take Dick on board with me, so he can't try to find where you are. You'll have nothing to worry about with him out of the way.'

'Was it Dick who tried to drown us in Neptune's Staircase?' I demanded.

'Quite possibly.'

'Possibly? Didn't you just say that he obeys your orders?'

'He does,' MacDuff told me. 'But he takes orders from others as well. And I know he has received instructions to keep an eye on you both.'

'You mean, to liquidate us? Perhaps by cutting our throats?'

'No,' MacDuff replied unmoved, 'I don't believe so. Not yet, in any case. That may come later.'

'And, nevertheless, you ask us to do you a service?'

'I regret to say that I have no other course.'

With some vehemence, I broke out: 'But who is it who gives such orders? And why?'

I couldn't reconcile myself to the idea of having Mary aboard my *Rustica*. True, for a moment, the thought of her being near actually appealed to me, but then I felt that her gaze would either bind me to her or make me want to flee from her.

MacDuff answered my question: 'That's just the problem. Nobody knows. Not even me. Well, possibly Mary knows. Of course you can ask her.'

'What does 'take care of' involve?'

'It's perfectly simple,' MacDuff assured me. 'I merely ask that you allow her to stay aboard your boat for three days. You and your friend, as well as Mary, need a little peace and rest. I suggest that you make a trip around Mull. Tomorrow morning, you could sail to Drambuie - there isn't a soul there at this time of year. If you feel a bit confined, you can always take your dinghy over to Tobermory and have a beer or two. Providing that Mary remains on board. Then on Thursday, you might find an anchorage off Ulva - you know where that little island lies. There are several good places, completely sheltered from wind and weather. And on Friday I'll meet you at Tinker's Hole - a perfect anchorage at the southwestern point of Mull. If you get there early, you could certainly make a little excursion to Iona. Just the place for you. It was on Iona that Saint Columba went ashore when he brought Christianity to Scotland. There's a cathedral and a burial ground. Lots of kings are said to be buried there - forty-eight kings of

Scotland, eight of Norway and four of Ireland. Something like that. So it's well worth a visit. Especially for a person with your interest in Celtic history.'

MacDuff seemed to be describing an innocent holiday cruise. He neglected to mention that the western side of Mull lay open to the full sweep of the Atlantic, with nothing but empty sea all the five thousand nautical miles westward to the mist-shrouded fishing banks of Newfoundland. Moreover, it was still winter. The weather could look very different in a few hours.

I pointed out: 'We might be delayed by the weather.'

'If you have sailed through Corryvreckan, you can surely manage a trip round Mull.'

'And what,' I asked, 'if something should happen to you? What shall we do then?'

'Nothing will happen to me.'

'But if something did?' I insisted.

MacDuff was silent for a moment - which I took as an admission that, in fact, disaster might befall him; something worse than sea and sky could bring upon him.

He replied: 'In that case you can do what you want. You can put Mary ashore where she wishes. You can take her with you if that's what she would like. But don't try to follow her or invent some feat of valour to 'save' her life. Remember that if, against all expectations, I don't come back, nobody in the world will be capable of lifting a finger to help you.'

We were quickly nearing Eilean Mor. The moon had risen, and it cast a singular shimmer over the cascades of Corryvreckan. MacDuff must have worked out our course from the sound of breakers and taken bearings from his own riding light. Not once did he turn round to check our position. He beached the dinghy in an invisible cove, well sheltered from the waves which had now become alarmingly high. We walked up to the top of the little island, and from there we perceived a grandiose and ghostly spectacle.

In the faint and glimmering light from the stars and from sea-fire in the water, the breakers appeared to be luminous, living creatures which reared up and sank down, disappeared and rose again in helpless confusion. Standing there, I had a sense of being in another world, and I understood how easy it must have been for the ancient Celts to abolish the distinction between reality and fable. For them, animals and people, untamed nature and civilization, were two sides of the same thing. Their tools were inhabited by spirits. Skilful craftsmen were looked up to as gods. We, who cannot live without drawing a line between truth and fiction, between certainty and mere belief, find it difficult to comprehend how a people could live with only truth and certainty. Nowhere in all the tens of thousands lines of poetry in old Irish manuscripts, is anyone said to tell a lie. The word doesn't exist. Nor had the Celts a word for what we mean by 'fairy tale'.

MacDuff remarked: 'Seeing such a thing can make a whole lifetime seem worthwhile.'

We stood still for many minutes. Then MacDuff broke the spell.

'Well,' he inquired, 'what is your answer?'

After a little time, I said: 'You are asking no small thing of us. And what are we to receive by way of thanks?'

'Nothing,' MacDuff told me curtly. 'I don't bargain. I am begging for help. I can't leave Mary here.'

'Why not?'

Now there came a hint of anger into MacDuff's voice, as if I *ought* to have understood.

'She would freeze to death.'

That was unanswerable. Once again, Torben and I were faced with an accomplished fact. I wondered if MacDuff had, quite coolly, counted on my being too good-natured to say no. Well, I wasn't going to give in easily. I could behave as uncompromisingly as he.

'Of course I must speak to Torben first.'

I could just see that MacDuff nodded.

'For my part, I accept. But on one condition. I must know more about the hazards involved.'

MacDuff was, I felt, already rebuffing my requirement.

'If I am to take responsibility for Mary during three days,' I told him, 'I must know what sort of risks and dangers are hanging over her. I want to know why Pekka had to die. I want to know what she was saved from.'

I realised that MacDuff was shaking his head. And I continued:

'You, if anyone, must understand that I can't simply transport Mary about as if she were a piece of luggage. I am not Pekka. I haven't saved her from anything. Only a few hours ago, she was fully prepared to shoot us. And now you are expecting me to take care of her without any safeguards at all.'

'She would understand how you feel,' said MacDuff. There was a touch of hesitation in his voice.

'That may well be. But I don't want to sail blindly about, not knowing what's at stake. Not with Mary. It would be as dangerous for her as for us.'

This seemed to have made an impression, because MacDuff didn't protest. He was silent for some time.

'I can tell you a part of it,' he then said, 'but not all. Afterwards you must decide for yourself if it's enough. There are certain things I can't tell you - even if they are of no importance to me.'

'Why not?'

'Because Mary would leave me if she found out.'

Having seen Mary and MacDuff together, I understood that it would be futile to go further into the matter. And it was clear that MacDuff had counted on this being my attitude.

'Well,' he said, 'where do you want me to begin?'

'Can you start by explaining why there are people who must die for the sake of the Celts?'

MacDuff stared out into the darkness before he answered.

'I ask myself that,' he said. 'A day never passes without my facing that same question.'

'And the answer?'

'There isn't one. A million people died in Ireland during the famine of the eighteen forties. The English could have prevented it. Why didn't they? Why did they allow it to happen? It can't even be explained as a matter of money. Letting people die of hunger was an economic loss for England - but that didn't end the English policy of impoverishing Ireland. Thousands of people died when Ireland became free. The English could have prevented that as well. Why didn't they?'

I protested: 'The Irish could have refrained from taking up arms.'

'Could they? That's just the question. Who can decide? In Dublin, as late as 1920, English employers who needed workers still put up signs with 'Irish and coloureds need not apply'. And do you know why old houses in Ireland have so few windows? Because the English, in their fanatical search for ways of fleecing the Irish, imposed a tax on windows. In Brittany, it wasn't until 1950 that elementary school teachers - who of course were one hundred per cent French and employed by the French government - stopped beating children who happened to speak a word or two of Breton, their mother tongue. Or an old clog was hung from a child's neck in the same spirit as Jews were made to wear yellow stars during the Occupation. The Bretons were treated as if they were immigrants. In 1969, a labour exchange wrote to various industrial concerns inquiring what kind of workers they desired: 'Bretons, Italians, Spaniards, Portuguese or

Moroccans'? Why do you think that France has never counter-signed 'The European Declaration of Human Rights'? For a simple reason. The Declaration obliges its signatories to acknowledge and support the languages of their minority populations. In 1810, the British government brought in a law declaring that all school children who were heard to speak Welsh in the classroom should be made to wear a sign bearing the words 'WELSH NOT'. At the beginning of this century, *The Times* wrote that the sooner Welsh was exterminated the better. I could go on forever. You ask why the Irish took up arms? I have no answer. You can put such a question to a state, to a dictator or to a government. You can put questions to individuals. But you can't ask a whole people the same question. And in any case, Ireland became free.'

'What is a people,' I demanded, 'if not a collection of individuals? It's people who kill, not a people.'

MacDuff said: 'Sometimes I wonder if there are any individuals. When a people has existed for over three thousand years, as the Celts have, then it's as if a whole people is to be found in each person. I have fought all my life for a free Celtic people.

'Sometimes I wonder why. Couldn't I have been satisfied with just being a pilot? I love my work, the sea, the mountains and the countryside, the people I meet. But no - I can't help doing it. And I mean exactly that. As long as the Celts are not a free people, then I'm not free either. I am as far as possible from being a romantic revolutionary, believe me. I'm not fighting for a future Celtic state or a Celtic nation. I detest states and nations, just as the Celts have always done. I don't fight for any form of government or even for democracy. I fight so that the Celts will be able to decide for themselves how they will live and die. That's enough for me. Later, when we are free, we can think about how we are to be as a free people.'

'Won't it be too late then?' I asked.

'Too late! It will be much worse if we are too early. That's what far too many fail to understand. They believe, as certain people in the Basque country or Northern Ireland do, that just some few can raise a rebellion and throw out the forces of occupation. Afterwards, those few will try to make the others understand what it was they all wanted and needed. That's the attitude of politicians. And we have some of that kind here as well. Dick and O'Connell are among them - power hungry individuals who always feel they know best.'

'All the same,' I pointed out, 'you transport weapons for them.'

'Not for them!' MacDuff told me vehemently. 'I sail weapons to places where they are needed. To create a threat - not to be used.'

He made a gesture to dismiss in advance any possible objection to this.

'They will be needed on the day when the Celts let the world know that we are a free people - whether in Scotland, in Wales or in Brittany. When we Celts cease to vote for foreign political parties and declare ourselves independent. That day is not far off. But our independence won't be accepted in England or France or Spain. It won't help at all that our freedom has come to us by democratic means. No more than in Latvia or Lithuania. The day that comes, we'll need weapons to show we are in earnest.'

I said: 'They didn't need any weapons in Poland or Eastern Germany.'

'No,' MacDuff admitted. 'Because the Soviets withdrew their threat. In our case, it would be the same as expecting the British government to tell Wales and Scotland: All right! Do what you like. If you want to be Celtic, be Celtic! We're not interested in ruling you any longer. Keep your oil, your regiments, whatever else you happen to have left. They are yours! ... They won't say that to us. So we must have weapons.'

I asked somewhat rhetorically: 'But surely some people want to use them now?'

'Certainly,' answered MacDuff. 'There are even people who already do use them. What am I to do about that?'

'Try to stop it!'

'How? By resorting to violence? Starting a civil war when we are on the way to becoming a free people?'

He didn't wait for an answer.

'You must understand that there are many people on the Celts' side. They are not all as sensible and rational as I'd like them to be. But they are Celts. There are romantics bent on violence, like Dick and O'Connell. There are all sorts of Druids, from pure philanthropists to heathen fundamentalists with a sickle in one hand and King Arthur's sword in the other. There are Celtic societies and Celtic language clubs and Celtic educational associations. There's Celtic music. I've got no monopoly on all that - or on how liberation should take place. But I hope it will be in a peaceful way. I am convinced that it will be so where we are concerned, with a few exceptions. The risk is simply that the violence of those few will be returned on a massive scale by England or France. That is one of the reasons for the existence of the Celtic Ring.'

MacDuff was silent. So was I - waiting tensely.

After a time, he went on: 'I am afraid that I must exact a promise from you. Even if you don't believe in promises. If you don't think that you can keep it, then tell me so now. For your own sake, for Torben's sake, for my sake and Mary's, you must never repeat what I am going to tell you about the Celtic Ring. Not even to Torben.'

I was torn between my desire to hear the truth and my unwillingness to keep it from Torben. How could I really promise to tell him nothing?

'I promise.' I managed to get the two words out, albeit without conviction.

'Well then,' said MacDuff. 'In all the Celtic regions there are at present people who, in their different ways, work for the freedom and independence of their countries. Everywhere in them, there are Druidic orders with, taken together, tens of thousands of members. At their ceremonies and festivals, they appeal for Celtic unity. All the countries have their Nationalist parties and more or less active resistance movements. There are Celtic radio and television stations which make no bones about their special character. Annual congresses are held, and they draw hundreds of delegates from all the Celtic countries. Put together, they make a powerful force - but separately they can't accomplish very much. Take those congresses, for example - they get barely visible coverage in the papers, where they are presented as a tourist attraction more than anything else. Or look at the Nationalist parties. Through the years, they have suffered from having to choose among the leading parties; whether the Socialists, the Liberals or the Conservatives. Nobody explained to them that the real line of division lay elsewhere. Of course the Celts have never believed in states or in nations - and what they want now is to live in federations: free associations of people who will decide themselves where they belong. In the past, the misunderstandings and mistakes of the Nationalist parties did a lot of harm. But that's over now - since the Celtic Ring was formed. The Ring is an inner circle of people from all the Celtic countries. It has a single task: to co-ordinate all efforts at liberation in those countries. Its symbol is a sickle - not the Communist sickle, the Celtic one. You will understand why if you place such a sickle on a map of Europe. You put the point of the sickle on the northwestern point of Galicia, and then the rest joins together Brittany, Wales, Ireland and Scotland. The aim of all is to have open boundaries and cultural exchanges.

But no common leadership.'

I realised how close Torben had been to the truth - even if he didn't dare believe that it was the truth.

'The Ring is secret,' MacDuff was saying. 'And all who know of it accept that it must be kept secret. In Scotland a governing council has already been appointed. It is to lead the country during the first years after independence. That's no secret. But in the other occupied Celtic countries members of each council would be in gravest danger if it became known that Celtic liberation was both organised and co-ordinated .'

'Has the Ring power?' I wanted to know.

'That depends on what you mean by the word. The Ring doesn't exercise any direct power over people in general. It has influence, great influence, but mostly by virtue of the members' daily efforts to promote Celtic culture. The Ring provides a groundwork. Without the Ring, the IRA would have lost out long ago - but the IRA doesn't know that it is only a pawn in a much larger game which can't be won by its methods. Even if Northern Ireland doesn't become Celtic when it gains its freedom, it won't be long before Scotland and Wales demand the same status. But whatever the Ring's outward power, it has almost unrestricted authority over those who - without being members of it - have agreed to work directly under it. That's what Mary and I have done. Dick is in the same position. So, for that matter, is MacDougall - no doubt you met him on Kerrera. O'Connell, on the other hand, knows nothing. He thinks that he is working for the IRA. That he is continuing Ruair O'Bradaigh's work when O'Bradaigh established contacts with the ETA in the Basque country. Well, O'Bradaigh had dreams of free Celtic countries, but all he got to fulfil them was fifty pistols from the ETA. And O'Connell is a dreamer too - of a kind that the Celtic Ring has no use for. We others have sworn on oath that we will always be faithful to the Ring. We obey orders, not from one another, but directly from the Ring. There is no hierarchy among us, except possibly what results from natural authority. Though we do obey orders, we don't do it blindly. An important and wholly decisive restriction applies. Each of us has the right to refuse obedience to a particular order, but not the right to prevent someone else from carrying it out. Have you now begun to understand? To grasp why I couldn't prevent your coming so close to death in Neptune's Staircase? I didn't so much as know that an attempt would be made on your lives. But even if I had known, I wouldn't have been able to stop it.'

I asked: 'Had you received an order when we met at Invergarry Castle?'

'Yes.'

MacDuff made a telling pause.

'But,' he then assured me, 'I used my right to refuse an order. And the Ring never gives the same order to two people at the same time. Of course that would undermine the function involved. Refusal to carry out an order is a safeguard against the abuse of power.'

'But the order was evidently confirmed in our case.'

'I don't know,' said MacDuff. 'Quite possibly it was decided that you two should be frightened sufficiently to keep you away from Scotland and Ireland. My word can sometimes carry weight. I justified my refusal by stating my conviction that you didn't know anything essential about the Ring, and nothing at all with certainty.'

'How was that received?'

MacDuff said again: 'I don't know.'

'And with Pekka?' I asked.

He turned hastily towards me, but in the darkness it was difficult to make out the expression on his face. I was afraid that I had gone too far.

'Pekka was dangerous,' MacDuff told me calmly. 'I don't know how he discovered the existence of the Ring. But such things can happen. He had read a great deal of history and seemed to have been fascinated all his life by more or less secret societies. He knew everything about the Druidic orders, the Masonic Lodges, the Knight Templars. Perhaps he'd only guessed, followed a trail, then used his imagination to fit the pieces of a jig saw puzzle together - and got it right. That might not have been enough for condemning him to death - if there was someone among us willing to carry out the sentence. But ... there was the matter of Mary.'

MacDuff fell silent and remained so for quite a time. I supposed that he had reached the point where, for his own and Mary's sake, he could tell me no more.

But suddenly he continued: 'Mary belongs to a Druidic order that places very heavy demands on its members. They adhere to all the old beliefs and maintain the traditions of a thousand years. They live like Holy Fathers and give a great part of their time to collecting knowledge and passing it on. Nothing is written down. Everything is conveyed by word of mouth. They believe in *Sid* - the Celts' paradise, you know. They think that nothing could be better than to go there. Only their earthly deeds on behalf of the Celts prevent them from committing suicide. Every other year they confer the honour of going to *Sid* on one of their members. Being chosen is apparently the highest distinction they can bestow.'

'Is it possible!' I interjected. 'Today?'

'Yes. Unfortunately it's not only possible, it occurs. Even the Celts have their fundamentalists.'

'But possible that Mary should be one of them?'

MacDuff didn't seem to hear my question.

'Last year,' he told me, 'it was Mary who drew the winning lot. The thing takes place in a complicated ceremony with a bit of burnt bread. The person who gets the burnt bit is chosen. I don't know exactly what goes on, and I don't want to know either. The Ring gave me an order to prevent Mary from

299

committing suicide. I refused to obey. Saving her life would have been the same thing as condemning our love to death. There was nothing I could do except hope that by some miracle she would survive. It was horrible. Afterwards I found out that the Ring had made an exception in Mary's case and given her a direct order not to commit suicide. Of course she refused. She had a complete right to do so. But at the same time she declared that the Ring had no authority over the Druidic order to which she belonged. They were free Celts; free to believe and act as they thought best. The trouble was simply that, as I told you, she had sworn absolute fidelity to the Ring. Of course that made her something of a risk to it. She was the only member of her order who knew of the Ring's existence, but as she was placing the Druidic order above the Ring, she would doubtless reveal what she knew about it - what she knew being most certainly valuable Celtic knowledge, which should be passed on to her brothers and sisters of the Druidic order. In some way or other, Pekka had found out where and when the death ceremony would take place. Mary was to be drowned, as a mark of honour to one of their gods. But what Pekka neither knew nor understood was that Mary changed her mind at the very end. She regretted her act when she believed that she was, in fact, already dead. On returning fully to consciousness, she was aboard Pekka's catamaran. She had lost everything. In the first place, she had turned from me. Then she had failed the Ring. And finally, she let down her Druidic order. So she sailed away with Pekka. For she had no longer any will to live.'

I was bold enough to ask: 'Why did she change her mind?'

'Because of her love for me,' said MacDuff simply.

I divined a kind of pride in his voice when he said this. But meanwhile, I understood how profound his despair must have been when he believed that Mary was to die. And I understood as well the all-pervading hope aroused in him when he realised that she was still alive.

'You know the rest,' said MacDuff. 'I brought Mary back. That was my intention when I followed Pekka. I'd never have believed that he would dare to sail through the Pentland Firth in such weather. That he should so endanger his own life and Mary's rather than fall into my hands - I couldn't comprehend it. Not even in my own desperation could I have done a thing like that. But he survived - perhaps because his catamaran was so light and fast. My fishing boat would have gone under before I'd got half way into the sound. When I knew that he had brought it off, I followed him to Anholt and then Dragør. I took Mary back with me. I could always refuse an order against this, so that was all right. But I prevented others from carrying out their orders. We have been traitors, both of us, Mary and I. Nobody knows about it except you and Torben - and he doesn't know with certainty. Dick and O'Connell guess or suspect something, but they know nothing. Now do you understand why I made you swear to keep silent?'

I gave him a nod to indicate that I did. But I wasn't sure that he caught it in the darkness.

'Dick and O'Connell would gladly kill the four of us if they got hold of something definite,' MacDuff added. 'And they'd do the killing without having received any orders.'

I said: 'I'm sorry that I have to tell you this. They already feel sure that Mary is alive. You made a mistake. You should have reported that Pekka died in Denmark.'

I told him what had been said at the end of dinner in Gylen Castle.

'Yes,' MacDuff agreed in a metallic voice that cut through the air like the edge of a sword, 'perhaps I should have told the truth about Pekka. But Mary? Without actual proof of her death, who would believe that I had murdered her with my own hands? And, for that matter, who would have believed that she'd happened to fall overboard somewhere near Denmark when I was close by? No one who knew me or Mary would swallow that. Everybody believed me when I came back from the Pentland Firth and reported that the *Sula* had gone down. No evidence was needed. The fact that the Pentland Firth is notorious, and my grief - because I was convinced that Mary *had* gone under - were proof enough. But then, only a few days later, I learned from a fellow pilot that Pekka was at Kirkwall, on Orkney. Naturally, I asked if there was a woman on board, but nobody had seen Mary. Pekka must have kept her hidden - or else she was so miserable that she didn't care what happened and just remained out of sight. In any case, nobody had seen her. So I decided that I'd stick to the story that she had drowned in the Pentland Firth, though Pekka had survived. And I was forced to say I finally got hold of him on the North Sea, not far from Orkney.'

He was silent for a few minutes.

'I had the impression that the Ring believed me. But next day you two turned up in Fraserburgh.'

'Didn't you recognize the boat on the North Sea?' I asked.

'No and if only I had! But we were sailing on auto-pilot. I slept and Mary kept a look-out. She reported that we had passed a sailing boat, but she hadn't a thought of it being you. Nor did I. Why should I?'

I asked: 'And in Thyberøn?'

'You must have sailed the same day I came back.'

I thought of the morning when I'd seen the *F 154* sail by on the North Sea. I had waved, but the wheelhouse was empty. And I realised that the fishing-boat we'd seen wasn't following us at all. Our belief that it was showed how apprehensive we had been.

'So, you see,' MacDuff continued, 'when you turned up in Scotland it was already too late. My story had been told.

And I was obliged to deal with you and Torben. The first thing was to find out if you knew anything about the Ring or about Pekka's death. Of course there was no reason to suppose that you did, since you must have left Denmark at about the same time as it happened. But I didn't dare take chances. So I organised that little visit aboard your *Rustica*. Unfortunately, I didn't guess that the Ring was keeping me under observation. Just a routine measure perhaps. But the result was pretty alarming. When, after half an hour of searching, I had found Pekka's logbook, I was caught unawares in *Rustica*'s cabin. So I had to explain somehow what I was looking for there - as I am not exactly known to be a burglar. (It wasn't my idea to take your passport and your money, incidentally.) And the most convincing thing to do was just to show Pekka's logbook there in my hand.'

'But wasn't that giving yourself away about Pekka's death?' I asked.

'No. You are forgetting something essential. I had terrific luck, for once. Because at the last entry in Pekka's logbook he was still in the Pentland Firth. And from the way he ended, it seemed very probable that Mary would have been drowned. That was plainly indicated by Pekka's notations on the wind and weather. Well, I said that my suspicions were aroused when I didn't find the logbook on board the *Sula*. So I was making sure that Pekka hadn't given it to you before he left Kirkwall. The fact that you turned up so soon after his visit there confirmed my suspicions - as did the logbook! I thought that this story was believed. But you must realise that I'd put myself in a precarious situation. A single word from you or Torben about having met Pekka in Denmark would have upset everything. That's why I avoided speaking about him when we met at Invergarry Castle. And again I was in luck. When you asked about Pekka, you didn't mention Denmark, and Torben didn't say he knew that Mary was alive. I managed to stop you in time.'

Perceiving now in what danger we had placed him, I asked: 'Why didn't you shoot us? It would have solved all your problems.'

'I have told you before. One day you and I must sail about together in the Hebrides. When all this is over and forgotten. And of course I believed that you weren't a danger to the Celtic Ring. But when I granted you what amounted to a free conduct, it was on the understanding that you would leave Scotland without speaking of Mary. I genuinely believed that you would take my threat in earnest. When I found out that you had boarded my boat and spoken to Mary, I had to change my mind. If you hadn't lied to the lock-keeper at Corpach and anchored behind the island on the other side of Loch Linnhe - well, it's fairly certain that you wouldn't still be in the land of the living. As you may realise, I didn't doubt that you had overstepped the bounds set for you.'

'And in Neptune's Staircase?'

'I still don't know why that happened.' MacDuff admitted. 'But Dick was aware that you had Pekka's logbook, which reveals far too much, and he is not a man to take any unnecessary risks. He doesn't trust people at all.'

'If only you had told us what was at stake!' I said.

MacDuff answered: 'Till this evening I didn't realise that I could depend on you.' He was silent.

'What will you do now?' I wanted to know. But no answer came.

'Mary was right,' he remarked, in a voice that sounded flat but not dejected. 'The respite couldn't go on forever.'

'It's my fault,' I said.

'No,' replied MacDuff. 'I should have foreseen the Ring would try to find out by other means what you two had in mind. As for me ... Even if the Ring had no proof Mary was still alive, it never totally accepted my word that she wasn't. I wouldn't have, either, in their place.'

'Can't the Ring change its decision?' I asked. 'Couldn't you convince them that you are no danger to them?'

'I might, yes. But it's hardly likely after this. And even if they did in my case, I must confess that Mary is no longer dependable.'

Suddenly, I rebelled against all the impossibilities hopping about us.

'How can you put up with it?' I demanded. 'You expose yourself to the risk of having to kill on order. And you accept that other people have the right to do it. Even when the person you set highest of all is to be killed.'

'But something important changes it all,' he said, 'Refusal to kill is an absolute right.'

'But what difference does that make in practice? When somebody else will always obey the order?'

'Not always,' said MacDuff. 'Because if you kill, you must yourself take complete responsibility for the deed. You can't blame it on others. Or make use of assassins. It's your responsibility, and yours alone. For you had the right to refuse.'

'And the head cult?' I asked sharply. 'Is that also a right?' Without any reaction to my tone, MacDuff said simply: 'It exists. Certain Druids revere it. But nowadays nobody kills just to have a head to play with - if that's what you imagine. That much has altered in three thousand years.'

That was not what I had in mind. I had wanted to know about Pekka's head - and what Pekka might have seen when he wrote about the head cult in his logbook. But I couldn't bring myself to ask. For that would mean asking MacDuff if he personally, with his own hands, had killed Pekka. And it was true, what MacDuff had said: I was afraid of the answer to that question.

On our way back to his boat, MacDuff seemed in some

way relieved, in spite of what was hanging over him. And I understood that I must have been the first person to whom he had told so much.

'I'd very much like to talk to Torben alone,' I said to MacDuff when we climbed on board. 'If you have nothing against it?'

'Nothing at all. But I must sail in half an hour.'

He called to Mary to come up on deck. And I went below to the cabin.

'There you are,' I said to Torben.

He was still looking just as pleased and satisfied as before. But there was something more in his expression, something vacant and out of focus, which was new to me.

'How was Corryvreckan?'

I answered: 'As it usually is, I expect.' And I went straight to the point. 'MacDuff wants us to take care of Mary for three days. Is that all right?'

Torben didn't reply at once.

'He can't take her with him to Kerrera,' I explained. 'For obvious reasons. And he can't just leave her here. She would freeze to death.'

I had expected objections, but he merely replied: 'Then it looks as if we have no choice.' He seemed less than displeased by the absence of an alternative.

I glanced at him but saw no change in his expression.

When I came back up on deck, I saw that MacDuff and Mary were standing by the gunwale, close to the wheelhouse. They held each other tightly, and they didn't observe my presence before I made it known. Then, very slowly, they released each other.

'You can sail when you wish,' I told MacDuff. 'Tinker's Hole, Friday! If necessary we'll wait all day Saturday. But no longer.'

MacDuff advanced towards me and, to my astonishment,

he gave me a bear-hug.

'I promise you, even if you don't believe in promises,' he said, 'one day we'll sail together in the Outer Hebrides. Just you and me.' I felt that this was more than reward enough for the service we were about to render him.

Mary said nothing. She was holding a leather rucksack in one hand and seemed to be waiting for the rest of us to make the next decision.

Sussi couldn't take the three of us. So I rowed Torben first over to *Rustica*. The wind had abated somewhat, and now one could actually tell that we were in a sheltered place - which previously, had been difficult to believe. It was a starry, sparklingly cold night, and the roar from Corryvreckan sounded like a thunderstorm moving away. When I got back to the fishing boat, MacDuff had already started his powerful diesel engine, and the anchor chain was up-and-down. Mary jumped agilely down into *Sussi* and didn't look back at MacDuff. But I did - meanwhile holding tight to the gunwale. Our eyes met.

'One thing more,' I said, 'before we go. You do owe me the answer. Was it you ...?'

I didn't finish the sentence.

'Yes, it was,' he answered. 'To save Mary's life.'

'And the head?' I got the question out at last. 'Why?'

MacDuff seemed to be turning away.

'I thought,' he said quietly, 'it would be the certain proof. But not even that helped. Not even that.'

I pushed off. As MacDuff got his boat under way, I thought: plus one and minus one equal zero. He steered northeastward out into Corryvreckan. Mary sat immobile in the stern of *Sussi*. It was too dark for me to see her eyes. That was my only solace.

Chapter 25

MY sleep was troubled, when I slept at all, on the port side berth of the 'saloon'. Over and over, I went through what MacDuff had revealed to me. Torben, I saw, was heavily asleep in the quarter berth, to starboard of the companion-way. The forepeak, usually my quarters, had been given to Mary. It remained empty, however. Each time I woke up, I saw Mary's silhouette out in the cockpit. And every time she was in exactly the same position. I thought repeatedly that I must get up - must go and tell her to come down into the warmth of the cabin. For the thermometer showed the temperature to be at three degrees below zero. I didn't understand how she could stand it. But I continued to lie in my berth.

First at dawn, I heard her open the creaking hatchway door and climb down the ladder. I wanted to stretch out a hand as she went by, and ask her to tell me what was upsetting her. But at the same time I was certain that she was a person who didn't want words of comfort. There are people who don't. I am one of them myself.

When I awoke next time, everything was different. The night seemed to have been a dream. Sunlight came in through the hatchway - which indicated a westerly wind. The day was now two hours longer than at the winter solstice - which could be noticed. It was already light at eight o'clock. Torben, I saw, was standing at the paraffin-stove, and I caught the smell of toast. The door to the forepeak had been closed, presumably by Torben so that Mary wouldn't be awakened.

It was pleasant to remain abed, without any need for haste, with nothing to be taken care of immediately. Until the turn of the tide, at about ten, it was impossible for us to leave. For that matter, I didn't know where we would sail to. MacDuff had suggested Loch Na Droma Buidhe, on the east side of Mull. How far away was the place? Well, I could find out later. Probably as a reaction to the experiences of the previous day and to the sleepless night before that, nothing now seemed more important than the toast and the patch of clear blue sky to be seen through the starboard portholes. I could note from where I lay that the barometer had risen. So we should have fine sailing, wherever we intended to go.

I let Torben call me when breakfast was ready. Not being a morning person himself, he fully understood that one might not want to talk for the first half-hour after rising. Our silent breakfast was delightful in its simplicity; toast, Robertson's Scotch Marmalade (long a favourite) and coffee. Since my years in France, I wasn't used to eating very much in the morning. After breakfast came the first, and best, cigarette of the day.

Its smoke curled upwards towards the cabin ceiling. In fact ivory white, the ceiling always turned a yellowish colour during winter months; the effect of my paraffin lamps, cooking, cigarettes and the heater. The windows had also suffered, and I saw that they needed cleaning on the outer sides as well, because salt had crystallised there.

When Torben and I cast off, the wind still came from the west. And Mary still slept, after her sleepless night. But the roar from Corryvreckan had died away, leaving an unnatural silence behind it. This time, we sailed through the channel between Eilean Beaq and Jura. To begin with, we felt the eddy that runs close to land, but as soon as we were out in Corryvreckan, the tidal water swept us quickly eastward into the Sound of Jura. Looking back to the northeast, we saw what now remained of the hell we had sailed through before: whirlpools, waves rising steeply, areas where masses of water shifted and displaced one another as if they were large floes of ice, circles of water which seethed and bubbled like lava in a volcano's crater. But now the place was merely fascinating to look at.

I hesitated to have a proper talk with Torben. I was afraid that he might notice some awkwardness in me and guess that I was again keeping something from him. But instead I caught something odd in him. Simply that he failed to ask what MacDuff and I had talked about at dinner, then afterwards on Eilean Mor, seemed strange.

At first, I ascribed the difference in Torben to his violent feelings in Corryvreckan the day before, and to his absolute conviction there that his passage through purgatory would end in some other world. That conviction must have left its mark. I have, since that time, tried to understand what happened to him. And I have come to the conclusion that his experience, especially his belief that his life was almost over, shook him to the depths of his soul and opened his heart and mind to forces which would otherwise never have entered there.

But that morning only the immediate cause of his being so absent became clear to me. And I did not want to believe that this was of importance.

Somewhere in Luing sound, I asked Torben what he thought of Mary. Of course he'd had a long talk with her.

He said: 'She is not like others.'

'What others?'

310

'Other people. I have never met anyone like her. How can I explain it?'

He seemed to be considering the matter for himself rather than for my benefit. I wanted to know what he and Mary had talked about.

'Actually, I don't quite know what we talked about,' he answered.

'What do you mean by that?'

'Well ... That we spoke about something altogether different from what we seemed to be talking about. We discussed Celtic history - but that wasn't the actual subject. At least not for me.'

'Really?' I said. 'What was it then?'

'Have you never found that words suddenly appear to lose their meanings? You go on talking, but in fact what you say signifies nothing. All that counts is what you do *not* say - a tone of voice, a glance ...'

I remarked jestingly: 'More or less what happens when you're falling in love.'

When I looked at Torben, I realised that my jesting tone was not in order, quite the contrary. He avoided my eyes, almost as if he feared what I might see in his own.

'Yes,' he agreed at last. 'I suppose so.'

He said no more, and I don't know what he had in mind just then. I didn't believe, nor did I wish to believe, that anything much was involved. But if Torben had been captivated by Mary's enigmatic personality, it was - in view of what MacDuff had told me, and her probable fate - about the worst thing that could happen.

To lead our thoughts towards something more tangible, I said: 'Well, certainly you talked about human sacrifice. I caught that.'

'Yes, we did,' he answered in a relieved voice, as if happy to have been provided with an escape from the real subject. 'She had a peculiar attitude towards history.'

'In what way, peculiar?'

'Everything is of the present-day.'

'That sounds,' I said, 'as if it were taken from Pekka's logbook.'

'Yes, I have thought of that. But at least he used the past tense in what he wrote. For Mary everything is in the present. I didn't know at times whether she was talking about something that happened a thousand years ago or just yesterday. I read somewhere that there's an island in the Pacific where they treat history in the same way - or have done. All that has taken place is of equal interest. One of the natives came running to the American governor and shouted that a murder had been committed. It must be avenged! When the affair was investigated, it turned out that there had indeed been a murder. But twenty seven years earlier! When you read about the incident, the attitude doesn't seem so strange. After all, you understand what you read. But when you meet it in reality, as I did yesterday, you realise what an enormous difference it makes. For long periods, I didn't know how to take it.'

Torben fell silent.

'I'd like to know,' he said at last, 'how it feels to live without a sense of the past. Of course, in a way it fits with the Druids' idea that all knowledge can be contained in the memory. That everything becomes dead knowledge when written down. But how could one live without books and the written word? I would be dead without them.'

He looked so that you could easily have believed that all the world's books had already vanished.

'Sometimes I wonder if they weren't right,' he went on. 'Actually, it might have been because the Druids kept the words alive in their memories that they managed to imbue words with such power. They did, certainly, know the real value of words. They could even stave off violence by words.

That every single word meant something to her was what I felt when I talked to Mary.'

I glimpsed what it was in Mary that could have fascinated Torben. It was what she stood for and believed she lived for: the Druids' conception of language and knowledge as the goal of existence. But only that? Wasn't it also Mary as a woman?

Torben had talked with her for hour - had been alone with her while MacDuff and I were on Eilean Mor. That would have been enough for her to make a great impression on him even without the susceptibility that derived from his recent experiences in Corryvreckan. Torben fell easily in love. I think it was a way of increasing his knowledge of the world. So he always encouraged his fleeting amorous feelings - and he liked others to take an interest in them.

There had been occasions when we devoted hours to discussing such feelings: how they were roused, what they were good for, why they were induced by precisely a certain woman and not another ... Now, on the contrary, he seemed dismayed and bewildered. What kind of woman was Mary?

But then, I had to concentrate on the navigation. We were proceeding at a good speed through Luing sound, hastened on our way by the tide. Because of the stream, landmarks and seamarks rushed to meet us, and we had scarcely time to identify what we saw. Meanwhile, I pondered on how I could distract Torben's attention from Mary. The easiest thing would be to take Torben ashore, while at anchor, and leave Mary alone on board. But it irritated me that I'd then be prevented from talking to Mary myself. Since my conversation with MacDuff, I knew much more about the Ring, but there were unanswered questions; and he had kindled a new curiosity which only Mary could satisfy.

We had already sighted Kerrera on the horizon when Mary appeared. Suddenly, she was standing in the cockpit, with a warm smile directed by turns at me and at Torben.

Gone was her burning gaze, gone her emphatic manner. She was simply a very beautiful woman who seemed to enjoy looking out over the water and allowing her long, ash-blond hair to be caught in the wind. She was wearing jeans and a large, thick woollen sweater of the kind popular among Scottish fishermen. I scarcely believed it could be Mary I saw. At the sight of her, there was evident joy in Torben's eyes. He had difficulty in taking his eyes off her.

'Where are we heading for?' she asked.

'Droma Buidhe,' I told her.

She seemed pleased with this reply. Either she knew where it lay, or she didn't really care where we were bound for.

Torben said tentatively: 'You must be hungry.'

'Yes. Now that you mention it, I am actually rather hungry.'

'Take the helm!' I told Torben, and I turned at once to Mary. 'I'll show you where everything is, so you'll be able to manage by yourself on board.'

'I always manage by myself. Especially on board.'

She explained to me that her father was a fisherman in Stornoway, and she had been practically brought up in a fishing boat.

'But you can tell me anyhow,' she added. 'There's always something to be learned.'

When breakfast was ready, we had Loch Spelve aport. There, Pekka had concealed himself before sailing in his dinghy over the Firth of Lorn to the Garvellachs islands. It was easy to understand his hesitation before the crossing. That he made it at all showed that he had no lack of courage. Furtively, I looked to see if Mary was noticing those islands. But she was preoccupied by our sails; she looked them over and trimmed them more expertly than I had ever learned to do.

We were speedily moving closer to Kerrera - still well to

starboard, however. I was drawn in two directions. I was torn between a desire to satisfy my curiosity and a desire to avoid attracting any unnecessary attention. Good sense and caution prevailed. I kept close to the east coast of Mull, on the opposite side of the firth. True, no more than three nautical miles lie between Mull and Kerrera. But not even through binoculars could anyone on Kerrera discern our sail number or type of boat. Moreover, I had exchanged my Swedish ensign for the Scottish courtesy flag, which was likely to make the identification of *Rustica* doubtful. But I couldn't repress an impulse to take out my own binoculars and scrutinise Kerrera. I caught no sign of life on the island. As I put the binoculars away, Torben looked at me questioningly but without real interest. Mary didn't seem to notice our covert glances. Perhaps she didn't know that MacDuff had sailed to Kerrera. It occurred to me that she might not even know what sort of expeditions he undertook. And I remembered his saying that she was not trustworthy.

But now all matters of that kind vanished into the glittering water, into the high afternoon air. We had fine sailing; it gave me more pleasure than anything I had done for a long time. However, I couldn't prevent Torben and Mary from sitting together on the foredeck. I was unable to hear what they said but I saw the smiles they exchanged, how their eyes met and lingered on each other. Now and then, the wind seized fragments of their conversation. I understood that they must still be speaking about Celtic culture and history, and I gathered that as a rule it was Torben who asked questions and listened.

Not long after three o'clock we rounded Duart Point. The sun disappeared behind the mountain of Mull, three thousand feet high, but it emerged when we passed long valleys. The shadows looked as if they had been sharply etched by an engraving tool. We sailed past Castle Duart, yet another of the countless old Scottish piles which, in recent times, have been acquired by descendants of the original owners - after ten, twenty or even thirty generations had come and gone. Where did the new owners get their money from? And why their wish to regain the castles? Had Pekka been right yet again? That everything lived on. Druidism in Celtic churches. The clans in their ancestral seats. Were the castles vast screens which concealed something beneath, hidden underground in dungeons and deep cellars? Were they junctions and places of co-ordination for a new Golden Road ...?

Twilight fell swiftly. The sky reddened, then became grey, and the keen edged shadows on the mountain slopes faded out. The tidal stream had turned, yet we reached Calve Island - outside the harbour of Tobermory - before dark. Tobermory, the largest town on Mull, may in summer be the sailing centre of Scotland's west coast, but now only a few solitary boats swung at anchor in the harbour, which was itself no more than a natural anchorage. We sailed past the entrance and then, on a new course, towards Aulistan Point. We steered our course with the help of light from the town astern. Out in the Firth of Lorn, we'd had sunken rocks with breakers to steer by. There were none now, and we were obliged to grope along in the little light that remained with occasional flashes from a torch. The worst came at the entry to Loch na Droma Buidhe, the approach there being a narrow inlet scarcely a hundred feet wide, with cliffs on either side. We crept along, and unaided by Mary we would certainly not have come through unscathed. Her eyes seemed to penetrate all darkness. She stood in the bows calling 'Starboard!' or 'Port!' At first I didn't wholly rely on her. But I soon realised that I had to. Otherwise expressed: I understood that I wouldn't have done so well myself.

When we were through, Mary sat silent in the cockpit. Since twilight, something had changed in her. We no longer heard her infectious, rippling laugh. She had taken part wholeheartedly in the entire sail: taken the helm, laid out courses, calculated the tides and made coffee. In short, *Rustica* had gained an ideal crew. But when darkness came she withdrew into herself. She piloted us into Droma Buidhe because it was necessary. But there was no joy when she called out her last instructions.

The change didn't surprise me. Her zest for life earlier in the day had given me more cause for wonder. Even if MacDuff had not spoken to her about the risks he ran, I couldn't conceive that Mary failed to notice, or sense, a difference now. True, I was an uninitiated observer. Even I, as nothing but an observer, had got the impression that their farewell on board Macduff's boat was final. On the other hand, it might have been that they believed every parting to be their last one.

We dropped anchor on the southern side of the loch, just inside the entrance. Then we went astern to make sure that our thirty-five pound plough-anchor had dug itself in properly. We had a nearly forty fathoms of cable out, which was a little on the short side.

While sailing to Brittany, I had learned not to be niggardly about ground tackle. The situation round Britain made the need still more evident. In view of the places where Englishmen commonly anchor along their shores, they would doubtless regard all the waters of the Stockholm archipelago, and those north of Gothenburg, as sheltered little anchorages. In Scotland it was almost impossible to find a harbour where one could moor at a quay. Even at Tobermory there were no landing stages. So yachtsmen lay at anchor or moored to a buoy and rowed ashore in a dinghy. The marine charts teemed with the marking *hr* for 'harbour', but that meant merely natural inlet, more or less sheltered from wind and weather. At least Loch na Droma Buidhe was one of the few really sheltered anchorages. But to my mind the basin in the middle was of alarming size - half a nautical mile straight across - enough to allow storm winds to whip up waves at least a metre high. Even so, Droma Buidhe was considered to be one of the safest anchorages on the entire west coast.

As soon as we had furled the sails, Torben helped me to launch *Sussi*.

'Now we'll sail over to Tobermory and go to a restaurant,' I told him.

'All three of us?'

'No,' I replied. 'I promised MacDuff that we'd leave Mary on board.'

Torben turned and looked at her but said nothing. His gaze made it very clear to me that I still couldn't tell him what I knew from MacDuff. It struck me suddenly that I was no longer prepared to put unreserved trust in Torben. A dreadful discovery, this. But, once formulated in my mind, I couldn't get rid of it. And what made matters worse was that actually he couldn't trust me either. After all, in giving my promise to MacDuff I had failed Torben. This might not have mattered under normal circumstances; Torben would have understood the situation. But with Mary close to him, I wasn't quite sure what was happening

Half an hour later we left in the dinghy. To Mary I said only that we were going to Tobermory. With thought of her becoming hungry, I'd shown her where food was kept. And she knew already how to light the paraffin stove.

She said nothing and seemed not to care where we went. I disliked having to leave her alone aboard *Rustica*. After all, it was my home. But I didn't appear to have a choice of my own in dealing with Torben, MacDuff and Mary.

The crossing took more than an hour and a half. We didn't get ashore until after eight o'clock. Using an Optimist as dinghy is pure luxury compared to the rubber boats - very difficult to row - that most sailors use. But with two men aboard, *Sussi* didn't exactly behave like a greyhound. And when her sails were up, the boat left you scarcely room to breathe under the boom and aft of the mast. Torben and I lay across the boat with our heads on opposite sides to balance our weight. Each time a gust of wind came along, the one of us with his head to windward had to lean out a foot or two beyond the gunwale to keep the boat from turning over. As *Sussi* didn't move very quickly, I was constantly obliged to adjust the sheet, slackening it properly when a stiff breeze arrived. We did manage to arrive without *Sussi* having turned over, but we had got pretty wet.

Safely ashore in Tobermory, we discovered that the town had a picturesque harbour front, the houses being painted all sorts of colours: yellow, red, bright blue, black, green ... We walked along the single street hunting for a restaurant in one of the colourful houses. We ended in a nondescript place up on a first floor. I don't remember its name - which is just as well left in oblivion. The bill of fare was plain, and we finally chose lasagne. This was brought, and with it on the plate came chipped potatoes and half a tinful of white beans in tomato-sauce. Torben and I looked incredulously at each other. But we found something interesting on the menu, especially for Torben: a *Scottish* wine. He summoned the waiter at once and wished to know what kind of imported wine took the liberty of calling itself 'Scottish'. To his amazement, he was told that the wine was actually produced in Scotland - at a monastery which possessed vineyards on southern slopes where the weather was particularly mild. We ordered a bottle of both the red variety and the white. Torben first tasted and then drank them both with his usual care and attention. Judgement was thereupon handed down: certainly not great wines but honest in character, good table wines without inherent defect, fully drinkable if they suited one's mood at the moment.

They suited ours, and we finished off both bottles. This, we felt, compensated for not eating the food on our plates. When leaving, we asked the waiter where we should go to have 'one for the road' before sailing home.

'Well,' he said, 'you have only to choose. Either you go to the MacDonald Arms or you go to the Mishnish.'

Torben asked: 'Which is the better of the two?'

The waiter, who looked as if he understood the good points and the shortcomings of pubs from long experience, considered the matter.

'Well, if it isn't the Mishnish,' he said, 'it is the MacDonald Arms.'

We went to the MacDonald Arms, which proved to be a typical Scots pub; distinguished from its English equivalents by the copious assortment of Scotch malt whiskies it could offer. My favourites, MacCallan and Old Fettercairn were on view, but also numerous other whiskies of all shades and all ages. Torben looked despairingly for a list of wines, and I suffered from awful indecision about which whiskies to try. I always drank moderately - not from fear of getting drunk, but because I hated to face a new-born day with a hangover. It would obviously be hard to keep within bounds. As I was regarding a whole row of brands new to me, I suddenly heard a voice behind me.

'I'd recommend Glen Morangie to start with. It's mild and round, and consequently best taken first.'

I turned round and found myself confronted by a man whom I had not, I was sure, seen previously.

He went on: 'If you'd like to try something more unusual, the Talisker is a good bet.' He cleared his throat significantly. 'It's a little bit rough!'

I was still somewhat taken aback.

'Don't look so surprised!' he said. 'My name is MacLean. I live a bit further down the coast. I saw you sail by there this afternoon. Every time a vessel passes, I reach for my binoculars. It's a bad habit I have.'

MacLean, I thought - either the laird himself or some kinsman also residing in Castle Duart. I was curious about the man, but I wished to be prudent. Even if I more or less assumed that Torben and I had been given a reprieve until we met MacDuff again, I felt far from secure. On the other hand, MacLean's regard was frank and open; he radiated goodwill. For that matter, so did most of the Scotsmen we met.

With no hint of undue interest, he inquired where we came from.

'Denmark and Sweden,' I replied.

'But weren't you sailing under our flag?'

I had forgotten about that. But how had he been able to recognise us when he'd only seen us through his binoculars?

Torben had drawn nearer when he saw that I had company.

He said: 'Our Swedish flag was blown to pieces a fortnight ago on the North Sea.'

'A fortnight ago?' said MacLean with much surprise.

Perhaps *too* much surprise, I thought. Or was I being exaggeratedly mistrustful? I seemed to feel that an emissary of the Ring was at my back wherever we went.

'Surely you don't mean that you sailed over the North Sea in January?'

'That,' said Torben, 'is exactly what I mean. But it wasn't my fault. It was the Skipper's idea. Blame it on him!'

MacLean announced to everyone about: 'These two gentlemen must have free drinks here this evening. They have sailed across the North Sea in January. Just to look in on us here in Scotland.'

I sensed that all eyes were turned towards us. And I wanted to make some protest. But it would be pointless.

'That *is* why?' MacLean asked, in a voice that was

somewhat lower but still perfectly audible to everyone present. 'Just to see how we live here in Scotland?'

'Yes, and because Scotland is a beautiful country. And no other people are so hospitable. And in winter we'd be free from all the tourists.'

I heard an approving murmur at close quarters. MacLean was pleased and he looked out over the room as if to tell all those present that he was right to have us drink at his expense. Of course I'd have preferred to be spared the attention. Sailing to Tobermory might turn out to have been a great mistake. But there was nothing I could do about it now except try to keep up appearances.

MacLean returned to his first topic.

'Well, which whisky is it to be?'

Wishing to postpone any decision about the Talisker, which was 'a little bit rough', I quickly answered: 'I'd like to taste a Glen Morangie.'

It was Torben who had to face the Talisker. He didn't dare confess his distaste for Scotland's national beverage. But his true feelings were betrayed by the grimace that distorted his face when he swallowed his first swig of the Talisker. I managed to distract MacLean's attention from the spectacle by praising with sincerity the mild and delicious taste of Morangie. Happily, Torben did the right and manly thing: he got down all that was left in the glass at one go. So it was empty when MacLean turned back to him.

With some difficulty, Torben declared: 'I have never tasted anything like it.'

'No, I'm sure you haven't,' said MacLean. 'There's nothing like Talisker!' He ordered another round.

Quick as a cobra, Torben now got in: 'I'd like to taste the other whisky as well.'

It was the first time since we had arrived in Scotland, perhaps the first time in his life, that Torben asked for a glass of whisky. After taking a tiny sip of the Glen Morangie, he looked thoughtfully down into his glass. Then he tasted it again. Whereupon, his entire face lit up with surprise.

MacLean regarded him with satisfaction.

Suddenly he asked: 'By the way, weren't there three of you on board this morning? I thought I saw a third in my binoculars. A woman, if I'm not mistaken?'

'Yes, there was a woman,' I replied. 'But she needed to rest this evening.'

'No wonder.' There could very well have been reproach in MacLean's tone. 'And have you dragged her with you across the North Sea?'

I didn't know what to answer. Nor did Torben, who simply stood turning his glass round with his fingers. But MacLean didn't seem to wonder about my silence and let the matter pass. I couldn't make him out. He asked us many questions that evening, but whether they sprang from perfectly ordinary curiosity or from certain suspicions was unclear to me. As the evening drew on, it became increasingly difficult to determine anything at all. Others at the pub wanted to stand us drinks, and when the MacDonald Arms closed both Torben's sense of judgement and my own were somewhat impaired.

In any case, I was happy that we two could have a long evening out together as if nothing had come between us. I began to hope that our conversation in the morning hadn't meant what I'd thought it meant. I told myself that all was really as before, that my misgivings were imaginary, that on Friday the whole thing would be over.

We put out again into the dark, each lying on one side of *Sussi*. Understandably enough, our navigation was even more awkward on our way back. And, when gusts of wind came along, I had considerably more difficulty in getting Torben to counter them with his weight. At one point, he almost sank the boat by moving out over the gunwale when the wind had already passed. In the end, I was forced to rely entirely on my own reactions (not that they were so much quicker) and slacken the sheet as the gust arrived.

At first, I steered by a constellation that lay straight to the east. But when we had got half way, I discovered that light was coming from some source directly on our course but well above the sea - presumably from a height to the other side of Loch na Droma Buidhe. But what was a light doing there? Had we been joined by another boat in the Loch?

The closer we approached, the more strangely the light behaved. Torben had fallen asleep, and finally I woke him up. He had raised himself drowsily, hit his head on the boom and nearly overturned *Sussi* with captain and crew. When he more or less recovered his senses, I pointed out the light to him. He said at once:'There's something burning up there.'

And I realised instantly that he was right. *Rustica*! I thought. Has Mary set fire to *Rustica*?

But of course the fire was higher up. When we were only a few cable lengths from the entry to the loch, we saw it clearly. We stared up at the height. At the top, spectrally silhouetted against the fire, someone stretched out both arms towards the sky and out over the sea.

An instant later, we heard a cry that echoed between the faces of rock. The silhouette vanished into the dark. After a few more seconds, the flames began to die down. It can't have been more than a minute before the fire was totally gone and darkness reigned supreme. All was silent.

Chapter 26

'I'm going ashore,' Torben said.

'What do you intend to do?'

'What do you think? See what has happened. Help her.'

'Her?' I asked. 'How do you know that it's Mary?'

'Who else would it be? Have you forgotten Anholt, with the fire and the woman up on the cliff?'

I hadn't forgotten. But if it was Mary who had cried out, perhaps she was not alone.

I said: 'There may not have been an accident. Someone must have put out the fire.'

'I have already thought of that.' Torben sounded irritated at what he presumably took as an objection to his landing.

'It can very well be our friends from Kerrera,' I told him.

'Does it matter who it is?'

I wanted to prevent Torben from going up. For his own sake, for our sake. We were under no obligation to Mary. Rather the contrary.

'You won't be able to see anything,' I pointed out. 'We haven't even got a torch with us.'

'I have,' said Torben. 'He drew out his head lamp from a deep inner pocket. 'Sail back to *Rustica* and wait for me there.

I'll whistle three times if I want you to come with the dinghy.'

We had now come close to land, and I tried to find a ledge where Torben could jump ashore.

I asked: 'Wouldn't it be better if you waited for me? I'll sail round the head and tie up *Sussi* on the lee side. Here, she'd break to pieces against the cliffs. It won't take me more than ten minutes.'

'Oh yes, it will.' said Torben, 'And in all events ten minutes is too long.'

'Then we'll leave *Sussi* here,' I told him half heartedly.

On the one hand, I didn't want to leave him. On the other, I was worried that if Mary hadn't been alone something might have befallen *Rustica*.

'No, we won't leave *Sussi*!' said Torben. 'We can't risk losing the dinghy. We must have it for Mary if something has happened to her.' There was stubbornness in his voice.

'Be careful!' I told him, when he had jumped onto a stone and was clinging to the slippery rocks.

All the good whisky I had drunk might have been to blame. In any case before Torben was out of earshot I shouted after him words that I regretted at the same instant as I uttered them.

'Don't forget!' I called. 'If it had been one of us, Mary certainly wouldn't have lifted a finger to save us.'

Torben didn't answer. He began, with wild haste, to climb up the headland. His head lamp cast a shaft of light either against the blackish grey rock or out into the dark, where it seemed to linger for a few fleeting seconds after it had been turned away. I pushed off with a foot to get *Sussi* clear of the cliff. The waves were not high, but I didn't want to keep her there any longer than necessary. She had already received a number of scratches and gashes on her freeboard.

When I came into the calm water of Loch na Droma Buidh, I realised what I had actually shouted to Torben. True, my concern for him lay behind my words then. But in his state of mind how could he understand that? Behind my outburst there had been, as well, a base instinct to get even with Mary. For him, this would appear even more contemptible if he was unaware that his eagerness to rescue Mary did not spring purely from brotherly feeling.

Shortly after entering the loch, I was struck by something else: Mary could not have been alone. If so ... How would she have got ashore?

Once back on *Rustica*, I stared out into the darkness without catching the slightest movement or light. Second after second passed, minute after minute. I tried to prepare myself for every conceivable occurrence: anybody at all turning up among the trees, a sudden outbreak of gunfire ... Astern of *Rustica*, *Sussi* lay ready for me to spring aboard, and I'd be on land in an instant or two.

But time passed and nothing happened. I was horribly cold. The alcohol had provided a certain superficial warmth that didn't last. Perhaps I would have been less anxious if I'd remained a bit drunk.

After the first half hour of waiting, my uneasiness increased and turned into fear that something dire had taken place. Not a sound could be heard except the lapping of waves against the hull. The height to the south, which Torben had climbed, was in total darkness. After a further quarter hour, I decided to wait one hour longer; then I'd go up the mountain myself. This decision calmed me somewhat, and I prepared for the expedition by putting on suitable boots and warmer clothing, and taking my torch. When ten minutes were left before the appointed time, I saw a beam of light moving slowly and fitfully through the woods down towards the shore. It advanced, remained still, briefly or not so briefly, then advanced again. When Torben blew his whistle, I was already sitting in *Sussi*, rowing with powerful strokes in towards land.

327

Now and then, I turned to make sure that I was heading directly for the spot where the light from Torben's head lamp fell on something white. Just before I got there I saw what this was: Mary's naked legs. I remember thinking as I jumped ashore: What would MacDuff say?

The first thing that came from Torben was: 'She is alive!'

He stood bent over Mary, I saw that he had placed his heavy sailor's jacket round her.

'We must get her into a warm place,' he added. 'She is frozen.'

I told him: 'We'll have to row her together. I could never lift her on board by myself.'

Even getting her into the dinghy was not easy. We placed her on the bottom between the thwart and the stern. So as not to overturn the boat, Torben and I were forced to sit side by side on the thwart, each with one oar. While Mary's legs were up on the stern and stretched over the water, her head rested on Torben's free arm. I felt through my trousers the cold coming from her body. And I wanted to row faster, but we didn't dare. For no more than two inches of *Sussi*'s freeboard remained above the waterline.

I still don't know how we succeeded in getting Mary up onto *Rustica* - only that we did succeed. We laid her on the port side berth with an aluminium-coated cover wound about her. (I kept one on board precisely for such cases). And we then put her into a down sleeping bag; after that, into a second sleeping bag over the first one. She mumbled something inaudible when we laid her down on the berth. I waited for her to scream with pain when warmth began to penetrate her limbs. From my days as a skin-diver, I knew how it hurts when warmth starts to spread in frost-bitten parts of the body. The fingers are worst. One feels that they are being torn to pieces. But not a sound came from Mary's lips.

Torben sat beside her, watching over her. I believe that he

scarcely took his eyes from her that night. He didn't spare me more than an occasional glance.

I asked him what had happened.

'It took me a long time to find her,' he explained. 'The last part of the way up, I didn't dare to have the lamp on. Like you, I was convinced that we weren't alone. It came to me then that, as we had taken the dinghy to Tobermory, Mary couldn't possibly go ashore by herself. Was that your idea, too?'

'No,' I answered. 'But exactly the same thought struck me when I had left you. Do you know how she got to land?'

'Yes. She swam.'

'Swam?' I supposed at first that I had misunderstood. 'It can't be done,' I said. 'After ten minutes a person would be more or less unconscious in the water at its present temperature.'

'She was naked when I found her. Have you any better explanation?' Torben demanded.

It almost seemed that he was reproaching me for our leaving Mary without any way to get ashore.

'How is it with her?' I asked.

'I don't know. It was hell reaching the spot without a light. I searched along the rock ledge under where we saw her. I thought that she had fallen down. But at last I found her up at the top, not much more than a foot from the edge of the cliff. And only inches away from ashes of the fire. She was lying like an unborn child, and she was naked. There were no signs of injuries. But she was ice cold, and at first I believed that she was dead. I couldn't find any pulse. So I held the glass on my head lamp in front of her mouth. When it became a bit misty, I knew that she was still breathing. I took off my coat and sweater, wrapped her in them and tried to rub warmth into her. It was a good five minutes before she showed the slightest sign of life. Then she opened her eyes and stared at me as if I were a ghost. After that, she became delirious. She thought she was in *Sid*.

Torben silently gazed for a long time at Mary's hand, which he was gently holding.

Then he said in a hushed voice: 'At the same time, she suffered. Not because she was in pain, but because she regretted what she had done. She was sorry that she hadn't reached *Sid* through her own will power. Again and again, she said that she was a deserter.'

Torben was silent once more. I wondered what he thought of the situation. Because of course I knew why Mary believed that she had deserted again. At last, slowly, as if it were difficult for him to produce his words, Torben told me more.

'And then there was MacDuff. She thought that she had failed MacDuff. She wanted to go back. She didn't want to stay in *Sid*. I didn't believe that she loved him so much.'

He seemed unaware of the despair he had put into those last words.

I felt an enormous relief. Mary loved MacDuff above all else, however impossible their love might be, however much it afflicted her. Meanwhile, I saw that Torben was suffering, as well as Mary. And I couldn't do anything to help him. Well, we would soon be leaving Mary behind us - and that would be that.

'When we sailed here,' Torben, mused mostly to himself, 'she said that she and MacDuff couldn't live together. She said they weren't engaged in the same struggle. Their time had run out long ago, she told me.'

I began to suspect that Mary had used Torben to strengthen her in her belief that she didn't need MacDuff - that for her Torben had been part of a momentary attempt to forget MacDuff. But now she had discovered, rediscovered, that their love had a stronger hold on her than teachings of the Druids and the culture of Celts. She lived for an idea, but she was the helpless victim of her emotions. I suddenly thought of her with a kind of sympathy, new to me about her since Dragør.

When I suggested that it might be best to sail to Tobermory and get a doctor, Torben finally looked up at me.

'She would never forgive us for that,' he said.

'But if she dies?' I wanted to know. 'What will we do then?'

'What will we do?' Torben repeated.

The idea of Mary dying appeared to be completely strange to him.

Finally he said: 'If she recovers, it's better that she finds herself here with me when she realises she is still alive.'

'With you?'

'With us.' Torben didn't change his tone.

There was nothing I could say to this.

'And the fire?' I inquired. 'Who put it out?'

'Nobody.'

'Nobody?' I protested: 'What do you mean? Somebody must have put it out!'

'No. It died out by itself. I felt the ashes. They were cold. And dry!'

Torben shrugged a shoulder - meaning that he wouldn't even try to explain how a fire could extinguish itself from one instant to the next, that he accepted the occurrence without question. It was not an attitude which normally would ever have been his.

'I am sorry,' I told him.

'For what?'

'For what I said about Mary.'

He reassured me: 'That didn't mean a thing.'

This answer came quickly, as if Torben too had feelings of guilt. It showed all the same, that he had caught and remembered what I'd said. And there was an emptiness in his tone that undermined the sincerity of what he said. I am not sure that he gave his forgiveness the slightest thought. He had merely uttered a phrase - oblivious to what words are for, to the fact that their magic and power was what he believed he would find through Mary.

As an explanation of what I had called after him, I said: 'I didn't know that Mary meant so much to you.'

To this he answered nothing at all. Perhaps he thought that I was lying to myself, or only to him, or to us both at the same time.

I left him bowed over Mary, went into the forepeak and closed the door.

Chapter 27

WHEN I woke up in the morning, I had a racking headache. I had slept out of sheer exhaustion, but the events of the evening had remained agitatingly with me. The sheet and blanket lay in a heap at my feet. It seemed to be quiet in the saloon, and I opened the door carefully so as not to awaken Torben and Mary.

The saloon was empty. Torben had been thoughtful enough to scribble a message on a piece of paper: 'Don't worry. We are coming back.' But the knowledge that Torben had gone ashore with Mary didn't exactly reassure me, rather the contrary. While I prepared breakfast and swallowed two headache pills, my worries turned to concrete questions. What had Mary felt when she recovered consciousness and discovered that she was not in *Sid*, that she, in spite of everything, had been faithful to MacDuff rather than to any fanatical Druid order? Joy? Gratitude to Torben for having saved her life? I realised what that might mean to Torben and how easily he might take it as justification for feelings of another kind.

I wanted nothing so much as to weigh anchor, sail round Mull and deposit Mary at the appointed place of meeting.

In the hope that the chilly morning air would clear my head, I took my breakfast to the cockpit. The sun was rising over the mountain to the east. Before me, *Rustica*'s bow pointed northward, past the island of Oronsay which made Loch na Droma Buidhe such a sheltered anchoring place. Round about, the summits of mountains were covered with snow. The sky was clear, and shadows cut sharp lines onto the granite grey mountain sides. It must have been magnificent, but my restlessness blinded me to its beauty.

My gaze roved between the shore, where *Sussi* lay moored, and the bush covered slopes to which I thought that Mary and Torben might for some reason have gone.

What were they up to? From where could Mary have got the strength to rise, sail ashore and go up among the cliffs surrounding Loch na Droma Buidhe? I hadn't the peace of mind to wait any longer. I put on my oilskins and made *Rustica* ready to sail. Whatever might happen, or whatever *had* happened to the two, I didn't intend to remain there any longer than absolutely necessary. Mary must be found and returned to MacDuff.

I had just put the anchor-chain on the windlass when I heard the creaking of rowlocks. I turned and saw that *Sussi* was on the way out from shore. Torben was rowing swiftly and methodically. Mary sat in the stern, erect, with her hair blowing in the wind.

When she saw that I was watching, she gave me a very warm and friendly smile.

I went astern to help them up. Torben said nothing and avoided looking at me as he climbed on board. He looked unutterably tired. But he seemed cheerful, almost happy.

'When do we sail?' Mary asked, in a voice which seemed completely unaffected by her pain and suffering.

'Now. At once. I don't want to be late.'

'For what?' she wondered distantly.

'We are to meet MacDuff tomorrow.'

Have you forgotten that? I was about to ask. But a glance from Torben stopped me. I stared at Mary, whose expression hadn't changed at all when I mentioned MacDuff. Yesterday I had been certain that she loved MacDuff and that all else was without significance for her. But now? My anxiety returned. What sort of game was she playing?

According to Pekka, MacDuff was dangerous. But with MacDuff I felt secure. It was Mary who gave me the feeling of crossing over ice in the spring or walking through a swamp. Suddenly a crack might open, or I'd sink into a quagmire while frantically seeking something to catch hold of.

At two o'clock that afternoon, we passed Ardmore Point on the north coast of Mull and I was already wondering where we ought to anchor for the night. After only a few more hours, twilight would fall upon us. I left the helm to Torben and gave him a safe course as the western side of Mull is treacherous, with plenty of rocks and shoals.

I sat indecisively with the chart in front of me. We were twelve miles from Iona, and we wouldn't be able to get there before dark. The Treshnish Isles didn't seem to offer very good shelter. Between Fladda and the larger island, Lunga, there were numerous shallow reefs and the sole anchorage was open to the northwest. Calgary Bay, on the shore of Mull itself, might be possible if the wind remained in the northwest, but Scottish weather was too unpredictable to take the risk. So that left only the channel between Mull and the island of Ulva. But once again prospects were doubtful. I read in the pilot that the sound was 'studded with rocks and sandbanks,' and that it should be 'passed with extreme caution'.

I cast a glance at the extra compass inside. Torben was roughly keeping the course I had given to him. I realised at the same time that I didn't check only because of our principle always check each other's navigation. I checked just as much because I couldn't help thinking that he was not himself, just like me perhaps. We had been by now in danger several times, and it would have been surprising if the experience had left us untouched. Inwardly I tried to make light of it. I assured myself that all would be as usual when we left Scotland behind. Tomorrow we'd deposit Mary with MacDuff and then be free to sail wherever we wished. The open sea lay before us. We could sail to the Caribbean. Or to Portugal. And nobody would miss us. On the contrary, there were those who would be happy to have got rid of us. Perhaps Mary was among them.

Why not do it? Why not do what they all wanted? Just as I was asking myself this question the hatch opened and Mary climbed down into the cabin. She placed herself beside me, put a hand on my shoulder and bent forward over the chart. Her cheek was only an inch or two from my face, and I felt the warmth of her hand. What did she want? Once more, I was on precarious ground. It struck me that perhaps she was quite simply trying to separate Torben and me, as a way of protecting the Ring from our intrusions. As long as MacDuff guaranteed our lives, there was nothing more she could do. Anger mounted within me. She did this although she might have been dead now, if we hadn't taken care of her!

'Where have you thought of sailing?' she asked.

I pointed at the sound of Ulva, and she gave me a startled look.

'I thought you knew better,' she said.

'Show me a better place! We could sail on all night if you prefer.'

'No,' Mary said, as if it were an order.

Rustica heeled over and she leaned against me. The swell from the Atlantic was obviously increasing. I pushed her away with both hands. She looked at me searchingly, with defiance, but she said nothing. This time I managed to meet her gaze without becoming lost in it.

'The sound of Ulva is the only place where we are safe from the swell,' I told her.

'We can go to Acar Mor,' she said, and again she leaned against me.

I was sure that she wanted to see whether I would push her away again or at least draw back. So I didn't move at all.

She pointed to the island of Gometra, which is separated from Ulva by a strait.

'Here,' she said, 'behind this islet, Eilean Dioghlum, there is a sheltered cove where we'll be safe from all winds. It's easy to enter.'

'But how deep is it? We draw more than six feet.'

'In the middle it's nine feet at low tide.'

'Does MacDuff use it?' I inquired.

'MacDuff?'

She repeated the name, as if she had never heard it before.

'Yes, MacDuff, who else!' I insisted. 'Have you forgotten him?'

For once it was Mary who looked away.

'Yes,' she said in a toneless voice, 'I have. I forget him every time we are apart.'

Her eyes were on me again. I could see that for once she was oblivious to everything about Druids or Celts; she thought only about her impossible love for MacDuff which time after time had caused her to betray all that she believed in. Her despair at that moment made her human. I spoke to her in a voice that was friendlier than I had intended.

'And Torben? Is he only a way of forgetting?'

'Torben?'

The wall that had just collapsed between us was again intact.

The rest of our sail was a wordless torment. When people

in a sailing-boat are as estranged as Mary and I were, a boat becomes more like a prison than a dream about freedom. Mary didn't show herself on deck until we were outside the entrance to Acarsaid Mor. I don't know how she could have known that we were arriving; she must have spent her life in the waters where we were sailing. Just as when we had entered Loch na Droma Buidhe, she placed herself in the bows and called back to me clear and indisputable words of command, which I obeyed to the letter. I was forced to rely on her because I hadn't had time to do my chart-work as I should have.

Inside Arcasaid Mor, the water was calm, but the westerly wind swept over the islet, and we still made good speed. I had to tell Torben that he must come up and take down the sails. All went so rapidly that I had to use the engine to prevent us from being driven up on the sharp rocks of Gometra. Mary helped with the anchor, and the chain followed it good-naturedly and without any kinks from the chain-locker. The whole manoeuvre had been slovenly executed and I felt only relief when the anchor had dug itself in. Silence fell.

Without explaining why, I launched *Sussi* and boarded her.

'I'm going to row ashore,' was all I said to Torben and Mary, without waiting for any reply. 'There's a rubber dinghy in the cockpit-locker if you want to do the same.'

This information made Torben look up. Did he believe that I had deliberately refrained from telling Mary that we had an extra inflatable when we lay in Loch na Droma Buidhe?

I landed on the little island of Eilean Dioghlum, a barren, rocky, treeless place, perhaps three hundred feet across and a few hundred more in length. At its northern end, there was a plateau some thirty feet above the rest of the islet. It didn't take me many minutes to scale up there, and I sat myself on the edge, facing the sea. Down below my feet, the swell exploded against the rocks, and atomised foam flew up into my face. A black and white ferry of the Caledonian MacBrayne line was on its way towards the Sound of Mull. Using the ferry as gauge, I could estimate the dimension of the Atlantic's huge and pulsating swell, created by some tremendous storm hundreds of miles away. At one moment, the black hull of the ship was seen swaying on the tops of waves, at the next, it had disappeared down the other side. The sky was a flaming inferno. Between the sun and the island of Coll on the horizon, heavy clouds were rolling up, illuminated from below by fiery red light. The sea was the colour of blood, and the islands formed the dark red crust on a healing wound. It was painfully beautiful.

But the beauty produced no relief. I felt only sadness. Never before had I known the same desire to leave *Rustica* as soon as we had come into harbour.

To the southwest lay the island of Staffa, famous for its basalt pillars which enclose Fingal's Cave and the source of inspiration for Mendelssohn's Overture to The Hebrides. Pekka had been on Staffa. I spoke his name aloud as a conjuration, but it no longer meant anything. He was dead; somebody had killed him. What difference did it make? Thousands of children died of hunger and famine every day. Why bother about Pekka? I realised that my search for the Celtic Ring was meaningless if it meant risking losing the most valuable things I had, my friendship with Torben and my tenderness for *Rustica*.

I remained sitting there until it was dark. I dreaded being again face to face with Torben and Mary. What could we say to one another? I persuaded myself that it would all be over tomorrow. I thought, with something like anticipation, that I would sail to Brittany, to my friends at Saint Malo. After all, I was free to sail where I wished.

Not a sound was heard when I rowed back to *Rustica*. I stayed for a little while in *Sussi* before I climbed on board.

Light came into the cockpit from the saloon, but I didn't see anyone. On coming below, I found that the door to the forepeak was closed. My uneasiness returned, but I didn't dare open the door in case Torben and Mary were sleeping there together. The idea came to me of looking instead in the cockpit locker. The rubber dinghy was gone. I supposed that Mary had gone ashore, and that Torben must be sleeping in the forepeak. He was certainly tired.

But after half an hour, I began to have doubts and, cautiously, I opened the door. The forepeak was empty. So they must have gone ashore together. I discovered that in actual fact I was relieved because I wouldn't have to see them. And an awful fatigue suddenly came over me. I got myself something like a meal, drank a glass of wine while eating it, returned to the forepeak, set the alarm-clock to ring at five next morning and having closed the door so that I wouldn't be disturbed I went to bed. If Mary and Torben could enjoy nocturnal prowls together, they could hardly object to both having berths in the saloon.

I slept heavily but was awakened at about one by the creaking of the hatch. I heard Torben's and Mary's whispering voices, but I couldn't catch what they were saying. I listened to the tone. Was it happy or sad? Impossible to say. But one thing came clearly: Torben saying that he would never, if he could help it, let anything happen to me. This convinced me further that Mary wanted to make a tool of Torben, that she was consciously trying to separate him from me, presumably with the aim of stopping us from taking too much interest in the Celtic Ring. She didn't realise that such a project was pointless and now too late. I hadn't the slightest desire to pursue our investigations because MacDuff had revealed the essentials to me. But there was no way I could make her understand this without breaking my word to MacDuff. Also, and even worse, she might risk her own life, along with

MacDuff's and our lives, in some dramatic attempt to protect him.

I didn't get back to sleep for some time, and I felt that I had just dozed off when, an instant before the alarm clock sounded, I found myself fully awake. I knew that I had had nightmares, even though I only remembered them for an unpleasant feeling that lingered on. I did recall one of them, however. Mary was kissing me over and over again. I tried furiously to push her away, to run from her, but my body refused to obey; my arms remained at my sides and my legs wouldn't move.

I got dressed in the forepeak, where my oilskins were hanging on the door. When I hesitated to go into the saloon, it struck me how much I had changed. I had always been one of those people who live without expectations, who count on nothing in advance, be it positive or negative. An optimist will never quite be happily surprised; a pessimist only regains lost territory when his forebodings prove to be unfounded. Now I had begun to understand that pessimism might be the wiser course. If there is a great danger of a setback, then it must be better to spread out the pain and start suffering in advance.

That was perhaps the reason why I felt scarcely anything at all when I saw that Torben and Mary were sleeping together in the portside berth. I simply took the thermos flask which I'd filled with coffee in the evening and went out on deck. First I got *Rustica* ready to sail. Then I sat in the cockpit, drank coffee, smoked a cigarette and waited for dawn. Daybreak brought a strongish wind, drizzle and a sad grey sky. So far, we'd had good luck with the weather: excellent visibility and no precipitation when we sailed, the contrary while in harbour. Although usually a cautious sailor, I hadn't listened to a single weather forecast after leaving the North Sea. There would have been no point in listening since we so seldom had been able to choose ourselves when to sail.

This wasn't a morning I would have chosen for sailing either. Of course we had only ten nautical miles to Iona. But for the whole passage, we would be completely exposed to the Atlantic. To be on the safe side, I took a reef in the mainsail and set the jib. In order not to awaken Torben and Mary, I put out under sail. The movements of the boat at sea would wake them up soon enough. I hoped that they wouldn't fall out of their mutual berth before I could stand on the starboard tack. For the rest of our trip, their berth would be the leeward one, and it might be so calm and comfortable that they wouldn't wake up until we arrived at our destination. I would prefer to remain alone on deck. I hoped that the wind and the rain could help clear my head and put a little order into my confused ideas about the Celtic Ring, about Torben and Mary, about Torben and me, and about the uncertain future.

After ten minutes on a northerly course, I tacked and put *Rustica* on a heading that would bring us close to Staffa. Not because Pekka had been there or because I believed that I could discover something; it was simply the shortest route to take. The waves were huge, but they didn't break, being mostly the result of a long and powerful swell. As usual, *Rustica* sailed gently and with dignity. Serenely, I thought. The Rustler is a fantastic sea-boat. I had never known *Rustica* to slam into a wave, however choppy the sea.

Half an hour later, we were off the coast of Staffa. The walls of vertical pillars at its side resembled the jaws of a blue whale. What could Pekka have been looking for there? The island was uninhabited and inaccessible. To that extent it might suit shady activities. But during the winter the swell that broke all around the island could make it impossible to land for months on end. Unless of course there was some tiny cove into which a seaman like MacDuff would be able to take a boat. As soon as weather permitted, Fingal's Cave became a great tourist attraction. But why choose a much visited island as a place for shady goings-on? If boat loads of trippers didn't serve to conceal transports of another kind.

Everything was possible, I thought as Staffa began to fade away into the misty rain. But the thought came as an indifferent observation in passing. I had no feelings about the matter; it didn't concern me any longer. In an hour our expedition, our whole adventure, would be over. We would deliver Mary to MacDuff. Then, if necessary, we could sail off to the end of the world.

Iona emerged gradually out of the mist. I kept close to land, where there was plenty of water. Tinker's Hole lay in the southern part of the sound. It wasn't more than a narrow passage between a tiny islet and the little island of Erraid. The latter was separated from Mull by a strait which dried up at low water. To my eye, Tinker's Hole seemed an unsafe anchorage, but according to the handbook it was sheltered from both wind and ocean. The only drawback was the tidal streams, which could run up to three knots between the cliffs.

The difficulty was rather to get in. From the north, it would be too dangerous to be called 'interesting' even by a British sailor. Entering that way required local knowledge. The entrance from the south couldn't be much easier. There was a large unmarked rock in the middle. And from quite some distance I saw the waves breaking all around the Hole.

While I pondered on the situation, the hatch opened and Mary climbed out as if she knew that I needed help. She didn't say anything or even give me a glance. Instead, she looked sweepingly round the horizon and seemed to take some bearings by eye.

'Steer 140 degrees!' she told me.

Mary had piloted us accurately twice before. I had trusted her twice and intended to do so once more. But not blindly. I followed her instruction but kept half an eye on the chart. I did not doubt her capabilities or knowledge, those she had proved, but I did not trust her sense of self-preservation. She seemed to be thrown between a zest for life and a longing for death, even if she herself couldn't tell life and death apart. Her longing to go to *Sid* had surely nothing to do with a desire for death. On the contrary, it was a desire for more life. But between someone who truly believes in an after-life and someone who believes fully and firmly the opposite, there is a gulf that can never be bridged. The risks that we ran while entering Tinker's Hole couldn't have the same meaning for Mary as they had for me. The word 'vital' in the sense of being vital for life and death could not mean anything to her.

To get a better view, I stood up and followed Mary's indications, but keeping an eye on the chart at the same time. We approached the breakers from the northwest where there should have been a passage we could have taken, but I didn't discover it until it was too late.

Without Mary's help, we would no doubt have run aground. After a few cable-lengths of dizzy rampage between the breakers, we reached the rocky islet which protects Tinker's Hole from the Atlantic. Above the wail of the wind and the roar of the waves, Mary ordered me to keep close to the islet's southern point.

Soon afterwards I turned to port. In the twinkling of an eye, Mary lowered and furled the sails. A moment later, the anchor-chain was running out through the hawse-pipe and *Rustica* settled herself comfortably. The silence that fell as we came into the shelter seemed as overwhelming as the noise had done before. It was broken by Torben opening the hatch with a bang.

'What the hell is going on?' he asked and rubbed his shoulder.

He had probably fallen from his berth when we made our sharp turn to port. He checked himself when he saw where we were.

'Were you really in so much of a hurry?'

'Yes,' I told him. 'And I want to leave as soon as possible.'

Torben looked at me as if he didn't understand what I meant. But he ought to have understood. Or was it only me who was afraid that we couldn't trust each other completely any longer? Suddenly, I felt that I didn't know anything with certainty any longer.

Torben closed the hatch and returned below. Through the plexiglass, I could see him roll up his sleeping-bag and start to prepare breakfast. I sat at the helm, poured out some coffee from my thermos and lit a cigarette. Mary was still standing in the bows and looking northward. Would MacDuff come that way? Or wasn't she thinking of MacDuff at all? Impossible to know. I could ask as many questions as I liked, but it was meaningless to try to guess the answers. Finally, I suceeded in suppressing even the questions. The only thing that remained was the waiting, which requires neither questions nor answers. Now and then I looked north or south, hoping to see the black hull of *F 154* appear on the horizon.

In due course, Mary came aft and sat down in the cockpit. I offered her coffee and a cigarette, both of which she accepted without a word. Time dragged by. Mary became more and more withdrawn. For the most part, she simply stared into space.

The rain had stopped and the sky was breaking up. The wind veered to the southwest and it had become noticeably warmer. As the end of February was approaching, one could imagine that a touch of spring was in the air. My spirits rose a trifle. But at the same time restlessness crept over me. Why didn't MacDuff come? Shouldn't he already have arrived?

Finally, I couldn't stand it any longer and launched *Sussi*. I went down and took the binoculars from the rack at the companionway. Torben looked up, but said nothing.

I rowed out to the little island that was the last outpost before clear water, unbroken horizons and the open sea. From there, Tinker's Hole much resembled a water-filled stone-quarry, flanked as it was by naked cliffs. The nameless island consisted of rocky hillside rising in two humps, and from the top of one I had a boundless view of the grandiose and breath-taking coastline.

Through my binoculars, I began to make a systematic investigation of all the bays, inlets and channels. At first, I focused on what lay furthest off and sought for boats around the horizon. The sea was empty as far as could be seen. There were no more signs of life on the islands to the south: Colonsay, Islay, Jura. Only smoke rising from the chimneys of occasional cottages.

I swept the binoculars over the horizon to the west. No life there either except the perpetual movement of the sea. From which direction would MacDuff come? I had no inkling. What was the good, actually, of my sitting there with binoculars? It was self-delusion on my part to believe that the end would come sooner if I saw MacDuff's boat appear in the distance.

I was already on my way back to *Sussi* when a reflection of the sun caught my eye. It was not like the usual glitter in the water, but rather something like lightning or a flame. It seemed to come from the two small islands, just south of Iona, known jointly as 'Soa', about two nautical miles west of Tinker's Hole. Seconds after the first flash and before I could raise my binoculars, I heard the muffled roar of a powerful explosion. Although the sound undoubtedly came from over the water, something made me turn around and look at *Rustica*. She was exactly as she was when I left her. But Mary stood up in the cockpit, looking in the direction of the sound. Torben's head emerged from the hatch. The rumble of the explosion had almost ceased to echo from the cliff-sides when

I finally had Soa in focus.

In the narrow strait between the two islands, flames rose several feet high, but it was too far away to make out what was burning. I thought I saw two or three figures moving slowly over the southern islet away from the flames, but facing the sun as I did, it was difficult to tell what went on.

Then I heard a lesser bang from somewhere above my head. I looked up. A bright red parachute-flare was slowly descending across the sun. It was a distress signal, which is only to be used when life is in danger. I began to run down towards *Sussi*.

Chapter 28

WHEN I came down to the shore, Mary was weighing anchor. She had already started the engine.

'What is it?' Torben demanded, as he helped me to hoist up *Sussi* and stow her on deck.

'There's somebody in distress,' I replied.

I pointed at the flare, which still gave off a powerful light, while I took the helm and put the engine in gear. Other people must have seen it, I thought. Mary had swiftly raised the thirty-five pound anchor and secured it. I turned to starboard and laid a course that would take us south of En nam Muc. I was in such a hurry that I forgot about the rock in the middle of the approach to Tinker's Hole. It was Mary who reminded me of it, quite simply by moving the helm over to starboard.

'Thank you,' I said, realizing my negligence.

'What did you see?' she asked.

'It came from Soa. An explosion. Something was on fire. I thought I saw people as well. But I'm not sure.'

'How many?' Mary wanted to know.

'Two, possibly three. It was difficult to see because of the sun.'

'And the distress signal?'

'That came after the explosion,' I said. 'But I didn't see from where.'

'Then perhaps it isn't too late.'

'Too late for what?'

'How fast can we go?'

'Six knots. If the sea isn't too choppy.'

'Twenty minutes,' Mary said to herself.

It was as if she had a picture of the chart in her head. She knew exactly the location of rocks and how far it was between the islands. She knew by heart even the depths of the anchorages.

'Do you think it's MacDuff?' I asked her as we rounded En nam Muc, just to the south of Tinker's Hole.

She didn't answer, but I was sure that I had guessed right: she believed that MacDuff had sent up the distress signal. Had Dick and O'Connell decided once and for all to put no faith in MacDuff, whatever explanation he might have given for his and Pekka's presence in Denmark? If so, it was pure madness to let Mary accompany us to the island, or at least that she should show herself so visibly. Her presence in the cockpit was deadly dangerous, for her and also for us.

Torben evidently thought the same, for he urged her to go below. But she didn't give him a glance. It was as if she wished to be seen. What did she think? When the might of the Druids was at its zenith, their words had had magical force. A warrior who was ridiculed in a satire was undone for the rest of his life. But invocations and incantations hadn't helped the Druids to defend Anglesey against the Romans. And today?

'What do you intend to do?' Torben wondered.

'No idea,' I answered. 'Sail out to the island and see if we can do something.'

It was obvious that he wished to say something more, but not in front of Mary. I tried to dismiss the idea that Torben might have no wish to sail to Soa if the purpose was to help MacDuff. But how could he believe that he himself counted in Mary's eyes?

MacDuff was the only person who gave her a desire to live. Surely, Torben must have begun to understand that now.

'We have to go there,' I told him. 'No matter who has sent up the distress signal.'

Torben glanced at Mary. She had taken out the binoculars, and she didn't let the island out of her sight for an instant. We had one mile and ten minutes left when she lifted an arm and pointed.

'A boat!'

She gave me the binoculars. There could be no doubt. To the left of the fire, two people were getting into a large inflatable. But we were still too far away to see who they might be.

'Perhaps they are clearing out because we're coming,' I suggested.

Mary looked at me as if I didn't know what I was talking about.

'In any case, they must have seen us,' I added.

Mary nodded. Just afterwards we heard the sound of an outboard motor, and we saw the large inflatable detach itself from the greyish black wall of the cliff. It headed in towards the Firth of Lorn at high speed, certainly making twenty or thirty knots, and it had soon disappeared astern. It was clear that they were avoiding us. If they had taken a direct course they would have passed only a few cable lengths from us. Instead, they had made a wide sweep round us, so wide that we couldn't possibly have identified them in our binoculars. But, unfortunately, they would have no difficulty in recognising us if they knew who we were. For one thing, we still hadn't met another sailing boat since we left the lock at Corpach; for another, we were again sailing under the Swedish flag. Changing our flag was the last thing I did before leaving Acarseid Mor on Gometra. I believed then that our feints were at an end, but I had been too quick in regarding our troubles as over.

I threw a last glance astern to see where the inflatable was bound, but it was already too far away for me to guess. If O'Connell was aboard, of course Kerrera would seem a likely destination. But perhaps they wouldn't dare sail that far on open water and run the risk of being observed. For other people than us must have seen the distress signal, and they might well be keeping a look out. I asked Mary where the nearest lifeboat station was, but she merely shook her head.

'Don't you know where it is?' I insisted.

For once, I cursed my sceptical attitude towards electronic equipment. I wished that I had a VHF radio on board. Our only means of summoning help was by sending up one of our white attention calling signals.

'MacDuff would never forgive you if you called for help from the lifeboat station,' Mary said. 'It's for people in distress at sea, nothing else.'

'But he sent up the flare, didn't he?' I asked.

'That was for me.'

'For you?'

We soon saw the fire clearly. My fears had been justified. The flames were rising from what was left of MacDuff's fishing boat. It lay in the little strait between the two islets. The wheelhouse was already gone, and amidships we saw a gaping hole, presumably made by the explosion we had heard. The bow was relatively undamaged, no doubt because it lay against the wind and the flames were blown astern. It could not be long, however, before the entire boat was in flames, and nothing would be left but bits of wreckage. I didn't mourn the *F 154* as a boat; she had not brought good fortune. But I was increasingly alarmed about him. Was he still aboard? Was he still alive?

Mary got the anchor overboard in an instant. As soon as it had dug in, we launched the dinghy.

'One of us must stay on board,' I said to Torben. 'This is far from being a secure anchorage. So it's you or me.'

The island was too small to stop the swell that came rolling in from the Atlantic and sent up cascades of water against its western side.

'I want to look myself,' Torben said.

'All right. But don't try to go aboard the fishing boat. When the flames get to the diesel-tank ...'

I didn't finish my sentence. Mary was pale but resolute when she got into the dinghy. Too late I realised that I should have had a look in the rucksack which now lay between her legs on the bottom of *Sussi*. If she had a firearm with her anything might happen. I sincerely hoped that there was no-one left on the island.

Torben rowed quickly towards a ledge of rock on the north side, some fifty yards from the fire. Mary evidently told him to go in stern first, because when they arrived he swung the boat half way round. He hadn't understood what she was up to. As soon as they touched, she dashed towards the fire. Torben stood nonplussed with the mooring rope in his hand. I thought at first that he would drop the rope and simply run after Mary, but then he drew the dinghy up onto the ledge. By then her lead was too great; very soon I saw her climb up on the still undamaged bow. She stood there for an instant looking into the flames, before she disappeared down into the hull. This was exactly what I had feared. Torben swiftly approached, and he would certainly follow Mary into the hull. I wanted to shout to him not to do it. But at least a cable or so lay between me and the island, and the roar of the fire would drown all other sounds. I pictured Mary down in the cabin, groping through the smoke in the confined space and

352

searching desperately for MacDuff, contemptuous of her own life.

Suddenly Mary stood on the deck again. Torben had just come over the gunwale to join her. Through my binoculars, I saw that she shouted at him, perhaps that he must climb back down. But he continued towards her. She opened her rucksack and dug a hand into it. I remember thinking: She's taking out her pistol! It's quite likely that I cried out as never before, because she looked briefly in my direction as if she had heard something without knowing what it was. But then her hand emerged filled with what looked like white powder. She threw it into the flames. A few seconds later, the flames shrank down, extinguished. It was magical. At least as long as one didn't know what the powder consisted of. I realised now how the fire could have gone out so abruptly at Loch na Droma Buidhe. The last I saw before I put down the binoculars was Torben's stupor and how Mary stood with arms hanging at her sides as she stared into the charred hull.

I went below and poured myself a substantial whisky. My hand was so unsteady that I spilled about half of it. Torben was safe, that was all that counted at that moment. Mary, too, was still alive. But what had happened to MacDuff?

I realised that his death might as well be taken for granted. And a pang passed through me. Of loss, of longing, I don't know what.

Then I began to worry about the consequences of MacDuff's being dead. I was no longer free to leave everything behind me and sail away into the west. I couldn't leave Torben and Mary to themselves, even if I fully understood how perilous it would be to keep Mary on board. Who would protect her now when MacDuff was gone? Torben and I? Pekka hadn't managed to survive. Our own chances of doing anything but take to senseless flight seemed no better. And, for that matter, did Mary want to go on living?

When I went back up on deck, I could no longer see Mary. Torben was standing in the bows and looking down into what had been the hold. Five minutes, possibly ten, went by before Mary became visible again. She had evidently searched through what remained of the boat and found nothing there. Without a glance in his direction, she passed Torben and clambered over the rocks. He hastened after to help her, but she shook him off. Then he followed her like a faithful dog to the dinghy. They put it back into the water and he began to row her back to *Rustica*. He rowed slowly, as if he didn't wish to arrive, as if he sensed that what came next would remove him from Mary.

She and I joined together in stowing the dinghy on deck.

'I must get to the Garvellachs,' she told me when we had finished.

The Garvellachs! Where Pekka had sailed to, where he had found Mary and saved her life, that very life that she hadn't wanted to keep. Once again, I thought of Pekka's words about the Golden Road that was supposed to have been re-established, about how the funds had been collected for the new Celtic states. In Roman times, the Druids' holy centre and the place where they hid their treasures had been the island of Anglesey, which was perhaps the legendary Avalon. Could the Garvellachs be the contemporary equivalent? Was it from those deserted islands, more sea than land, that the revolt and liberation of the Celts would come? If so, it was very probable that Dick and O'Connell, it they were responsible, had taken MacDuff there.

'Why the Garvellachs?' I asked Mary.

'If MacDuff is alive,' said Mary, 'he is there.'

'And if he is dead?'

She didn't answer at once.

'In that case, too, he is there,' she said finally.

I looked at my watch. Three hours left before twilight and

twenty miles to the Garvellachs.

'We can't get there before dark.' I pointed out.

'I know. I'll find the way.'

'It's not easy even in daylight. I have looked at the chart.'
Mary's eyes narrowed.

'What interest have you in the Garvellachs?' she asked.

'Pekka was there. It was there he saved your life.'

'My life? That's such a relative thing. How do you know
that he didn't take life at the same time?'

For a brief moment, it seemed that we two were in the
same universe and spoke the same language.

'Do you never feel sorry about Pekka ?' I asked.

'In the same way that I feel sorry for you.'

'For me?'

'Yes,' Mary said. 'You ought to hate both me and
MacDuff. And you ought to put less faith in Torben since he
believes that he can trust me. But you don't.'

'No. Why would I do that?'

'To help you survive.'

'Torben hasn't deserted me, if that's what you mean. I
can get along without hating people.'

The idea hadn't occurred to me before, but the more I
thought of it, the more I actually began to believe that I would
survive, whatever happened. Perhaps Mary was right. I had
reason to hate in some sense. But now I felt that my only
strength and advantage over people like her was not to hate
and nothing else.

'Shall I haul up the anchor?' Mary asked.

'How can you be so sure that I intend to let you go to the
Garvellachs?'

'You know that as well as I do.'

Would I really expose myself to danger in order to try to
save the life of MacDuff, of the man who had personally killed
Pekka? I tried to persuade myself that it wasn't only for

MacDuff's sake. It was also for Torben's sake. If MacDuff was still alive, everything would be so much easier.

'What's happening?' Torben asked me in an empty voice when I got back to the cockpit.

'Mary wants to go to the Garvellachs. She believes that MacDuff is alive.'

I didn't know with certainty that Mary believed this, but I wanted Torben to get used to the idea. The last couple of days, he had behaved as if he had never seen the tenderness between Mary and MacDuff when we met them in Corryvreckan.

'Where are the Garvellachs?' Torben asked.

'North of Corryvreckan. Twenty miles from here!'

'Is it far from the mainland?'

Why did he ask that? At the same instant, Mary called that the anchor was aweigh, and I had other concerns.

'Wake me up when we arrive,' Torben said as he went below. 'It went alright this morning. Till I woke up!'

This was intended as a joke, but he sounded so cheerless that it came as a reproach.

Mary set the mainsail and the jib, and before long we raced forward, rising and sinking in cadence with the long rhythm of the swelling sea. The mild southwesterly wind laid a gauzy haze over the water. Astern, the sun had already begun to blur away, and the sharp outlines of land disappeared ahead. I began to worry about fog. There is no particularly great likelihood of mist or fog in Scotland, but what does probability matter against what really is?

Thus far, it was I who navigated. I had laid out a course that took us in close to the southwestern point of Mull, on the other side of Torran Rocks, a large area with sunken rocks which raised their sharp and broken tops only at low water. At high tide, as now, the reef looked rather innocent, as if it didn't exist. But I knew that a southerly course of only five degrees more would have been a disaster for *Rustica*'s plastic hull.

After Torran Rocks, there was open water, except for the Corryvreckan, which put out a greedy finger a few miles away to the east of the Firth of Lorn. So as not to be drawn into Corryvreckan - sailing there once, in cold blood, more than sufficed - I had plotted a course leading to the most northerly island of the Garvellachs, Garbh Eileach.

When darkness fell, we still had five miles before us, less than calculated because the tide was with us. During the last hour I had been able to see the lighthouse on Eileach an Naoimh, the southernmost of the four Garvellachs. It flashed every seventh second, ever more brightly in the gathering dark. I confirmed our course at regular intervals by taking bearings on the lighthouse. The current set more and more to the northwest, and it was important to compensate for it by heading more to the south. With the lighthouse in sight to starboard, I had no great difficulty in calculating the drift.

But then came the fog that I had feared from the outset. In only two or three minutes, the light disappeared. The fog became so heavy that it felt like soft rain against my face and on my hands. Moisture crept in everywhere, and soon it dripped from the boom and the sails.

I looked at Mary. She had lifted her head and seemed to be smelling the wind and the fog.

'What shall we do now?' I asked.

She glanced at the compass, then looked again out into the fog where there was nothing to be seen.

'Steer ten degrees more to the south,' she told me.

'But that will put us on the rocks!' I protested with some vehemence.

'Just do what I tell you,' she answered sharply.

'I hope you know what you are doing.'

'The fog is the best thing that could happen,' she said and made it sound as if she were responsible for its arrival.

That meant that there must be more threatening dangers than the rocks of the Garvellachs. In the faint red glow from the compass and the log, I could make out only the contours of Mary's face. But the tone of her voice was just as hard and relentless as when she had pointed a pistol at Torben and me in MacDuff's cabin. There was also a complete self confidence and superiority in her way of telling me how I should steer. At least *her* belief in what we were doing could not be doubted.

'There's a strait between Garbh and Eilean an Naoimh,' she explained. 'It's narrow, very narrow, but deep enough. When I tell you what to do, you must obey my orders exactly. One little mistake, and you will put your *Rustica* on the rocks.'

I ought, then and there, to have turned back and groped my way out to sea and open water. But I didn't.

It wasn't long before I heard the characteristic sound of breakers. If asked to give a rational explanation of Mary's ability to navigate in the dark and in the fog without aids, it could only be that she was somehow able to *listen* her way through. I know that there are Eskimos who navigate by the cries of birds flying towards land, and that there are Polynesians who can steer correctly from the sound of breakers. But Mary's hearing must have exceeded by far what may be called normal.

For my part, I heard merely a confused roar that closed in on us. It felt as if we were in a tunnel with an invisible roof and walls. Finally, I listened only for Mary's commands. Out of the corner of an eye, I saw sea-fire from crests of waves breaking a few yards away.

We came through. It still appears to me as a pure miracle. It took about five minutes before I could suddenly hear the sound of breakers from astern. But the time is something I have extrapolated later. While it went on, time did not exist, not even in the shape of a hope that all would be soon be over.

Once through, I lit a cigarette with shaking hands. My chest was bursting from the strain, and I could count the beats of my thudding heart. I allowed the match to burn longer than necessary. In the flickering light I could see that Mary had an ecstatic expression in her face. I have wondered many times since why we had to take just that passage. I can understand why we didn't sail to the south of Eileach an Naoimh; for when that was possible we were not yet wrapped in fog and we would have been visible a long way off. But I suspect that Mary actually wished to expose herself to the tension, to the ecstacy of exceptional experiences and to abolish time.

'You trusted me,' she said. 'That's good.'

'I had no choice.'

'Oh, you did,' she said and I imagined that she was smiling in the darkness. 'You could simply have turned around and headed out to sea.'

'Yes,' I replied, 'I could have done that. But it wouldn't have helped us, neither Torben nor me.'

It was intentional that I didn't include her. It was easier to say things as they were when I couldn't see her. But she made no reply.

'Where do we anchor?' I asked. 'The only anchorage at Eileach an Naoimh is open to the southwest. With this wind, somebody will have to remain on board.'

'We'll drop anchor at another place. I'll tell you when to come about.'

The usual anchorage was already to windward of us. But one tack out in the sound would suffice, if that was where we were heading. When we had gone about, Mary lowered the mainsail to slow us down. That she hadn't taken in the jib instead was certainly no accident. With her feeling for boats and sails, Mary would have guessed that *Rustica* sailed better to windward with the jib than with the mainsail alone.

'Who is going to stay on board?' I asked.

But I had already decided that Torben should keep anchor watch. If MacDuff was still alive, it was better if Torben didn't have to witness his reunion with Mary. And if MacDuff was dead? The question faded away into the heavy fog.

'I'm going ashore by myself,' said Mary, 'and I forbid either of you to follow me.'

I didn't bother to ask by what right she issued orders.

'Bring her up into the wind now!' she said at the same time as the jib glided down on deck.

While I held *Rustica*'s bow into the wind, Mary dropped the anchor. Although she prevented the chain from rattling by letting it run through her hands, I could still hear that she let out a lot of it. The water must be deep. I looked about, but there was still nothing visible through the fog: no glimmer of light, no hint of shape or form. How would we know if we were beginning to drag, having no way of taking our bearings? Torben would have to make soundings at regular intervals to see if the depth changed. That was the only way. For whatever Mary might say and wish, I intended to accompany her when she went ashore.

'Help me with the dinghy!' she said as soon as she had made the anchor fast.

The dinghy weighed nearly a hundred pounds and wasn't easily launched by a single person, not even by someone so adroit as Mary.

'Wait a minute,' I told her, 'I'll have to tell Torben.'

'We don't have time!'

'I have. And I don't intend to leave *Rustica* without anchor watch.'

'But you are not coming ashore with me! Just help me launch the dinghy,' said Mary.

'In any case I'm putting you ashore,' I told her. 'You don't imagine, do you, that I'd risk not having the dinghy if something should go wrong?'

I turned around and went below. Torben wasn't asleep.
He sat fully clothed on the edge of his berth.

'Where are we?' he asked.

'At the southern island of the Garvellachs.'

I showed him on the chart.

'Mary is planning to go ashore alone.'

'She must not do that!' Torben exclaimed.

'Well, she has forbidden either of us to go with her. All
the same, I'll row her ashore.'

Torben was about to put forward more objections, but I
cut him short.

'You'll have to speak to her yourself.'

He shook his head.

'Actually,' I told him, 'I think we might only be in the
way.'

'Be a hindrance in saving MacDuff's life? Is that what
you mean?'

'Yes.'

Torben looked down, but he said nothing.

'I'll wait for Mary in the dinghy,' I said. 'If she isn't back
in an hour I'll come and fetch you. And we'll look for her
together. Is that all right?'

'Yes. I suppose so.'

'Back in an hour, then!'

I took the torch, matches and the hand-bearing compass. I
tore out the page on the Garvellachs from the pilot-book. Then
I switched on the anchor light on the masthead, but within
seconds Mary's head emerged from the hatch.

'Put that out!' she said.

'We have to find our way back,' I objected.

'Take a bearing! But no lights! Otherwise it's far from
certain that we'll get away from here at all.'

'You won't be able to see the light very far in this fog,' I
pointed out.

'Far enough. Besides, the fog is going to lift. If I find MacDuff I won't be able to control it any longer.'

Stunned, I looked at her. Did she, in complete seriousness, mean that the fog was her own doing? Or imagine that it was akin to the mists that hid Avalon from the surrounding world? I turned to Torben, but he had evidently reacted only to the name 'MacDuff'. For an instant his eyes met Mary's, but there wasn't a trace of tenderness or recognition in her eyes. At that moment, I am sure that Torben could have been anybody at all. As I could have been.

'Here!' I said to Torben and I put the lead-line on the table. 'Every fifth minute should be enough to see if Rustica is dragging. We probably have lots of water astern.'

Hoping that he'd be kept occupied by this task while Mary and I were gone, I turned and left him.

Mary and I climbed into the dinghy and pushed off. It wasn't easy to keep a course in the fog and without the faint gleam from the paraffin-lamp behind *Rustica*'s curtains, we'd have had nothing at all to guide us. Mary gave me a course which I repeated over and over to myself. If I forgot it, I'd have no great chance of finding the way back.

She sat in the stern, and from a weight against my feet I realised that she had again placed her rucksack between her legs. She was barely visible and I couldn't discern her face at all.

'What are you going to do?' I asked her without getting any reply. 'What do you think has happened?'

Mary remained mute.

'Is it the Celtic Ring?' I asked as a provocation, but to no avail.

'Quiet now!' she admonished a little later.

A sense of unreality overcame me. What are we afraid of? Why is the fog so dense that we can't see anything? What am I doing here in a dinghy in the middle of the night with a woman I don't know and can't see?

The feelings of unreality didn't disappear until I asked myself what would happen next. Since then, it has struck me that what we call the future perhaps only exist to make the present real and that history, the stories of what has been, are alone in being real in themselves.

I had not yet decided what I would do when *Sussi*'s keel touched bottom, but I was not prepared for Mary's next move, although her arrival earlier on Soa should have forewarned me. I had scarcely caught hold of a projecting rock in order to keep the dinghy still, when she leapt ashore. She was instantly engulfed by darkness and fog. But I had the presence of mind to snatch up the hand-bearing compass and take an approximate bearing from the sound of her vanishing steps.

Chapter 29

I tried to think. I already knew that I would follow after Mary, but beyond that I had not the slightest idea of what could be done. If a chance existed that MacDuff were alive, then I couldn't just wait and hope that Mary would find him. What, for that matter, was she likely to accomplish alone against such people as Dick and O'Connell?

I listened, and I looked into the darkness. Nothing to be heard or seen. I took from my pocket the page I had torn out of the pilot. I smoothed it out on the thwart, placed the torch beside it, lit a cigarette, and examined the sketchy map. This showed only the island where we were, Eileach an Naoimh. The island was little more than half a mile long, a fifth of a mile wide, and its highest point, Dun Bhreanuim, rose to 250 feet above sea level. On the west side, cliffs descended steeply into the sea from a plateau pierced by a mountain ridge. Ascent appeared to be easier from the east.

The island was described as uninhabited and completely without trace of modern civilization. But it abounded in historical remains. As early as 542 A.D., Saint Brendan, the same Irish monk who according to legend sailed in a leather boat from Ireland to North America, founded the first

Christian colony on Eileach an Naoimh. When Saint Colomba came to Iona twenty years later, he made his religious retreat on the island. A number of Scottish clans had afterwards used the Garvellachs - or 'Garvellocks', as the name was also spelled - as a place of refuge. On the northernmost island, itself a single rock no more than a few hundred yards in circumference, the remains of an almost impregnable stronghold were accessible only with great difficulty, even in fine weather. The fastness was thought to have belonged to Conall Cearnach, a legendary figure of Irish folklore who lived shortly after the birth of Christ. In the thirteenth century, the fortress was rebuilt by the Clan MacDougall.

I reread this last sentence incredulously. Was it truly possible? Had the MacDougalls possessed a castle on the Garvellachs? It was another piece that fitted into the puzzle. I understood its significance when I saw that from immemorial times Eilean an Naoimh had been called 'the Holy Island'. It seemed that I was being led into one of the labyrinthine designs engraved on many Celtic graves. I felt that, whatever I did, the Celtic Ring would close ever more tightly about me.

Looking again at what was marked out on the map, then at the descriptions, I asked myself where I should begin to look for Mary. *Chapel* it said at one spot on the map. This turned out to be no more than twenty one feet by nine in size, and nothing was left of it except the walls, which were a yard thick and must have withstood the sea wind for fifteen centuries. Closer to the water, remains could be seen of the walls that had belonged to a rather large monastery. And near these there still stood intact two 'beehives': round stone huts, each about ten feet high, with a domed roof and space enough to accommodate a meditating Druid or monk. The 'beehives' were connected by a passage, and together with this they formed the number *8*. Round about the island, there had earlier been quite a few stone crosses with Celtic inscriptions, but most of them had disappeared. Somewhere, dungeons were supposed to exist; one of them had been used by particularly penitent sinners who sought to purify their souls. In approximately the middle of the island, a stone marked the grave of Arthne, thought to have been Saint Columba's mother, the Princess of Leinster. The stone was a foot and a half high and had a cross engraved on one side.

Was it there Mary had gone? Or to the chapel? Or to another of the sacred sites? I couldn't guess. I didn't even know with certainty where I was myself. I noticed that the usual anchorage lay directly southeast of Arthne's Grave. It was sheltered by some islets, but had been unusable for us because of the southwest wind. As far as I could see, there was only one other place where we could have anchored. Since we hadn't felt the swell, Mary must have anchored *Rustica* north of three tiny islands that lay close under the coast.

In that case, I ought to be just south of a landing-place shown on the map. On leaving *Rustica* I had steered at about 250°, and Mary had disappeared almost directly westward into the island. That could mean only one thing: she had gone towards Arthne's Grave.

I made fast the dinghy and filled my pockets with small shells. I laid out one of these every fifteen yards, that being about the distance reached by the beam from my torch. By counting the number of shells each time, I could calculate how far I was from the grave. Getting there was considerably more difficult than I had expected. In order to use the hand-bearing compass, I had to walk in a straight line, and that meant clambering over blocks of stone and rock formations which lay before me. If I went round them, it would have been hard to know when I had completed a half circle.

Now and then I stopped to listen. I had to assume that Mary and I were not alone on the island.

The first, and terrifying, foreboding of what had occurred

came to me when I was about a hundred and fifty yards from Arthne's Grave. Out from the fog and the darkness came a piercing scream. It didn't last long and broke off as abruptly as it had begun. But the horror of it continued to echo within me after the sound had ebbed away and all was complete silence again. I don't know how long I stood transfixed, whether for some seconds, ten minutes or longer. But I hope that I will never in my life hear a scream of that kind again.

I tried to make haste, but this resulted only in bruises when I hit myself on the sharp rocks. I realised that it might be wiser to switch off my torch for the last fifty yards to Arthne's Grave. If it was Mary who had screamed (and who else could it have been?) she must have been able to see. And if she had seen, there must have been some light. And if there was light, somebody else must be there.

Cautiously, I approached the spot where the gravestone should stand. The ground rose steeply, and I had to climb rather than walk. It was a slow process as one hand was occupied holding the hand-bearing compass. The compass was supposed to have internal illumination for emergency use, but at sea I had never known its faint greenish Tritium light give enough light to navigate. The fact that I could read it quite distinctly that night on Eilean an Naoimh shows how dark it must have been.

At last, I was up on the plateau, which was covered with ferns about three feet high. I walked slowly on, even more warily than before. Suddenly, my leg struck something hard. I investigated with one hand. It was certainly the gravestone.

I moved back a few steps and listened. Not a sound. Nor was there the slightest glimmer of light. It seemed unlikely that anyone could still be close by, if somebody had been there at all. After a moment I took the risk and switched on my torch.

The sight that met my eyes can never be erased from my

memory, and as I write now I feel the nausea well up again. The ray of light from my torch revealed a severed head standing on top of the stone. The head was still bloody and the eyes stared inertly out into nothingness. The head was MacDuff's.

I don't recall much about the moments that followed. No doubt I was sick. I hoped that I didn't scream like Mary. I know that I dropped the torch and its light went out. That saved me, for the moment at least. What I had seen didn't vanish with the light that went out from the torch, but a remembered image is always a little less real than reality itself, unless you have definitely gone mad.

The head cult! I thought mechanically. This was what Pekka had witnessed and dreaded. But what was the meaning of it? To ascribe magical properties to heads, to keep the skulls of friends and relations who had died, that was one thing, and they still do it on the island of Madagascar. But this was brutal murder quite simply placed on view. On view for whom?

Thoughts rushed through my head. This didn't fit at all with what MacDuff had said. Nobody killed for the sake of the head cult, he had said. Nor was anybody killed because of the head cult.

Of the thoughts that came to me then, a single one could be called logical. If MacDuff's head had been placed up on the stone to be seen, the intention was that Mary should see it. Why? To terrify her out of her wits and thus remove all possibility of opposition? But who had done it? Dick? As instructed by the Celtic Ring? Or was it someone from Mary's own Druidic order?

I crept away from the stone until I dared try to turn on my torch. I was lucky. The switch had simply been pushed back when it hit the ground. In my other hand I was still clutching the hand-bearing compass.

Should I return to Rustica and Torben? Impossible to do

that now. If Torben heard that MacDuff was dead, that Mary was still on the island and perhaps in the hands of those who had killed him, nothing could make him stay on the boat. He would go ashore and look for Mary. Should I go back to *Sussi* and wait there in the hope that Mary would reappear? I looked at my watch. Little more than half an hour had passed since I left the boat. Back in an hour! I had promised Torben. If I hadn't returned by then, he would inflate the rubber dinghy and leave *Rustica* to her fate.

But what could I do? It became clear to me how helpless and harmless to anybody I actually was. And MacDuff was dead, nothing could change that, not even revenge, if I had been capable of carrying it out. It wasn't through revenge that I would ever be able to sail with him along the western coasts of the Outer Hebrides.

If only I could have hoped to persuade Torben just to weigh anchor and sail away. But the only possible course for me was to try to find Mary before the hour was up. Perhaps we actually were alone on the island now, she and I. MacDuff's head might have been left behind only as a grotesque warning.

I began to walk towards the Chapel. Although I found a path, which made progress easier, I was still so shaken that I had to concentrate on every step. I stopped sometimes, turned off the torch and listened. But I heard nothing except the sighing of the wind, the faraway cry of a seagull and waves breaking in the distance. Otherwise, all was silence. And darkness.

I had about a hundred yards left when it became clear that it had been wishful thinking to believe that Mary and I were alone on the island. I heard the sound of voices, and they became more distinct as I drew closer. I had switched off the torch and was groping along with an arm outstretched before me. Suddenly, my hand touched a stone wall. The voices came from the other side of this; I couldn't make out anything they said because they were speaking in a Celtic language.

I groped on, following the wall to find an opening. It was certainly a wall of the chapel and, since the roof had gone, people on the other side could doubtless hear the slightest sound I made. To avoid tramping on a branch or kicking a stone, I felt my way with each foot before putting weight on it. Now and then I bent down and felt what my foot had prodded. That was how I discovered Mary's rucksack. Had she thrown it from her before she went into the chapel?

The rucksack was open. I quickly put a hand down into it and felt Mary's pistol lying at the bottom. My hand gripped the butt, but I had to force myself to draw it up. Holding the weapon in my hand, I wondered if I could ever get myself to use it. If I hadn't had to keep absolutely quiet, I would no doubt have tossed the gun away, such loathing did I feel of just holding it. But it was still in my hand when I came round the first corner of the wall. Further on, I saw a light coming from what looked like a hole or window in the wall. But when I reached the spot, I found that the top of the wall had quite simply caved in along with the roof.

I heard more plainly now the same voices as before. None was Mary's. Three men were speaking. Even though I did not understand the Celtic words, I didn't have to hesitate about the tone: they completely lacked any touch of humanity.

With infinite care, I raised my head above the edge of the wall. The first thing I saw was Mary sitting huddled on the ground with her back against the wall furthest from me. Before her, a fire burned in a copper globe, casting flickering flame shadows on her face. Three men stood round the globe. I recognised the one on the left. It was Dick, holding a sub machine-gun just as nonchalantly and naturally as at Invergarry Castle. The other two wore white cloaks.

I stood petrified. Fortunately, the attention of the three was directed in the opposite direction, at Mary. She sat lifelessly, with blank and staring eyes, before them. I had no need to understand their words in order to grasp that a kind of interrogation was taking place, a ritual trial with three prosecutors and an accused who was already condemned. Implacably, one of the men put a question to Mary, waited and repeated it. Mary neither gave nor showed any response; she continued to stare at nothing. Abruptly, Dick moved closer to her, produced a thin band of braided leather thongs and placed it around her neck. I watched terror-struck. He was preparing to garrotte her! She would be strangled as a sacrifice to some god of the Druids. I thought with extreme revulsion that the Celtic Ring couldn't lie behind it. Her own Druids must have got hold of her first. Or was it simply Dick's morbid idea of punishment and revenge?

I felt something break within me, and that my hands were clenching. I scarcely noticed that one of them clenched round the butt of Mary's pistol. I am one of those people who are considered unnaturally calm and collected, and I have always felt that anger and rage could only debase. But at the same time I have also always feared what might happen if I ever began to feel that anger or rage was justified. I knew how I had felt before when, on a few occasions, I had come close, but never had I known such hatred and repugnance as came to me when Dick secured the leather snare around Mary's neck.

Her head fell to one side as Dick tightened the loop. There was no resistance in her. It seemed as if he could have broken her neck with a sewing-thread. He took a step backward and waited. Mary didn't lift her head again. Dick looked at the two others and they nodded. I understood from their manner that they were pronouncing their verdict and that the sentence was death.

Dick went forward once more to Mary, and he slipped a small peg through a little loop in the leather band. At that instant, it seemed that my arm, the hand, the fingers of the hand were foreign objects and didn't belong to me at all. The arm lifted itself out across the top of the wall and the hand directed the pistol at Dick. Its forefinger closed round the trigger.

The gun went off a first time with an ear splitting detonation. Dick gave a cry and collapsed to the ground. The two other men looked at Dick, thinking that it was he who had fired the shot, before they realised what was happening. I fired two more shots at random. One of the figures shouted something at the other who extinguished the fire by giving the copper globe a kick. A moment later I heard them dashing heedlessly towards what must once have been the entrance to the chapel. I was in luck, I thought. If they had thrown themselves on the ground, it might have been necessary to try to shoot them as well. But they had realised that it was a death-trap to stay inside those walls, not knowing where the shots came from or how many did the shooting. Their footsteps faded away into the darkness and fog.

When I got down into the chapel, my foot struck against Dick's body. I switched on my torch, bent down and felt for his pulse. He was dead. Plus one and minus one equals zero, I thought. What had I done? I looked at Mary. She lay on her side, and I supposed that she must have fainted. I could see no wound. Plus one and minus one. It could just as well have been minus two if Dick had managed to draw the noose. I removed it from her neck. How meaningless! I thought. I had killed to save a life. My legs seemed to be made of lead. I began to feel sick.

I tried to look at Mary to convince myself that the killing had been for her sake. Yet was she of so much more value than Dick merely because he had wished to kill her? How did I know that she had never killed anyone herself? Or that killing Dick was more defensible than his garrotting of Mary would have been? Plus and minus. I kept working out the equation mechanically. But I was saved from the operation by the realisation that the sum was not yet established. The two men might well return. And Torben, what would he have done when he heard the shots? I had to get back to *Rustica* before he had time to pump up the rubber boat. If he went ashore and ran into the two men, my act was likely to become an even greater absurdity than it seemed already. I picked up Dick's machine gun and hung it on my back. The two weren't going to use the thing, that much I'd see to at least.

I lifted up Mary and carried her out of the chapel. When I'd got some fifty yards, a dreadful fact became plain to me: I no longer had the hand-bearing compass. Unthinkingly, I must have laid it down when I took the pistol from Mary's abandoned rucksack. Even if the fog gave us safety for the moment, I didn't dare leave her temporarily and go back to look. In the first place, I was already uncertain of the way back, and in the second, I was sure that the two men would return when they had got over their scare. To them as well, the fog must give a certain sense of security and renewed courage. Moreover, the importance of Mary to them was obvious; they wouldn't give her up without a struggle.

I paused indecisively, well aware that I had to make up my mind. We had to reach the edge of the water; from there I could find the way back to the dinghy. But in which direction lay the shore? I did hear the crashing of breakers but I knew well enough the deceptions involved in attempting to find one's way from sounds in a fog. Sure enough, when I moved in one direction the waves were heard from another. Panic rose within me. If I didn't get back to the boat in time, Torben would be ashore without knowing what had happened and the risks he faced. He had certainly heard the shots, and it would never have occurred to him that I had fired them. If he believed that Mary or I, or both of us, had been shot at, he would have thrown all caution to the winds.

Something had to be done. But what? The fog was just as thick as before and I could feel the microscopic drops of moisture on my face. Mary murmured something inaudible. I wanted absolutely to get her out to *Rustica* before she regained consciousness. But holding her as I did, under her knees and under a shoulder, I found that my arms had started to grow numb. Soon I'd be forced to lay her down somewhere. I was sweating heavily and at the same time was chilled by the wind.

The wind! I suddenly thought. Without a compass, without a light or sound to go by, I still had the wind. When we arrived at the island it had been southwesterly. On the way to the water it should be against my right cheek. I started walking again as fast as I could manage while carrying Mary. But before long it was impossible for me to go any further. I put Mary down and rested for a moment.

Then I heard a faint cry, dampened by the wind, which seemed to come from the chapel. The two men had evidently returned, found Dick's body and discovered that Mary was gone. At almost the same time, I did see something through the fog: what seemed to be two black holes cut into the darkness. These gradually assumed the shapes of domed stone huts, of the beehive monks' cells. But at that moment I was filled by desperation and despair. For there would be no point in returning to the dinghy. Without a compass and only the wind to give direction, my chances of finding *Rustica* before the fog lifted were almost non-existent. Plus one and minus one, I thought again. Perhaps all was in vain. Torben would come ashore before I could stop him. He would wander blindly about on the island. At best, he might have found the extra compass that lay in the navigation drawer. But the map of Eileach an Naoimh was in my pocket. The chart could have provided his only guidance, and its scale was far too large for it to give him more than a rough idea of the place.

I felt totally balked. What could I do? The pistol

remained in my pocket and the sub-machine gun still hung on my back. So I was armed, but I was convinced that I couldn't bring myself to use a firearm again, except perhaps to send warning shots straight up in the air.

Mary gave a moan. It was damp and cold on the ground. I carried her into one of the stone huts and put my jacket about her. And I wondered what would happen when she emerged from her state of shock. Would she really wish to return to *Rustica* now that MacDuff was dead? At moments I considered leaving her in the hands of Providence while I went and tried to warn off Torben from advancing into the island. I recalled with bitter irony my telling Mary that I could get along quite well without hating anybody. Well, now I had truly hated someone and what had come out of it? I had killed one human being and might be the cause of three more people losing their lives.

Time dragged by. I did nothing at all, merely waited and listened. I have no idea how long. Nothing happened. But then what might happen? Finally, I couldn't stand it; anything was better than sitting idly at Mary's side waiting for a catastrophe. But when I was about to lift her again, I heard footsteps approaching. And an instant later Mary gave a groan of pain. I put a hand over her mouth, but it was too late.

'What was that?' one of the two men asked in English.

The Celtic language had no doubt only been used for the death rites' sake.

I held my breath. The speaker couldn't have been standing more than a few yards from the stone hut.

'What was what?' the other asked.

'Didn't you hear it? Sounded like a moan.'

'I didn't hear anything,' came the answer, to my relief. 'Where did it come from exactly?'

'From somewhere in the distance. But with a fog like this you never can tell. In any case, they can't be far away.'

I took a breath again, but meanwhile I was in a cold sweat. Somehow, I sensed that Mary had opened her eyes at the sound of the voices. But she didn't move her head away from my hand on her mouth.

'We've got to be careful,' said one of the men. 'Considering that they took Dick's tommy-gun with them.'

'Don't I know it! But we've got no choice. We'll have to find them, that's all. The others will be back when this fog clears. And you know pretty well what it will mean if we haven't found Mary by then.'

'And found the Swede as well. He's no better than that Finn was, whatever MacDuff tried to make out. Well, where do we begin?'

'They must have a dinghy somewhere. If we get that out of commission, we can take things a bit easier. They won't be able to get away.'

'Then we'd better begin at the landing place. But don't forget Dick's tommy-gun. They may be down there with it already.'

'I doubt that. Stupid of them to leave their compass behind. They won't get far without it. Anybody can get lost on the island in this weather. A pity that we hadn't our pistols with us from the start. We lost a good quarter of an hour getting hold of them. But who would have thought it could turn out like this? Dick was supposed to be on guard instead of foolishly letting himself get carried away.'

My heart sank. I heard them moving off and I took my hand from Mary's mouth.

In a weak and barely recognizable voice, she asked where we were. She sounded as her eyes had looked when I saw her first, in Dragør.

'In one of the beehives,' I answered.

Without a sound and very slowly, Mary sat up. I surmised in the darkness that she raised her hands to her neck, feeling for traces left by the garrotte.

'Leave me here!,' she said abruptly, despairingly.

'I am sorry,' I answered, 'I can't. Torben must have come ashore by now and is trying to find us. If you are not with me, I'll never be able to get him back to the boat.'

'It won't help,' she said. 'The respite is over.'

'Not for Torben and me, it isn't,' I protested and felt a form of resolution returning to me. 'When Torben and I have got you back on board *Rustica*, I promise you that you may do whatever you wish. You can come back to Eileach an Naoimh and be sacrificed a third time, if that's what you want. But the least you can do now is to help me protect Torben. You owe that much to us both.'

'Why?' asked Mary.

I was about to reply that I had saved her life. Then I realised that this might be exactly what she expected to hear. Since MacDuff was dead, she would say that she no longer had a life that was worth saving.

'Because I helped you when you tried to rescue MacDuff,' I told her instead. 'And because MacDuff saved my life and Torben's. Do you want him to have done that in vain?'

I didn't bother about the pain my words might give Mary. It had to be said. She didn't answer. She wept.

'Do you?' I repeated.

'No,' she said at last in a voice that revealed all her sorrow and suffering.

I helped her to stand up, and she held on to me tightly around the waist. I noticed that her legs were shaking. But after a few minutes she could stand by herself.

'What do you want me to do?' she asked.

'You know the island. Start by showing me the way to the dinghy. It may be too late, but we must know what has happened to it. If we're in luck those two can have begun looking for *Sussi* in the wrong place.'

I knew it was a risky business, but no matter how I tried, I couldn't think of a better alternative. Without Mary I might perhaps have taken the chance of remaining invisible in the foggy dark until I found Torben. But even if I were alone, the problem would remain of how to dare make my presence known if I heard someone coming close. And how could I find my way about the island without Mary's help?

We had scarcely emerged from the stone hut when we heard a horrible cry of terror.

'What was that?' I said and heard the fear in my voice.

Mary made no answer. She had stiffened in the middle of a step. From deep within herself, she must have caught an echo of her own cry when she saw MacDuff's head. I listened, but all was silent again. Torben? I thought in awful anxiety. There was nothing we could do but to move on.

I took Mary by the arm and shook her. Then, slowly and mechanically, she continued to walk in front of me towards where she knew the water to be. It took us a good ten minutes to cover a hundred yards. But I then heard the lapping of waves and within seconds we stood beside the dinghy. It lay precisely as I had left it, except that it was now filled with water. Two gaping holes had been made in the bottom.

So we were too late. The two men must have deduced that we had not come ashore at the usual anchoring place because of the onshore wind. In that case ... I didn't get time to finish my thought when I heard a voice from behind us.

'Don't turn around!'

I didn't budge. I felt all the muscles in my body tighten. Plus one and minus one, I thought again. It must not have been meaningless. I was about to throw myself on the ground or make a dash for it when I heard the voice again:

' ...which translated into good Danish would mean something like stand still!'

It was Torben.

Relief after so much strain caused my legs to give way, and I slumped down to the ground. Torben came up to me and helped me onto my knees.

'I'm sorry,' he said. 'I had to use the same trick again. But I didn't dare do anything else. You have a machine gun, and in the circumstances you might have shot me first and asked me who I was afterwards.'

'Mary!' I stammered out and looked round for her in alarm. She hadn't moved at all. She stood beside the dinghy and she stared as if paralyzed at what could be seen of Torben. It was only then that I realised that he was wearing MacDuff's coat and that he had blood on his face and hands.

'What has happened?' I asked.

'I'll explain on the way out to *Rustica*.'

'Yes, but the dinghy,' I said and pointed my torch at the two holes.

'That doesn't matter,' Torben assured me. 'I took the rubber dinghy.'

He took a few steps towards Mary but it wasn't until he came close that he caught the panic in her eyes.

'It's me, Torben,' he told her gently and he took off MacDuff's coat before her.

He had his own underneath.

'I'm sorry,' he said, 'but I had to scare your Druid colleagues into flight.'

Mary still didn't appear to understand what he was saying.

'She is in a state of shock,' I told him in a low voice. 'We must get her to *Rustica*.'

'We will. Don't worry!'

There was a calm confidence in Torben that I hadn't noticed for a long time.

He took Mary's arm and led her along the shore. She seemed too dazed to know what was happening. I followed after them. Some thirty yards away we came to *Rustica*'s red and yellow rubber dinghy. Torben placed Mary in the prow and himself in the stern. I sat on the thwart in front of him and prepared to take the oars.

'I found the extra compass,' he said.

We needed it now. I rowed as quickly as I could and Torben directed me when we got off course. Soon we heard shouts that seemed to come from somewhere further to the south.

'Well, well,' said Torben in his new assured manner, 'they have found their fine inflatable that could make thirty knots. It can't any more.'

Torben must have had time to do to it pretty much what they had done to our *Sussi*.

A few minutes later, we reached *Rustica* where she lay like a phantom-ship on the still water sheltered by the small islands. We helped each other to lift Mary on board, for her body didn't seem to obey her any longer. I remember wondering if she would ever be able to regain her strength? We put her on the port side berth and set up the lee-board to prevent her from rolling off if the sea should be heavy when we came out on open water.

I had never before seen Torben work so quickly and efficiently on deck. The rubber dinghy was hoisted up, deflated and stored away in the briefest possible time; very soon the anchor lay on deck and the sails were set. I have rarely been pleased to sail in fog, but I was that night. I laid out a course that would take us west of the islets which lie southeast of Eilech an Naoimh. To starboard as we put out, the two men could be heard shouting commands at each other. They had evidently thrown all caution overboard. We understood how desperate they must be when they began to fire wild shots at us in the dark. None of these came anywhere near us.

'Now, tell me what happened!' I asked Torben when all sound of the pair had faded away behind us.

'I heard a horrible scream and decided to row ashore as you can imagine. I took it for granted that you and Mary had been hurt or were captives. But of course I didn't know where you were, or even if you were still alive. I remembered that you had the map with you. But I found a description of the place in one of your guide books, with a bit on the chapel and Arthne's Grave. When I got to the shore, the first thing I did was to find *Sussi* and disable the poor thing.'

'So you were already ashore when the shots were fired? And it was *you* who made those holes in the bottom?' I asked amazed. 'Why?'

'What else was there to do? I didn't know anything. I had to consider every possibility. My reasoning was that, if you were still alive and had got away in the fog, you'd try to get back to the dinghy sooner or later. But our enemies would figure that out too. I wanted to stop them from lying in wait for you. There must be no reason for them to hang around the dinghy. So I tried to make them believe that you wouldn't bother coming back, since you had gone aground and badly damaged the boat when you landed. It worked. When they found the dinghy they were overjoyed.'

'How do you know?'

'I heard them.'

'Heard them?'

'Yes. To begin with I had discovered your shells when I was looking round the dinghy for traces of you. And I guessed that you had dropped them to find your way back. I'd have done the same thing. I followed the trail till I got to the gravestone and then ... I saw what you must have seen.'

Torben stopped.

'Well ... It was some time before I had recovered. I looked about for any sign that you or Mary had been there.

There was none. But a bit further on I found some clothes of MacDuff's. And his headless body.'

Torben stopped again. I fully understood his reluctance to go on.

'I didn't know what to do with myself. I felt totally helpless. At the same time sickened and enraged. I thought I was above revenge, but I wasn't. And that's when I heard the shots, which didn't make things better. But I had no weapon at all. Only a knife, but what can you do with a knife against people who stop at nothing? You have to realise that I was desperate when I got the idea that the only thing I could do was to frighten them half out of their minds. The Celts are highly superstitious. The one thing that would send the two fleeing with terror was MacDuff's ghost. So I put on some of his clothes. And I took his head with me.'

Torben waited for me to say something. But what could I say? I saw how afflicted he was by the image he had of himself wandering about in desperation with MacDuff's bloody head in the crook of his arm. Yes, Torben too had experienced something that day which he would never be able to forget.

He told me then how he had hastened to the chapel and found the two men there.

'I had tremendous luck, because they'd returned in a hurry with their weapons and were inclined to be careless. I couldn't make out what they were doing in the chapel, but it was clear to me that you two had escaped them and must at all costs be captured. I followed after them, overtook them on the way to the dinghy, and while they were looking at it, I appeared to them out of the fog as MacDuff's ghost. I must have been a truly fearful sight. Never in my entire life have I beheld anyone so terror-stricken as those two were. They vanished back towards the centre of the island. I found their own rubber boat and made quite sure that it couldn't be used again. After that, it was just a matter of waiting for you and Mary to show up. Which you did and, happily, before the pair got over their shock. I don't know at all what I'd have done if they had come back.'

He vainly attempted to make what we had been through sound as if it had been nothing but an adventure. But the worst part remained to be told, and I knew that he would ask.

'There's one thing I don't understand,' Torben said. 'Who fired the shots? And where did you get the sub-machine gun from?'

I explained what had happened and that I had killed Dick. Torben gave me a long and searching look and I knew that he understood what my feelings were, and that nothing would ever be the same for me again. But he said nothing. There was nothing more to be said.

'Go below to Mary.' I told him. 'She'll need you when she wakes up. I can manage alone here.'

When he had gone, I finally added up the sums. Plus three minus one equals two. That was my sum that I had to live with for the rest of my days. Just like MacDuff.

I laid out a new westerly course, straight out into the Atlantic. After that, I had nothing further to do. When we came into the Firth of Lorn, I dropped the tommy-gun and Mary's pistol into the sea. I would rather live in constant flight all my life than use a firearm again. The world and its oceans are so vast when your boat is your home that it must be possible to live a tolerable and undetected life somewhere.

At three o'clock in the morning I could note in the logbook: '*Fog cleared. Passed Dubh Artach lighthouse in a southerly wind, Force 4 . Full moon. Starry sky.*' I had gone down and looked at Mary, who was sleeping deeply and, it seemed, peacefully. Torben had watched by her since he went below. When I arrived, he gave me a glance that contained our entire friendship. He was himself again, and yet totally different. As I realised that I was myself.

I returned on deck and sat alone in the cockpit. For thousands of nautical miles beyond Dubh Artach, there was nothing but open sea. The mild spring air brought a kind of hopefulness. As the steering vane took us westward, *Rustica* raced along under the stars. For several days, there would be no need to decide where we were sailing to. MacDuff's words about the immensity of the sea came back to me. I had something of his feeling now. I lit a cigarette, poured out more coffee for myself and felt a freedom, a sense of extreme relief and even something that could be called happiness. Unbroken horizons, perpetual change, joy in being alive: that was what MacDuff must have known and lost. Trying to learn to appreciate it to the full and to the best of my ability would be my way of remembering him.

EPILOGUE

FIVE months have passed since the light from the lighthouse at Dubh Artach faded away into the darkness of the Hebridean night. As yet, I do not dare to say where we are. But the world is wide for a sailing-boat like *Rustica*; from the mist-shrouded banks of Nova Scotia to the Amazon delta, from the fiords of Chile to the coral reefs of Madagascar. It might take a lifetime for someone to find us.

When I sank Dick's sub-machine gun and Mary's revolver into the sea, it was to prevent me from ever using them again. That's why I was convinced that the only possible future for me, Torben and Mary was one of flight. What I knew was in itself enough to make us live under a constant threat. With Mary on board and alive, there could be no doubt of what would happen to us if the Ring, or any of the fanatical organisations of the kind Dick and O'Connell represented, should get hold of us.

But since then Mary has gradually begun to live again; she and Torben left *Rustica* a long time ago, and they are now far away. Perhaps it was for the best. Although Mary and I made awkward attempts at becoming closer to each other, we never succeeded. Torben and I are still friends, but something has changed.

With time, I have realised that in a way his love for Mary existed in him long before they met each other. It was a longing for the limitless and the absolute. Torben's aversion to symbols, myths and theories perhaps derived from a sense of loss. The belief in the force and importance of words, in fiction and reality as two sides of the same thing, in knowledge as the very essence of life, all that which the Druids had taught and lived for, had always been a part of Torben.

Nothing must happen to him and Mary. That is the reason why I have written this book.

Not because I wish to expose or stop the Celts' efforts to become free peoples. On the contrary, I would wish that the Celtic peoples became Celtic first and independent if they wish. Every people which is a people, and which wants to be free, must be allowed its freedom. MacDuff made me understand that there exists a human right which has to do with the identity of each and everyone, a right that has always been oppressed in the holy name of nationalism. To deprive someone of his name is a way of killing him, said the ancient Celts. That is exactly what England has always tried to do in Scotland, Ireland and Wales, and what France has often succeeded in doing in Brittany.

No, I have not written this book to deny the Celts the right to their name. I have only written it so that Mary, Torben and I will not have to live the rest of our lives in fear. For, surely, the more people who share the knowledge of that which according to some must remain secret, the less risks we will run. I well know that there are writers who have been thrown into prison or condemned to death for writing what they believed to be the truth. But I refuse to believe that the Celtic Ring will pursue us to the end of the world out of pure vindictiveness. Truth has always been honoured by the Celts and the word placed above acts of violence. It is my hope, and my belief, that they must be able to achieve their freedom without making a mystery of their efforts and without causing bloodshed, without counting human lives as simple sums to make up.

I have also written this account as completely and truthfully as possible, and I give my word that I know nothing more than what I have told. Removing me, Torben and Mary from this planet would thus safeguard no further secrets. Those points which remain obscure in the text do so because they are also unclear to me. I owe my readers an apology for sharing with you the threat that hangs over me, but I have not found any other recourse available to me.

On Board *Rustica*, August 1991.